FOUND
ART

Center Point
Large Print

Also by Susan Page Davis and available from
Center Point Large Print:

The Priority Unit
Fort Point

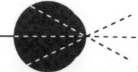

**This Large Print Book carries the
Seal of Approval of N.A.V.H.**

FOUND ART

MAINE JUSTICE
· BOOK 3 ·

SUSAN PAGE DAVIS

CENTER POINT LARGE PRINT
THORNDIKE, MAINE

This Center Point Large Print edition
is published in the year 2018
by arrangement with the author.

Scripture quotations taken from the New American Standard Bible® (NASB), Copyright © 1960, 1962, 1963, 1968, 1971, 1972, 1973, 1975, 1977, 1995 by The Lockman Foundation. Used by permission. www.Lockman.org

The text of this Large Print edition is unabridged. In other aspects, this book may vary from the original edition. Printed in the United States of America on permanent paper. Set in 16-point Times New Roman type.

ISBN: 978-1-68324-750-0

Library of Congress Cataloging-in-Publication Data

Names: Davis, Susan Page, author.
Title: Found art / Susan Page Davis.
Description: Center Point Large Print edition. | Thorndike, Maine : Center Point Large Print, 2018. | Series: Maine justice ; Book 3
Identifiers: LCCN 2017060446 | ISBN 9781683247500 (hardcover : alk. paper)
Subjects: LCSH: Large type books. | GSAFD: Mystery fiction.
Classification: LCC PS3604.A976 F68 2018 | DDC 813/.6—dc23
LC record available at https://lccn.loc.gov/2017060446

FOUND ART

Chapter 1

Thursday, September 16

An unexpected bonus turned up in the tobacco smuggling case we'd been working on for weeks. My best detective, Eddie Thibodeau, had investigated and identified the suspects. We'd raided their nondescript beige ranch house at dawn and sent the prisoners off in a marked unit.

Arnie Fowler was in charge of cataloguing the contraband we found in the garage. A red pickup with a Maine license plate and a green SUV with a Quebec plate were parked in there, and the SUV was ready for the run to Canada, where the taxes on cigarettes are extremely high. The boxes were piled in the back seat and behind it in the cargo area, with a tarp thrown loosely over them.

"How could they take all this over the border?" Nate Miller asked. He was the newest detective in the Priority Unit, and Eddie's partner.

"They wouldn't try to go through the customs gate," Arnie said.

Eddie nodded. "Yeah, they had a contact scheduled to meet them on a woods road. The border patrol plans to meet them at the drop tonight."

There were places, lots of places, along

the world's longest unguarded border, where people and contraband could cross undetected, bypassing the checkpoints. A four-wheel drive and a little nerve went a long way. Although it might seem small potatoes compared to some drug operations, smuggling tobacco could be very profitable, and these guys had figured to make a bundle on the cargo of cigarettes.

Arnie turned to me, clipboard in hand. "All set, but there's something odd here, Harvey. Help me set it out on the floor, Nate."

They lifted a large, flat box out of the cargo area of the SUV and set it on the cement floor in front of me.

"This was behind the tobacco," Arnie said.

"Did you open it?" I asked.

"Not yet." Arnie handed Eddie his completed inventory of the items in the SUV. "You want me to?"

I stepped closer and looked it over carefully. A large cardboard box with "Panasonic printing with option—" on the side had been trimmed to fit the contents and taped around it, making a flat, rectangular box about three inches thick. When I picked up the package and shook it, it didn't make any noise. I took out my pocketknife and carefully slit the filament tape along the seams and laid the cardboard back. Eddie, Nate, Arnie and his partner, Clyde Wood, stood silently watching me. The edge of a nice, hefty frame showed in the opening, and I lifted it out.

"A painting," Eddie said.

"A good painting," Arnie agreed. "What do you think, Harvey?"

I didn't recognize the picture or the artist. It was an oil painting of fishing boats nuzzling each other in their harbor slips. A fretful, brown sky lowered over them. It reminded me a little of the Turner in the chief's office, but it was newer and brighter. The boats had numbers on their bows—numbers with ME in front of them, the state's designation.

"Not an old master, but it's good," I concluded. I squinted at the signature in the lower right corner and made out *E. L. Nevar*. "All right, Arnie, add it to your inventory. I'll take it back to the station myself and do a little research."

Arnie took the clipboard and scribbled on it, then handed it back to Eddie.

"Okay, guys, let's do a thorough search of the house," Eddie said. "Don't want to miss anything."

The others went inside, but I called to Eddie to stay for a minute as I wrapped the cardboard around the gilt-framed painting and stuck the tape back in place as well as I could.

"Good job, Ed," I said. "Everything under control?"

"I think so. We'll get the stuff to Evidence and go over the vehicle more thoroughly."

"The prisoners didn't mention this at all?" I nudged the cardboard box with the painting in it.

"No. Do you think it's stolen?" he asked.

"Could be."

"I've got enough paperwork to do," he said. "If you want to handle the painting . . ."

"Sure." I looked at my watch. It was 6:30 a.m. "Okay. I'll head out."

I was home by seven, and Jennifer, my wife of two months, met me at the door.

"Thought you'd be sleeping," I said. I couldn't keep my smile in. She looked great in her worn jeans, long-sleeved T-shirt, and moccasins, and her long, golden hair was pulled back in a ponytail.

"I can't sleep when you go to work at 4 a.m." She kissed me, and I shut the door and walked through the entry to the kitchen with my arm around her.

I kissed her again before I let her go. She poured coffee for me, and I sat down at the table with a contented sigh. Jennifer, home, and hot coffee, in that order. What could be better?

"So, everything went okay?"

"Yes. Eddie did fine. Three people in custody, and the border patrol will handle the other end."

"Nobody hurt?"

"Not in our unit."

She frowned. "Did you fire your gun?"

I looked down into my coffee and nodded. It

10

was the first time I'd fired my pistol outside the shooting range since a bombing suspect had hit me on my Kevlar vest several months before. "Yeah. I was wondering how I'd do when it happened again."

"I guess you did fine," she said.

I shrugged. "Those guys were lousy shots."

"I'm glad you don't do this every day. I'd be a nervous wreck." She sat down beside me.

"It doesn't happen very often." Before Jennifer married me, I think she had the vague notion that cops got into shoot-outs every day, the way they do on TV. I'd tried to reassure her on that score, and yet it seemed I was going into more high-risk situations since I'd met her. I sipped my coffee, and I could tell immediately that it wasn't decaf.

"You can't drink this," I said.

"That's okay, I thought you'd need high-test. You only got five hours of sleep."

"Don't remind me."

The bell on the microwave rang. She got up and rummaged in the cupboards and came back with a cup of tea for herself and a plate with two muffins on it.

"Are you eating this morning?" I asked.

"I feel great."

I smiled. She'd had a couple of days when she couldn't keep breakfast down. I was forty-one. We'd both wanted to start a family right away, while I was young enough to keep up with the kids, and God had smiled on us. Unfortunately for Jennifer, morning sickness was part of the deal.

Jennifer was the woman I'd thought I would never find, the one steady spot in my chaotic life. She had settled into our new home easily, content to be Mrs. Harvey Larson, and made no secret that her main goal in life now was making me happy. I tried to just enjoy and appreciate that. Otherwise I started to feel inadequate.

I called her every day from work. She didn't usually call me. She was afraid my phone would beep in the middle of a court hearing, or when I was trying to arrest someone. The day she'd learned the news, I'd been very busy at work but took a break at noon to call her. Her first words were, "Are you coming home for lunch?"

"Too much paperwork," I said.

"Can't it wait?"

"Have to keep up my image of efficiency."

"I wanted to talk to you."

There was a little edge to her voice that got my attention. "Talk. I'm listening."

"Well, it's one of those bad-news-good-news things. I was really hoping to tell you in person."

Things went into slow motion. "Give me the bad news."

"Well, it's going to cost money, and we have to do more decorating."

12

Relief hit me. She was teasing me. "So? That's not so bad. Decorate all you want."

"Are you sure?"

"I'm sure. What's the good news? Your sister got a job at Maine Medical, and she's moving in with us?" Abby, one of her younger sisters, was a nurse with a hankering to move to the city. I wouldn't mind helping her out.

"No, not that," Jenny said.

"What, then?"

"I—I really want to see your face. I'll just wait until you get home tonight."

My brain was in gear, finally. Good news that had to be delivered in person. I said, "I'll be home in fifteen minutes."

I grabbed my jacket and went to the locker room. Eddie was in there, poking around in his locker.

"You ready for lunch?" he asked.

"Ed, I'm leaving for the day." I opened my locker door.

He looked at me in surprise. "Okay, Harv. Everything all right?"

"Yeah, I'm sure it is. It's just something personal." From the top shelf, I pulled a teddy bear, soft and snuggly, with stitched eyes that babies couldn't choke on. "You know I don't do this often."

"You never do this."

"First time for everything," I said.

13

"Sure." Eddie kept up with me as I set a quick pace for the stairs. He eyed the teddy bear as I punched the security code at the door. We had to have doors that locked from both sides, in case one of our prisoners decided to take a walk.

"Make sure everybody gets their reports done," I said.

"Okay. Congratulations."

I hit the driveway in twelve minutes. Jenny opened the door before I got the key to the lock and fell into my arms. "How did you figure it out?" she asked, cradling the teddy bear.

"Hey, gorgeous, I'm a cop." That was a line she had never let me get away with, but this time she laughed as I pulled her into the house and shut the door.

A week had passed since that day, but we were still in the euphoric stage. I'd wake up in the morning, and it would hit me: I was going to be a father. I smiled a lot those days.

"Want to see what we found on our raid this morning?" I took out my phone.

"Is it gruesome?"

"No, I think you'll like it." I showed her a picture I'd snapped of the painting we'd con-fiscated.

"That's pretty nice." She nodded at the screen. "Your kind of art," which I took to mean classic and realistic.

"Yeah, I kind of like it," I admitted. "It's

14

probably hot, though. I'm trying to find out where those guys stole it."

After we finished breakfast, I got a shower and dressed in a suit and tie befitting a police captain. My shoulder holster went on under the jacket, and I clipped my badge on my belt, pocketed the rest of my gear and picked up my briefcase. Never thought I'd be carrying a briefcase to work, but I was getting used to it.

The men weren't back at the office yet when I arrived, and I set the boxed painting down beside my desk, opened my briefcase, and pulled out the paperwork I'd taken home the night before. Requisitions for office supplies, preliminary notes for upcoming evaluations, and profiles of candidates for the position of deputy chief of police.

The paperwork wasn't urgent, and I couldn't resist getting right on my computer and looking for information about the artist, Nevar, and any recent art thefts. Evelyn Nevar seemed to be a fairly new artist, still living, who painted things that looked old. I flagged her name in a special computer program Jennifer had designed for me and checked the painting's box and the frame for fingerprints. Nothing I could use there.

About nine o'clock, I called Mike Browning, the police chief, in his office on the fourth floor, directly above mine.

"Something interesting turned up on our

tobacco case this morning. Can I come up there and brief you?"

Mike knew me very well, and immediately told me to come. I took the stairs, carrying the painting with me.

I was now privileged to have the security code for the top floor, so I let myself in there. Mike had a private secretary, Judith, who was old enough not to take offense if people called her a secretary instead of an administrative aide, or whatever the newest term was. She nodded soberly at me. "Go right in, Captain." She never smiled.

"What's this?" Mike eyed the box. "A present for me?"

"No, but you might wish it was." I peeled back the tape and took the framed picture from the carton.

"Nice," he said. "I like it. It looks pretty good to my untrained eye."

"It was in the vehicle with the cigarettes bound for Quebec."

"No kidding. Somebody up there wanted a Maine coastal scene hanging in his den?"

"I think so. The artist lives in Ohio, but has a summer home on Swans Island. Evelyn Nevar. She's done a lot of Maine scenes. They sell in the neighborhood of two grand."

He whistled.

"I've been checking the updates to see if

16

one's been stolen lately, but I haven't turned up anything yet."

"So, you know a little bit about art?"

"Not much. I guess I could bone up on it fairly quickly."

Mike smiled. "See, that's what I like about you. Whatever I need an expert on, give you a week and you're it."

I shrugged. "I'll never be an art expert, Mike."

"Well maybe an art aficionado will do." He stood the Nevar against the wall on top of a bookcase that held his reference books. "You'd better talk to Ron Legere. His detectives had a couple of art thefts not long ago. Let's see if he can come up here."

He made the call, and soon Legere, the detective sergeant, joined us with a manila folder in his hand. Judith came in with extra mugs and fresh coffee.

Sergeant Legere nodded at me and sat down, looking slightly harried. "You've got something related to the art burglaries?" he asked.

Mike had replaced the old chief's antique but uncomfortable wooden chairs with upholstered armchairs, and I was making myself comfortable with the coffee.

Mike nodded toward the painting. "Harvey's latest loot. We're thinking it's stolen, and you two ought to work together."

"Well, we've had two art thefts this year, and

17

we think maybe they're related." Legere frowned at the Nevar.

"Thefts from where?" I asked. "Galleries? Museums?"

"Nope, private collectors," said Mike. "Brief him, Ron."

Sergeant Legere opened the folder and said, "Sunday we got a call from a homeowner in the West End. Someone had broken into his house Saturday night and made off with a bunch of stuff, including four works of art. Three paintings and a framed sketch, valued between three and ten grand each. He had some other prints and things hanging in the house, but the thieves didn't touch them. Anything worth less than a thousand, they left. But they also stole his computer, his TV and VCR, a video game setup, and an antique platter and some Depression glass."

I ran my hand through my hair. It was getting too long in the back. "So, they knew what they were after, as far as the art goes."

"Right," said Legere. "But they grabbed some small stuff, too. They did the job in the early morning, when the owners were asleep."

"They were in the house?" I didn't like the sound of that.

"That's right. That's what made me connect it with a case we had in February. I handled it with Clyde Wood." Ron looked at me over the top of the folder. "He's in your unit now. He can tell you about it. Same M.O. Thieves broke into a rich guy's house in the night, stole all his good art right from under his nose. The guy got up in the morning, and the walls were bare. We haven't caught them."

"So, you think maybe they waited seven months and struck again?" I asked.

"Maybe. More likely they were operating someplace else in the interim."

"Can you check on that?" Mike asked me.

"Sure, I can tap into back records in the area, Cape Elizabeth, South Portland, maybe Westbrook, and see if they've had anything like it." I had computer links with law enforcement agencies all over. "I can also flag the type of crime in Jennifer's program. Then, if any new art thefts turn up in the state, we'll catch it right away."

"It works with things like that, not just names?" Mike said.

"Sure, I can flag some phrases like 'local artist,' 'stolen paintings,' and so on." I'd hit pay dirt a few months earlier with "car bomb," but that was painful history and I didn't mention it.

"When's your wife going to market that program?" Mike asked. "I think it's time we had it installed on a few more computers, including mine."

"Well, I don't know, Mike. Jennifer's not in the software business anymore."

"Somebody else could market it for her. She's sitting on a gold mine."

"I'll mention it to her." Jennifer had gladly given up her career designing computer programs before we got married, but she knew Mike was intrigued by the program she'd customized for me.

"All right, so you'll do some cyber checking on this art thing?" Mike got up and refilled his coffee mug from the pot Judith had left on a hotplate.

"Sure," I said.

"I was thinking I'd hand the whole thing to Priority. What do you say?"

I wasn't sure how Legere would take that. His detective squad was good, but my smaller unit was considered the elite. We got the sensitive cases—the high-profile murders and the industrial espionage—anything likely to make the mayor's blood pressure rise. I didn't want to cause hard feelings between the Priority Unit and the detective squad, though.

"We're kind of busy right now." I looked at Legere. "Who's handling this latest burglary?"

Legere said, "Joey Bolduc and Bob Marshall. But I've got a lot of other things I could use them on."

I nodded. "Fine. We'll take it from here."

He handed me the folder. "It's all yours. I'll have the boys send anything else related to this up to you."

"Thanks, Ron," Mike said. Legere got up and left.

Mike held up the coffeepot and arched his eyebrows.

"I'm good," I said.

"So, what's up with Jennifer?" Mike sat down and put his feet up on the antique desk that came with his office. I figured Judith sneaked in there before he got in every morning to polish the scuff marks off, because it always gleamed.

"A little morning sickness. Other than that, she's great."

"Well, Poppa, I guess that comes with the territory." Mike's three kids were grown, so he could be casual about it. "How are things in the unit?"

"Good. We wrapped up the smuggling case this morning. Three arrests."

"I'll look at the reports today."

I nodded. "The new men are settling in." Nate and Clyde had both come into the Priority Unit within the last two months.

"Good. Keep me posted on this art thing," Mike said. "I feel better with you handling it. Ron's good, but he knows nothing about art, and Joey's even worse. Bob Marshall is a fair detective, but he's got no finesse, either. We need someone with some class on this."

"You're looking at me?" I almost laughed.

"Well . . ." he swung his feet to the floor and

stood up. "Face it, Harv, a lot of our guys are culturally illiterate. You've got a broad education and twenty years of experience. You don't let yourself stagnate. If I had to pick one man to handle something like this, I'd pick you."

"That's flattering, but a little scary. I really don't know that much about art."

Mike smiled. "You will."

Chapter 2

I'd been in charge of the Priority Unit less than three months, and I was still getting used to my new position and the personnel changes, but overall I felt we were on track. We were coming up on evaluation time, and I thought about how I would rate each man.

Eddie Thibodeau had been my partner before my promotion, and I figured his evaluation would be easiest, since I knew him best. At Jennifer's and my wedding, he was the best man and in charge of banishing reporters—at which even he would admit the results were mixed. He'd just passed his twenty-eighth birthday, and he was single and loving it. Seeing him organize and execute the raid that morning told me he was ready for leadership.

Arnie Fowler was my senior detective. He was fifty-seven, and planning to retire at the end of the year. He'd been Mike Browning's partner back in the day and brought continuity to the job. I knew I would miss Arnie's subtlety and polish. We'd have to bring a new man in when he left.

Clyde Wood, in his early fifties, had worked downstairs on the detective squad for fourteen years. He'd come into the unit when Arnie's partner left. I'd known Clyde slightly for years, but hadn't worked much with him. He was a big man with a large mustache, and moved slowly. Sometimes it seemed he thought slowly, too, but he usually reached the right conclusions in the end, unlike Arnie, who was good at making quick decisions under pressure, but didn't always jump in the right direction.

Nate Miller, at thirty-five, was a family man, a good cop, steady, methodical, and so grateful to me for taking him out of uniform it was sometimes embarrassing. I'd brought him on board in July, when I'd taken my promotion, and hadn't regretted it.

"Captain, you want me to go to court with Eddie for the hearing?"

"Yeah, that would be good, Nate." We were all on a first-name basis in the unit, but Nate was so new, it was still hard for him to call me anything but Captain. I was trying to give him experience in all phases of our work, and observing a few court hearings wouldn't hurt him.

"Yes, sir."

I was going to have to work harder at being friendly to him.

None of us were emotionally close to the new men yet. Eddie, Arnie, and I had worked with Mike for a long time, and dropping two new men into the mix had changed the dynamic. I wanted Nate and Clyde to be an integral part of Priority by the time Arnie retired.

Supervising Eddie and Arnie was also strange, when we'd worked side by side for years. I was still struggling with the management end of the job, and Mike was my main support. When he was named chief of police, I had stepped into his old job with trepidation, but he gave me free advice whenever I wanted, and sometimes when I didn't.

I made a few notes on each man's file and put the paperwork away. I was working on a computer fraud case of my own at the moment, so I buckled down on that for a while.

Clyde and Arnie came into the office about ten o'clock. They'd been working nights on a drug case all week and had joined us for the sunrise raid. I sent them home to get some sleep.

The office was quiet all morning, and I sent out e-mail requests for information on stolen paintings to the state police and several municipal police departments in the area. Then I went back to my computer fraud case until Eddie and Nate came in just before noon, fresh from the smugglers' bail hearing.

"Going to eat lunch, Harvey?" Eddie asked, pulling off the striped necktie he'd worn to the courthouse.

"Brought it with me. I'll eat here."

"How's Jennifer doing?" Nate asked.

"Pretty good. I'm hoping her sister Abby will come stay with us for a while. She's coming tomorrow for a job interview at the hospital."

Eddie's ears pricked up. Abby bore a striking resemblance to my wife, who was high on Eddie's list of favorite people. He'd met Abby and the third sister, Leeanne, at the time of the wedding and had kept up a steady flirtation with both of them while they were around for the festivities.

He hovered near my desk, and I said, "Abby's staying for the weekend. Why don't you come over Saturday night and visit?" He rewarded me with a huge smile.

When he and Nate left for the café down the block, I dialed my home number. Jennifer answered.

"Hey, gorgeous, how you feeling?"

"Not too bad."

"Did you eat any lunch yet?"

"No. I'm thinking about it."

"Make sure you feed that baby." I was feeling very tender toward her. I'd wanted kids for years, but had been deeply disappointed during my first marriage. After it ended, I'd stayed single so long I'd about given up. "I invited Eddie to come over Saturday night, is that okay?"

"Should be. Abby can help me fix dinner."

"Okay."

"I'm going to get her room ready this afternoon."

"Don't push it."

"I'm fine," she said.

The whole pregnancy thing was so new to me, I wasn't sure what she was and was not capable of. I leaned toward feeling guilty if she had the least discomfort, but her doctor, Margaret Turner, knew me well enough to try to counteract that. She was a good friend, and she'd sent some books home with Jennifer. Evenings I'd been reading a little, and I was starting to believe that most women in the "delicate condition" weren't all that delicate. I was still a little dazed by the fact that Jennifer had married me, and we had this enormous joy of a coming child added. I didn't deserve it.

Eddie brought his sandwich up to the office, and we ate together in the break room. He gave me all the details on the bail hearing, and I thought he had things well in hand.

Mike walked into the room at quarter to one. He frequently left the cushy chief's office upstairs to visit us in his old stomping grounds.

"Harvey, can you boys handle one more case?"

"Besides the art thing? I guess so. Eddie and Nate are about done with the tobacco smuggling. They'll have arraignments and paperwork."

"Well, you'll need Eddie on this one."

Eddie's eyebrows shot up, but his mouth was full, so he didn't say anything.

"What is it?" I asked.

"A 911 call came in ten minutes ago from the

Québécois Club. They've sent four ambulances over there. The lunch guests are dropping like flies."

"Mass food poisoning?" I asked.

"That was the first impression. But the club manager insists it's a deliberate poisoning."

"You're joking."

Mike shook his head. "He says it's a hate crime."

"Oh, brother!"

"What's so amazing?" said Eddie. "Lots of you Anglos hate Frenchmen. Francophones were persecuted in Maine right up until the 1960s."

I scowled at Eddie. "Listen to you! You're my best friend, but when somebody says 'hate crime,' you're lumping us all together as Anglos! I happen to be Swedish, you imbecile!"

"Careful," Mike said, "that might be construed as an ethnic slur. Anyway, take a couple of guys on over there and see if you can sort it out. If it doesn't make any sense, say so, and tell the press that. Come up and see me when you get back, Harvey."

I called to Nate, and he went with Eddie and me in my vehicle.

"What is this place, anyway?" he asked, when we got out in front of the Québécois Club. The old, three-story brick building had a discreet sign over the steps. A rescue unit was parked in front, and an ambulance pulled up behind it.

"It's a private club for French people," I said.

"For French *men*," Eddie corrected.

"Isn't that illegal?" Nate asked. "I thought gender-based organizations went out a long time ago?"

"Not illegal, just politically incorrect," I told him.

Eddie said, "It's mostly old guys. They come here to get a good lunch and *parler français* to each other and get away from their wives."

We went up the steps and inside, where pandemonium ruled, in French. Everywhere, elderly men sat waving their arms and chattering away *en français*. EMTs were examining one moaning customer who lay on the floor. The place smelled like fresh bread and vomit.

A white-haired man in a tweed jacket stood by, wringing his hands, watching the EMTs anxiously. I stepped over to him and held up my badge.

"I'm Captain Larson. Who's in charge here?"

He turned toward me and let loose a stream of rapid French, of which I caught, "*C'est mauvais, c'est horrible.*"

"Eddie," I said.

Eddie stepped up and started talking to the man in French. One of the EMTs stood up, and I approached him.

"What happened here?" I asked.

"At least six people got bad abdominal

29

cramps during lunch. Sudden onset, and violent symptoms. We're taking this man in, and there's one more who probably ought to go. That will make seven total—we already transported five."

"What caused it?"

"We don't know."

I went back to Eddie.

"He's the manager," Eddie said, nodding toward the man he'd questioned. "All he knows is, people started getting sick and collapsing. It happened really fast. He doesn't know what caused it. He called 911 for the first man, and by the time the ambulance got here, there were three more."

"Seven now," I said.

"Well, he's all upset, of course, because this place is known for the best French food. I mean, you have to be French to come here, and they won't put up with anything second class. But he insists it wasn't the food."

"All right, we need to know what every sick person ordered. Food, wine, everything, right down to the toothpicks."

Eddie turned back to the manager. Nate and I found our way into the kitchen. The chef was better at English, so I talked to him. Nate interviewed a college-age busboy who spoke fluent, if slangy, English.

The chef insisted that there was nothing wrong with the food. Everything was fresh, fresh, fresh!

I tried to calm him down a little, but he thought everyone was accusing him of poisoning the *vieux messieurs*.

Nate asked the busboy to locate the waiters' order slips for him, and I abandoned the chef and helped him line up the waiters and sort out who had waited on the men who subsequently became ill. The three waiters went through their order slips and identified the ones for people who'd gone to the hospital.

Nate made a careful list of everything on each order form. I asked what else the patrons had had access to. There wasn't a salad bar, but they were served water in the dining room, and there were salt, pepper, and sugar containers on the tables.

I left Nate questioning the chef about the ingredients of each dish served and went into the dining room in search of Eddie.

"What have you got?" I asked.

"He says this was done to kill French people. He thinks it was a frog-hater."

I stared at him. "I can't believe you just said that."

Eddie brought his hands to chest level, palms open. "Not me. I'm telling you what he said."

"Okay." I shook my head. "Eddie, you know I love you and your colorful but charming people. I suppose there could possibly be a francophobe behind this, but really, those attitudes went out with the 1930s, didn't they?"

"Not according to my pop. But anyway, that's what this guy was saying, that it was a hate crime. I don't buy it."

"I'm glad to hear you say that. I don't buy it, either. Maybe it was a woman," I said. "Some misanthropic women's libber who wants them to open the club up to females."

"To me, that's more believable. Anyway, these guys want to leave." Eddie nodded toward the healthy diners, who still sat at their tables, talking away with fluid gestures. The ambulance crews had moved out with the last of the stricken.

I thought about it for a few seconds. "Let's take names and addresses and let them go." As long as we could contact them later, I didn't see any point in holding them all. If they stuck around, we could possibly have more sick people on our hands.

We went around the room, cataloguing the information. I could handle some of the names, like LaChance and Pellotte, but fell down on Ouellette and Quirion, and started yelling for Eddie when I met Monsieur Poissonier. When we had all of their addresses, they left singly or in pairs, shaking their heads. A few of them asked us if their friends would be all right. Eddie spoke soothingly to them in French, and he seemed to have a calming effect on them. Score one for Portland P.D.

When the club had emptied except for the

32

manager and staff, I took Nate's notebook and went through the list of foods and drinks served. Several wines were served, but the sick people didn't share any bottles. Besides water, there was one common item for the victims, crème brulée. I sent Eddie to the chef.

"Get his recipe, then get a sample of every ingredient, from the container he used. And ask him if he put anything in it today that's not in the recipe. It could turn out to be a simple case of tainted supplies."

We took away an untouched serving, and partial portions from the dishes of two of the victims. The rest had already gone to the dishwasher. I detailed Nate to get the dishes to the lab, along with the samples of ingredients.

"Can we open tomorrow?" the manager asked me.

"I'm sorry, but you need to wait until the lab reports are in. I'll try to expedite it," I said, but he looked back at me with a blank expression, so I called Eddie over to translate.

The manager and the chef weren't happy, but I told them there wasn't room for a repeat performance the next day, and the club couldn't serve any food or drink until we gave them the okay. They seemed to accept my verdict, and we left.

At the station, I briefed Mike and went back to my computer job. Eddie and Nate worked furiously on the poisoning case all afternoon, then stayed late to complete their reports on the tobacco smuggling.

When I got home that night, Jennifer met me at the door. I set my briefcase on the top step and kissed her thoroughly.

"How you doing, gorgeous?"

"All right."

We watched the local news broadcast, which played up the mysterious outbreak at the Québécois Club. Then I ate my supper while Jennifer picked at hers. I figured she had given me an optimistic version of her health report.

"What would taste good to you?" I asked her.

She considered that at length. "Maybe . . . a jelly doughnut?"

I laughed. "You can't keep saltines down, and you want jelly doughnuts?"

She looked hurt.

"Oh, Jenny." I put my arms around her and pulled her over onto my lap. "I'm sorry. If you think you can eat 'em, I'll go get 'em."

I drove to the nearest Dunkin' Donuts and bought half a dozen jelly doughnuts. When I got home, Jennifer very slowly ate one, and I ate three.

The stack of messages on my desk Friday morning took me a while. I wasn't used to all the administrative clutter, and I appealed to Paula, our unit's secretary. Civilian aide, that is. She thumbed through the notes and handed me three.

"You need to return these calls right away. If you want, I can schedule the appointments you need. Ignore the rest."

"I can do that?"

Paula assured me I could.

I returned the calls Paula had selected while my men worked on their open cases. Eddie and Nate were going over the lab report from the Québécois Club, which had come in surprisingly fast. No doubt after the evening news report, Mike had called the lab techs and put a little pressure on them.

"The crème brulée was definitely the culprit," Eddie told me.

"Food poisoning?"

"Arsenic."

I stared at him. "You're not kidding, are you?"

"No, it was in the cornstarch."

"Suspects?"

"Everyone who worked there, at least." He shrugged. "I suppose any of the guests could have gone into the kitchen, too."

"Ask the chef and the kitchen workers and waiters who was in there."

"It could have happened on Wednesday," Nate put in. "The chef prepared the dish yesterday morning, and he had used cornstarch for something else on Wednesday. It was fine then. So, the arsenic was put in it between Wednesday morning and Thursday morning."

I said, "All right, between that and the smugglers' arraignments, it sounds like you two have your day's work cut out for you."

They left, and I turned back to the stack of messages. I was invited to sit in on interviews of candidates for the deputy chief's slot the next week, and I didn't feel I could refuse. A social worker wanted to discuss plans for a girl Eddie and I had arrested on a drug charge that spring. An assistant district attorney needed to see me about a pending case.

I gave Paula notes for my schedule and finally got down to work on the computer fraud case. I needed blocks of time to set up dummy accounts for myself as a potential customer for the swindler I hoped to catch. I wanted to resolve that case to free myself up to pursue the art thefts. I had a feeling that case could turn out to be very important.

At noon, Eddie and Nate weren't back. I hoped they weren't eating at the Québécois Club. I called home, and Abby answered.

"How was your interview?" I asked.

"I got the job, Harvey. I can start anytime, nights."

"What did you tell them?"

"I'll give a week's notice in Waterville and start here next Saturday."

"Fantastic, Abby. Your rent's free, as long as you want to stay with us."

"Thank you. I can stay now until Sunday afternoon if you want me to. I came prepared."

"That would be great. How's Jenny doing?"

"Not bad. We were just eating lunch."

Jennifer came on the line and said, "Hi, honey."

I smiled at the caress in her voice. "Hey, Abby says you're holding your own."

"I think so. Half a sandwich so far. It's really good to have her here."

"Is there anything I can bring you tonight?" I asked.

"Just you."

"I'll be there as early as I can be."

I walked down the street to the café that the cops for some reason called "the diner," even though it wasn't one, and made myself eat a sandwich and drink a glass of milk. Mike came and sat down opposite me.

"Hey, Harv, what's up with the Québécois?"

"I'm letting Eddie and Nate handle it, and I'm trying to put my computer fraud case to bed." I told him what they had so far on the food poisoning.

"How's Nate working out in the unit?"

"Great. I'm really glad we got him."

"And Clyde?"

"Too soon to tell. Ask me again in a week."

"Older guys take a while to settle in on a new

assignment." He smiled. "But then, you know how that is. Had a chance to do anything on the art theft yet?"

"Some. I put out a few feelers, and I had Eddie question the smugglers they brought in about the painting, but they claim ignorance, which is odd, since it was in their vehicle."

"Hmm, yeah." He tipped up his bottle of Moxie and took a big swig.

"So, what are you up to, Mike?"

"Looking for a new deputy, tightening up security a little, trying to get department heads to start thinking about their budgets for next year. That would be you."

"Already?"

"Just get a copy of last year's budget and look it over and start thinking about it. Paula might have some suggestions. She did a lot of work on the unit budget last year. And don't forget you've got a management seminar October first, and your IBIS training is coming up next month."

I felt a little steam-rollered. Eddie and I were scheduled to go to the Maine State Police Academy near Waterville for two days of training on an updated ballistics identification system. That would be interesting, but the management seminar sounded like a huge bore.

"Jennifer and I are going to stay at her parents' house when I go up there for IBIS training," I said. "Her folks are only twenty miles or so from the Academy, and I'd hate to leave her right now."

"Because of the baby?"

"Yeah. Did Sharon have morning sickness?"

"Yeah. Well, with Mike, Junior she did. I don't know about with Debbie. I remember with Tommy, Sharon was crabby the first three months, and miserable the last three."

"So the middle three are the best?"

"Hey, every woman's different, they say. Let me ask you something. Does a baby have a soul before it's born?"

Mike wasn't a Christian, but his wife was, and lately he'd been coming up with these theological questions for me. He and Sharon must have some interesting discussions at home. At least he was willing to talk about God, and I tried to be patient with his questions, even though Mike didn't seem to make any progress spiritually. We batted that one around for a while, then I went back to my desk.

I spent most of the afternoon on the computer, setting up the swindler. We'd gotten the tip on the racket from a local woman who had been taken for over five thousand dollars in phony investments. I'd spent several days unraveling the scheme, and had now tracked the thief electronically to York, Pennsylvania.

I made some calls and filled in the local police down there. They would make the arrest, and I started faxing documentation they would need to press charges. At four-thirty, they phoned me to say the swindler was in custody, and I felt like I'd done a good day's work.

Eddie and Nate came in and discussed the Québécois case with me. They had a promising list of suspects and were leaning toward a former employee of the club who had been fired for rudeness to the elderly patrons.

"Aren't you disappointed it wasn't an Anglo?" I asked, "or maybe a Scandinavian?"

Eddie rolled his eyes. "Oh, come on, Harv."

"Yeah, yeah," I said.

Nate actually chuckled, which told me he was getting used to me and knew I wouldn't bite his head off over small stuff.

They decided to come in on Saturday and carry on with the case. Paula said goodnight and went home. While the guys polished off their reports, I went back to the art case. I pulled up copies of the reports on Legere's two art thefts, then entered several key words into my flagging program. I did some research on the artists whose works had been stolen. There were no artists in common for the items stolen in the two burglaries, and there weren't any Nevar canvases reported stolen. I contacted the police departments in several more area towns and asked for data on any art thefts within the last year.

Arnie Fowler called me and said he and Clyde

were making progress on their case and would call it a day. I trusted Arnie to file a thorough report. Eddie and Nate e-mailed me their daily reports and stood up, ready to head home.

Nate headed for the locker room, and I said, "Eddie, look at this." The police chief in Kennebunk had responded to my e-mail inquiry, saying a Nevar and several other artworks had been stolen in his jurisdiction a few weeks earlier.

Eddie leaned over and read my screen. "You think that's our painting?" His dark eyes gleamed. "I mean, the one we confiscated?"

"Could be. I'll have him send a description of the stolen Nevar, and if it's a match one of you guys can take it down to Kennebunk Monday."

Abby was setting the table for three when I got home. I greeted her and walked on through to the sunroom, where I found Jennifer on the wicker settee, with a book of poetry on her lap. She was wearing navy sweat pants, white socks, and my old Harvard T-shirt. Her hair was loose and full, and I knew she'd washed and blow-dried it.

"Feeling better?" I asked, smiling as I bent to kiss her.

"Much. Abby won't let me help her with supper, but I think I'm actually going to enjoy eating tonight."

"Great." I sat down beside her and put my arms around her. "Mike wants the department to buy more copies of your flagging program."

41

"Tell him I'll install one on his computer for free."

"He wants it for the entire system, or at least for several officers. Wants to know if you're going to market it."

"Oh, that would be a big project. Marketing is not my forte."

"How about that guy who bought the rights to your programs from Coastal?"

"John Macomber?"

"Yeah. He's marketing your other programs." Her former coworker at the software company had made a deal with her earlier in the year.

"Maybe I should call him," she said.

"Do it tonight?" I gave her my most persuasive smile.

"Okay. Now, kiss me again."

I was happy to oblige, and I rubbed her tummy lightly. "Do you think our baby has a soul?"

She pulled away and frowned at me. "That's kind of out of the blue."

"Not really. Mike asked me."

"Oh." She nodded with total understanding. "I don't know. I guess so. I hadn't really thought about it."

As if Mike hadn't give me enough to read up on, with the art case. I kissed her again.

Eddie came over late Saturday afternoon. Jennifer was having a nap, and I took him out to the back yard, where we sat on the lawn swing. Abby brought iced tea out and joined us, sitting beside me.

"I made mashed potatoes for shepherd's pie tonight," she said. "Do you think Jennifer could eat that? She always liked it as a kid."

I thought about it and shrugged. It sounded pretty bland—potatoes, corn, hamburger. "Worth a try. I'm sure she can eat the potatoes, if nothing else. And she tells me the nausea goes away later in the day."

"Yeah, that's why it's called morning sickness."

Eddie asked about her nursing job, and Abby was soon regaling us with stories of the ER in Waterville, where she had spent the last few months. Eddie was very attentive, and I started feeling like I was the one who should go cook the meal.

Finally Abby looked at her watch. "I'd better start supper!" She jumped up and ran into the house.

"She sure looks like Jennifer," Eddie said. "She's smart, too."

"Eddie . . ."

"What?"

I shook my head. I was having enough trouble being Eddie's boss. I wasn't sure I could handle it if he started dating my sister-in-law.

I went inside to check on Jenny. She was asleep, her shimmering hair fanned out on the pillow. I thought I could touch it, ever so softly, without disturbing her, but her eyelids flew open.

"I'm sorry. I didn't mean to wake you up."

She struggled to sit up.

"What time is it?"

"Five o'clock. Eddie's here. Abby's making dinner."

She got up and put on her Portland Sea Dogs sweatshirt, and we went out to the patio. Eddie still sat on the swing. He stood when I opened the French door.

"Jennifer! Are you feeling better?"

"Yes. I'm glad you could come, Eddie."

She reached out to him, and he kissed her shyly on the cheek. He was still coming to terms with Jennifer being pregnant and tended to blush at first, every time he saw her, which was amazing because Eddie is very outgoing and usually in his element around women.

We talked a little, and Eddie updated us on the Thibodeau clan. His grand-mère was knitting him a sweater, and Cousin Rene's baby, Danielle, was rolling over.

After a bit, Abby came and told us the meal was ready, and we went inside. Jennifer ate as if nothing was wrong, and my nagging uneasiness began to fade. I settled her afterward in front of the fireplace in the living room, lit the fire, and brought a crocheted afghan to the armchair where she sat. Eddie volunteered to help Abby with the dishes, and she accepted with alacrity. Girls seemed to fall all over themselves trying to get Eddie's attention, and I saw the signs in Abby, but he wasn't making it difficult for her. He wielded that dishtowel like a pro and kept up a running banter with her while they worked.

I set up the Trivial Pursuit game, then went through the study that had been the previous owner's dining room and pushed the kitchen door open. Eddie was hanging up his dish towel while Abby swabbed out the sink.

"You guys ready for a little trivia?" I asked.

"Only if I can be on your team," Abby said. She looked at Eddie. "Has anyone *ever* beaten him?"

"Once that I know of," Eddie replied, "and then it was bad luck rolling the dice. But Jennifer's pretty good, too."

"You can be her teammate."

I frowned at Abby. "Don't I get a say in this?"

"Nope. Come on, I'll let you be team captain."

Team Eddie had some luck with rolling the dice, but when it came down to it, Abby and I beat him and Jennifer.

"It's because this is an old game," Eddie said.

"Yeah, I think you're right." Abby nodded soberly. "If they had an updated version, Harvey wouldn't know all the music and movies. Maybe that's what I'll get you two for Christmas."

"Yeah, a Millennials version," Eddie said. He

was always ragging me about my age, but now Abby was ganging up with him.

"Eddie's just a sore loser," I said.

"Now, children." Jennifer put on her most adult tone. "I believe it's cookie time."

After the cookie break, Eddie was ready to head out. It was nine-thirty, and we all needed sleep. I walked out to his truck with him.

"So, did you and Abby talk much while you were doing dishes?" I asked him.

"Yeah. I told her how I go to church with you all the time now, and she said she'll go with us in the morning. I like her a lot, Harv."

"Well, take it easy. I don't know if I could handle having you in the family."

Chapter 3

Sunday, September 19

Jennifer insisted she felt fine Sunday morning and was adamant that she did not want to miss church. I gave in, and she dressed demurely in a navy jumper and white blouse. Abby wore nice pants and a plaid blouse. She put her own hair up and did Jennifer's for her. They might have been twins. I didn't actually see Jennifer eat any breakfast, but she told me she was all set, and I decided not to make it an issue.

When we got to the church, Eddie was sitting with Jennifer and Abby's brother, Jeff. He had recently been hired by the Portland Fire Department and moved down from the family farm in Skowhegan. Sitting between Jeff and Eddie was Jennifer's old roommate, Beth Bradley. She'd sparked a minor rivalry between Jeff and Eddie that summer, but Jeff seemed to have carried the day, and Eddie had backed off.

Jeff came into the aisle to hug his sisters, then had Abby sit beside him. Jenny wanted to sit on the aisle, in case she needed to tear for the ladies' room. I didn't say "I told you so," but sat between her and Abby without comment. I couldn't help wondering if she was really going to be okay, and how long this would last. Anxiety for Jennifer kept me so preoccupied I didn't get much from the sermon, but she made it through the service and seemed to be feeling fine afterward.

I said to Eddie, "Do you have a place to eat lunch?"

He leaned toward me and whispered, "The Hammonds invited me." The Hammonds had a cute twenty-two-year-old daughter, Lydia, who worked in personnel at the B&M Baked Beans cannery, and three younger children. Lydia was in the singles Sunday school class Eddie had been attending.

"Great." I should have known Eddie would find a new social life in his new circles. He said goodbye to Abby and the others and ambled off to join Lydia and her parents.

During lunch at our house, Abby was rather subdued. She had to head north that afternoon and finish out her last week of work in Waterville.

"I hate to go home and leave you," she said to me when Jennifer had left the table for a nap. "What if she's worse tomorrow, and you have to go to work?"

"One of her friends could come and stay with her, I guess. I'm really glad you'll be staying here with us for a while, though."

"I'd do anything for Jennifer."

I smiled at her. "I know. Thank you. It's a big relief to me that you're willing to move down here and do this for us."

"Well, I wanted this job change, anyway. The timing was right for everybody, I guess." Abby got up and started clearing off the table, and I took my dishes to the sink.

"I'll clean up," I said. "You need to pack."

"Okay. I'll be back Friday, and I'll start at Maine Medical Saturday night."

"Bring down your books and things," I said. "Whatever you want here."

"Thanks." She wrapped up the leftover food and put it in the refrigerator, then left the kitchen. I started the dishwasher and wiped the table and counter.

After Abby said goodbye to Jennifer, I carried her luggage out to the car. She gave me a watery smile, then embraced me. "I'm glad she got you, Harvey."

"Thanks. That means a lot."

She flipped her long hair over her shoulder, got in her car, and drove away.

I went back to Jennifer and stretched out beside her on the quilt. She lay quietly in my arms, and I held her until she fell asleep.

Eddie and I had been running together three times a week for years, and he met me at the corner Monday morning. When we got back to my house, the coffeemaker was running, and Jennifer was making pancakes.

"Hey," I said. "You're supposed to be sleeping."

"I did that already. Sit and eat, both of you."

Eddie poured himself a cup of coffee and sipped it uneasily, watching Jennifer over the rim of the mug.

He caught my eye. "Maybe I should just leave and see you at work."

"No." Jennifer brandished the spatula at him. "I am healthy, and I'm cooking a big breakfast. You can't leave."

He gave in and helped himself to a stack of pancakes. I made a mental note not to tell him any details if Jennifer had more stomach upsets. To my surprise, she sat down and ate a pancake, too. Maybe things were on the uptick. Eddie started making jokes, and she laughed at them. Definitely a good sign.

When we arrived at the station, Arnie and Clyde went up the stairs with Eddie and me. I gathered them around to talk about their cases, and Nate came in while we were planning the day for the unit.

I updated them on the art theft case. Kennebunk had e-mailed me a digital photo of the Nevar painting stolen there. It matched the one we had found on the raid, so I sent Arnie to Kennebunk with the painting. Their department would document it as evidence and return it to the owner.

Clyde had to spend the morning at the court-house, and Eddie and Nate planned to pick up the Québécois Club suspect for questioning.

A report came in from the chief in Cape Elizabeth after the men had left. They'd had an art theft in May. A couple's home had been burglarized while they were out of town. The security system had been deactivated. In addition to artworks, the thieves had stolen their electronics, two collector shotguns, and a target pistol.

Hard on the heels of that e-mail, I received a fax with a chilling report from the Westbrook P.D. In late July, a night burglary had gone awry, and the homeowner had been shot with his own weapon. He'd survived, but had undergone extensive rehabilitation. I wondered why I hadn't heard about the case, until I realized it had happened during my honeymoon. Small sculptures, a coin collection, a portrait, and guns had been taken.

I called upstairs to see if Mike was available. He was, and I went up to discuss the new developments with him.

"Could be the same guys who did the two jobs in Portland," he said thoughtfully, chewing gum as he looked over the printouts. His jacket lay over a chair, and his tie hung around his neck untied.

"Should I look farther afield?" I asked. "Portsmouth, maybe?"

He shrugged. "They could be crossing the state line."

"Yeah, I'm pretty sure that Nevar painting was headed for Quebec."

Mike snapped his gum, frowning. "Let's concentrate on Maine. You can catch new crimes from the updates. How about you check with Scarborough, Biddeford, and Saco P.D.'s for past cases?"

"Yeah, I've sent out inquiries. And I thought I'd visit the Portland Museum of Art today and broaden my education."

Mike grinned. "Atta boy! Go for it."

I drove to the art museum and told the curator about the art thefts. He had heard about a couple of them, but was surprised to learn we'd found several more in the area. I asked him how museums went about buying artworks, and how they knew they weren't stolen. He explained a little bit, the novice version, I'm sure, about how they investigated the provenance of each piece they acquired. He was also able to tell me some things about the sculptor and a couple of the painters whose works had been stolen in the recent burglaries.

He put a print-out in my hand. "Here's a list of organizations and e-mail sites we offer free to our patrons. You can go online and sign up for notices for art shows and auctions."

"Great." I folded it, tucked it in my pocket, and

gave him my business card. "Please call us at the Priority Unit if you notice anything not quite right—or very wrong."

"I'll do that."

It was one o'clock when I left the museum. I grabbed a sandwich and went back to the office and tried to concentrate on work.

Eddie and Nate came in and asked me to run over to the Québécois Club with them. They had brought in the disgruntled former employee, Thomas, and questioned him, but now were having second and third thoughts about his guilt. We drove to the club in Eddie's truck and talked some more with the manager, the chef, and the waiters.

"I don't like that waiter, Jason," Eddie said. "He's evasive."

"Something's a little off with him," Nate agreed.

We had given the club the okay to open for lunch that day, and a dozen or so men sat in the dining room. After a quick chat with the manager, we went out to the kitchen. Eddie cornered Jason and talked to him some more while Nate and I assured the chef that we were working hard on the case.

"I am tasting," he said with a grave nod. "I taste everything now."

I hoped he used a clean spoon.

Eddie rejoined us, and I looked a question at him.

"I don't know. Nothing solid."

"Let it rest for now," I said.

We went outside, and Nate said, "Captain, do you think we're on the wrong track?"

"Maybe. Just let it simmer for a few hours, Nate. Sometimes things sort themselves out."

Eddie laughed and looked at Nate. "That's Harvey's favorite method of investigating—thinking."

"It's the best tool in the toolbox," I said. "Your favorite is legwork, and that's a good one, too, but sometimes you just need to let the dust settle."

I stopped on the sidewalk and called Jennifer on my cell phone. Nate and Eddie walked on toward the truck.

"How you doing, gorgeous?" I asked.

"Pretty good."

"Sure you're okay?"

"Well," she said, "I think I could eat a jelly doughnut right about now."

"Great! I'll send some over." I had lost my skepticism about jelly doughnuts.

Nate had climbed into the jump seat, and I got in front with Eddie. We were ready to head back to the office, and I said, "Just pull in at the doughnut shop for a minute, Ed."

He stopped at Double D, and I ran in and came out with a box of jelly doughnuts. There was a florist practically next door, so I told Eddie and Nate to hang on, and went in there and got half a dozen pink roses, then asked the florist to call me a cab. While she did, I scrawled a note to Jennifer on a card: "Precious Jenny, you make me very happy."

I paid for the flowers and went out and stood at the curb. Eddie and Nate were waiting for me in in the truck. Eddie spread his hands in a silent but unmistakable "What are you doing?" I signaled for them to be patient.

The cab pulled up, and I opened the passenger door and laid the box of doughnuts and the flowers with the card on the seat beside the driver.

"Can you deliver this stuff to 137 Van Cleeve Lane within the next fifteen minutes?" I asked. I held up a twenty-dollar bill.

"Not a problem."

I took out my pocket notebook and wrote down the telephone number for the cab company and the number of the car. "All right, buddy." I handed him the twenty. "Here's the deal. I've got your number. In fifteen minutes, I'm going to call my wife. If she's not eating jelly doughnuts, I'm calling your boss. Got it?"

He looked at my badge, the twenty, and me. "Got it. And thanks."

I shut the door and walked back to Eddie's truck and got in.

"Do we want to know what that was about?" Eddie asked.

"Jennifer's got a craving for jelly doughnuts."

"That's a good sign," said Nate.

"How can she eat jelly doughnuts?" asked Eddie. "She barely keeps breakfast down."

"Don't ask me, I'm just glad she's hungry."

When I got back to my desk, I called her.

"Hey, gorgeous! Whatcha doing?"

She laughed. "Eating doughnuts."

"Fantastic." I was content.

"The flowers are beautiful."

"Are you sick of roses?"

"As if."

I smiled for the next hour.

When I got home at quarter past five, Jenny was asleep in our bedroom. I tiptoed in, and she opened her eyes. I scooped her into my arms, sitting on the edge of the bed.

"How you doing?" I asked, pressing my cheek against her hair.

"Good, but I'm thirsty. I've been really lazy today. I should have done some computer work, but I'm so sleepy."

"You needed the rest." I went to get her some fresh water. When I got back into the bedroom, she was thumbing through a book her obstetrician had given us, on pregnancy and childbirth.

"Listen to this, Harvey! Our baby is an inch long."

"That small?" I pulled a little tape measure out

of my pocket and looked at the first inch mark. "That's pretty tiny to be causing you all this trouble."

"Oh, and his heart is beating already. Can you believe that?"

"Wow."

"Mary Rowland called, and I asked her if babies that tiny have a soul. She thinks they do."

"I'll tell Mike." If our pastor's wife said it was so, it probably was so, although Mike would give me an argument, just on principle. I think he just enjoyed arguing.

I went to the other side of the bed and took my shoes off and moved over beside Jennifer. I held her close while she read to me what babies are like at eight weeks after conception. I couldn't remember being so happy.

The next morning I offered to call one of our friends from church to come and keep Jennifer company and do a little housework, but she insisted she didn't need to be baby-sat. I wasn't totally convinced, but I said, "Okay. I'll run home for lunch if I can."

Eddie and Nate were at the office when I got there, already working on the poisoning investigation. They got out their notes and hashed it out, arguing a little and reading bits to each other from their interviews. All of the Québécois Club's arsenic victims had survived, but three were still in the hospital. The doctors said the poison had been too diluted to be fatal. I got coffee and checked the e-mail and crime updates on my computer, keeping one ear on their conversation.

"The guy that got fired, Thomas, was in there late Wednesday," said Nate. "He could have done it."

"But his new boss says he was at work," Eddie reminded him. "He's got an alibi."

"But they don't watch him all the time," Nate argued. "Somebody saw him at the Québécois."

"Who?"

They both pawed through their notes.

"Jason," Nate said. There was a moment's silence.

"Who else?" Eddie asked, his voice rising.

Silence again.

"Jason was the only one to see Thomas in the club," Eddie said at last. "Suppose he wasn't really there."

"Why would Jason lie?" Nate asked.

Their eyes met, and they were out the door.

Paula answered the phone on her desk and said, "Just a moment, please." She pushed a button. "Harvey, line two. Those boys sure are persistent, aren't they?"

"Yeah, I think they're close to breaking this case. Who is it?" I nodded toward my blinking desk phone. I didn't like surprises.

"The social worker on the Hadley case."

"Thanks." I took the call, rescheduled the appointment I'd made the previous week, and went back to my pursuit of fine art.

Nate and Eddie reported to me an hour later. The waiter, Jason, had skipped work that morning without an explanation. When they heard that, they went right to his house and picked him up. He was hustling his girlfriend to pack, about to leave town. They took him into custody, but he refused to talk without a lawyer present.

"He's down in the holding cell. Terry's going to call us after he has a chat with the lawyer." Eddie flopped down into his chair.

I filled them in on what I'd been doing on the art case while they waited. Finally Terry called Eddie, and he and Nate went down to get the prisoner. They took him and the court-appointed lawyer into the interview room. After they'd talked for a while, Jason Cuvier was ready to confess.

"That idiot thought he could extort money from the manager," Eddie told me later. "How stupid can you be? He practically closed the whole club down."

"What, he was threatening to poison the food again if they didn't give him money?"

"Something like that," Eddie said. "He thought he had this brilliant plan, but when he saw how sick people were, he got scared and didn't ask the manager for money. I ask you, how profitable is it to blackmail someone whose business you ruin?"

"Really bright guy," I said.

"Yeah. He must be Swedish."

"Oh, tell me about it," I said, but I smiled.

He and Nate were doing all right. They were learning to make their different ways of working complement each other, and I hoped they'd be good partners in the end. Eddie definitely had the edge on Nate in experience, but Nate had a way of seeing the whole picture that I thought would be helpful, if Eddie would listen to him.

After they'd returned the prisoner to holding, I checked the crime updates on my computer, keeping one ear on their conversation. A painting by one of the artists I'd flagged was reported stolen in Yarmouth, to the north of us. I printed out the data and took it to Eddie.

"Can you call the Yarmouth P.D. and get a complete report on this?"

He scanned the sheet. "Another painting stolen."

"Yeah, they're very active."

"Maybe there's more than one set of burglars," Nate said.

"It's possible." I went back to my desk.

Eddie at last hammered out a plan of action for the rest of the day, and he and Nate left the office. Paula brought me a fax from the police chief in Biddeford. They'd had an art theft in their city a month before. The thieves had broken in while the family slept, disarming the burglar alarm. They had stolen a good painting and some antique ink bottles. Also, two televisions and a computer with a laser printer, a CD player, and a motorbike.

"Motorbike?" Arnie Fowler's eyebrows shot up when I told him. "These guys haven't stolen anything that big before."

"Right. Computers and TVs were the biggest items, other than paintings."

I went home for lunch. Jennifer had it on the table, and she ate with me, just a little macaroni and a few carrots, and a couple of bites of my piece of pie, but she was drinking milk today, and she smiled into my eyes while she did it.

"Janice brought the pie," she said.

Bud and Janice Parker were our neighbors, in a well-kept ranch across the street. Bud had given me lawn care advice, and Janice had been friendly to Jennifer. They were nearly sixty, and Bud was looking forward to retirement from his insurance career. Janice was a dedicated homemaker and had helped Jennifer keep the flower beds healthy through August. Jennifer had gone over when they bought a new computer and helped set it up, and she'd taught Janice how to Skype with their Air Force colonel son.

That afternoon I looked at the unit's budget for the previous year. I went through it three times and asked Paula a few questions before it totally made sense.

Eddie and Nate were busy on another robbery case, wrapping it up and doing the paperwork. I put Arnie onto compiling the details from all the art thefts, so we could spot common factors, and I asked Clyde to try to determine where the victims had bought their artworks.

I continued educating myself on the artists whose works had been stolen. Most were respected, living American artists. Their media varied. Most were oils or watercolors, but two acrylics had been snatched, as well as the three small sculptures in the Biddeford burglary, and small antiques from several homes.

About three o'clock, I called Mike to see if he could pay us a visit. Mike had been going through his own budget woes and was glad to take a break. He came through the stairway door smiling.

"This place smells like home."

All of the men welcomed him, though Nate seemed a bit shy with the chief. The rest of us were on a first-name basis with Mike, and that must have seemed odd to Nate. I'd been a little scared of the last chief myself, in the old days, and anyone called upstairs to his office knew it couldn't be for anything good. But I knew Mike so well, I didn't think he could scare me—unless he started talking about retiring again.

I went over what we had with him and let Arnie and Clyde add their bits. Some of the stolen items had been bought directly from the artists at shows, some through galleries, and a few at auction.

I folded my hands on my desk and looked at Mike. "My preliminary theory is this, and I could be absolutely wrong, but it seems to me that the art thefts are for one person or group, and the electronics are for another. I'm not sure about the antiques and coin collection yet. They could go either way."

"So, you're saying the thieves split the loot between at least two buyers?" Mike asked.

"Yes, or maybe they're commissioned to steal the art, and can pick up whatever else they want for themselves at the same time. So far, they haven't gone into bedrooms when the owners are at home, and they haven't lifted any jewelry. But electronics have been taken at all of them, and guns wherever the homeowners had them. The one man who was shot woke up when they were in the house and walked in on them."

"What's with the motorbike?" Mike asked.

"You got me. One of them took a fancy to it, I guess. But TVs and DVD players they could unload pretty quickly for cash. Not a lot of money in used ones, but some. The motorbike was probably a bonus for them."

"You may be right, and there's an art dealer or

collector who sets up the thefts and sends a crew in to do it for him."

"So now what?" asked Arnie.

"For one thing, look at people who've been arrested in the past for stealing electronics," Mike said. "Whoever's behind the art thefts may have hired some small-time crooks to do the heavy lifting for him."

"I think we should go around to galleries and warn them," I said. "Their customers may be targeted. I don't see a lot of purchases from the same dealer, though."

"Somehow, the thieves know who's got the art," Mike mused.

"There's some connection," I agreed, "some way they get word on that. If we could figure out how, we might figure out where they were going to strike next, and then we can catch them."

Arnie and Clyde set out to make the rounds of galleries in town, telling the owners there had been a rash of art thefts in the area over the past year and suggesting they advise their customers to take extra security precautions.

I said to Mike, "I wonder if it would do any good for one of us to go undercover and start buying art at auctions and shows."

"Too expensive," Mike said. "We'd have thousands of dollars tied up for a long time. And it's such a long shot. If they were victimizing the customers of a particular dealer, it might work."

We both went back to our budgets, but it churned in the back of my mind.

Jennifer was working on her cross stitching when I got home. Beth Bradley had gotten her started on that while they lived together. She had done a little laundry and had a casserole in the oven, which told me she was feeling pretty good.

When supper was ready, she sat down with me, and I brought her a plastic bottle of Poland Spring water from the refrigerator.

"I don't need expensive water," she said. "I can drink tap water."

"Nothing but the best for my baby." I set the bottle on the table and leaned over to kiss her. Her left hand went up to the back of my hair, and her fingers twisted in it.

"Your hair's curly."

"I know. I need a haircut."

"Let me do it."

"You'd better try to eat something first, and drink some water. Margaret will be over here sticking needles in you if you don't hydrate."

"I guess this has been pretty awful for you," she said.

"No. I just feel helpless."

"That's what's awful for you." She laughed. "My lord and protector, and you can't do anything about this. Eddie must be really revolted. He hasn't been around for two days."

"He's very concerned about you, but he feels

a little out of his element. He was just getting used to the idea of us having a baby when you started being nauseous all the time. That's pretty unnerving for a single guy."

She shook her head. "The Invincible Duo, reduced to jelly."

She really did seem better that evening and sipped away dutifully at the bottle of water while we watched a new British drama on PBS. I felt as if I'd been wound up tight, and very slowly I was uncoiling.

"I wanted to call John Macomber tonight," she said around eight o'clock.

"Do you have his number?"

"It's in my computer desk."

I got her address book for her.

"You know, I think I could eat another jelly doughnut now."

I laughed and went to the kitchen to get it for her, and when I came back she was talking on the phone to John. I sat and listened to her end, and it sounded like John was very interested. They were discussing whether Jennifer should sell her program to him outright, or take royalties on sales.

"It has a limited market," she said to me when she'd hung up.

"But it's a fairly large one," I pointed out. "Once police departments learn about its capabilities, they'll all want it."

"If they can get it into their budgets, which you know is very hard." She took a bite of the jelly doughnut. "How come food tastes good one minute and awful the next?"

"I dunno. You okay?"

"Yeah, this is great. But don't let it near me before ten in the morning."

"You're beautiful with jelly on your nose."

She laughed and grabbed a tissue to repair the damage.

"We need to talk about names." She took another bite.

"What kind of names? For the computer program?"

"No, baby names."

"You mean, like Bubby and Junior?" I laughed.

"Harvey Junior."

"No, no, no. I refuse to name my son Harvey Junior, or Harvey Anything. Or Anything Junior, for that matter."

"Well, what will we call him, then?"

"Are you so sure it's a boy?" I asked.

"Oh, I don't think a little girl would be this ornery. And it's what you want. A son."

"I don't care," I said honestly. "I really don't, as long as—"

"As long as he's healthy?" she asked.

"That's what everyone says, isn't it?"

"Not everyone. But lots of people."

"I really mean it. A boy or a girl, I don't care,

as long as you feel good again and it's a healthy child." I tried not to think about the nameless baby who would be in college now if he'd lived. I didn't even know if it was a boy or a girl. Pastor Rowland said I would see my child in heaven. I'd wrangled with it, and with God's grace, I'd reached a place where I could live with that.

"I hope it's a boy." Jennifer sounded wistful, and I wondered if she'd read my mind and caught a hint of sadness. She held out the plate with half a doughnut on it.

"Had enough?" I asked.

"For now." She took a drink from the water bottle and leaned back on the couch. "So, should I take royalties or a lump sum?"

"What did he offer you?"

"Ten percent of profits or two thousand dollars."

"What will it retail for?" We talked it over, and I did the math. "He might sell it to hundreds of departments."

"Maybe. In time. I think I'll take the two thousand."

"He might give you more when he sees it in action. And I'll write a glowing testimonial telling how it's helped me solve cases."

She smiled and stroked my stubbly cheek. "I'll talk to him again tomorrow. We'll see."

Chapter 4

Wednesday, September 22

The art theft case lay dormant. Eddie had been in court half the day Wednesday, for Jason Cuvier's indictment in the poisoning episode and hearings on the smuggling case. We'd been handed a triple homicide, and I put Clyde in charge of it because he had so much homicide experience, and because I wanted to observe him. Arnie and Nate supported him.

They had the killer in custody almost from the beginning, but handling the evidence was tricky, and all of the officers had to practice meticulous care. It was new territory for Nate, who hadn't been in on many homicide investigations. I watched Clyde closely and was satisfied with his procedure and management.

While they handled the details, I sat in on interviews for three candidates for the deputy chief's position. All were from outside Portland. One was the current chief in Ellsworth; another was the female deputy chief in Dover-Foxcroft. The third possibility was a chief from New Hampshire. The city council grilled them all and argued over their qualifications.

"Looks like a toss-up to me," Mike said when

we'd retreated to the Priority Unit after the meeting.

"Nobody in our department qualifies?" I asked.

"Can't think of anyone. At least no one I'd want to work with that closely."

"I hope they don't take the New Hampshire guy. Too many of the laws are different."

Mike shrugged. "That can be dealt with. Anyhow, the council thinks we need to consider women more."

"Do you want a woman deputy?"

"I don't suppose it would matter much, and it would make the city look good."

I was surprised that the idea didn't make me uncomfortable. But not the woman we'd just interviewed. She had a condescending streak. "Get another bunch of candidates in here."

"I dunno. I'm thinking maybe they'll pick the Ellsworth guy." Mike left me, and I put it out of my mind.

Abby came back to Portland on Friday. I took my lunch hour late so I could meet her and Jennifer at Margaret's office for Jennifer's checkup.

"You're better," Margaret pronounced after taking Jennifer's vital signs. "Still not eating enough, and maybe a little dehydrated, but better than you were last time I saw you."

Jennifer smiled at Margaret and me. "I feel better."

Margaret set her up for an ultrasound. It was the first time either of us had seen it, and it took my breath away.

"Look, Jenny. We can see our baby." My eyes filled with tears. She squeezed my hand tight, watching the monitor. Margaret pointed out the organs that were developing, but still so immature. The beating heart eclipsed everything else for me. I stared at the screen and squeezed Jenny's hand.

"You'll see a lot more in another month," Margaret said matter-of-factly.

I took a deep breath and fumbled for my handkerchief. Jennifer kissed my eyelids and said, "I married such a softie."

Margaret made some notes on Jennifer's chart. "All right, keep eating. You've lost four pounds, and you can't afford to lose any more. We need to get the scale going the other way. Harvey, keep buying doughnuts, or whatever she'll eat. Jennifer, when you can, drink milk. You might have some nausea for another few weeks, but you need to try to get back to a balanced diet. And keep up those vitamins!" She laid down the clipboard and smiled. "I want to see you again in two weeks."

It seemed to me that two weeks was pretty soon, so either Jennifer was special or Margaret was more concerned about the morning sickness than she let on.

71

She popped a disk out of the sonogram machine and handed it to me. "Home movies of the baby. Enjoy." She kissed Jennifer on the cheek and was out the door to see her next patient.

Jennifer got dressed, and I sent her home with Abby. I left them with orders for naps all around. Abby had worked from eleven to seven the night before and hadn't had any sleep.

A touchy new case landed on my desk that afternoon, and I had to supervise Nate and Eddie closely, leaving Arnie and Clyde to close out the homicide. The new one was the kind of case that's emotionally draining, a sexual assault that left the victim in the hospital and the perpetrator at bay.

Eddie and Nate laid the groundwork and got a solid I.D. from the victim. They brought in the rapist early that evening, but he was still arrogant. I felt filthy just looking at him. Nate and Eddie were pumped because of their success, and I was glad they had the guy off the street.

When I got home from work an hour later than usual, Jennifer and Abby were both zonked, and I started scrounging for food in the refrigerator. There was plenty, including an uncooked meat-loaf. I put it in the oven and decided I could microwave some leftover mashed potatoes. I was working on a salad when Jenny came padding out in her sock feet, her white terrycloth robe over her baseball shirt nightgown.

I kissed her and sat her on a stool where she could watch me cut veggies. "Have you watched the video?" I asked.

"Six times. He's so . . . perfect."

I laid down the knife and put my arms around her. "This is going to be great, you know."

"I'm starting to believe it."

"It is. He's going to be healthy and strong, and he's going to look like you."

Jennifer laughed. "I hope not, if it's a he."

"Like Jeff, then," I corrected. "Boys who look like you will look like Jeff."

"I'll be ecstatic if he looks like you," she said.

I pulled back and frowned at her. "You know all my baby pictures are funny looking."

"You were cute."

"You're just saying that."

"I am not!"

"What's to eat?" Abby said from the doorway. "I'm starved. Are you cooking that meatloaf I left in the fridge?"

"I certainly am."

The three of us got the dishes and the food onto the table, and I sat down with Jenny on one side and Abby on the other. Bookends.

"This is weird." I looked from one to the other. Jennifer's face was much thinner now, and she still had little dark smudges under her eyes, but otherwise it was uncanny for two women who weren't twins. They both had the Rapunzel look that night, with one long braid dangling over a shoulder. Jennifer's was a foot longer than Abby's, but even Abby's was long.

The next morning, Jennifer was sick again. I made her rest all weekend. The only way she would stay in bed was if I stayed in there with her, so we read a Mrs. Pollifax mystery out loud to each other and started a new Tess Gerritsen.

By phone, she cemented a verbal contract with John Macomber for $2,500 for the computer program, and he said he would bring the papers over on Monday. She would deliver the program to him within two weeks. She was definitely feeling better, and chafing at my bed rest orders.

"John says he'll pay me in full when I give him the program, with the understanding that I'll work with him to fix any bugs he finds," she said. "I should start working on it."

"Only if you work on the laptop, in here."

She frowned at that. "John's excited about it, and he's ready to talk to his advertising firm about a marketing campaign. Oh, and he said the programs he bought from me before are doing well. He'd like me to do some freelance programming later."

"We'll see," I said. "You need to gain some weight and quit tossing your breakfast first."

She pretended to pout, but she wasn't stingy with her kisses, so maybe she was secretly glad

I was pampering her. She conducted her business from the sleigh bed in the master bedroom, sitting up against a bank of pillows with her day planner and calculator and file folders spread out on the comforter and a bottle of spring water on the night stand.

"Knock, knock." Abby came to the doorway late Saturday afternoon in faded jeans and a Skowhegan Indians T-shirt.

"Are you ready for your first night on the new job?" Jennifer asked her.

"All but the uniform. Can't wait." Abby came over and sat on the foot of the bed.

"Are they going to make your high school change its mascot?" I asked, looking at the Indian profile on her shirt.

Abby shook her head. "I don't think so. There was a big to-do about it a decade or so ago, but the school board stuck to their guns on it being a heritage thing. Funny, the Maine Indians aren't insulted. It's the militants out west that want it changed."

"I hope they don't change it," Jennifer said. "I can just see it—the Skowhegan Moose."

"How about the Skowhegan Skunks?" I suggested. Abby lunged for a pillow to throw at me.

I retreated to the garage, and Bud Parker wandered across the street when I put the overhead door up.

"What are you up to, Harvey?" he called from the driveway.

"Thinking about mowing the back lawn one last time for the season," I said. "Come on in."

He stood around and talked for a few minutes, getting an update on Jennifer and asking me about the homicide Clyde and the other men were working on. It had been major news in the paper and on the local TV broadcasts, and I'd made Clyde handle the publicity.

"Figured you'd be in the middle of it." Bud sounded a little disappointed.

"No, I'm just watching from the sidelines. The men are doing a good job."

"You aren't just pushing paper now, are you?" he said anxiously.

"No, I'm working on some other things, and if they need me I'll be there, but I think they've got it under control. I've got some good men."

"I kind of hate to see men get promoted out of what they're good at," he said.

"No, Bud, I'm still kicking down doors once in a while. But mostly I tell the other guys when to do it."

"So what are you working on now?"

"Well, there's a burglary ring we're looking at, and there was a violent rape case yesterday. My two most experienced men were busy with the homicide, so I had to get in on that. One of my men had never handled a rape case before, so I went through it with him and Eddie."

"Don't they have policewomen for that kind of thing?"

"Well, yes, we had a female officer work with the victim, but when you go to arrest the perpetrator, that's not the case you want to send a female out on," I told him.

"I don't know, women these days think they can do anything."

"I know it. Maybe they can, but somehow it doesn't seem right to me," I said with a shrug. "We've got female cops who think they should be assigned just like the men, and for the most part they are, but on a case like that—well, I guess I'd better not spout off too much or someone will be calling me a bigot and demoting me."

Bud laughed. "I guess management has its pitfalls nowadays."

"You got it." I had the lawnmower ready to go, and started it up. Bud went back across the street.

Eddie met me at six Monday morning to run, then went home to shower and change, but came back to eat breakfast with me at seven-fifteen. Jennifer got up and sat with us, but I made breakfast. She was drinking water—milk was still too much in the morning—and nibbled at a scrambled egg and dry toast. Eddie and I ate a pile of eggs and sausage and toast.

Abby drove in, returning from work, and joined us for breakfast—her supper.

"Hey! How's the job going?" Eddie asked as she sat down and reached for the orange juice.

I put my arm across the back of Jennifer's chair, watching her eat while they talked. I tried not to count the bites she swallowed and reminded myself it was a lot more than a week ago.

Abby seemed optimistic about things at the hospital. She told us about her shift and some of the things that were different down here than at the Waterville job.

"And the hospital is so much bigger," she concluded. "I'll probably lose weight just walking from the parking lot to my station."

"How are your folks doing?" I asked her.

"Pretty well. I think they're worried about Jennifer, and they miss Jeff, too. Now that I'm down here, it probably seems really quiet to them."

"Empty nest." I was glad we wouldn't go through it for twenty years or so.

Eddie pushed his chair back. "We'd better get going."

"Right."

Abby got up and walked outside with him. I leaned over to kiss Jennifer goodbye.

"Take it easy today," I told her. "I'll call you later, and I want you to still be feeling as good as you are now, or better." She kissed me again, and

I knew she was more than I deserved. The baby was a bonus, a precious, sacred gift.

Eddie and I drove separately. We'd tried to keep carpooling after the wedding, but since I'd moved and had different duties, it hadn't worked very well, so we took our own vehicles now. We'd managed to preserve our three-times-weekly running routine, although it took a major effort sometimes. Jeff ran with us on days when he wasn't on duty at the fire station, and we took a few minutes to pray together on those days. That was something new for all of us, and we grew closer because of it.

I didn't even get to my desk before the latest crime was dumped in my lap. Terry Lemieux, the day patrol sergeant, called to me as I went through the foyer to the stairway.

"The chief told me to tell you as soon as you got in," he said. "There was a burglary early this morning in Rosemont."

"Don't tell me," I said. "An art theft." A run-of-the-mill burglary wouldn't have been steered to my unit.

"That's right." Terry handed me a copy of a night shift patrolman's report. I took the file with me to the third floor and read it twice, then called Mike.

"You want me to take this art theft case in Rosemont?" I asked.

"Well, it's what we've been waiting for.

Another burglary within the city limits, same M.O."

"Does Ron Legere know?"

"I'll tell him."

I said, "Okay, I'll touch base with Ron after we do some preliminary work."

I sent Nate to the courthouse for a hearing on his last case and kept Eddie with me on the art theft. Arnie and Clyde were meeting with the district attorney at nine, and I briefed them on the new theft before they left.

"We may be getting somewhere," I told Eddie as I worked at my computer. "One of the paintings stolen last night was by the same artist as one stolen two weeks ago. Maybe these thieves have a customer who admires Lance Redwall."

"Lance Redwall? Yeah, I saw the name, but I'd never heard of him before this case," Eddie said.

"He's building a reputation in the art world. His landscapes are selling for four to six grand. He's been painting for ten or fifteen years, and his recent works are better than the early ones, but even the early ones are commanding big prices now."

"How do you know all this?" Eddie asked.

"Hey, I'm a cop."

"So am I. You can't snow me."

I smiled. "I've been reading up on all the artists whose works we know were stolen in the area recently."

"Is this artist local?"

"Nope. Lives in New Jersey. But this painting was purchased through a gallery on Market Street."

"Where was the other one bought—the Redwall that was stolen two weeks ago?"

I checked my computer file on the art thefts. "An art auction in Boston three years ago."

"So, if the thieves are learning who's got art, they've been keeping track for a long time. Or looking at old records."

"Word of mouth would be more like it," I said. "If they all came from the same source, the records would make sense but . . ."

"Do art collectors brag about it?" Eddie asked. "I thought they kept their mouths shut for security."

"I dunno. Maybe they tell their friends. People they trust."

"Their art dealer," said Eddie.

"That's true. There could be a dealer masterminding this thing." I sat back, mulling it over. "Hey! Where would you go if you wanted to chitchat about art and up-and-coming artists?"

"A gallery, I guess. A show for one of these artists on the list."

"Or . . . ?"

"What are you thinking?" he asked.

"Come at it a different way, Eddie. Let's say you wanted to learn about archery or flying or stamp collecting. Where would you go?"

"The library?"

"To meet people with the same interest."

"An online chat room?"

"I was thinking real face time."

"A club," he said.

"Bingo."

"Is there an art club in town?" he asked.

"I don't know, but I'm going to find out." I turned back to the computer.

He left me alone, and I immersed myself in local organizations, via the chamber of commerce website.

"Got it," I told Eddie ten minutes later.

"What, the art club?"

"Yes. I just talked to the vice president. They only meet once a month, though."

"And the next meeting is . . ."

"October eleventh. They meet the second Monday of the month."

"So, you're going to join?"

"Correction. *We* are going to join."

"Undercover as art lovers?" Eddie asked.

"You got it."

"I'd better do some homework."

"Yes, you'd better." I gave him a list of local artists and the name of a woman from Connecticut who would be the guest speaker at the next Portland Visual Arts Society meeting. "See what you can find out about this artist, Mandi Plunkett. She'll be speaking on layering acrylics, and demonstrating her technique. I want to know what she paints and what her work sells for and who buys it."

"How do I find out all that?"

"Internet, library, whatever works. Give me a report before you leave tonight."

"Oh, brother." Eddie had not done well on term papers in school.

I stood up and reached for my jacket. "Let's go visit the house that was burglarized last night and interview the owner. You can do your homework this afternoon."

Eddie and I drove to Rosemont in my SUV. Ralph Carter had not yet gone to the local insurance agency where he worked. A couple of crime scene techs were dusting for fingerprints in his living room, and I sent Eddie to talk to the patrolmen who had interviewed the nearest neighbors, to see if they'd seen or heard anything unusual in the night.

Carter sat down with me in the dining room. His wife brought us coffee and then headed out for an appointment at the hair salon.

"It was about three a.m.," Carter told me. "A noise woke me up. I didn't know what it was, but it wasn't one of our house's regular sounds."

I nodded with perfect understanding. I'd been living in my house for almost three months, and I was still getting used to its sighs and groans.

"I went out into the hallway and turned on

a light," Carter said. "I heard someone running away. When I got to the kitchen, the back door was wide open."

"I know you made an initial report," I said, "but could you please tell me what was taken?"

He exhaled heavily. "The biggest thing was the Redwall painting. It was a gift from my wife's parents." He shook his head. "The biggest *pain* was the computer, though. Not only did we lose a lot of files, but the thieves now have a ton of personal information about us."

"I'm sorry." People know they should back up everything externally, but they forget. They know they shouldn't leave sensitive information on the hard drive, but they do. I think it's because we're lazy by nature.

"What else?" I asked.

"The printer, a video camera, and a CD player. The TV and DVD player were sitting in the middle of the living room floor. There was also a family photo in a sterling silver frame worth a few hundred bucks. We can get a copy of the picture from the studio, but my wife was more upset about that than anything else. But the computer—I'd only had that one eight months."

"How much was the painting worth?"

"My in-laws paid six grand for it. That was the most expensive item."

I nodded. "We'll do everything we can to get your stuff back. The electronics will probably be sold quickly to a fence, but the thieves may have stolen the painting for a particular collector. It might be harder to trace, because it won't go on the open market."

I got a few more details from him, and a photo of the stolen painting. They had a laptop that had escaped the theft because his wife had taken it into the bedroom the night before, and I advised him to get on it and change all his passwords immediately. I went into the next room, where the techs were packing up their gear. They reported that the thieves had apparently worn gloves, because they didn't get any prints except the owners', not even off the TV and DVD player they had obviously handled. I promised Mr. Carter to get back to him soon and went outside to collect Eddie.

That night Abby sat with us in the sunroom, watching an old Fred Astaire movie. She'd slept all day and was alert for the evening. Jennifer was still eating lightly, but seemed to be doing well.

"So, what are you guys naming the baby?" Abby asked when the movie was over.

"Anything but Harvey," said Jennifer. "That's as far as we've gotten."

"Well, as the little chub's aunt, I think I should have a vote."

"Any suggestions?" I asked.

"Well, there's George for Dad. What was your father's name?"

"Neil."

"That's not bad."

"I don't like it," said Jennifer. "How about Alan?" Alan was my middle name.

"Doesn't go with Larson," I said. "Alliteration or something. I don't know why my mother named me that."

"Why did she name you Harvey?" asked Abby.

"I think when she was pregnant she kept seeing this giant rabbit."

Abby laughed. "Oh, right. I should have known."

"It was her father's name," I said. "Harvey Connor."

"Name him Connor," said Abby.

"Connor Larson." Jennifer nodded thoughtfully. "It's a possibility."

"Let's keep thinking," I said.

When Abby left for work, Jennifer and I settled down for the night. I was almost asleep when a thought hit me.

"Why don't you like Neil?"

"Hmm?" she was nearly asleep.

I rolled over. "Why don't you like the name Neil?"

She opened her eyes. There was enough moonlight that I could see them gleaming.

"Did you want to name him that?"

"Maybe. I don't know. I'm just curious as to why you don't."

"Oh, you know, associations. Like that kid that beat you up in sixth grade."

"It was third grade, and his name was Elmer. You wouldn't want to name our son Elmer, would you? Regardless of bullies, I mean."

"Guess not."

"Well?"

She didn't answer right away, and that was like waving a red cape at me. "It was him, wasn't it?" I said.

No answer.

"Jenny, tell me."

"Yes, it was him, but it's not important. Just forget it, okay, Harvey?" She was earnest, pleading.

"Oh, boy. I can't now." I flopped back on my pillow.

"Well, I had, and I think you should. We've dealt with this."

I said, "I know, but I didn't know his name was Neil."

"It's not a problem. Please don't stay awake thinking about it."

I stared at the ceiling, where moonlight bounced off the tilted dresser mirror and made a ball of light above us.

Jennifer's breath was even and soft, but my heart was pounding. She had told me all about it before we were married. Well, not *all* about it. She'd never mentioned his name. In my mind, I kept seeing a man—a young man whom she had once trusted—grabbing her satiny braid and pulling her to the floor.

I knew I was going to be tired the next day, and I decided to take her advice and forget it, but I couldn't. I rolled over and forced myself to think about other things. Mentally, I went over all the paintings that had been stolen, and the artists. I planned out the assignments for each of my men to carry out the next day. But Neil kept leaping out at me with a sneer on his face, which was pretty strange when I didn't even know what he looked like.

I push the light button on my watch. One a.m. I stared at the gray rectangle of the window.

Chapter 5

Tuesday, September 28

Eddie had made a decent effort on his report, and I read every word. The art club's speaker, Mandi Plunkett, was renowned in the comparatively new medium of acrylics. Serious painters traditionally used oils, but acrylics had become accepted and appreciated over the last three or four decades. The fact that they dried fast was a boon to painters.

At the club meeting, she would demonstrate techniques that were possible only with acrylics. She did shows several times a year, and her works were on display at four prestigious galleries down the East Coast. One was hanging in the Museum of Modern Art in New York. She had spent the summer in Maine, at her cottage in Harpswell, and would go back to Connecticut the day after the club meeting. Eddie was bored stiff by his assignment. I gave him an A- for content and a C for mechanics.

I went through several cups of coffee, fighting drowsiness. Online, I used my law enforcement exchange software for profiles of art thieves. They were somewhat rare, especially in New

England. None of the M.O.s seemed to quite fit that of the local thieves.

I signed up for several newsletters and began to receive notices of art shows and auctions throughout New England. I glanced through the brochures and online ads, but as I worked, Neil was always in the back of my mind, and the pain he had caused Jennifer rankled there.

At noon I drove home, stopping at a bookstore first. When I got to the house, Jennifer was sitting at her computer in shorts and a knit shirt, working on adjustments to her program for John Macomber.

She stood up. "Hi! I thought you weren't coming home. You didn't call."

I put my arm around her and walked into the living room with her. "I'm sorry. I thought it would save time to just come. I was busy all morning. You okay?"

"Yes. Abby's sleeping. I don't have lunch ready."

"That's all right. Sit." She sat on the sofa, and I sat down beside her and looked at her, not sure where to begin.

"Is something wrong?" she asked.

"Yes."

"What is it?" She put her hands on mine, and a little frown creased her forehead between her eyebrows.

"It's about last night. And Neil."

She looked down at the rug. "I wish that didn't bother you. You helped me get over it. It's the past."

"I'm sorry, Jenny. Will you forgive me?"

"Forgive you what?"

I sighed and pulled my hands away from hers.

"I hate that guy." I shook my head. "I think I hated him when you first told me about him, but I let it go. I was just so glad that you were all right, and that you were with me, not some creep like him. But last night, I just couldn't quit thinking about it. Before that, to me he was the man who had hurt you. He'd never had a name before, in my mind. Did it have to be Neil?"

I could feel the tears coming, and that made me mad. I stood up and walked across the room and stood looking out the window at the front yard. The leaves were half turned to red on the maple in Bud and Janice's yard.

I heard her come softly across the rug. Her hands came around my waist, just above my belt. I didn't move. She leaned against my back. Finally, I turned around.

"What can we do?" she asked, looking up at me.

I drew her to me, and her hands went under my jacket and around me.

"Jenny, I can't stand to think about it."

"Then don't. I don't." We stood there, not saying anything. After a while, she said softly, "Nothing happened."

"Yes, it did."

"No. I was stupid, and he was a jerk, and it ended."

"He hurt you."

"Not really. He scared me badly, and I got a few bruises, but I got away from him that night, and I never saw him again. It could have been a lot worse, baby, but I'm fine."

"It bothered you for years."

"It hasn't lately. Not since I told you. You helped me not let it hold me back."

My chest ached, and for some reason I couldn't accept what she was saying. "His name was Neil," I said, too loudly. "My father's name."

"Yes." She rubbed my back a little, then tucked her left hand under the strap of my shoulder holster, where her four fingers just fit, taking up the slack. "Had you thought of naming our baby Neil?"

"I don't know. But I can't think about it now. Not ever. He took something away from us. He upset you so badly; you still have an aversion to his name."

"I can get past it now." Her soft voice calmed me. "And your dad meant so much to you. If you want to use his name, it's okay, Harvey."

"No, I can't. Not now." I took a deep breath, and let it out in a sigh. What would that scum think if he ever heard she'd named her first baby Neil?

She brought her right hand around to my chest and closed it around my badge. "Do you want to pursue it now? It's been three years."

"That's not too long," I said.

"But it is a long time, and it would be my word against his. For what? Terrorizing?"

"Attempted rape. Assault. You had bruises."

"No witnesses."

"You said there was someone who helped you."

She scrunched up her face. "I don't even know that guy's name. He came running when I screamed, and he kept Neil busy while I ran. That's all I know."

"Tell me Neil's last name."

She hesitated. "Can't we leave it to God?"

"Jenny."

"I know you'd find him. You're too competent not to. Harvey, this is not right. You've got to let go of it."

I sighed. "You can say he didn't hurt you, but he did."

"A few minutes ago, you asked me to forgive you," she said. "Have you forgiven yourself?"

I was quiet because I couldn't say yes. She pulled back and looked at me. I met her eyes for a second, then looked away. She was right. I knew it.

"I've got to go back to work," I said.

"Please don't go yet. We need to resolve this."

"I'll try. I'll really try. I need to think about it."

"Harvey, please. Drop it."

I pulled her hard against my chest. "Jenny, I'm sorry. I couldn't help it. No, that's a lie. I could. I don't think I want to help it. I want to hate him."

She cried then. I took her over to the couch and sat down and held her. I couldn't understand why I was acting this way. It was so unlike me to be unable to compartmentalize the personal stuff. After a minute, she reached for the tissues.

"When I think about him hurting you, I don't know if I can ever forgive him," I said.

"Carrie hurt you, and you let her," she said in a very small voice.

We sat for a while, not saying anything, until I looked at my watch. "I need to go."

"You haven't eaten anything."

"I can't." My hand touched the bookstore bag I'd dropped on the couch when I came in. I pulled the book out. "I brought you this."

She looked at the cover. "*Baby Names*. Five thousand of them."

"Four thousand, nine hundred ninety-nine."

Her eyebrows puckered. "This isn't over, is it?"

I kissed her quickly and stood up. She followed me to the door.

"Harvey, please."

I turned back. She looked at me with those big gray eyes. I hugged her again and said, "Take a nap, gorgeous," and got in my Explorer and drove back to work feeling lousy.

I snapped at Eddie in front of Nate that afternoon, and he was hurt. I went back later and apologized. Then I apologized to Nate. And I still felt rotten. I buried myself in work. I was scheduled to be in court most of Wednesday, and I was glad. It meant I had a lot of work to do, preparing for hearings, and I wouldn't be in the office the next day, thinking about what I shouldn't be thinking about.

When I got home that night, Beth was there and Abby was fixing supper for four while Jennifer set the table. Beth was perusing the baby name book.

"How about Archibald? Call him Archie."

"No, thanks," said Jennifer. She came to me and kissed me, then looked searchingly into my eyes.

"I'll be back." I went through to the bedroom and set my briefcase down and peeled off my suit and laid my gear on the dresser and my cell phone on the night stand. I still felt awful, and I still hated Neil. The longer it went on, the more I detested him. Wasn't it right of me to feel protective of my wife? I put on jeans and a T-shirt and went back to the kitchen. Abby was ready to put the food on the table, and we ate.

Beth flicked a glance my way as she cut her pork chop. "So, Harvey, what's up in the world of crime?"

"Lots of illegal stuff."

"Ooh, you're grouchy tonight."

"And you're mouthy." If I'd said it with a smile, Beth would have smiled back and kept on teasing me. We'd had a genially antagonistic relationship for months. But I wasn't smiling, and neither was she. I felt guiltier.

"I'll be so glad when tonight's over," said Abby. "Two whole days off. I can hardly wait."

"How's school going?" Jennifer said to Beth, who taught kindergarten.

"Not bad. My kids are mostly sweethearts." She eyed me apprehensively. "Harvey, I'm sorry I pushed the wrong button."

"We've got a difficult case now," I said, as an excuse. Jennifer's gray eyes had that hurricane's a-comin' look.

I couldn't eat much, although I should have been starving, and I didn't see Jennifer eat anything.

"Jeff has tomorrow off," Beth said. "He's taking me out to dinner."

"That's great," said Jennifer.

I thought back to the days when I would sit on the steps of Jennifer and Beth's house until Jenny got home from work, willing to take her anywhere just so I could see her. I still wanted to be with her every minute, but I wasn't sure she wanted to be with me right then.

Beth left soon after the dishes were done, and Abby asked if we wanted to watch TV.

Jennifer said she was tired, and I followed her to the bedroom. She was wriggling into a long, sleeveless nightgown. I went over and put my arms around her.

"Mad at me?" I asked softly.

"No." she adjusted the front of the gown and leaned against me. "Do you want to talk about it now?"

Did I? I still had that knot in my stomach. "I don't think so."

"Tell me when you're ready."

"I will." I released her, and she went into the bathroom. I could hear her brushing her teeth. I turned the quilt down for her.

When she came out, she went straight to the bed. I stood there, watching her climb in. She looked up. "I'm sorry, Harvey. I'm really tired."

"It's okay." I was tired, too, but it was too early for me to get into bed. My brain was going a mile a minute. I sat down on the edge of the mattress to kiss her. "Are you really feeling okay?" I asked. "You didn't eat much."

"I just need to rest. But tell me if you want to talk."

"Okay."

"I mean it. Wake me up, even." Her eyes pleaded. I kissed her forehead and went out, turning off the light.

Abby was watching the national news. I slumped down in an armchair and looked at the

TV, too, but I wasn't thinking about it. After a while I got up and walked into the study and flipped the light on. There was a whole bookcase full of Jennifer's books—her old college textbooks, computer texts, philosophy books, and reference books. My hand went out to her college yearbooks and rested on the binding. Four tall, brightly colored volumes of the Prism in a row. I took my hand away and sat down at my computer.

I hadn't checked my stocks for days. I looked at the closing quotes. We were gaining steadily. I checked the Maine weather site for the next day's forecast. Sunny and warm for the season. My mind kept coming back to the man Jennifer had dated her senior year of college. Neil Somebody.

I stood and went back to the bookcase and took down the last yearbook. The binding felt cool in my hand. It should have burned me.

We'd never looked at her yearbooks. Why not? They were just there, like my Harvard yearbooks that I'd stuck in a box in one of the spare rooms upstairs. Veritas . . . Truth. Not what I wanted to think about.

I sat down with Jennifer's final yearbook and found her photo among the seniors easily. Gorgeous, as always, but about three years younger. If anything, she was more beautiful now.

Wainthrop was near the end, and from there

I went to the last page and searched backward, slowly. Surely I had a right to see what he looked like.

Her class at the university had more than 500 members. I thought fleetingly that I might find him faster on the computer. It would be no trick for me to access the school's records. I kept turning pages backward and got to the T's. Neal Truax. Neal with an A? He had glasses and was a little wimpy looking. Math major. Debate society. Math honor society. Couldn't be him. He didn't look strong enough to pin a salamander, let alone a healthy young woman.

I kept looking. S, R, Q, P, O, N. I was being foolish. I was being deceitful. No, I wasn't, I hadn't told Jennifer I wouldn't look for him. But my conscience kept telling me I was.

Had she ever actually said he was in her class? I laid the book on my desk and went into the living room. Abby was watching a cop show and laughing. Buddy cop shows, a trend in television that season.

"Is this the way you guys do it?" she asked. The lieutenant was a kick boxer, and the detective was a former chess champion who spoke fourteen languages.

"Not quite," I said.

A commercial for cat litter came on, and Abby turned down the sound.

"Jennifer seems a lot better," she ventured.

"Maybe."

"She was good this morning, anyway. But it seemed like she didn't feel very well tonight. She didn't eat."

"I thought so, too."

"She was always so healthy," Abby said. "It's hard to see her this way."

I sat down in the armchair. "I'm glad you're here. You're a nurse, and if she has a bad spell, you'll be here."

"If I don't sleep through it," she said ruefully. "We really ought to fix up some way for her to call me when I'm up in my room. A bell, maybe."

"How about an intercom? I could buy one tomorrow and set it up tomorrow night. From our bedroom to yours."

"I don't know," she said.

"Why not? If she felt sick, she could buzz you. And we can use it later to listen to the baby when he's napping."

"If you want."

"She's never been sick, has she?" I asked.

"Not that I can remember."

"Never missed school?"

"I don't think so."

"She played softball in high school and college," I said, remembering the days I'd searched out the tiniest details about her.

"Yes, she did a lot of things."

"I'll bet she had boyfriends."

"Not too many."

"Oh, come on," I said, trying to sound jovial, "she must have had a few."

"There was this kid in high school who had a crush on her for ages. Brian Wentworth. She couldn't stand him."

"Didn't she go out?"

"A few times, I guess. Craig Weir. He was okay. Then there was Andy House."

"How about in college?"

"Mm, she was pretty serious about her studies then."

"No guys, huh?"

"Why, are you the jealous type?"

"Who, me?" She was too close to the truth.

"We went to different schools," Abby said. "There was one guy she brought home at Christmas once. Her senior year, I guess."

"Yeah? Computer major like Jennifer?"

"I don't think so. He was good looking. I thought she was sold on him. But when I came home in the spring, it was all off."

"Did she tell you about it?"

"No, just said they broke up. She got out a couple of weeks before I did, and I guess it had been over for a while."

"You didn't go to her graduation, did you?"

"No, Mom and Dad went."

"So, that was your sophomore year?"

"Yeah. That was a tough year. Anatomy and physiology, and microbiology."

Her cop show came back on, and she turned the sound up. I thought about what she'd told me. Jennifer said she hadn't seen Neil again after the night he attacked her. But hadn't he graduated that year, too? I guessed the graduating class was so large she might have avoided him during the ceremonies. Or had her anonymous champion beat him so badly he'd missed graduation? Maybe he wasn't in her class after all.

"What was the guy's name? The one she went with in college?"

"Daniel or something like that."

"Daniel?"

"I forget." She was trying to listen to what the kick boxer was saying.

I went to the bedroom doorway. Jennifer lay quiet, and I didn't go in. Would a guy named Daniel go by Neil as a nickname? I didn't think so.

Back at my desk, I opened the book to the seniors again and turned to the D's. Neil Daniels. It had to be him. Art history major. Longish blond hair, serious eyes, mouth in a set line. Looked like a rapist to me. I closed my private mug book and replaced it on the shelf.

Chapter 6

Wednesday, September 29

The next morning I went to Eddie's to run with him and Jeff. During our usual prayer time, I felt hypocritical and said a short, generic prayer. When I got back home, Jennifer was up and had coffee ready. I took a shower and sat down at the table with her. I coaxed her to eat a banana. She took three bites. I finished it and ate raisin bran and drank a cup of coffee.

When I went into the bedroom for my gear and my briefcase, she followed me.

"Harvey," she said as I was putting on my holster, "we haven't talked about Neil."

I froze. How could she just say it like that?

"What's to talk about?" I adjusted the strap and pinned on my badge, then reached for my suit coat. The small stuff went into my pockets: notebook, pen, handkerchief, plastic bag, tape measure, key ring, cell phone.

She watched me silently. I picked up my brief-case and turned to face her.

"I'll call you." I leaned down to kiss her, and she lifted her face to me, but the tears swarmed in her eyes. The kiss was perfunctory. I started to leave, and she threw her arms up around my neck and kissed me again.

"You know I love you." She sounded a little desperate.

"Yes, I know, Jenny." I was hurting her, and I hated that. I tried mentally to justify my actions because of my love for her and my loathing of what he had done to her when she was innocent, when she had trusted him. If I did nothing, now that I knew who he was, wouldn't I be letting her down? I couldn't let it go now. I held her against my shoulder for a minute, then gently pulled myself away. "I'll call you."

Abby was coming in from work as I left the house.

"Hello, goodbye," she said.

"Sleep tight."

I got in the Explorer and drove to the station, arriving ten minutes early. When the men came in, I went over everything with them. Eddie was still working on the art theft in Rosemont. Arnie and Clyde had fallout from the triple homicide to handle—preparing their testimony for a probable cause hearing. I asked Eddie if he needed Nate, and he said he didn't. I told Nate I had a different assignment for him, and gave him instructions for a background check on Neil Daniels.

I entered the name in my flagging program, checked the updates and e-mail. It was all I had time to do before I had to go to the courthouse.

At lunch, I called home and told Jennifer I would be eating at a restaurant near the courthouse. She sounded bleak.

"Are you eating?" I asked.

"A little."

"Eat more. For me."

"I'm not hungry."

"If you won't eat for me, do it for the baby. Please."

"Harvey—"

"What?"

"Harvey, I love you."

"Even when I'm being mean to you?"

"You're not mean."

"What then?"

"I don't know. I wish you could forget about him."

I pulled in a breath. "I'll see you later."

I hung up and hated myself. How could I do this to her? I loved her more than anything. I'd sworn I would never hurt her.

I went into the restaurant and ordered coffee. An assistant D.A. I'd worked with came over and sat down and started talking. I was attentive enough to keep the conversation up. His lunch came and he ate, still talking between bites. I looked at my watch and excused myself, walking back to the courthouse alone. I pulled my wits together before I had to testify. As soon as they excused me, I went back to the office.

Nate came over to my desk. "I haven't found much yet, Harvey. I checked with the university, like you said. He's in their alumni directory. His new address is in Lexington, Mass. He was a good student and graduated cum laude. He has a Massachusetts driver's license and a clean driving record. That's it so far."

"Check for a criminal record, please. Also, I'd like to know where he works. And Nate, this is just between you and me."

Eddie brought me his reports a few minutes later. "Nate working on a new case?"

"Yeah. Background check on something of mine."

He looked at me. I always told Eddie about my cases.

"Is Jennifer feeling okay?" he asked.

"She's better than she was."

He stood there for a moment. "Harv, are you mad at me?"

How many times had Eddie asked me that in five years? Quite a few, but not lately. More guilt to add to the load. I looked up at him.

"No, Eddie, I'm not mad. I'm sorry if I made you think that. Come for supper."

Abby was cheerful that evening. She'd reached her equivalent of the weekend and had slept all day. Now she was ready for some action. When I told her Eddie was coming, she flew around the kitchen. I dragged into the bedroom and set down my briefcase. Jennifer came out of the bathroom. She had just had a shower, and her hair was rolled in a towel. I stood there wondering what she would do. She was so gorgeous. She had said she would always love me. My heart said it was true. My head said she wouldn't, especially if she knew what I had Nate doing at work.

She walked slowly toward me in her white robe, and on the last step put her arms out toward me. I hugged her, then kissed her violently. The towel slipped from her hair and hit the floor. She gasped a little when I let her go, and her hands clutched the lapels of my jacket. I looked deep into her eyes, and they were true and steady.

"You really do love me, don't you?" My voice came out hoarse and harsh.

"Always," she said.

I was furious with myself. I turned around and started slapping my gear down on the dresser. Badge, notebook, pen, phone, key ring, plastic bag, handkerchief, tape measure, extra ammo clips. I peeled off my jacket and threw it at the bed. It fell short, and Jenny picked it up and stood holding it, watching me. I took the holster off and put it with the rest and pulled at my necktie.

"Please don't be angry," she said timidly.

"It's not you I'm mad at." I headed for the bathroom, pulling the necktie off.

When I came out to the kitchen in clean clothes,

Eddie, Abby, and Jennifer were obviously waiting for me. Supper was on the table.

"Mystery casserole out of the freezer," said Abby. It was one someone had brought over the week before. Kielbasa and cheese mostly. Eddie thought it was great. Jenny couldn't eat it. I felt like I never wanted to eat again, but I took a few bites so she wouldn't fuss at me. She ate fruit salad and half a roll. Abby and Eddie ate and talked like normal people. When we were done, Eddie said he would do the dishes with Abby again.

"You two go watch the news," he said. "We're getting pretty good at loading the dishwasher."

We went into the living room and sat down, and Abby followed with a cup of coffee for me and Jennifer's bottle of water.

"You want to watch the news?" I asked Jennifer.

"No. Do you?"

"No."

We sat in silence.

She stirred, reaching toward the coffee table, and I realized she was going for the tissue box. She swiped at two tears that had run down her cheeks.

"Jennifer—"

"I'm sorry. I know you hate it when I cry." It sounded as though she could barely get it out.

"I don't hate it. It just makes me feel—helpless. What can I do to make you feel better?"

"Forgive him."

I sighed. "If I could, I would."

She wiped her eyes again and said quietly, "I should have told you when you asked me."

"Jenny, Jenny!" I leaned my head against the back of the couch and looked up at the light fixture. Here she was, apologizing to me, and she had done absolutely nothing. "You are too good for me. Don't make yourself into the culprit here. I know who's at fault, and it's not you."

"His name is Neil Daniels." She swung around to face me. "You asked me to tell you. That's it. Neil Daniels. Do whatever you have to do."

I didn't move, as the guilt hit me full in the face. She got up and walked into the sunroom and beyond, to our bedroom.

I sat there another ten minutes, trying to process what had happened and where our relationship was headed. I didn't like our prospects, unless I changed.

Eddie came to the doorway. "Uh, Harv?"

"Yeah?"

"Are you going over to the church?" Jennifer and I usually went to the Bible study and prayer time on Wednesday. I didn't want to go, and I wasn't sure Jennifer did, either.

I stood up, weary to the bone. "I'll see if Jennifer's up to it."

At the bedroom door, I knocked softly and

pushed it open. She was lying on top of the quilt with her Bible beside her, but she wasn't reading.

"Do you want to go to prayer meeting?" I couldn't quite meet her eyes.

She sat up. "Do you?"

I stood there for a few seconds, trying to get the weight off my chest. It wouldn't budge. Did I really want to feel like this for the rest of my life?

"Yeah," I said.

To my surprise, she got up and started getting ready. Eddie and Abby went, too, though I wondered if Abby only went because Eddie was going.

The pastor led the Bible study, and when he was done he took prayer requests. By that time, I was scraping bottom emotionally. It was time to pray. We always formed small groups, men with men and women with women. Jennifer took Abby off with Beth and her sister-in-law, Ruthann. I had some options. I could step out into the parking lot and wait it out. I could go with Eddie and Jeff or a couple of other guys and try to act normal. Or—

I got up and walked slowly over to where Pastor Rowland had sat down with Rick Bradley and Dan Wyman.

"Pastor, I really need to talk to you."

"Certainly." He excused himself and took me into his study. As we left the auditorium, I looked over my shoulder and saw that Eddie and Jeff had joined Dan and Rick to pray. I shut the study door behind us.

"What is it, Harvey?" Pastor Rowland asked. "Jennifer looks stronger."

"She is. It's not that." I sat down and leaned forward, twisting my hands together.

"Are you all right, Harvey?"

"No. I'm miserable. Pastor, I've done something really rotten."

He looked at me silently, not condemning me, just waiting. The same technique I used on suspects.

"I've hurt Jennifer badly. On July seventeenth, I promised to love and honor and cherish her, and today I just—I just trampled all over her feelings. I guess I have to tell you the story before you'll understand."

"I'm listening."

I looked at the rug. "There was a guy Jennifer used to date in college. He—well, to make a long story short, he hit her a couple of times, and he tried to rape her. She got away, but it always bothered her in a big way. We are talking major psychological damage. When I first met her, she was very timid and distrustful of men. We talked about it some, and I think that helped. When we got saved, it didn't seem to be an issue anymore. She's okay with it now, and she's even forgiven the guy."

I looked up at him. He shifted a little, but didn't say anything.

"The trouble is, I haven't. I didn't realize how bitter I was about it until a couple of days ago. It came up innocently enough, but I suddenly found out I still hate him, and I wanted to do something to him. Confront him at the least. Maybe something worse, I don't know, make his life miserable. If I thought a criminal charge would stick, I'd go arrest him." I sighed. "But, anyway, I've been letting this thing control me. Jennifer's all upset. I asked her yesterday to tell me his last name, so I could find him. She wouldn't." I twisted my wedding ring and sighed.

"Have you talked to the Lord at all about this, Harvey?"

"Some. I asked him to help me be willing to forgive the guy. But I haven't really been able to yet. I sort of want to, but I sort of don't. I guess I've enjoyed hating him. That's pretty perverse, isn't it?"

"Have you asked God to forgive you personally?"

I hung my head. "No." I knew why not. Because then I'd have to stop hating Neil Daniels. I swallowed. "She wouldn't tell me his name, but I found out anyway. And today I did something even worse."

"What, Harvey?" he asked gently.

"I asked one of my men to do a background

check on Neil Daniels." I felt defensive, and said quickly, "We do background checks all the time. It's not unusual."

"But only on people you suspect of crimes."

"Well, we do them on people who apply for concealed weapons permits, things like that, too."

"But only if you have an official reason."

"Yes."

"And you had no reason today to check on this man Daniels."

"Not really."

"Harvey, what I'm hearing is that you abused your position to help you satisfy a personal grudge. Isn't that unethical?"

"It's against the rules. It's a sin, too. I know that. That's why I'm here. And I dragged my man Nate Miller into it."

"Did you tell him that it was personal?"

"No, I told him it was for one of my cases."

"So you lied, too."

I sat there for a few seconds, then looked him in the eye. "Yes."

Pastor Rowland was silent. I wondered if he thought I was beyond hope.

I said, "Tonight, I felt so guilty. I've been crabby with people for two days. I know I've been nasty to Eddie and Abby and Beth, not to mention Jennifer. She's told me in the past that being with me made her feel secure, and that helped her forget about her experience with Neil. Now I've undone all of that. Pastor, she came to me tonight and told me the guy's name. She thought I was mad because she wouldn't tell me when I asked her. She knows I'm wrong, but she's willing to submit to me. What can I do? I don't deserve for her to forgive me."

The pastor looked at me dispassionately. "I think you know what you have to do, Harvey. You know what the scripture says, don't you?"

"I know God hates lying."

"That's a start. Let me just step out to the auditorium for a second and ask Dick Williams to close the service. I'll be right back."

He left then, and I took out my handkerchief and wiped my eyes. Suddenly I wanted Jennifer badly.

When the pastor came back, he pulled his chair around next to me. We had a session of about twenty minutes, looking at what the Bible said on lying, deceit, hate and bitterness.

"I know you want to please God," he said. "You've committed your life to the Lord. This week, you've let yourself fall into sin. But it can stop right now. Get back into harmony with God, and with Jennifer."

He opened to Proverbs 28:13 and read to me, "He who covers his transgressions will not prosper, but he who confesses and forsakes them will find compassion."

I said, "I guess that's what I need to do. Confess and forsake."

"Yes. And leave the vengeance to God."

We prayed then, and I confessed everything. I asked God to forgive me, thanked him for saving me and for giving me Jennifer.

"Wait here," Pastor said. In a minute he was back, with Jennifer, and he closed the door softly on the two of us. We stood there a moment, eyeing each other. I opened my palms and held them outward, down by my sides, half afraid to put my arms out to her. But she ran to me and threw her arms around my neck, almost knocking me over.

"Jenny, I'm so sorry. Please forgive me. I was terrible to you. I love you so much."

She kissed the wrinkles at the corners of my eyes, where the tears were spilling out.

"You won't go after him?" she asked.

"No. Not because of what he did to you. But if I ever hear he's hurt someone else, or committed another crime—"

"Then it would be your duty," she said.

"I don't hate him anymore." I meant it. He was scum, but the rush of feeling was gone.

"Thank you."

"Thank God. I couldn't let go by myself. Jenny, I betrayed your trust. I went looking for that guy. When you told me his name tonight, I already knew it. I felt so convicted. I wasn't mad at you. I was mad at myself. Please forgive me."

"I do. I have."

"How can you love me?" I asked.

"It's easy," she said. "It's very easy." I held her close, with the baby between us.

When we went out to the auditorium a couple of minutes later, Abby was sitting in the back pew, waiting for us. She looked alone and apprehensive. Pastor Rowland stood near the door.

We walked down the aisle, and I stopped in front of Abby. "I need to apologize to you."

"What for?" She turned wide eyes on me.

"I tried to use you to get information about a man. Neil Daniels."

"That's it!" she cried, then stopped, looking at me in confusion. "You were trying to find out about Jennifer's old boyfriend."

"Yes. I wasn't honest with you. It wasn't a casual interest. I'm sorry. I shouldn't have done it. Will you forgive me?"

"Yes, of course." She looked at Jennifer and me, still a little perplexed.

"I'll tell you all about it tomorrow," Jennifer said.

We went out onto the steps.

"Thank you, Pastor." I shook his hand, and he said goodnight and walked toward his house.

Jeff's truck and Eddie's were still in the parking lot, and they stood together near them, talking with Beth. I gave Jennifer my car keys and walked over to them alone.

"Hey, Harv," Eddie said, his dark eyes sober.

I nodded. "Beth, I'm sorry I was mean to you yesterday."

"It's all right Harvey."

"No, it's not. Something was bothering me, and I let it affect everything I did and said. I was rotten to you, too, Eddie. I'm sorry. Please forgive me."

"Sure."

Beth put her hand out and touched my sleeve. "Are things better now, Harvey?"

"Yes. I've made my confession."

"Did you have to confess to Pastor Rowland?" Eddie asked. I knew the priest connection he'd been raised on still bothered him.

"No, Ed. I had to confess to God. Pastor helped me sort it out."

Jeff had been silent, but he put out his hand then, and I took it. "Take care of my sister," he said.

"I'll do better now."

Eddie clapped me on the shoulder. "Whatever happened, it's okay."

"Well, it's not just being grouchy. I had Nate do something personal for me at work. I lied when I said it was for a case."

"You don't lie anymore, Harv."

"I did today. I lied to you and Nate. It was a sin, Eddie."

He looked at me in the light of the street lamp,

as though he couldn't believe it. I recalled a time when I was training him for undercover work, when I had instructed him specifically on how to lie without looking nervous.

"God will forgive you," he said at last.

"Yes. He has."

Jennifer and Abby were waiting for me in the Explorer. We drove home in silence, but I held Jennifer's hand all the way.

When we got home, Abby said, "I'm exhausted, so I'll see you guys in the morning," and headed up the stairs. I locked the door. Jennifer had gone into the bedroom. I got a bottle of water and followed her.

"You still need to hydrate."

She was sitting on the bed, taking her braid out. She reached for the water and took a long drink.

"You're better," I said.

"A lot better now. I think tomorrow is going to be a wonderful day." The smile she turned on me was genuine, the glorious one I hadn't seen in days.

"Jenny, I love you so much. I don't know how I could do what I did to you."

"It's over."

"Yes."

She set the water bottle down on the night stand and opened her arms to me. I sat down beside her and held her and buried my face in her hair.

Chapter 7

Thursday, September 30

The next morning, I went first to Mike. He listened to my story, shaking his head.

"I thought you learned this lesson, Harvey."

"I thought so, too."

"Last time, you used the department's computer system to get the goods on a beautiful woman you wanted to date. Now it's revenge. What's it going to be next time?"

"There won't be a next time, Mike. I promise, it will never happen again."

"So, you're saying I can trust you with a computer?"

"I hope so. It was wrong, I know. I'm sorry."

He looked at the print that hung on his office wall, the Turner seascape he'd inherited from the last chief. "Let's just say you suspected this subject of criminal behavior and let it go at that."

"You're not going to discipline me?" He could fire me if he wanted to.

"I think you've disciplined yourself." Mike leaned back in his chair and linked his hands behind his head. "Harvey, if you've got a weak spot, it's your emotions." That hurt, because for years I'd prided myself on keeping my feelings inside. "Jennifer is good for you, but she's your soft spot. Emotion has its place, even in police work, but it shouldn't be in the driver's seat."

He sat up and opened a desk drawer and took out a paper. "I've been talking with the patrol sergeant. We need some officers in the department with extra computer training. They all come in with the basics, but we could really use some people who could get online and find information, track down cyber criminals, and use the specialized software that's available, the way you do. I'll set up some training sessions, and you can instruct."

"Oh, Mike, come on—" I stopped. I had no right to protest. I held up my hands. "All right."

"I'm not punishing you. We really need this. Every day we get complaints about scams offered by e-mail, or sex offenders preying on kids by way of the computer."

"All right, I'll do it," I said. "Are these remedial students or ones with aptitude?"

He considered. "We need a cadre of sharp computer people."

"I could stand to teach people who enjoy it and understand what you're going for."

"All right. I'll ask the department heads to nominate people for special computer training. What's the limit on the class?"

"Six, maybe." I was thinking of the computers available in my unit and the logistics.

"We'll screen you six people with computer aptitude and willingness to upgrade. Afternoons?"

"I'd rather have them fresh in the morning."

He made a note. "Nine a.m. to noon. How long?"

"I could teach them a lot in a week. Start out with simple stuff—make sure they know how to do DMV checks, background checks, data searches. Then go on to interacting with the crime databases and cracking these electronic scams."

Mike said, "If we had six people we could depend on for advanced stuff, I'd feel pretty good. I call on you a lot right now."

"So does the detective squad. They should be able to do it themselves."

"Should they be top candidates?"

"Only if they like it. I'll set a fast pace, and I don't want someone who hates it dragging us down."

"Anyone from your unit?"

"Sure. Eddie and Nate."

"Clyde too old to learn new tricks?"

"I'll sound him out, but he hasn't shown a great admiration for his computer."

"One thing, Harv. Impress on these people that personal use is taboo."

"Got it."

"Because you don't want to be in the position of having to discipline people who've abused our computer system, do you?"

"No way."

Nate's report on Neil Daniels was lying on my desk.

"Eddie, where's Nate?" I asked.

"Locker room, I think."

I picked up the report and walked down there. Nate was closing his locker, with a jacket in his hand.

"Nate, this report—"

"Is it okay? I called his employer, and I might be able to find something else, but I'm not sure what."

"Well, actually, I haven't read it yet."

He looked at me, puzzled.

"Nate, I lied to you yesterday." His expression became even more baffled. "This background check wasn't for an open case. It was personal. I'm sorry. I shouldn't have asked you to do it. I wanted to check up on Daniels. I shouldn't have done it in the first place, but if I were going to, I should have done it at home, on my own time and my own computer."

He turned away from me, reaching into the pocket of the jacket. "No big deal."

"Yes, it is a big deal. I'm sorry I got you involved in it. I just came from Mike's office, and

I told him about it, and that I used the equipment and your time for my own purposes. I'm sorry, Nate, and I want you to know I won't put you in that position again."

"Okay."

"And, Nate, there's one more thing. Mike wants me to give some advanced computer training for a few officers. Would you be interested in that? You've shown some capability, and it would help us in the unit. I thought I'd nominate you and Eddie for the training."

"Sure, I'd do anything that will help me do a better job up here. I don't exactly feel as though I'm carrying my own weight yet."

"I think you are, but this would enhance your job performance."

"Great. But I wish you'd read my report." He smiled a little. "I worked hard on it."

"Why don't you brief me right now?" I said. "Has this guy been involved in any criminal activity?"

"I don't think so. Clean as a whistle. His employers like him."

"Then I tell you what I'm going to do. I'll file this away, and if we ever need it, it will be there. I think right now that I should leave this thing alone."

Nate still looked a little uncertain, but he said, "Okay, Captain."

I talked to Eddie about the training, and he

was willing to go through it, although he rightly pointed out that I'd taught him a lot of computer skills already. But I knew there was a lot more he could learn, and he was quick at picking up new things.

At noon, my desk phone rang.

"Captain Larson? This is Greg Prescott. I don't know if you remember—"

"Of course I remember. You flew Jennifer and me to New York on our honeymoon. Good to hear from you!" Greg was the navigator on our plane in July, and he'd come out into first class and chatted with us for a few minutes. I'd given him my business card and told him to call when he was in Portland, but hadn't heard from him since.

"Well, I'll be in Portland this weekend. I thought maybe I could take you and your wife out to lunch on Sunday."

"Come eat at our house," I said. "We'll be going to church in the morning, but we'll be home by twelve-thirty. We'd love to have you come."

I started giving him directions, but he cut me short, saying, "How about if I just meet you at your church?"

"Well, sure, if you want to, that would be great."

When I'd told him how to find the church, I called Jennifer and told her about Greg's call.

She and Abby were enjoying the day together and had baked brownies and cleaned the refrigerator.

"Oh, good. I'll cook a pot roast on Sunday," she said.

"Don't overdo things, gorgeous."

"I won't. And you'll be happy to know I'm eating right now."

"What are you eating?"

"Peaches and a muffin."

"Want me to bring you anything tonight?"

"Just you."

"I'll be there. Take a nap this afternoon, okay?"

When I'd hung up, I sat for a minute savoring the joy of being married to Jennifer. It was so much better when I wasn't keeping secrets from her.

I spent a quiet afternoon doing research on the art case and preparing an outline for the computer training.

Jennifer came bouncing into the garage as soon as I drove in. I barely got out of the Explorer before she was in my arms. I picked her up and swung her around so that her hair flew out behind her, and then I set her down and kissed her.

"Eddie called Abby a little while ago, and she invited him for supper."

"Great. Man, it's good to see you looking like yourself again!"

"Abby and I talked this afternoon." She lowered her voice and glanced toward the house.

"And?"

"She was touched by your apology last night."

"I was an idiot."

"No. Well, maybe, but anyway, she said she couldn't believe at first that you would be so sneaky, and especially that you lied to people. She thought you were above all that, I guess."

"The impeccable Harvey Larson fell off his pedestal," I said regretfully.

"Oh, honey." She hugged me close. "I love you."

"If I didn't have you, I'd be pretty miserable right now. I don't ever want to do anything like that again."

I headed for the shower. Jennifer came into the bedroom as I was putting my shoes back on.

"I never did cut your hair. Let me do it now," she said.

I got the barber scissors and a comb and sat on a stool in the kitchen for her. Abby watched in amazement as she ruthlessly attacked my hair. Before shearing the curls off the back, Jenny ran her fingers through them and sighed mournfully.

"Hate to do it," she said, but off they came.

"They'll be back in a month," I told her.

Eddie arrived as I swept up the pile of hair.

"Need a trim, Eddie?" Jennifer clacked the scissors at him.

"No, thanks." Eddie handed her a carton of ice

cream he'd brought along. "My mother says I eat here too much, so I thought I'd better contribute."

Jennifer laughed. "You don't, but thanks."

His smile drooped. "I think it's because I haven't been home much lately."

"Still avoiding your folks?" I asked.

He sighed. "Every time I go over, she nags me about confession. I tried to explain it the way you did, Harvey, but I don't think she's buying it."

"Well I, for one, was shocked at Harvey's behavior," Abby said.

I winced. "I'm really sorry, Abby. I'll never try to manipulate you again. I promise."

She nodded. "I'm going to hold you to that. I'm sure God will, too."

I wasn't sure how to take that. Did Abby believe now that God was my master, or even that he was real? I tried to be extra nice to her that evening, and I wished I could read her thoughts as she watched me eat. She was solicitous of Jennifer and jumped up to get me coffee. Eddie and I talked a little shop, but Abby put a stop to that.

"This is family time, Captain. No discussing murders and robberies tonight."

I smiled guiltily. "All right, sister, dear, bring on the familial camaraderie."

After a protracted game of Risk, we had dessert. She honored Eddie, the winner, with an extra scoop of ice cream. Jennifer and Abby sat on the couch, giggling and making plans for decorating one of the spare rooms upstairs for a nursery.

Eddie watched them with amusement. He turned to me with a smile. "Aren't they great? Look at them!"

"They are." Jennifer was the great beauty, I thought, although she was still too thin. Her eyes were more sober and gray. Abby's were bluer, and sparkling. Their hair was the same shade, Abby's in a pony tail that night, and Jennifer's in a braid.

"Do you think—"

"What?" I asked.

Eddie shook his head. "Nothing."

After he left, Abby and Jennifer got on the telephone extensions and called their parents. Jennifer gave them a glowing report of her health and the baby's. Her youngest sister, Leeanne, begged to come down for the weekend, and Jennifer told her to come.

"You'll be too tired," I said, when she filled me in.

"No, Abby will help me." Abby backed her up, so I braced myself for the Wainthrop Sisters Pajama Party.

"I feel like eating a jelly doughnut," Jennifer said at quarter to ten.

"Oh, boy, I guess that's my cue," I said and headed for the garage.

"Take me with you!"

"Me, too!"

I turned back with a smile. Jennifer was scrambling for her shoes, and Abby was pulling on a sweater.

The seminar on management was my lot for Friday. Mike wouldn't listen to my protests, and I drove early to Augusta and came home late. Jennifer met me at the door when I went in, trailing my briefcase in my left hand. She was tired, and I was tired. I put on jeans and a sweatshirt and sat in the lawn swing with her, out in the back yard. The frost had killed the grass and bushes, but it was still nice to have our own bit of earth to enjoy in peace. Abby brought us hot tea and an afghan, which she tucked over Jennifer's knees.

"Did you eat, Harvey?"

"No, I'm not hungry."

"Feed him," said Jennifer.

A few minutes later, Abby brought me a plate of warmed up leftovers, and I ate them.

Jennifer asked me all about the seminar and seemed to be interested in what I'd found extremely boring.

"Didn't you learn anything new?" she asked.

"Yes, I learned I hate management."

Leeanne drove down before lunch on Saturday, and the three sisters were giddy with joy at being together. I was happy for them, but I needed to get out and find some masculine company. I called Eddie to see if he could play basketball. That afternoon, I spent a couple of hours in the old neighborhood with him and his cousins Dave and Rene and a couple of other guys.

Back on Van Cleeve Lane, the Wainthrop Girls' Festival had toned down to ecstatic. They were cooking for the anticipated dinner with Greg Prescott the next day. I told them to make extra food because I'd invited Eddie, too. When he'd heard Leeanne was in town, he had been unable to keep from inviting himself. He hadn't been with both sisters together since our wedding, and it promised to be an interesting day.

Sure enough, when we arrived early for Sunday school the next morning, he was on watch by the church doors, and we sent Abby and Leeanne to his class with him.

"This won't ruin your status in the singles class, will it, Ed?" I asked.

"No, all the guys in there will be after me to introduce them, though."

"Share the wealth," I advised.

Jennifer and I went to our usual group in the auditorium. After the class, I went into the foyer to watch for Greg. I saw Eddie and the girls coming up the hallway from their classroom. As Eddie had predicted, two or three other young men were trailing along after them.

Beth's brother, Rick Bradley, came and stood

by me for a minute. "Got a houseful of women this weekend, Harvey?"

"Yup."

"Guess you're hoping you get a boy in there soon."

I smiled. "Were you disappointed your first one was a girl?"

"No. I thought I would be, but when I saw her, I wasn't." He grinned. "But I sure was happy that the second one was a boy!"

Greg came in wearing his airline uniform, and I went over and shook his hand.

"Great to see you, Greg."

"Harvey! I came straight from the airport," he said. "I thought I'd have time to change, but we were a few minutes behind schedule."

"That's okay." I took him into the auditorium, and Jennifer moved over to make room for Greg. Past her, Eddie was sitting between Leeanne and Abby.

Jennifer greeted Greg warmly, but that was as far as we got before the pianist began to play. After the service, we corralled our dinner guests and introduced them to Greg and made sure everyone had a ride to the house. Once we got there, we men took off our jackets and ties, and I gave Greg a quick tour of the house.

We all sat down to pot roast, potatoes, green beans, biscuits, and squash. Pies followed, and I learned that Leeanne had inherited her mother's

131

touch for excellence there. Greg gave abundant praise for the meal, and Eddie did it *en français*.

It was a warm day, so we went into the back yard. The three sisters sat in a row on one side of the lawn swing. Eddie sat on the other side with Greg, and I pulled up a lawn chair.

"Do you have to fly out today, Greg?" Jennifer asked.

"No, we're stuck here until tomorrow morning early. I'm staying at a hotel by the airport."

"Can you stay and go to church with us again tonight?"

"That wouldn't be too much for you folks?"

"No," I assured him. "We love company. Jennifer might need a nap, though. For the baby."

Greg did a double take. "You guys have a baby coming?"

Jennifer blushed. "Not until next April."

"Hey, congratulations!"

"Thanks." I couldn't help smiling. "It's something I've waited a long time for."

Abby started to get up. "I was going to bring the lemonade out."

"I'll get it." I stood up, and Greg did, too.

"Need some help?"

"Sure," I said. "You can get the glasses."

We went inside, and I found the tray laid out on the counter, and the pitcher of lemonade in the refrigerator.

Greg said, "Captain Larson, would it be too

forward of me to ask which of your sisters-in-law your friend Eddie is here for?"

I grinned. "I don't think Eddie knows. And call me Harvey."

We took the lemonade out, but it was clouding over and getting chilly, so we soon moved inside. Greg, Eddie, and I sat down in the sunroom and started talking baseball, and Jennifer, Abby, and Leeanne went to the kitchen to do dishes.

Greg watched them go with an awed expression.

"Their parents must be gorgeous. Three beauties in one family."

I laughed. "They've got three boys, too, and not one of them is ugly."

Eddie was watching Greg with a calculating look.

Chapter 8

The sunroom was light and pleasant, but the breeze had become sharp, and I closed the patio door. I had come to love the room, with the white wicker furniture, bright cushions, shelves full of books, a small oak table and chairs, Jennifer's print of Van Gogh's *Starry Night*, and the sampler Beth had stitched as our wedding gift.

Eddie and I pumped Greg for a few minutes about the aircraft he flew. I could tell Eddie liked Greg, but he didn't seem sure that he wanted to. Definitely a potential rival.

I suggested the old standby, table games. We got the girls to come in and vote for their favorite games. Greg claimed to have an I.Q. of 97, which I strongly doubted.

"I could probably handle Monopoly if someone else will count my money for me," he said.

"I thought pilots had to study math and physics and all sorts of things like that," Leeanne said, wide-eyed.

"That's why I'm a navigator, not a pilot." Greg didn't crack a smile.

Abby elbowed Leeanne. "He's kidding. The navigators do all the math."

Leeanne blushed.

We let the women choose their tokens first. Our set was an old one Jennifer had bought at a thrift shop, with the older tokens. Abby took the dog, Leeanne the wheelbarrow, and Jennifer the thimble. Eddie chose the cannon, and Greg the car. I took the hat. I wondered if the tokens said anything about personalities, and why nobody wanted the shoe or the iron.

The game progressed until Mike called me about four o'clock. "There was an attempted break-in last night in Deering, Harv. The alarm went off, and nothing was taken, but the owners did have a couple of nice paintings inside. One of the detectives got their statement. Take a look at it in the morning."

"Okay. Do you think they're safe now?"

"Well, the owners are certainly more alert. If it was your art thieves, those people were lucky last night."

Jennifer lost all her cash in the game and turned down the offer of a loan from Abby. She went into the kitchen to start supper. I was losing anyway, so I sold out and followed her. She was getting out a frying pan.

"Moms-to-be don't have to fix food for six people, seven counting the baby," I said.

"They're having so much fun. Don't interrupt the game."

"Oh, it'll be over soon, anyway. Greg's piling up cash, and Eddie and Leeanne owe him bigtime. You're not supposed to be able to borrow in Monopoly, you know."

"We always did," she said.

"So I gathered. They're playing by the Wainthrop Rules."

She was getting out eggs and milk.

"What are you doing?"

"I thought we'd have breakfast for supper. French toast."

"Let me or Abby cook it. You sit down."

"Harvey, I'm not an invalid. I'm fine."

"A week ago you had me scared silly. Just sit." She relented, but gave me some coaching on French toast, and while the first batch was cooking I started some microwave bacon. About ten minutes later, Abby and Leeanne came into the kitchen, complaining loudly about how Greg had trounced them all, and I was flipping the toast onto a platter like a pro. The girls set the table and arranged the leftovers and syrup and drinks, and then we got the guys in there to eat. Greg seemed to be right at home by this time.

When the meal was over, Leeanne shooed Jennifer and me out of the kitchen. "You two haven't had a minute alone together all day."

"Leeanne warms my heart," I told Jennifer, settling on the couch in the living room beside her. "She always puts herself last." We could hear laughter and bantering from the kitchen.

"What do you think of Greg?" Jennifer asked.

"What about him?"

"He's eyeing my sisters very carefully."

I shrugged. "Can you blame him?"

"He's awfully good looking to be thirty-something and single," she said with a little frown.

"He seems like a great guy."

"I suppose we'll never see him again after today, so it doesn't matter."

I leaned away from her so I could see her face. "What do you mean?"

"Oh, Abby . . ."

"What, Abby's attracted to him?"

"Well, I thought it was pretty obvious."

I considered. Maybe I was dense. "It seemed to me like he was impartial with the girls."

"But she was partial to him," said Jennifer. "Besides, she's closer to his age."

I gave up thinking about it and put my arms around her. "Still love me?" I just wanted to hear it.

"Of course."

I smiled.

Greg left about six-thirty, saying he would meet us at the church. Eddie hung around and took Abby and Leeanne in his truck, and the old married folks followed sedately in Jennifer's Escort. It was quiet. Jenny leaned on my shoulder. When we got to the church, they were all standing in the foyer talking to Ruthann, Rick, and Beth. Jeff was on duty that night. Jeff and I were getting to be good friends, and I missed him. Several people going in stopped to inquire about Jennifer's health.

Mrs. Driscoll paused beside Eddie and said, "Would you like to eat dinner with us next Sunday, Eddie? Amanda's coming home over Columbus Day."

Eddie shot a glance toward Leeanne and Abby, then said, "Thank you, Mrs. Driscoll, that would be very nice."

I smiled to myself. Even the Wainthrop invasion wasn't hampering Eddie. It would take quite a woman to tie him down.

We decided it was about time to go in and sit down. I whispered to Jennifer, "Who do you think will sit beside Abby?"

"Don't take any bets," she said.

When the dust settled, I sat on the aisle with Jenny beside me. Beth had claimed the spot on the other side of Jennifer, and Leeanne, then Eddie were beyond her. Abby sat between Eddie and Greg, who had the far end. I saw Charlie Emery, a senior at Colby College who was home for the weekend, looking our way. He eyed the flight crew uniform and Eddie. He cast one last longing glance along the pew before he turned away and sat farther back, with Lydia Hammond.

"I am so glad I'm not dating, or trying to," I

told Jennifer and Beth, and they both laughed.

"Your sisters are causing quite a buzz in this church," Beth said.

Jennifer gave an exaggerated sigh. "It's only begun, I'm afraid."

I looked down the row. "I'm standing in for their father, I guess. Should I give Eddie and Greg the third degree?"

Jennifer looked down the row. "I saw Greg checking his calendar in the foyer, trying to figure out when he'd have another layover in Portland."

When the service was over, Greg left for his hotel, promising to stay in touch.

Jeff and Eddie came early to run the next morning. Leeanne was up and had her car packed when I came back to get ready for work.

"I hate to go," she said. "This has been a really great weekend."

"Classes today?"

"Yes, I'm heading straight for Farmington. My first class is at 9:30. I really should leave now, but I was hoping to see Abby for a second when she gets home."

Jennifer was puttering in the kitchen, and Leeanne hung around just long enough to hug Abby when she came in tired from the hospital. "There's a chance I may be able to switch to the three-to-eleven shift," she reported. "That way, I

139

could be awake all day with Jennifer and sleep when it's dark."

Leeanne left us, and I sat for a second cup of coffee while Abby ate.

"I'm going to work on the software some more today," Jennifer said.

"I'll make sure she doesn't overdo it," Abby assured me.

"Good, because you know, once Jennifer gets into a computer program, it can be hard to talk her down."

I got my briefcase, and Jennifer followed me into the garage.

Her hair was caught back in a silver barrette, and I let my hand run down the length of it. "There's an art club meeting next week on Monday night. Eddie and I are going. Want to go with us?"

"Art club? Do we have to draw or anything? Because I'm really bad at that."

"No, we're just going to meet artists and art lovers. For a case."

"Undercover work?"

"Sort of. We won't tell them we're policemen unless they ask. We just want to see how it feels there. We're trying to find out how the thieves know who has valuable art in their homes."

"How do *you* know when people have something valuable?"

I thought about that. "Well, I guess a lot

of people in this neighborhood might have some pretty good pieces." We were living in a neighborhood beyond our income. We had gotten a good deal on the house from a church member, and I had saved money for years while I was single, making the purchase possible.

"You don't think they just look for ritzy houses to hit?" Jennifer asked.

"They seem to know specifically who has what. Sometimes I think they go for particular pieces. Sort of a steal-to-order business."

"That's interesting. Mrs. Harder has several nice paintings. She has an N.C. Wyeth illustration hanging in her entry."

I was startled. "Is it real?" I collected Wyeths in a more modest way—old books with dust jackets bearing his illustrations.

"Yes, she told me her father bought it years ago."

I whistled. "She shouldn't have told you." Mrs. Harder was a widow, living in a little stone cottage down the street with her niece. She walked her toy poodle daily, and Jennifer had struck up an acquaintance when we'd moved in. "She's only known us a couple of months. That might be exactly how these guys find out things. Just being friendly."

"And Bud and Janice Parker have a pair of Wallace Nutting prints in their family room."

"You're right. I'd forgotten. I'll check and

see what those are worth. How many other art collectors do you know?"

"Hmm . . . Can't think of any more offhand, but I haven't been in most of the houses on this street."

I kissed her passionately before I put the garage door up. "I'll call you."

"I'll be here."

"Do you know how much that means to me?"

"I think I have an idea."

I read the report of the attempted burglary that happened Saturday night, and I decided to send Eddie and Nate out to interview the homeowners to see if the detective had overlooked anything that would tie it to the string of burglaries we'd already investigated. I also wanted to know what art they had that the burglars had hoped to filch.

On the Internet, I checked values of Wallace Nutting prints and N.C. Wyeth illustrations. There was a wide variation depending on subject and quality, but there was a great deal of interest in them, and the values astonished me. Highly collectible, especially Wyeth.

I called Mike and asked if he had a minute to discuss the computer training. He told me to come up.

In his office, I scrutinized the Turner print carefully. A seascape with a sailing ship amid waves and a turbulent sky.

"You like that painting?" he asked.

"I love it, but it's a print, not a painting."

"Yeah, we can't have valuable paintings hanging in the police station."

"True. The print itself is pretty old. Might be fairly valuable," I said. "I've just been checking the values on some prints, and you'd be amazed." I walked to the opposite wall and looked closely at the Tom Sparr original Mike had hung the day he took over the office. It was a watercolor of a fishing rod and creel lying in long grass. Mike was an avid fisherman. "Do you mind if I ask how much you paid for that?"

"Sharon got it for me. About a hundred and fifty, I think."

I nodded. Not valuable enough to draw the thieves' attention.

"So how's the art case going?" Mike asked.

"Eddie and I are getting educated. We're going to an art club meeting next week. Jennifer might go with us."

"Good. That will lend you credibility. How about this computer thing?"

"I've got several names. Eddie and Nate for sure. Cheryl Yeaton ambushed me in the parking garage this morning and asked me about it. Did you mention it to her?"

"I told the sergeants, so they could see who was interested in their units. Cheryl probably got it from Terry Lemieux."

"So, what do you think?"

"She'd be good."

I said, "Don't laugh, but I was thinking of Tony Winfield. His uncle's got nothing to do with it. He's a smart kid." Tony was the governor's nephew, and his mind seemed to be in fast forward all the time. I'd used him as backup on a couple of cases, and I liked his intuition.

"Let me think about that one. He's very new."

"Does seniority count on this?" I asked.

"If someone with a few years under his belt wanted it very badly, I think it might."

Now I was curious. "Anyone in particular in mind?"

"Yes. Terry." Mike was looking steadily at me, as though gauging my reaction.

"Terry? Great. Is there a problem?"

"No. I'd like to see him do it. Terry's a good man, and he's done well as patrol sergeant."

I eyed Mike with speculation. "You know, Arnie mentioned him to me a while back when I was talking about replacements for our unit."

"Doesn't surprise me. His name has come up before."

"When?"

He said slowly, "Before we got Eddie."

"You picked Terry for the unit."

He nodded.

"I didn't know that. I knew Eddie wasn't your first choice."

Mike said, "Oh, I have no problems with Eddie. You know that. He's turned out fine. But I always felt like Terry got the short end of the stick when the old chief passed over him and stuck me with Eddie. Terry's done very well where he is, but it was a big disappointment to him."

"Do you think I should consider him when Arnie retires?"

"If you want to. He'd be terrific in Priority."

"But he'd lose rank, wouldn't he? And they'd have to train someone else downstairs."

"Not your headache."

I nodded. "If you think he's serious, I'll consider him. I was also thinking of Jimmy Cook for my unit." Jimmy was an experienced patrolman, and Nate's best friend.

"Jimmy's good," Mike said.

"So, what about this computer class? Any more names?"

"Well, Ron gave me a couple of detectives' names. Joey Bolduc and Emily Rood."

"Okay. So, how many is that?"

Mike counted them out on his fingers. "Eddie, Nate, Cheryl, Tony, Terry, Joey, and Emily. Seven. Can you handle seven?"

"How can I cut one person? They'd resent me forever."

Mike said, "I guess the question is, do we have enough computers available at one time? If you do this in your office, there are six."

"That's counting Paula's. What do we do, boot her out during the training?"

"Well, I don't think you can do it downstairs during peak hours."

"The logistics are up to you," I said. "If we can set it up, I'll take them all. Otherwise we'll have to cut one or two people."

"I'll see if I can scrounge up a couple more computer terminals. Short of that, laptops. Can you start Monday?"

"This art thing is keeping us busy, but I think so."

"Good. Take these." He handed me two folders.

"What's this?" I opened the top one. "Cruelty to animals? You've got to be kidding."

"Nope. Ox pulling at the fairgrounds. We got a complaint that they're hurting the poor oxen. They've already called the SPCA. I want an officer to go out there and see that there's no steamrolling done."

"Can't a patrolman handle this?"

"Probably, but I thought some diplomacy might be required."

"So, Arnie?"

"Excellent choice."

I opened the second folder. "Not another sex case."

Mike shrugged. "The detectives downstairs are swamped. We need someone experienced on this one."

I went down to my office and sent Arnie to

the fairgrounds and Clyde to the hospital on the sexual abuse case. Nate and Eddie spent the morning with me on the art theft case, compiling more information.

At noon I drove home and collapsed on the couch in the living room. Jennifer brought me a plate of leftover pot roast, potatoes and green beans.

"I really didn't come home for food," I said. "I just needed to be out of the craziness for a few minutes."

"So eat anyway." With that smile, she could talk me into anything except when I was under great stress. "Abby says she's put her name in for that three-to-eleven shift."

"That would be so great. She'd be here and awake all day, I'd have you to myself evenings . . ." I took a bite and realized I was hungry.

"What's up at the P.D.?"

"All kinds of crazy cases."

"Like what?"

"Oh, ox abuse, child abuse, you name it. The detective squad is all tied up, too, and we're getting their overflow."

"What you need is a nice, restful espionage case," Jennifer said with a twinkle.

"Something like that. Something that makes you think and has some logic to it."

"I've told you before, you should have been a scientist."

147

"Huh. Not enough field work for me." I was starting to relax.

When my plate was empty, Jennifer took it. "Why don't you put your feet up for a few minutes?"

"No, I'm not tired exactly. Maybe mentally."

She went to the DVD player and put a disk in.

"What are we watching?" I asked.

"Our baby."

She came back, and I pulled her onto my lap, and we watched the two-minute tape three times. Finally I clicked it off and just held her.

"Feel better now?" she asked.

"Much."

Chapter 9

I studied art all week, thought about the unit's budget, and prepared for the computer training. The six-month evaluations were still hanging over me, too. I couldn't put those off any longer.

I remembered how Mike had handled the process, telling me what he considered my strengths and weaknesses, and always giving me a chance to respond. I used that for a model.

Clyde first. He was still the unknown quantity. I'd been warned he might challenge my authority, but he hadn't shown that tendency so far. I'd thought hard before picking him at the end of July. I'd have taken Jimmy Cook then, but he was still having some problems with his leg, from a wound he'd received on duty. I realized I had been mentally reserving Jimmy to replace Arnie at the end of the year. Now I had Terry Lemieux and the gender imbalance to consider.

I'd been watching Clyde, and he was doing well. We'd had a messy shooting case, and I had deliberately put Arnie in charge to see how Clyde handled being second chair. He'd carried out his duties with no problems. But then, Arnie hadn't tried to order him around or override him on anything. His experience was an asset. I still wondered how he would react if somebody tried to pull rank. I thought back to the tobacco smuggling case and realized he'd deferred to Eddie, a man twenty-five years his junior, without complaint. I gave him mostly good marks.

Arnie pleased me very much. He had handled the ox pulling case with aplomb, and the event kept running. The SPCA had been suspicious at first, but had ended up agreeing with Arnie that there really was no abuse of the animals. The protesters that filed the complaint weren't happy, but Arnie had let them understand that the oxen's rights were limited, and so were theirs. Arnie had handled the shooting well, though he was perhaps a shade too deferential to Clyde. Maybe he was trying to ease his way out of the limelight. I realized I had less than three months left with Arnie, and I was going to miss him.

Nate was a steady worker, no matter what I assigned him. He was always attentive and thorough. He always showed me respect and was conscientious about putting in his time. Like Arnie, Nate could call someone cold, begin a pleasant conversation, and come away with what we needed. We'd had a conversation about honesty, and he'd seemed surprised that I considered his fictions in the line of duty to be lies. He definitely wanted to please me, and even asked me hesitantly if I'd prefer he wore a suit every day. I told him to dress comfortably, but to keep a coat and tie in his locker for occasions that warranted it.

With those three done, I picked up Eddie's folder. He was my best detective. I was proud of that, since I'd given him most of his training. Of course, he'd come to me with a natural ability. His friendship buoyed me through a lot of difficult spots. He was upbeat nearly all the time, but ready to cry with me when I hurt. I was surprised how difficult I found it to give a balanced view of his work. He was a little impulsive, but had a flair and instinct when it came to second-guessing criminals.

I thought back over the last six months. I'd worked the first half of it side by side with Eddie: days of painfully pulling together scraps of evidence needed to make a case, hours of boring surveillance together, and moments of stark terror when shots were fired.

After my promotion, I'd felt the gulf between us, but Eddie hadn't needed discipline since I'd become his supervisor. He'd undergone a department investigation in July, after a shootout with a suspect in the case against Coastal Technology. He'd accepted the standard suspension in the days before the hearing and handled himself well when he testified. He was exonerated and didn't complain about the mandatory counseling afterward.

I could see him maturing. He was a better cop than he'd been six months before. He was still happy-go-lucky, but with a serious side he hadn't had as a kid. He submitted to me in our profession the way Jennifer did in our marriage: willingly, with loyalty and love.

It was hard to write an evaluation of a guy like that and not make it sound too good. His weak points were disappearing on me. Finally, I printed the report for Mike and attached a handwritten note: "Mike, I'm seeing a real maturing process in Eddie, and I'm having trouble spotting things I don't like. Your comments?"

When I spoke to Eddie about his evaluation, I praised him and told him frankly how much I appreciated his commitment.

He said, "You've chewed me out enough times in the past, Harv. Maybe I'm finally learning some of the things you tried to teach me."

I met with Mike in his office on Friday about a new computer scam. They were becoming more frequent. In this one, the scammers were sending out e-mail notices that looked very much as if they were from a popular software company. They offered updates on widely used programs for a small fee. But it was all fake, and the money went into an account Mike figured I could trace and shut down.

"This might make a good project for my class," I said.

"Sure. Just don't let things lag. If the students aren't making quick progress, clean it up yourself."

"Will do." I nodded toward the seascape on the wall. "By the way, your Turner print is worth seven hundred and fifty dollars."

"You don't say."

"I do. And the fishing one by Tom Sparr has appreciated. When did Sharon buy it?"

"Three or four years ago."

I nodded. "You could sell it today for four hundred."

"We didn't buy it as an investment," he said. "I just liked it."

"Well, that's the way to pick art, I guess. I'm just sayin'."

"About your evaluations . . ." He opened a folder. I recognized my report, with the sticky note on top. "Eddie's perfect now?"

I shrugged. "Didn't mean to imply that. He's a good cop all around."

"Yes, he is. Maybe a bit impetuous?"

"A bit, and I said so. Not as much as he was six months ago. Three months, even."

"How does he handle the public?"

"The public loves him."

"Hasn't offended anyone lately?"

"Only the girls he hasn't called for a second date."

Mike rubbed his chin. "His reports any better than they used to be?"

"What, you want me to criticize his punctuation and grammar?"

"No, although I'll bet he hasn't mastered it yet. I was thinking of completeness."

"I've tried to show him how to improve in that area."

"And has he?"

"Yes, I think so. Some."

"Then say so. 'Shows improvement in paper-work.' Something like that."

"Who's going to look at this report?"

"You never know."

I sat back in my chair, thinking. "Is there something you're not telling me?"

"I've had an inquiry."

I didn't like the sound of that. "What kind of inquiry? What are you talking about?"

"I'm not supposed to say anything."

"Mike!"

"It's nothing bad. Somebody was wondering about offering him a new position."

"Within this department?"

"No. In another city." Mike closed the folder.

I eyed him warily. "Does Eddie know about this? Because he hasn't—"

"I would say he doesn't. You guys are so close, he'll probably come to you the minute the bomb drops. That's if it does. Maybe nothing will come of it."

"You've recommended Eddie for a different job, and he doesn't know about it?"

I stood up and walked slowly over to the windows. The same view I had, but ten feet higher. I could see the roof of the law office across Franklin.

When I could speak, I said slowly, "How could you do this to me?"

"To you? I'm not doing anything to you. I'm doing something for Eddie."

"No, you're not. You can't mess with some-body's career like that, without asking him."

"They'll ask him if they decide they want him."

"But he should know they're considering him, whatever it's for. You gave them his name. You're going to show them his records." I turned around. Mike was leaning back in his chair, looking at the fishing print.

"Harvey, I'm sorry you're taking it this way. I wasn't looking at it like that."

"You're the chief now, Mike. Man, I used to sweat bullets every time someone mentioned the chief, and if I had to come up here for something, I thought I'd have a heart attack."

"That the way the men feel about me now?"

"I hope not. Most of them know you a lot better

than we knew Leavitt. But you start acting like this, and it makes me kind of nervous."

He stood and walked over and looked down at Franklin Street with me.

"Mike, you're not having regrets, are you?" I asked.

"Sure, all the time."

"You hate this office?"

"No, the office is fine. I just wish I was out there doing stuff. I know what I'm doing now is important. By George, I've tried to make sure everything that comes through this office is important. I don't waste time up here. But I need a deputy, and then Fairfield comes down here and wants to steal my best officer." He turned and looked me in the eye. "Harv, they wanted you. I can't let you go. I told them maybe we had somebody almost as good, someone you've trained."

"What? This is insane." I just stared at him until I could talk again. He stood there, waiting. "Who wanted me for what?" I demanded.

"Fairfield is looking for a new chief. I told you, I can't let you go now. You just took over in Priority."

A lot of things went through my mind. "Don't you think that's up to me? If I wanted to spend the rest of my career in another city, shouldn't I be able to say so?"

"Harvey, please. Calm down. I'm sorry. Really.

156

I think I panicked when they asked me about you."

"When did this happen?"

"Late yesterday. The town manager and two council members came down here. They knew a lot about you. You've had a lot of high-profile cases lately."

"Not for the last three months. I've hardly done anything since I got promoted."

"Hardly anything except show that you can run a crackerjack unit. Harvey, I have no deputy chief, and they were going to haul you out of here!"

"I wouldn't have gone."

"You wouldn't? You mean that?" He put his hands on my shoulders. "I'm so glad you said that, because I was afraid they'd come to you anyway, even after what I told them."

"What did you tell them?"

He turned away. "Let's not go there."

"Oh, man!" I wanted to skin him alive.

"No, Harvey, I think we should just forget this. See, I told them it was true, you were really good, but I need you, so I suggested Eddie."

"Why didn't you suggest someone like Terry or Ron? They're both in management now. Eddie couldn't be a chief. I couldn't, either."

"It's a much smaller department. Little town. They wanted you, so I figured Eddie was the closest thing I had to a Harvey Larson clone."

"Somerset County, right? Hey, that's right near Jennifer's folks. Practically next door to Skowhegan. Maybe I should meet with those guys."

"Women. All of them were women."

"You don't say?"

"Harvey, you wouldn't move up there just to be near Jennifer's family, would you?"

"I think I should at least ask Jennifer about it."

"Oh, no. You can't."

"Why can't I?"

"You just said you wouldn't go."

I held his gaze and said very distinctly, "Mike, do you know now how wretched I felt when you told me last summer you were going to retire? I thought our unit would collapse. You were very casual about it. 'You'll be fine, Harv. You'll get some new guys in, and everything will be peachy.'"

He shook his head. "If I could do it now, I'd nominate you for my deputy chief. But the mayor says I can't."

"That's ridiculous. I just took the Priority Unit. I'm as high up in this building as I want to get. I don't want to be totally in administration. Do you hear me? I don't want to be a deputy or a chief, here or elsewhere. I like my job. I'm staying put. Get a grip, Mike. We interviewed three plausible candidates for deputy last week. Close your eyes and pick one." I turned on my heel and headed for the door.

"Harvey, wait!"

I stopped with my hand on the doorknob and turned around.

"I'm sorry. I don't usually do things like this," he said.

"You're right. It was totally out of character."

"Look, there's a guy up in Bangor . . . a captain. Maybe we could interview him for my deputy." Mike looked slightly more hopeful than before.

"And what about the Fairfield people?" I asked.

He sighed. "I'll call the town manager and tell them to buzz off."

"If they're seriously interested in Eddie, you have to tell him and let him decide for himself."

"Okay, okay. Can I tell them I asked you, and you're not interested?"

"Yes. Or if you'd rather, I'll call them myself."

I called Fairfield, and the town manager was excited that I had actually made the call. She gushed over my perceived qualifications, my character, my accomplishments. For a fleeting moment, it was tempting. The pay was about the same, maybe a little higher. It was a small town between larger towns. Small department. Lower crime rate. True, they were just coming out of a period of upheaval, but I could sort through that. Jennifer would be within twenty miles of her parents. They would have their grandchildren nearby.

Then I thought about the flip side. I'd be going to a town tired of scandal, critical of its public officials. Jeff and Abby had just moved to Portland; Abby, at least, because we were there. We'd be leaving our dearest friends. Our church. Jennifer's doctor. We'd have to give up the house we'd just bought. I'd have to get used to another new job, this time in a strange place with strange people, and with everyone watching me.

I said no, thank you.

I was still pretty keyed up over the whole episode. At eleven-thirty, I told Eddie I was leaving and would be back by one. When I got home, Abby was in the kitchen, and Jennifer was having a nap.

"You're early," Abby said with a curious smile.

"I know, I just needed a dose of Jennifer."

"Well, I'll have lunch ready in twenty minutes."

"Perfect."

I went through the sunroom to the bedroom, took off my jacket and tie and shoes, and climbed on top of the comforter on my side of the bed. Jennifer opened her eyes, yawning and gorgeous.

"Hey, sweetheart!" She melted into my arms.

"Oh, boy, am I glad to see you," I told her. "The most bizarre thing happened this morning."

"Really? What?"

"I was offered a job as chief of police in Fairfield." I nuzzled her hair. It smelled like green apples.

Her eyes flew open and she pushed me away. "Fairfield? That's—" She eyed me keenly. "You said no, I hope."

"I did, but why do you hope?"

"You'd hate it. You're already strangling as a captain."

"Think so? Should I resign my commission so to speak, and go back to the rank and file?"

"No, I think you just need less interviewing personnel and evaluation forms, and more sleuthing."

"Yeah, well, it's happening to Mike, too. He's going berserk in the chief's office. He needs some action."

"Get him in on this art thing. Send him under-cover to an art gallery or something."

"He's too well known. They'd spot him in a second. His undercover days are over in this town, I'm afraid."

"Too bad. He loves police work."

"Maybe I can get him in on a case next week. He thrives on it."

"So, you turned Fairfield down?"

"Like a bedspread, as Bertie Wooster says. Hope you're not disappointed."

"No. It would be nice to be near the folks, but we're not too far from them now."

"I told Mike I have no aspirations to higher management, here or anyplace else."

"Good." She took my hand and placed it on her stomach.

"Baby kicking yet?" I couldn't help smiling.

"I can't feel it. Not for another month or two, I guess. I've been reading." She reached up and carefully pulled my glasses off. "Thought so."

"What?"

"Your eyes are crinkly. You're happy."

"Extremely happy."

Abby knocked on the door. "You guys want room service?"

When I got back to the station, Eddie was watching for me in the parking garage. I got out of the Explorer and locked it, and he was beside me.

"Harvey, the weirdest thing happened right after you left."

"What?"

"I got a call from the town manager in Fairfield. Do you know where that is?"

"Yes."

"Well, they need a new police chief. She said they wanted to know if I was interested."

"What did you say?"

He laughed. "I said they must have the wrong number. It's stupid. Me?"

I smiled. "Maybe not so stupid, Ed. You're good."

"Ha! They obviously haven't tried to read one of my reports. Imagine me doing evaluations."

"That would be pretty strange."

"I told her she should call you."

I smiled. "I wouldn't want it, either, Eddie."

"You sure?"

"Positive, but thanks."

I did some preliminary work on the computer scam and laid out my lesson plans for the class. Mike called me at four o'clock. "Harv, your class is cut to six people. You can do it in your office."

"Who'd we lose?"

"Terry. He's . . . going to Fairfield for an interview Monday."

"For real?"

"Yup."

I laughed. "You recommended him?"

"Yes, I did. And I think he'll be good at it. I don't know why I ever thought Eddie could do it. His handwriting is atrocious, and he can't write a decent paragraph."

"He's getting better."

"Well, he's too young, anyway."

I took out my day planner and made myself a note to send Terry a congratulatory gift if he got the job.

Chapter 10

Saturday, October 9

Jennifer woke up feeling terrific on Saturday, and we decided to celebrate. She'd been wanting to go to Fort Knox for a while, and I decided it was now or wait until the next summer. Eddie was wild to go. He'd been once as a fifth-grader. Beth, Jeff, and Abby were all free and wanted to tag along. We put the third seat in my Explorer and packed a picnic. Eddie and Abby scrambled into the back, with Jeff and Beth in the middle and Jennifer and me in front.

"We haven't seen half the forts yet," Jennifer said. We'd planned to get to them all that year, and the lighthouses, too. We hadn't realized how many there were, or how far flung.

"Next summer," I told her. "We still have a lot of places to explore."

"We'll have the baby then."

"I'll carry him," I promised.

It was cool and windy near the shore that day, and I kept Jenny bundled up. She had on a sweatshirt and a windbreaker, but I ended up putting my leather bomber jacket on her over it all. Outside the granite walls of the fort, I was freezing even with a sweatshirt on, but inside, out of the wind, it wasn't too bad.

We explored the fort together and in pairs, yelling to each other when we found something new. There weren't many people there that day, and we climbed a spiral granite staircase and sprawled out on the grass-covered roof with our picnic lunch, overlooking the river.

We found the powder magazines down near the shore. Eddie had remembered them as dungeons. Long underground stairways led down to them from the fort, with dim light bulbs shining at intervals overhead. When we got to the bottom, Jennifer wasn't sure she wanted to climb back up all those stairs, so we walked outside, examined the batteries and the hot shot furnace, and went around to the front entrance again, and in onto the parade ground.

Eddie climbed all over the big guns that pointed out at nonexistent warships. Everyone took pictures constantly. It was the best fort yet, we all agreed. Restoration work had been going on during the summer and the long, dark corridors with brick floors no longer had water sloshing in the low spots. Some of the masonry had been repaired. The wooden floors in the officers' quarters was solid. We went into the underground storage rooms with flashlights and examined the men's quarters and the bread ovens.

Finally Jennifer declared she'd had enough, and

I sat on the edge of the wall with her downstairs near a big cannon, looking out on the parade ground.

"Keep me warm," I said, putting my arm around her.

"You'd better take your jacket back."

"No, as long as you cuddle up, I'm fine." I still shivered a little. The cold granite we were sitting on didn't help.

"There's Eddie," she said. He and Abby appeared on the roof, on the opposite side of the parade ground. I waved, and they waved back.

Jeff and Beth came out of an arched opening to one side, and I whistled. Their heads swiveled toward us, and I waved. They started walking across the grass toward us.

"Seen enough?" I asked, when they were closer.

"It's so neat," Beth said. "I'd like to come back sometime in the summer."

"Yeah, when it's about ninety degrees." I stood and gave Jennifer a hand up.

Eddie and Abby came laughing down the spiral staircase.

"Your lips are blue, Harvey," Abby said.

We all went out and up the trail to the parking lot. I put the heat on, and we headed southwest. Abby made me stop for coffee and cocoa. A large cup of Tim Horton's helped, and Jennifer leaned on my shoulder. I was finally warm again.

Back at the house, I turned the furnace up and lit a fire in the fireplace while Abby and Beth heated up frozen pizza. They wouldn't let Jennifer help, so she went to change her clothes and came out in faded jeans, thick socks, and my old Harvard shirt. I finally shed my sweatshirt as the house reached a comfortable temperature.

We ate pizza and played a game of Yahtzee. Jennifer leaned sleepily against me toward the end. Beth kept getting after me for not paying attention. It was like old times, bantering with Beth. Finally Abby won the game, and we put it away. I just wanted to be with Jenny, but I didn't want to toss Jeff and Beth and Eddie out.

We moved into the kitchen for ice cream sundaes, and Jennifer was definitely feeling well. She ate a huge bowl of ice cream. Afterward, the three women started cleaning up the kitchen, and Jeff, Eddie and I, unchivalrous, sat and watched.

"So, how are things at the fire station?" I asked.

"Not bad," Jeff replied. "We had a house fire Thursday. I went in the ambulance, and we had a couple of cases of smoke inhalation. And there was a wreck on 295 yesterday. Routine stuff, other than that."

"You getting a lot of calls?"

"Quite a few. Not as many as in the summer. We're selling T-shirts to raise money for another thermal imaging camera."

"Great. Bring me six."

His gray eyes, so like Jennifer's, widened. "Six? Just like that?"

"Sure. Jenny, Abby, Leeanne, Travis, Randy, and me." Travis and Randy were their younger brothers, still in high school.

"What colors do you have?" Abby asked.

Jeff smiled. "Blue or blue."

"Then I guess I'll take blue," she laughed.

"Make mine extra large. I'll sleep in it," said Jennifer.

Jeff gave me a strange look.

"What?" I asked.

He said in a low tone, "I thought new brides wore skimpy lingerie at night."

I laughed. "I don't think Jennifer would know what to do with it."

"What are you guys whispering about?" Abby asked suspiciously.

"The size for the T-shirts," said Jeff. "What do you want?"

"Medium, I guess."

Jeff looked at me pointedly.

"How about Beth?" I asked.

"Oh, I didn't know I was getting one," she said.

"Sure, why not? We'll make it seven."

"I was going to get you one," said Jeff.

Beth smiled. "Thanks. I'm with Jennifer, I think. Extra large."

I gave him the look. Eddie started laughing.

"What is it with you guys?" Abby's voice rose with a tinge of paranoia.

"Just buy yourself one and wear it few times, then give it to her," I said to Jeff.

"Come on," Jennifer said with a smile. "I need to sit down for a while. You guys can build up the fire." She went with Jeff and me into the living room and curled up in an armchair. Eddie stayed in the kitchen, claiming he was now an expert in putting away dishes at our house.

Jeff insisted on making the fire up, so I just picked Jenny up and sat down with her on my lap. She didn't complain, but Jeff turned a couple of shades of red, or maybe it was the reflection from the fire. We sat, watching the flames leap.

"Can I talk to you sometime, Harvey?" Jeff asked.

"Sure. You can talk to me right now."

Jennifer turned her head toward her brother. "Is this a guy thing?"

"Well, uh, not really, but . . ."

She stood up. "Go on, you two. It's quiet in the study." I got up, and she wrapped an afghan around her and sat in the chair again.

Jeff followed me into the study, and I shut the doors to the living room and the hallway. "Have a seat."

He took Jennifer's swivel chair. "So." He nodded firmly and swung around to face me. "Harvey, something happened to me."

"Okay." I wasn't picking up any clues yet, so I just waited.

He let out a big breath. "It's been eating at me, and after what happened to you last week, I'm wondering if I'm hanging on to the past too much."

I swallowed hard. Personally, I didn't think I was the right guy for someone to ask these kinds of questions. I'd blown it royally with Jennifer.

"What sort of thing?" I asked.

"Maybe Jennifer's told you." He darted a glance at me, then looked away. "When I was a kid, my best friend was killed. Murdered."

I felt a little sick for him. I've handled plenty of murders, but when it affects someone I love, it hits home hard.

"No, Jenny never mentioned it."

He shrugged. "I'm sure it didn't affect her much. She was only five when it happened."

I sat up, doing the math. "How old were you?"

"I was eight."

I nodded slowly. That would make a huge impression on a kid, usually one that lasted a lifetime. "Do you want to tell me about it?"

He picked up a pen Jennifer had left on her desktop and clicked it a few times. "I haven't ever really told anyone about it. Not all of it."

"You don't have to now unless you want to."

"I want to. Because I want to know if God holds me responsible."

I hadn't expected that.

"Okay, just start at the beginning. Tell me about your friend."

"His name was Philip Madder. The kids all teased him about his name. They'd say he was madder than a hornet, or . . . whatever. I called him Flip."

I nodded. Jeff's eyes had a hollow look as he remembered.

"He and I hung out all the time. We were in the same grade, rode the same school bus. We lived half a mile apart, and that summer we rode our bikes all over. You've seen where we lived. There are lots of farm lanes and cottage roads. We sneaked out at night a few times." He looked over at me. "We wanted to go swimming together. There was this pond." He stared, his eyes unfocused, at the desktop.

"What happened?"

Jeff drew in a deep breath. "We'd agreed to meet at eleven o'clock. I knew my folks would be in bed by ten. But that night Leeanne was fussing. She was the baby that year." He gave me a rueful smile.

"So your mom was up with her?"

"Yeah. I had to wait until she settled down. I was fifteen or twenty minutes late, getting my bike and riding over to the pond."

I didn't know what to expect, unless he told me his friend had drowned, but he'd said murdered.

"Was Flip there waiting for you?"

Jeff inhaled carefully. "His bike was there. Flip wasn't."

A searing grief swept over me for eight-year-old Jeffrey.

"I'm so sorry. What did you do?"

"I looked around, and I called his name a few times. I didn't hear anything except frogs and wind in the trees. I waited half an hour or so, but the longer I stayed, the scareder I got."

I nodded.

"I went home and got in bed. I told myself I'd see Flip in the morning and he'd tell me what happened. At that point, I guessed maybe his dad had followed him and made him go home, and they'd left the bike there. I couldn't think beyond that. But . . . in the morning . . ."

"You learned Flip was dead."

"Yeah." He looked at me with questions in his gray eyes.

"I think I remember the case. It happened while I was at the Police Academy. We all talked about it." The Academy was only twenty miles or so from the Wainthrop's house. Time had dulled my memory of the details, but it was big news at the time.

"I was terrified," Jeff said. "I guess I was in denial, too. Harvey, my folks tried to keep it from me, but I heard what that guy did to Flip."

I leaned over and laid a hand on his shoulder. "I'm really sorry."

Jeff's breath was shallow. "I heard Mom say to Dad, 'George, that could have been our Jeffrey.' And I couldn't tell them."

"That you'd been out there?"

"Yeah." He made a small sound in his throat like a sob. "I never told them. Mom couldn't handle it. But neither could I."

"You never told anyone?"

He shook his head. "I was afraid if I did, they might put me in jail."

I had heard stories like it before, and I knew it wasn't unusual for a child that age to blame himself for a tragedy, especially when he'd been on the fringe of it.

"It wasn't your fault, Jeff."

"I was supposed to meet him, and I didn't."

"You couldn't help it."

He sat still for several seconds, then said, "I go round and round with it in my head, even now, twenty years later. If I'd gotten there sooner, if I'd obeyed my parents, if I'd gone back that night and told my folks he was missing."

"They caught that guy," I said.

"Yeah. Finally."

"He couldn't hurt other kids after that."

"I know. And I know he's still alive, in the state prison."

That was unfortunate, I thought. It might be

easier for Jeff if the murderer was dead. The fact that he was keeping tabs on the prisoner told me Jeff wasn't understating how much it had affected him.

"You asked me if God would hold you responsible."

He nodded and turned wide, anxious eyes on me. "I want . . . I want to do what's right now. Like you. I want to confess. Should I tell my parents now? Should I tell Flip's family? What should I do?"

I thought about that.

"What brought this crisis on? Why is it urgent now?"

Jeff frowned. "I think it was you. And Beth. Both of you trying so hard to show me what God wants. And going to church and thinking about things. I'm not sure I can get rid of this thing, or that God will forgive me."

"Is that what you want?" I asked.

He nodded.

I sat back in my chair and folded my hands in front of me. "Remember the first time you stayed with me at the apartment?"

"Yeah."

"You asked me if I thought you were a sinner."

"I remember."

"And I said yes, not because of this thing. I didn't even know about it. But because all of us are sinners. We do things all the time that don't make God happy. I could tell you a thousand things I've done, not just the ones you heard about last week. For example, I used to swear all the time, and God doesn't like that. It's one of the ten commandments, but I did it a lot. And for a while there, I drank a lot."

"But you got over it."

"I didn't get over it, Jeff. I repented and stopped doing it. That doesn't make me perfect now. I still get angry. I still get jealous. You know that. And you're like me and everybody else. You've got a ton of sins, too. Am I right? Lies you told, hurtful things you said to your sisters, cheating on a test, taking something that didn't belong to you."

He nodded.

"Any one of those makes you a sinner. And this awful thing that happened with Flip, well, I don't know if your folks had specifically told you not to go out at night or what, but I'm guessing you knew it was wrong."

"I sure did. Dad would have tanned my backside if he'd caught me."

"Yeah. So you disobeyed your parents. God will forgive that, just like all the other sins. None of them is more horrible than another. But it seems that way, because your friend died."

"But if I'd—"

"Enough with the ifs, Jeff. You didn't kill Flip. You know that. If you'd gotten there on time that night, you might be dead, too."

"I guess so." His voice shook.

I patted his shoulder again. "Maybe you let your friend down, but if Flip had known what would happen, I'll bet he wouldn't want you there. He'd want you to stay away that night. And one other thing."

Jeff looked up. "What?"

"You asked if you should tell your folks now, and maybe Flip's parents, too. I don't think that would help anyone."

"But shouldn't I tell them so they'll know why he was out there?"

"They know what happened to their son." I hesitated. "I'm not an expert on either theology or psychology, but it seems to me that would only hurt people and open those wounds all over again. The fact that you had planned with Flip to meet there doesn't change what happened."

He didn't look convinced.

"You should tell God. Definitely confess it to God." I felt like I wasn't getting through. "You know what? I think Pastor Rowland would be a good person to talk to about this. He knows far better than I do what God expects of us. Would you feel comfortable talking to him about it? I mean, I know it's not a topic that you'll be comfortable with under any circumstances, but I think you should get another opinion. Because I can see that you really want to settle this and do it right, whatever that entails."

He swallowed hard. "What about Beth?"

"What about her?"

"Should I tell her?"

I sighed. My first instinct was to say, "Are you nuts?" But then I remembered how healing I'd found it to confide in Jennifer about an incident that had haunted me for years. "Jeffrey, talk to the pastor. Ask him these questions. And then, after you settle up with God, if you think Beth needs to know about it, tell her. But if she doesn't need to know, I can't see the point of telling her something painful."

After about ten seconds, he said, "You may be right."

"I can call the pastor right now and make you an appointment."

"Would you?"

"Yes." I took out my phone immediately, because I didn't want Jeff to have a chance to change his mind or to blurt it all out to Beth before he'd settled it in his own heart. The pastor was happy to make an appointment, and I handed Jeff the phone and went out to the sunroom.

Jennifer, Abby, Eddie, and Beth had started a Trivial Pursuit game, and I sat down with Jenny.

"Want to play?" she asked. "You can be on my team."

"Only if Jeff can be on mine," Beth said. She was looking past me, toward the doorway.

Jeff came in and handed me my phone. "Thanks."

"No problem." I took it and stuck it in my pocket. "I think you're joining Team Beth."

Abby gave up her seat on the wicker settee for him and sat on a chair beside Eddie. We had a rousing game, and Jeff perked up considerably. An hour later, the three guests headed out.

"See you at church," Eddie said.

Beth kissed Jennifer's cheek. "Thank you. You too, Harvey."

I smiled at her without a hint of sarcasm. "You're welcome here anytime."

Jeff stuck his hand out. "Thanks, brother."

I clasped his hand. "You going to make it to church tomorrow?"

"Yeah, I'm off duty, so I'll see you there." He and Beth went out together.

As soon as the front door closed, Abby pounced. "Is Jeff okay?"

"Yeah," I said.

"Oh. I thought maybe something was wrong."

I winked at Jennifer. "Your brother may be a little lovesick."

"Well, we knew that," Abby said. "I'd better get ready for work." She went up the stairs.

Jennifer was eyeing me closely. "Now tell me."

"Okay. He's worried about something, and I helped him set up a talk with Pastor Rowland."

She nodded, watching me with big, gray-blue eyes. "Anything I should know about?"

I shook my head. "Just something he needs to work out for himself. And if he does, I think we'll all be happy. Him, you, me, Beth. Even Abby."

"Really?"

"Yeah, really." I put my arms around her. "When I married you, I knew I was getting a big family, and that made me happy. But I didn't realize how rough it can be sometimes."

"So, it's something bad."

"No. I mean, he hasn't done anything wrong. It's something that's been bothering him, but I think God will work it out for good in his life."

"I hope so."

She didn't ask me for the details, and for that I was grateful. I didn't like to say no to her, but I realized she would take Jeff's sorrow to heart if she knew how deep it went, and Jennifer already carried a weight of sadness for me. I didn't want to add to that.

I bent and got a good grip on her and stood up, lifting her and rocking a little to keep my balance. Being able to pick her up and carry her gave me an inordinate feeling of strength and, okay, masculinity—not that I wanted to enter the Wife Carry at the next lumberjack's competition or anything.

"Where are we going?" Jenny asked, holding tightly around my neck.

"You need to rest." I carried her through the sunroom. Abby was just coming back downstairs.

"Are you going to bed?" She sounded dis-appointed. "I guess it's Me and Bogey until it's time to go."

"Goodnight, Abby," said Jennifer.

"You guys are rotten hosts. Kidding." She turned on the TV.

I'd just set Jennifer down on the bed when my phone rang. I grabbed it.

"Harvey? It's Greg."

"Hi! Where are you?" I asked.

"At home."

"Home? As in New York?"

"Yes. Listen, would it be all right with you if I called your wife's sister?"

"Which one?"

"Abby."

"I guess so. She's here, spending a boring evening with Humphrey Bogart until her eleven-o'clock shift at the hospital. Can I ask you something, though?"

"Sure, anything."

I glanced at Jennifer, and she was listening, frowning. "Well, this is a little bit delicate. I don't want to insult you."

Greg gave a nervous laugh. "You want to know my income?"

"No. It's just . . . well, we don't know you very well, and I'm sort of standing in for her father, since she's living with us now."

"So?"

"So, you're not married, are you?"

"No. Is that all? I . . . I was engaged once. It didn't work out."

"I'm sorry. Jennifer and I don't want to be nosy, but we felt like we ought to know, or at least that Abby ought to know, if you were interested in her."

"So, I pass muster?"

"As far as I'm concerned. Want me to see if Jennifer has any more questions? She's great for asking personal questions." Jenny swatted at me with her hair brush.

"Would you like to talk to Abby now?" I asked. "She's out in the other room."

"Uh, that would be good," Greg said.

"Tell you what. Why don't you call back on the other phone, and I'll ask her to answer out there."

"Okay."

I gave him our landline number. We hung up, and I raised my eyebrows at Jennifer, with a smile.

"You always were a sneak," she said.

The house phone rang. I walked over to the doorway and yelled, "Abby, can you get that?"

"Okay." The TV went mute, and I heard her pick up on the third ring and say, "Hello? Well, hi!"

I shut the bedroom door.

Chapter 11

Sunday, October 10

Abby was pensive the next morning. By mutual consent, Jennifer and I didn't mention the phone call.

"How about we name the baby Jeffrey?" Jennifer asked, sipping her tea at the breakfast table.

"No, your brother will want to use that name."

"The rate he's going, his kids and ours will be in different generations," she said scornfully.

"I don't think so."

"You may be right, but cousins can have the same name," she said.

Abby was eating her oatmeal silently.

"How you doing, Abby?" I asked. "You look tired."

"I am. I should have had a nap yesterday afternoon. It's tempting to just fall into bed. If I fall asleep in church, don't wake me up."

"You could have slept last night after Jeff and Beth left," said Jennifer.

"Probably should have. But then . . ."

"What?" asked Jennifer.

Abby looked up at us, then back at her oatmeal. "Greg Prescott called last night."

I said innocently, "Oh, was that who called?"

I guess we were just smiling too much, because she got all mad and said, "You guys knew, didn't you? What did you do, Harvey, listen?"

I shook my head, laughing. "No, I was talking to him earlier, and I knew he wanted to call you."

"Oh. I'm sorry."

"That's all right. We shouldn't have held out on you."

"Do you like him?" Jennifer asked eagerly.

"Well, it's kind of soon to tell, but yeah."

I went to the counter for more coffee. "He seems like a nice guy."

"So, you're the watchdog now?" Abby asked.

"And griller of suitors," I said. "Would you like some coffee?"

She held out her mug, and I filled it.

"He's older than me," she observed.

Jennifer and I looked at each other and burst out laughing.

Abby shook her head. "I take it that makes him more eligible in this house?"

"How old is he?" Jenny asked. "I'm guessing thirty-two."

"No, he's not that old," I said. "He's about thirty."

Abby said, "You're both wrong. He's thirty-four."

"Whoa!" said Jennifer.

I shrugged. "He doesn't look it. Maybe he *is* too old."

Abby said, "Correct me if I'm wrong, but don't the critics have a sixteen-year age spread?"

Jennifer looked at me. "Maybe he's *not* too old."

I said, "How long did you guys talk?"

"Oh, half an hour or so."

"Did you learn anything interesting?" Jennifer asked.

"Well . . ." Abby smiled a little. "He lives in Brooklyn, has an apartment with his cousin Bill, who is an insurance adjuster. Drives a Camaro and loves to ski, but doesn't get to do it often. He flies mostly to Florida and Atlanta and places between there and New York, but once in a while he does a New England run, usually Boston, but occasionally to—ta-da!—Portland."

"And when's the next Portland run?"

"He's not sure. He might see if he can swap with somebody and come up next week."

Jennifer looked at the clock. "We'd better get dressed for church."

"Abby, I thought Charlie Emery cast a wistful glance your way last Sunday," I said.

She frowned at me. "Well, he'll have to do more than cast glances if he wants to get acquainted."

I got the shock of a lifetime between Sunday school and church, when Mike and Sharon

Browning walked into the auditorium, spotted us, and came up the side aisle to where we were sitting. I jumped up and said, "Mike! Sharon! Great to see you."

Sharon said, "He refused to go to my church, but he said he'd go to yours, so here we are." I knew she'd been begging him for years to go to church with her, and Mike had been just as persistent in his refusal.

We moved in, and Sharon and Jennifer sat together between me and Mike. There wasn't much time before church for conversation. Eddie got a quick greeting in, and then went to sit with the Driscolls. Red-haired Amanda looked very nice that morning. Abby seemed unconcerned. She sat between me and Jeff, taking notes during the sermon.

After the service, I conferred with Jennifer, and we decided to eat out. I invited Mike and Sharon to join us and Abby. Jeff told me he was eating lunch with the Rowlands, which put me in a great mood. We drove to a nice restaurant that had a good Sunday buffet.

Jennifer didn't eat very much, but she ate and wasn't nauseous, which was enough to make us both happy. Mike launched into a discussion as soon as we were sitting down with our plates filled.

"Your pastor was saying something about the Holy Spirit," he began. "How the Holy Spirit does all these things, comforts people and teaches people and all that."

I nodded.

"Well, if he's a spirit, like a force, that doesn't make sense to me."

Sharon said, "He is a person, Mike. You have God the Father, God the Son, and God the Holy Spirit. Three people."

"But the Holy Spirit is a spirit. See, if he's a person, why don't they call him the Holy Person?"

Sharon groaned.

I said, "I don't know, Mike. I just know he's real. He works in people's hearts. If you know you shouldn't have done something, that's the Holy Spirit working on you."

"Really? I never heard that. Is that in the Bible?"

"Yes," said Sharon.

"Okay, so when I tell a lie and then I feel guilty, that's the Holy Spirit?"

"You tell lies?" Abby asked with interest.

"Well, you know."

"No, tell me about it."

Mike was nonplused. Sharon said, "Yes, Mike, tell us about it."

He looked at me and said, "Well, let's say Fairfield calls and tells me they want to hire Harvey, and just, not thinking, you know, I say, 'Can't. He's got an unbreakable contract.' That would be a lie. And then when Harvey finds out, I feel guilty, and that's the Holy Spirit, making me feel guilty?"

"So *that's* what you told them." I shook my head. "The town manager was really surprised when I called her. She said something like, 'I thought you were committed to Portland for at least five years?'"

Mike winced. "Oh, boy. What did you say?"

"I said, 'You must have received the wrong information. I can leave here anytime I choose with two weeks' notice.' That would be in my contract, wouldn't it, Chief?"

"Uh, right. I guess it would."

Jennifer was smiling a little, eating chicken and potato salad.

"You had a job offer in Fairfield?" Abby asked incredulously.

"Right. But I turned it down."

"Why? That would have been great."

"Long story," I said.

"So, has Eddie got a new girlfriend?" Sharon asked in a not-too-subtle effort to change the subject.

"Oh, I don't think it's serious," Jennifer replied. "The Driscolls invited him for lunch today, and their daughter is attractive, but Eddie's still very much playing the field."

"He ought to settle down," Sharon said. "He's a nice boy."

I nodded. "He's grown up a lot this year. I consider him the best man in my unit now."

"How do you like being the chief's wife?" Jennifer asked.

Sharon's eyes sparkled. "Well, we've been to more dinner parties that I can count and have social obligations booked into the new year. To be honest, it's exhausting."

Mike said, "Speaking of parties, I've got another question for you, Harvey."

"Leave him alone, Mike," said Sharon.

"That's all right," I told her.

"Well, now, at your wedding you didn't have any liquor, but I know you used to drink quite a lot—"

"Harvey used to drink?" Abby asked, staring at me.

"Now, why is that?" Mike asked, waving a french fry at me. "They drank wine in the Bible, didn't they?"

I had that one down. "And do not get drunk with wine, for that is dissipation, but be filled with the Spirit."

"That's the same verse Sharon gives me, but it doesn't say not to drink any," he said.

"No, but we're not supposed to let it control us, and I was definitely having that problem back then. We're supposed to let the Holy Spirit control us."

"Oh, yeah," Mike said. "So, getting back to

the Holy Spirit, you were telling me that's your conscience."

"Well, he's a lot more than a conscience," I said.

"A conscience that's a person."

I nodded, wishing I could explain it better. "Sort of."

"Like Jiminy Cricket," Mike said.

Sharon moaned softly.

Mike finally quit asking theological questions, and we enjoyed the rest of lunch. I was glad he had come. Mike occasionally threw philosophical questions at me out of the blue, and I was used to it, but Sharon seemed a little embarrassed, and Abby found it highly amusing. I invited the Brownings to come to our church again and told Mike that maybe he'd have a chance to ask Pastor Rowland some of his questions. Sharon seemed eager, and Mike said he would think about it.

Abby was just about asleep at the table, so we went home, and she headed for bed. I convinced Jennifer to take a nap, too, and had settled down at my computer when Eddie arrived unexpectedly.

"Hey, Ed, did you enjoy your visit with the Driscolls?" I asked.

"Yeah, it was fine. I just felt kind of funny hanging around after, like Amanda was getting ideas."

"And you weren't?"

"Oh, I don't know. She's nice." He sat down in the chair at Jennifer's desk and swiveled to face me.

"She's pretty," I said.

"Kind of."

"What's the matter, Ed?"

"I think I should look for a woman I can be content with for the rest of my life."

"Amanda doesn't fit the bill?"

"Maybe, but I'd have to work at it."

"Ouch. Better keep looking."

"I guess I'm getting picky. I used to just think about having fun. Now I want what you and Jennifer have." He turned on Jennifer's computer, and looked up at the wall. Jenny had insisted on hanging a poster-sized picture of me in the Kevlar vest that once saved my life beside her computer. She'd wanted it in the bedroom, but I'd vetoed that.

"Jeff's serious about Beth," I said.

"I heard." Eddie sighed. "Beth's really nice. I lost out on that one."

"She wouldn't be right for you. You're both headstrong."

"Beth can be sweet and quiet."

"I know, but she's also opinionated and independent when she wants to be. That's not bad, really, but you'd be butting heads constantly."

"So, Jeff is a milquetoast, or what?"

"No, I just don't think it will be an issue for him. For you, it might."

Eddie frowned, in seeming consideration. "You mean, I enjoy confrontation, and he doesn't?"

"Jeff is the kind of guy who would give up a lot to avoid an argument with the woman he loves."

Eddie fiddled with the mouse for a minute. "Is Jennifer ever independent?"

"Well, I've heard her express opinions, but she's mostly content to let me lead. I'd do anything her way, just to see her smile, but she almost never wants things differently than I do."

Eddie clicked a few times and opened a computer game.

"Do you still think I ought to leave her sisters alone?"

"Did I say that?"

"I thought you did, back before the wedding."

"Eddie, I once asked you to go slow because I thought Leeanne was too young for you."

"What about Abby?"

I shook my head. "You'll have to act fast if you're interested in Abby. Major competition is on the horizon."

"Who?"

"Greg Prescott."

"The airline navigator?"

"Yes. He called her from New York last night."

"He's ancient. You're telling me I'm too old, and you're letting him into the nursery?"

"I'm not sure about that metaphor, Eddie, but Abby's twenty-three. She can make up her own mind."

"How old is he?"

"Thirty-four."

He clicked on the game. "How old is Leeanne?"

"She's twenty."

He was silent.

I said, "Eddie, I gotta tell you, part of my apprehension about Leeanne was that you used to be a little wild. I think things are different now."

He glanced at me, then back at the screen. "You do?"

"I think you're more . . ."

"What?"

"I'm not sure how to put it. I wasn't sure we wanted to see Leeanne get involved with you a few months ago. Since then, you've shown more gravity and maturity. I think I could trust my little sister with you now."

"Really?" His face was serious, but suddenly he grinned. "That's reassuring."

"Well, if you took Abby or Leeanne out, you wouldn't take them to a bar, would you?"

"Of course not."

"So . . . where would you go?"

He clicked a few times. "Maybe to church. Or here. I don't know. In high school, we used to take girls bowling and stuff. That seems pretty lame now. How about a movie?"

"Just be careful what you pick. These girls are my sisters now."

"So I'd do like you do, get some old black and white thing with dead people in it, and bring it to your house and watch it on TV with her."

"Sure, with Jennifer and me chaperoning."

"Talk about lame." He smiled. "Okay, I can live with that."

"Great. Anytime you want to bring a girl, including one of my sisters-in-law, here for a date, it's okay. We'll even throw in refreshments. Or you could take them to a concert or a Sea Dogs game or the museum. Whatever you both like."

"You really think Abby's out of the picture?"

"Not yet, but Greg got her attention."

"She and Leeanne are a lot different."

"Yes, they are. Do you have a preference? You seem to have fun with both of them."

"I do. They're nice girls. Abby looks so much like Jennifer . . ."

"She does, but I think in some ways, Leeanne is more like Jenny inside. She's quiet and thoughtful, and she doesn't want to take a step until she's sure she's not making a mistake."

He nodded and said slowly, "Sometimes I think I really want to get married. Dating is . . . well, it's hard. It seems to get harder, not easier."

"Tell me about."

"Life must be a lot easier once you're married, and you don't have to look anymore."

I smiled. "It is, Eddie. It's good, knowing you've got a woman who loves you unconditionally, and that she'll always be there. Really good."

His dark brown eyes flickered to me. "Abby going to church tonight?"

"I'm not sure. She was really tired this morning. She went to bed right after we got home from lunch, but if she goes to church, she'll still only have about five hours of sleep in."

"Is Leeanne coming back down soon?"

"We could invite her."

"How about we do another fort next weekend?" he asked.

"I don't know. It's getting pretty cold. Besides, do you know which sister you'd want to invite?"

He turned back to the game and clicked a few times. "Maybe I'm not ready for this."

I didn't think Eddie had ever thought this deeply about dating. In the past, if he saw a woman he thought was pretty, he'd start flirting and let nature take its course, until he met another cute girl. I could remember times when he'd dated three or four different women in one week. Now he was actually considering a long-term relationship, and he seemed a bit lost.

He was still hanging around when Jennifer got up, and we scrounged supper for three in the kitchen. Nobody was very hungry.

At six-fifteen, Jennifer went upstairs and

knocked on Abby's door to see if she wanted to get up and go to church. She said she did, and twenty minutes later, she came downstairs, dressed but yawning. She ate a container of yogurt, and we were ready to go. Eddie invited Abby to ride in his truck with him, and she did.

"Well," said Jennifer, as I backed the Explorer out of the garage.

"Well, what?"

"I can't figure Eddie out. Or Abby either, for that matter."

"I think Eddie's making a test run," I said. "He's not sure if he wants to ask Abby out or not. He's still thinking about Leeanne, too. I told him Greg called Abby, and I think he figures he needs to make up his mind now or never on her."

"Why is dating so complicated?"

"Eddie's feelings exactly."

"Maybe it's just them," she said. "I never had to decide between two or three guys. And when you asked me out, that was it. I never looked at another guy."

"I think Eddie wants that, too," I said. "But he's used to taking different girls out. He's more outgoing than I am. It sort of comes naturally to him. You and I were both a lot quieter."

"Did you date many girls when you were young?"

"Me? No. Not many at all. I was kind of like

195

you, I guess. Stand on the sidelines and look until you're sure you want to jump in."

"Abby's had more dates than I ever did," Jennifer said. "It's easier for her somehow. Maybe she and Eddie would make a good pair."

"They enjoy each other's company." I turned into the church parking lot. "He's got a serious side, though."

"Édouard?"

I laughed. "Yes, believe it or not."

"I've seen it once or twice," she admitted.

I went around and opened her door, and we followed Eddie and Abby inside. They were laughing together, and Eddie sat down beside her about a third of the way from the front. Jennifer and I sat with them.

When church was over, we had the usual buzz of conversation as people lingered to talk. I saw Charlie Emery speaking to Abby, and I craned my neck, looking for Eddie. He was standing near Jeff and Beth, talking to Jeff, and Lydia Hammond was beside him, talking to Beth. I looked to where Jennifer was conversing with Ruthann Bradley, and she met my gaze. I nodded toward Eddie and company, and she looked, then shrugged a little.

When we went out, I collared Eddie and said, "Did you ask Abby out?"

"No."

"Change your mind?"

He said, "I like Abby, but . . ."

"Not mate-for-life material?"

"I'm just not sure."

"Okay, buddy. No problem."

"Can I do the date thing at your house next weekend?" he asked.

"That depends. Who are you bringing? Lydia Hammond?"

"Lydia?" He seemed genuinely surprised. "Not Lydia."

"Well?"

"Leeanne?"

I stopped walking. "I haven't talked to Jennifer about this yet. I'd better ask her. And what do we tell Abby? 'Sorry, Abby, we've got a double date with Eddie and Leeanne, and you can't come'?"

"Oh, Abby could be there."

"Five people on a date? Get real, Eddie. You want a date with Leeanne?"

"I think so."

"Why don't you think a while longer?"

"Okay, we'll talk in the morning. Running at your house?"

"Yes, we'll talk then."

"What's going on?" Jennifer asked me, as she and Abby got into the Explorer.

"Eddie is not nearly as settled as I gave him credit for."

197

Abby said, "Charlie asked me to go to the gem show at the Civic Center with him on Saturday. What do you think?"

Jennifer said, "Gems? Are you interested?"

"In Charlie, or in rocks?"

"Either. Because if you're not interested in Charlie, I can't see any point in going on a date you have to study up for."

"He likes rocks, I guess," Abby said.

"Maybe he was just trying to come up with something creative for a date," I suggested.

Jennifer said, "If you like him but not the rocks, tell him you'd like to go out, but not to the gem show. See what he says."

"I don't want to insult him."

"You think that would be worse than just saying you don't want to go out with him?" Jennifer turned around to look at Abby.

I said, "Who knows, you might have fun at the gem show. It might be interesting."

"I told him to call me tomorrow night," Abby said.

"Making Charlie sweat it out for twenty-four hours?" I asked.

"Well, it caught me by surprise. I just wasn't sure . . ." I looked in the mirror at her, and she looked a little embarrassed. "Guess I should have just said no."

"Charlie's a nice guy," said Jennifer. "Aren't you going to give him a chance?"

We were home, and the discussion continued over popcorn.

"What if it had been someone else who asked you to go?" I asked. "Would you have said yes?"

"It would depend on who it was."

"How about Greg?" asked Jennifer.

"Well, sure," she smiled a little and looked away.

"How about Eddie?" I asked.

"Maybe. I don't think Eddie would want to go to a gem show, though."

I threw up my hands. "Help! This girl isn't ready to date. Let's lock her in her room for another year."

Abby scowled at me as fiercely as my sister Gina ever had.

"Sorry," I said. "It was a joke."

"Well, I'm an adult," Abby said. "If I remember correctly, you were married when you were my age."

Ouch.

"That's true, but I hadn't made a very wise choice."

"He's telling you he was young and foolish," Jennifer said, "and he doesn't want to see you make the same mistake he did." She leaned over and kissed me. "This is good practice for you. I think you'll make an exceptional dad."

Chapter 12

Monday, October 11

Eddie came at six the next morning. As we stretched in the driveway, I told him, "Whatever you do, if you decide to ask Abby out, don't ask her to go to a rock show."

Eddie frowned. "She told me she hates rock music."

"No, I mean the gem show at the Civic Center."

"Oh, okay." He gave me a funny look, and we set off on our new Monday route.

When we had gone the three miles and were cooling down, I told him Jennifer was going to the art club with us that night. "You might want to take a date," I said. "I'm not sure how conspicuous we'll be. The V.P. told me about fifty people or so usually go to these things, and there are always some visitors."

"So, should I ask Abby?"

"Not if you don't want to date her."

"She'd like to be in on the case, wouldn't she?"

"I don't know. Ask a female officer if you want someone to work on the case with you."

"No, I'm not doing that again for a while." I wondered if he was still hurting a little from his last relationship, with officer Sarah Benoit.

"Do what you want," I told him. "We'll go separately."

"Do we know each other? At the art club, I mean."

"Hmm. Probably better if we don't. Unless we see someone we know. If there's somebody there who knows we work together, they'd think it was strange that we were ignoring each other."

"Well, we'll hope that doesn't happen," Eddie said. "We don't want them to know we're cops, do we?"

"Not if we can help it. Just mingle and chat and see who's willing to talk about their collection, and who's listening."

At that moment, Abby drove her white Sentra into the driveway, home from work. I went inside, leaving Eddie talking to her. Jennifer was in the kitchen, and I said, "Eddie doesn't have his head on straight, that's for sure."

"Why do you say that?" she asked.

"He's out there right now, and I'll bet he's asking Abby to go to the art club."

"So?"

"So, last night he wasn't at all sure he wanted to date her."

"He slept on it and made up his mind." Jennifer went into the entry and looked out. "He's leaving." She ran into the kitchen and sat down innocently at the table and picked up her English muffin. I poured my coffee and was heading for the table when Abby came.

"Hey. Eddie asked me to go with you guys tonight," she said.

"Are you going?" Jennifer asked.

"Yeah. He said it was for the case, so it's not a real date, I guess, but he was really sweet."

At the office, I spent the first hour getting organized, reviewing the crime updates and e-mail, making sure our cases were under control, and talking to Mike. I got the outline for the first computer session out of my briefcase and found a note from Jennifer: *Have a great day, Captain! All my love.* I smiled and added it to the bundle in my bottom desk drawer.

At nine o'clock, Cheryl, Tony, Joey, and Emily came into the office. I sent Arnie and Clyde out to interview more art gallery owners. We were finding some of the art dealers were very discreet, but others talked more than they should.

The class zoomed through the basics, and I got a feel for what each of them knew and needed to know. They'd all done background checks. Tony was the least experienced of the six. He and Cheryl, as patrol officers, didn't spend a lot of time on the computer except for reports. The detectives used it more.

I ran down the first few things I would do when I got a new computer fraud case, showing my students some tricks that could help them track down the people behind those schemes. I detailed the permissions and clearance they would need to access some databases, and the point at which they would need a warrant.

Then I presented the case Mike had given me on Friday. I had them arrange their computers so they could see what I was doing as I worked on my terminal. I explained to them how I traced back the origin of the phony messages. Once I'd backtracked through several servers, I found out where the hacker's account was registered.

"We'll get a warrant for that," I said. "Next we want to close down the account the victims send the money to."

They were all impressed by how efficiently I managed foiling the scammer. I made out requests for warrants needed to prosecute and sent them electronically to the courthouse.

Several more complaints had come in about e-mail fraud, and I let Tony use my computer so everyone could join in while I walked them through it. Of course, there were a lot of hackers out there, but similar messages convinced me that one person was particularly active in the Portland area.

It was a pretty simple online scam that hacked users' e-mail contacts and sent messages that looked as though they came from the owner. If the recipients responded, the crooks were able to get personal information from them. I guided my students through tracing back the origin, and in less than an hour we had shut the guy down and notified his server. Most of them weren't that easy and took you through multiple servers all over the globe. I was glad this one was simple, since it made a good practice problem. The server cooperated in giving us the user's name, and I had Eddie call the police in Phoenix, Arizona, give them the information we'd gathered, and trust them to pick up the hacker.

After a coffee break, I introduced another case I'd worked on a little bit the previous week. It involved a chat room for kids, where I was pretty sure pedophiles were lurking, posing as youngsters. We talked about the type of information a stalker could gain from a child over the Internet, and how seemingly innocent revelations could mean trouble.

"Most of the kids are in school now," I said. "Around three o'clock, you all need to log on and see how it works. A molester will pose as a kid and gain a child's confidence in the chat room, then initiate private e-mail or messaging. I want you to just watch at first, see what the kids are talking about. See how many clues you can pick up as to where they live. That's your homework for tonight."

We only had a half hour left, and we moved on to the art case. I handed out assignments, asking for profiles of art dealers and gallery owners.

"We want to know if they've had so much as a traffic ticket," I said. "Somewhere out there is a dealer who is knowingly buying and selling stolen art, maybe even commissioning the thefts. Find me a gallery owner with a record, and we'll have something to investigate."

They began their electronic research, and I went from desk to desk, suggesting ways to get at more and more information. Cheryl's subject had gone bankrupt twice in other states before moving to our area and opening an avant-garde gallery. Nate's was a woman with a five-year-old marijuana conviction. Other than that, they seemed pretty clean. If you wanted Maine seascapes, Eddie's and Joey's dealers were quite expert. For nudes, Cheryl's man was the one to see. Antique portraits were a specialty at Emily's shop, and I thought of the former owner of my house. Mr. Bailey had owned an Early American portrait that hung in the living room before Jennifer and I moved in there. I ought to call him at his daughter's house, where he lived now, and remind him to take security measures.

"I wonder if any of these people would buy a painting if they knew it was stolen," Joey Bolduc said.

"How could we find out?" I asked him.

"Hmm . . ."

"Anybody?" I said, looking around the room.

205

Tony said, "We could take a painting around and say we wanted to sell it, and see if they wanted proof of ownership."

"Good. That's one way," I said. "If we had a valuable painting."

Nate said, "We could ask informants where to sell something like that."

Joey nodded. "Maybe we should try that. We have informants who might give us names."

"Do it," I said. "If you don't have a case this afternoon, ask Ron if you can work on this. My unit will work on any clues you turn up."

Emily said, "How could we get hold of a decoy painting to show dealers?"

"Well, I can think of a couple of ways," I replied. "I know a few people with moderately expensive artworks. We might be able to borrow something. But I think it would be safer to use something the department owns."

Tony's eyes lit up. "You mean we have paintings and things in Property?"

"What, stolen things we've recovered?" asked Joey. "I've never heard of anything like that. Stuff that's not claimed by the owners usually gets sold."

"No, I was thinking of a print hanging on the wall upstairs." I jerked my head toward the ceiling, and they all stared at me in silence.

"In the *chief's* office?" Nate breathed at last.

"Yeah, there's an old print up there. I checked it

out, and it's worth about seven hundred and fifty dollars. That's not quite in the price range these thieves have been shopping for, but it might be pricey enough to tell us what we want to know."

Tony said, "Where did the department get this print?"

"Excellent question, Winfield. That's your next assignment. Investigate the provenance of the Turner print in Chief Browning's office. Was it donated? Bought with budgeted funds? Recovered as evidence? Left behind by a former chief? Look into that for us."

It was nearly noon, and I sent them all off to lunch. When I drove out, heading for home, I saw them sitting together at the café down the street. It was cool, but not too chilly for lunch on the brick sidewalk. They looked like excited college students, arguing over a tough assignment.

When I came back after a half hour with Jennifer, Tony was waiting for me. "Sir, I talked to the chief's secretary. She's been working in the chief's office for twenty-five years."

"Good thinking, Winfield. What did she tell you?"

"The picture of the boat has been there since before she started working here. I mean, it was in the chief's office in the old police station, before this one was built."

I said, "That's great. It's been out of circulation. None of these dealers is apt to recognize it. Of course, it's not an original. There are probably more like it. But they wouldn't take one look and say, 'Oh, the city bought that two years ago.' "

"Right," said Tony. "I'm trying to find out how it got to be in the old office."

"Great. Keep at it when you have time."

I went up to see Mike and sound him out about the possibility of borrowing the print from his office.

"You want to borrow it?" His eyebrows almost met in the middle. "What for?"

"To show people and ask where we could sell it."

"I don't want to sell it."

"Of course not," I said. "But we could use it for a decoy, to get the art dealers talking."

He laughed. "Judith said Winfield was up here looking at it."

"Yeah, I've got him trying to find out how the department came by it."

"I like that painting," he said.

"It's a print, not a painting."

"But there *is* a painting somewhere? The original?"

"Of course."

"Where?"

"I don't know."

"I thought you were a good cop."

I sighed. "I'll tell you before five o'clock."

"Bet you don't."

"Guaranteed."

I called him at four-fifteen. "The original Turner painting is hanging in a museum in Boston. It's currently valued at sixty-five thousand dollars."

"No kidding. I told you, anything I need an expert on, give you a week and you're it."

"So, can we use the print as a decoy, Mike?"

"Take good care of it?"

"Of course."

"Terry Lemieux was just in here."

"Back from Fairfield?" I asked.

"Yup. He wants the job."

"Do they want him?"

"Dunno yet," Mike said. "They'll probably call if they do, for a detailed background. I'll have Ron do it."

"We'll miss him."

"Yeah. Harv?"

"What?"

"Thanks for staying. Come get the painting whenever you want."

I let Eddie and Nate work on the kids' chat room after three o'clock. Nate came to me, pleased with his success but troubled by what he'd found.

"There's a girl named Melissa in the chat room," he said.

"Might not be her real name," I reminded him.

"Right. But I talked to her for a while. You know, on the computer."

"Yeah?"

"She plays soccer at school. Her junior high has a girls' team. It's her favorite thing right now."

"Is she in Maine?"

"Yes. When I first went on there, I took your advice and said I wanted a pen pal in Maine."

"So?"

"She didn't tell me where she lives, but her mascot is the Black Raiders. Can we trace that?"

"Sure can." On my computer, I pulled up a file I'd gotten from the state Department of Education, and searched for "Black Raiders."

"Winslow," I told him.

"Wow. I had no idea you could do that so fast."

I grinned. "I've got all kinds of tricks up my sleeve. If the bad guys had what we have, there would be a lot more crime out there. We need more time and manpower to make the most of it, though."

"I've tried not to lie," he said. "I know you don't want me to. But I've let her think I'm a kid."

I said, "I understand, Nate. It's a fine line, and undercover work usually involves deception. The FBI has a whole unit that does this all the time. They pretend to be kids and wait for pedophiles to try to lure them into meeting them. It's about the only way to catch them."

"I don't know if I'd have the stomach for it," he said. "My own kids are in the right age group."

"I know. People who do that kind of work have to have periodic psychological exams. It's a very difficult field."

"So, what do I do? Warn this girl? I can't blow my cover in the chat room."

"No, don't do that. You have several options. You can ask her to e-mail you. That's the way the molesters do it. When she does, e-mail back and tell her you're a cop and you're concerned about her safety. Or you could call her school and have a chat with the principal. Or call Winslow Police and ask them to go to the school and talk to the principal, maybe speak at an assembly and warn the kids how easy it is for a molester to track them down."

"But then we wouldn't have warned her personally, and we wouldn't know for sure she got the message."

"True. Why don't you spend a little more time in the chat room and see if she'll e-mail you?"

Eddie came to the house for Abby at six-thirty, bringing a small bouquet of wildflowers.

"Men don't buy flowers if it's not a real date," Jennifer whispered to me.

Abby had slept most of the day and dressed for the evening in plum-colored pants and a white tailored blouse. She put her hair up on the back of her head.

Jennifer dressed differently and braided her

hair, "So people won't notice we look sort of alike," she told me, which struck me as sweetly naïve. She wore a plaid jumper over a black turtleneck. She looked like a high school girl, and I felt like the B.M.O.C., taking the head cheerleader out for milkshakes.

We left about five minutes after Eddie and Abby, and they were already seated in the meeting when we arrived. A few people introduced themselves to us and asked us if we painted. I said, "No, but we're interested in art and artists."

Mandi Plunkett gave a rather amazing demonstration with acrylics. Jennifer said, "She makes it look so simple. I almost believe I could do that!"

I smiled at her. "Get some paints and try it."

"Oh, no, I'm sure that I'd be very disappointed. Things never turn out the way I think they should."

"Your cross stitching is coming along. I like that moose picture you're making."

"It's supposed to be a horse," she said. "That's a fox hunting scene."

"Oh. Sorry."

The club president gave an assignment to the members. "Using any medium," she said, "paint a view from a porch, including the railing."

The members would bring their efforts the next month and display them and criticize each other's work.

"Sounds like fun," I said.

"Sounds masochistic to me," Jennifer replied. She hated putting herself out there to be criticized, which might be why she chose the computer field. No one ever wonders who designed the program.

I looked around at the assortment of people in the crowd. "It's a funny sort of club, no dues or anything. Just show up and you're in. I guess we're members now."

"Do you think they keep a membership list?" Jennifer asked. "That might be helpful to you."

The crowd broke up into buzzing clusters as members and guests discussed the demonstration and other art-related topics. I managed to catch the president for a moment and ask her if they had a membership list.

"We have a mailing list," she said. "Would you like to be on it? We send a newsletter once a month. Sign up with your e-mail, or if you want it postal, it's five dollars or twelve stamps for a year's worth."

I gave her Jennifer's e-mail.

"Do you ever give out the mailing list?" I asked.

"Occasionally we sell it, to raise money for the club. Only art-related businesses and organizations."

"Like what?"

"Magazines, art supply companies, museums. We sold it about a dozen times last year."

I drew her to one side and said, "Ma'am, I'm a police officer." I opened my jacket and exposed my badge for an instant, and her eyes grew large. "The Portland P.D. would very much like to have a copy of your mailing list. We're investigating a burglary ring, and several collectors have had artworks stolen recently."

"Of course," she said. "You think—oh, dear. I've heard about a couple of thefts. I do hope we haven't been indiscreet."

"Criminals will take advantage of everything," I said. "The club may want to reconsider selling its mailing list." I gave her my business card, and she promised to send me a copy of the list the next day, and the names of the businesses and organizations that had bought the list. I went back to Jennifer, who was listening to a middle-aged man expound on his oil paintings. She looked a little relieved when I reached her side, and he definitely looked disappointed.

Eddie and Abby, across the room, were talking animatedly with four other people, one of them Mandi Plunkett. Abby was really sparkling, and Eddie was watching her, smiling a little, and punctuating the conversation with apparently witty comments, as the others laughed whenever he opened his mouth.

"Quite a pair," I said to Jennifer, and she looked at them.

"Do you think . . . ?"

"I don't know what to think anymore. He was talking about taking Leeanne out."

We mingled during refreshments and struck up a conversation with a sixtyish amateur artist, Lucille Goodale, and a gallery owner, Nicholas Dore. Dore was the owner Joey had researched that day. He talked freely about the art market, and on impulse I said, "Mr. Dore, we've got an old J. M. W. Turner print I'd like to have valued. It's been hanging around for a long time. Could we bring it to you for an appraisal?"

"Certainly."

Jennifer wasn't quite looking at me. I said, "Perhaps my wife and I could bring it to your gallery tomorrow."

"Anytime between 10 a.m. and 5 p.m.," he said.

I nodded, and we moved away.

"Are we lying?" she whispered.

"No. It's hanging in Mike's office. I never said I owned it. The department's had it at least twenty-five years, and Mike said I could use it. Feel like working with me tomorrow?"

She was smiling now. "That's one of my fantasies."

"Really? Maybe I should send you to the Academy."

"That man doesn't know you're a police officer."

"If he asks me what I do for a living, I'll tell him. If he doesn't . . ." I shrugged.

We passed fairly close to Eddie and Abby, and I heard Abby say, "I'm a nurse, actually. I work at Maine Medical."

"And you, sir?" an elderly woman said to Eddie.

"I work for the city, ma'am."

"Ooh, City Hall?"

"No, my office is on Middle Street."

Jennifer darted a glance at me and whispered, "Should we laugh or be upset?"

"I think he's doing okay."

We met several more painting enthusiasts, and one man gushed over the bargain he'd gotten at a Boston auction a few weeks before. I didn't recognize the name of the artist, but he'd paid 'only' eight thousand for his Barrington original.

"Ever see a Redwall at auctions?" I asked, trying to use the innocent look I'd drilled into Eddie.

"Not often. They're climbing in value, though. Are you a Redwall fan?"

"His work is interesting." I tried to recall details from the photos the owner of the recently stolen one had shown me. "A bit stylized, but—"

"Exactly," the man exclaimed. "But very powerful images."

"Yes. I've been watching the prices lately."

"Well, if you're thinking of buying one, the Alexi gallery will have several of his paintings on display soon. You probably know about it."

"No, I hadn't heard."

He gave me the details of the exhibit, and I jotted it down in my pocket notebook.

"Is anyone here from the Alexi tonight?" I thought that was Nate's assigned gallery.

"No, I don't think so. Sometimes Roger Blaisdell is here, but not tonight."

Eddie and Abby were making their way toward the door. Abby needed to get home in time to change into her uniform and get over to the hospital. We chatted a few minutes longer, and we found a woman who gave instruction in oils and watercolors.

"Take a class," I told Jennifer. "You'd enjoy it."

"No, I don't think so. Not now."

When we got home, Eddie was gone and Abby was in the kitchen fixing herself a snack before going to work. The flowers from Eddie were in a crystal vase on the table.

"Did you have a good time?" Jennifer asked her.

Abby's blue eyes widened. "It was really exciting, wasn't it, being sort of undercover?"

Jennifer laughed. "Yes, but it was strange. I love mysteries, but I never realized how close open inquiry can be to deceit, when you're trying to get information."

Abby said, "Eddie was very good at it. He said he got several good tips for the case. I didn't realize how smart he is."

"Eddie's very quick," I said.

She nodded. "He picked right up on things people said, and he knew what to ask. And he's so funny!"

I looked at Jennifer. She had the what-can-I-tell-you look.

"I don't know, Abby," she said. "I kept worrying that I'd say the wrong thing and blow Harvey's cover."

Abby was about to leave for the hospital when the phone rang. Jennifer answered it and handed it to her sister.

"Oh, Charlie! Hi! I'm sorry; we went to an art club meeting tonight. No, I'm just about to leave for work."

Jennifer drew me into the study and around to the living room, where we couldn't hear. "Don't you want to know if Charlie's suit has any hope?" I asked.

"She'll tell us." Jennifer reached to turn on a lamp, but I pulled her against me and kissed her in the near darkness.

"I enjoyed working with you tonight. Sorry if your scruples were uneasy."

She laughed. "Silly. It was fun. Really. But I wouldn't make a good cop. Or a gambler, or anything else where you have to keep a straight face."

"Go to the art show with me."

"What, the Redwall exhibit?"

"Yes. It will be more formal. I need a gorgeous woman to take with me."

"You wearing a tux?"

"No, but my suit from London."

"How about taking one of the female officers?"

I frowned at her. "I hope you're joking."

"I am. I wouldn't let you go out with another woman, even in the line of duty."

"Couldn't trust me?"

"Of course I could trust you. It's them I'm worried about. If some of them saw you dressed up like that, they'd throw themselves at you."

It wasn't true, but I didn't argue. "Wear your green dress," I said, preparing to kiss her again.

"Jennifer, where are you?" Abby called. "I'm leaving now."

Jennifer pulled away and went out to say goodbye to Abby. When we went into the bedroom a couple of minutes later, she switched the light on. "Poor Charlie," she said.

"She turned him down?"

"Afraid so."

"Because of Eddie? Or Greg?"

"Who knows?" She pulled her jumper off over her head and hung it in the closet.

"I think Eddie scored some points tonight," I said.

"But did he want to? Eddie's charming all the time. Do you think he was really coming on to Abby?"

"Those flowers." I lined up the creases on my pants and snapped the wooden hanger over the cuffs.

"That's right. Flowers are semi-serious, aren't they?"

"I never saw him give a girl flowers before. Doesn't mean he never did."

She said, "The first time you sent me flowers . . ."

I'd only met her twice, but I knew, even then. I reached over and pulled the covered elastic from the bottom of her braid. "I remember."

Chapter 13

Tuesday, October 12

Four of my six students had definitely made contact with a youngster in Maine through chat rooms designated for young people.

"These chat rooms are supposed to be safe for kids," Cheryl said in an injured tone. She had contacted a girl who had revealed her school, street, nickname, and classes.

"Thinking it's safe makes them less wary," I said. I gave Cheryl some pointers, and within twenty minutes she knew exactly where the girl lived.

"A man could hang out on the corner after school and watch for her," she said woefully.

"My kid is in South Portland," said Joey. "I'm sure of it. It's a boy, unless it's a girl masquerading as a boy. He described the place he and his friends go for snacks after school. It's within two blocks of his elementary school. I could find it."

"You want to go out there this afternoon?" I asked. "Call South Portland P.D. first if you do, just a courtesy."

"What do I do when I find him?" Joey asked.

"Don't approach him. Go for the parents, if

they're around. Tell them how easy it was for you. Let them take it from there."

He nodded. "I'll ask Ron if I can do that today. These kids are starting to worry me. They're so vulnerable."

Nate said, "I called the principal in Winslow this morning. He said there are two Melissas on the soccer team, but when I told him she hates her red hair, he immediately knew who it was. He's got a female guidance counselor. He thought she might be the appropriate person to talk to Melissa, and he'll call her parents. He'll also talk to the students as a group, without mentioning her, and tell them how dangerous it is to give out personal information over the computer or the phone or anything like that."

"Good job, Nate," I said. "I have another assignment for you."

"More homework? My wife will love this."

"It's something I think you'll find worthwhile. I want you to write an essay about this assignment. I talked to the commissioner of education this morning. The department of ed will print it and send it to every school principal in the state. If they want, they can copy it and send it home to the parents. You can reach thousands of families with it, and alert school administrators and faculty all over Maine."

Nate looked pleased, and I felt good about it. His reports were always lucid and direct. He might soon be in demand to speak at schools and parent groups. I knew the managing editor at the *Portland Press Herald*, and I thought he would publish the essay as well, but I didn't tell Nate that yet.

"How do we reel in the pedophiles?" asked Emily.

"You tell me," I said.

"Pose as a kid?"

"That's what you'd have to do. Go into the chat room with a new screen name and see who contacts you. They'll ask questions, and eventually ask you to e-mail them. Then they can send you private messages, which, believe me, can get pretty disgusting. They count on kids being curious. After a while, they'll want to set up a meeting, and you can sting them. I'll warn you, though, the process can be sickening."

We moved on to the art case. Eddie and I briefed the others on the tips we'd gleaned at the club meeting. I told them Jennifer and I would take the Turner print to Dore's gallery right after lunch and would attend the Redwall exhibit the next week. Eddie would follow up on some contacts he had made.

We had discovered that if you could talk even a little knowledgeably about art, enthusiasts would generally rhapsodize about their work, their favorite artists, and their collections. Most of those we'd met were not collectors in a big way. Some were poverty stricken, a few were wealthy, but most were middle class hobbyists who enjoyed painting and talking to other artists.

Eddie said, "If they don't own good art, they'll tell you who does. I mentioned a couple of these Maine artists, and people would say, 'Oh, so-and-so has one of his watercolors.' Even if they didn't talk about what was in their own houses, they told me about everyone else."

"That's important," I said. "The thieves, or the person who hires them, might be locating artworks in that very way. Hang around these art people long at all, and you start learning where the art is."

I gave them new assignments for checking the location of the works of certain artists, and I had the names of a couple more dealers for them to check out. I also requested background checks on the officers of the art club.

By noon we'd accomplished a lot, and our art files were growing thick. Jennifer came up the stairs looking absolutely stunning. Her hair was in a French twist, and she wore a cranberry tailored jacket and gray pants. Joey and Tony had seen Jennifer before, but not in the power woman mode, and I caught their glances of admiration. Jennifer greeted Cheryl warmly.

I dismissed the class and sent Eddie to the drugstore for some brown wrapping paper. Jennifer and I went up the elevator to the fourth floor. I keyed in the code for Mike's office suite.

Judith, the secretary, was out to lunch, and I feared I'd missed Mike, too, but he was sitting with his feet up on his desk, talking to Sharon on the phone.

"I've gotta run, sweetheart. Mr. and Mrs. Larson just walked in here looking like a million bucks. Well, Jennifer does. Harvey looks like half a grand."

I was wearing a blazer and the tie that Eddie said gave me panache.

"So, you came to borrow my painting." Mike swung his feet to the floor.

"Print," I corrected. I knew he knew and was saying it to annoy me.

"Going undercover, Mrs. Larson?"

"I'm not very good at it, I'm afraid."

"You're hiding that baby pretty well."

Jennifer blushed scarlet. I scowled at Mike.

"How you feeling, poppa?" he asked.

"Good, thank you."

He nodded and lifted the frame from the wall. "I want this back up here today."

"Understood," I said.

He kissed the edge of the frame and handed it to me. I shook my head, knowing he was more attached to the fishing rod and creel painting than he was to the Turner.

"How's Sharon?" I asked.

"Not bad. We're staying home tonight. She's cooking lasagna."

"Sounds good."

"I've got another case for your unit, if you can handle it. Or are you too busy on this art thing?"

"What is it?"

"Rich guy thinks someone's trying to kill him. I was going to have Ron send a detective to talk some sense into him."

"And?"

"While we were on the phone, someone shot the guy's living room windows out. A marked unit's there now, but they need a detective or two. Your guys or Ron's?"

"Why don't you take Arnie and go yourself?" I asked. "My men are all deep in the art thing, but I can spare Arnie for a few of hours."

Mike jumped at it, and came downstairs with us to look for Arnie, his old partner from his detective days. Eddie was back with the wrapping paper, and he said Arnie was eating at the diner with Clyde. Mike went down the stairs two at a time.

"This is a fine print," Nicholas Dore said, examining the Turner carefully. "It's been in this frame for some time?"

"At least twenty-five years," I said.

"It's been kept in a good environment," he said.

"No water stains. We often see them on prints of this age."

"Is it worth anything?" Jennifer asked timidly.

"Not a lot, but a modest amount. If you'd like to look around for a few minutes, I'll check my sources." He disappeared into another room.

We looked at the dozen paintings mounted in the showroom.

"I like that," said Jennifer, pointing to an oil of autumn foliage.

"You ought to," I said, after checking the price tag.

"Do I want to know?" she asked.

"You could buy it with the money in your software account." She had about fifteen thousand dollars now.

She walked on to the next exhibit, a watercolor portrait of a baby in a yellow hat, laughing and reaching for the sky.

"It's not that good, but it's a happy picture," she said.

"Only twelve hundred bucks."

"No thanks. I'll wait for a picture of our baby."

Next was an oil of a little girl in pigtails, standing on the bottom rail of a weathered fence, looking off over a field of grass and milkweed. Her face was sweet and hopeful.

"It's you," I said.

"No."

"Yes. It could be. It's really well done!" I

checked the price. "Only two grand. It's a bargain."

"Don't be silly."

"I love it."

"Harvey, it's worth more than the Turner."

"Who's the artist?" I checked the tag and wrote it in my notebook. "Cecile Caron."

"Cecile Caron? She lives in Skowhegan," Jennifer said. "There's an art school there. She might be one of the instructors."

I looked at her, and my jaw must have dropped. "Jenny, it *is* you."

"Oh, come off it. It's not me." She looked at the painting again. "Although, that does resemble the fence in my dad's lower pasture."

Dore came back smiling. "Well, your print is valued at about eight hundred dollars," he said. "It might bring slightly more in some markets. If you're interested in selling it, I have a client who would probably pay that amount."

"Right now?" I looked at Jennifer, startled.

"Oh, let's think about it," she said. "I know you're partial to it."

Dore pressed me just a little, then gave me his card and said, "If you decide to sell it . . ."

"What's the commission?" I asked.

"Fifteen percent."

He wrapped the framed print and handed it to me.

"Thanks. That Caron painting over there . . ." I nodded toward the girl on the fence.

"A delightful piece," he said.

"Do you have any information about it?"

"We occasionally have works of Mrs. Caron's to sell. That is one of the best I've seen yet. It will no doubt increase in value."

"What about the subject? Was it painted from a model?"

"I have no idea."

In the Explorer, I kissed Jennifer and said, "You get bonus points for undercover work, gorgeous. You're right—I am partial to this print. So's Mike. Of course, I could be more partial to that painting of you."

"It's not me."

"I don't care. I still love it."

"Harvey, Cecile Caron is a living artist, and she's not that well known."

"I'm not talking about buying it as an investment. As something to enjoy."

She shook her head. "If you want to drop two thousand dollars, let's buy a piece of equipment for Jeff's ambulance or something."

I sighed. She had a point. But I was always good at logic, and I cast about for a new argument. "You've got your Van Gogh print."

"It cost me five dollars, and twenty more for the frame."

"I don't suppose the poster of me is comparable?"

"That was only eight bucks, and it's really

you, wearing the vest that saved your life. It's priceless."

"Okay, okay. But you're much better at this game than you think you are. You might want to consider doing some investigative work."

We took Mike's print back, and he was sober.

"Terry's going to Fairfield," he said.

"Wow." I shot Jennifer a look. "That was fast."

"They want someone quick. I told them he'll be excellent."

"How did your field work go?" I asked.

Mike smiled. "Clyde and Arnie are setting up protection for the gentleman and looking into it. It was good to get out of here for a while."

"Your print is now worth eight hundred bucks." I hung it carefully on the nail in the wall.

"The price is rising."

"Yes, and the dealer didn't ask for proof of ownership or question the print's past."

"Winfield's not in your unit. How does he figure into it again?"

"The computer class. I assigned him to try to find out how the department got it."

"Oh, right. Look at this." He picked up a framed, black-and-white, eight-by-ten photograph from the top of a file cabinet. I took it and held it so Jennifer could see. In it were two men in suits at the old police station. At the bottom was handwritten, 'Mayor John Carleton and

Police Chief Edward Brewer, 1954.' Behind them on the wall was the Turner print.

I gaped at Mike. "It sure has been around for a while. Where did you get this?"

"Spotted it in Mayor Weymouth's office. There are lots of old pictures along the hallway there, mostly former mayors. She let me borrow this one, but we have to take it back."

"I guess you checked to see if the Turner was in any of the other pictures."

"It wasn't."

"This is a great find, Mike."

I took Jennifer down to the parking garage and sent her home in her car, then went up to Priority. I told Tony about the photo Mike had discovered and sent him to the *Press Herald* with a handwritten note for John Russell, the managing editor, authorizing Tony to spend the afternoon in their morgue, searching for a news item about the redecoration of the chief's office in or before 1954.

I looked for Cecile Caron in the Waterville-Skowhegan telephone directory and got the number, but no response. Next, I dug around for the name of the art school Jennifer had mentioned and located her there.

"Mrs. Caron, I've been looking at a painting of yours. '*View from the Fence.*' Can you tell me about it?"

"Oh, that's at the Dore gallery," she said.

"Yes. I live here in Portland, and I saw it today. I'm interested in it. When was it painted?"

"I did it earlier this year."

"Oh, so it's not old?"

"Oh, no. It's one of my latest works."

"I liked it very much."

"Thank you."

"It reminded me of my wife. She lived in your area, and I had this crazy idea it might have been her."

"Your wife? What's her name?"

"Her maiden name was Jennifer Wainthrop."

"How old is she?"

"Twenty-five."

"Well, Mr. Larson, anything is possible. I did that painting from an old photograph. I was painting a barn years ago, and a little girl came and climbed on the fence near me. I thought I'd like to paint her, but I was in the middle of this other project, so I snapped her picture. It sat in a box for years. Then last winter I was cleaning house, and I came across it again. I sat down and started to paint."

My pulse was pretty rapid by then. "Do you still have the photograph?"

"Yes."

"My wife and I are coming to Skowhegan in a couple of weeks. We'd love to meet you. And could I see the photograph when we come?"

"Why, I guess you can."

Progress on all fronts. I was feeling pretty good.

Tony came back at five minutes to five with a poor copy of a document made from old microfilm.

"The city bought the Turner from a local dealer in '51," he said. "Paid twenty-five bucks. The dealer's long gone."

"Fantastic. You get an A on provenance, Tony."

I called Mike and told him, and he laughed. "Give that boy a gold star, Harvey. And make sure I get a copy of his report. I knew this class was a good idea."

Chapter 14

Wednesday, October 13

Nate, Eddie, and I kept at the art case all week. Arnie and Clyde split their shifts to work on the attempted murder, with Mike consulting. Patrolmen stayed at the man's house at night. They had a short list of suspects, and were eliminating them one by one.

The computer class worked the cyber fraud reports and the child molesting case. I let the students help each other on the last one. Emily, posing as an eleven-year-old girl, had been contacted by a man. At first she thought it was another youngster, but when he started e-mailing her, she knew it was an adult. The other officers helped her word her responses to keep him interested without tipping him off.

"He's asking really offensive questions," she told me, horror darkening her eyes.

I looked at the latest e-mail on her screen. She was right. No child should get messages like that.

"Okay," I said. "You want to go through with this?"

"Well, I sure don't want him out there preying on other little girls. I mean real little girls. You know what I mean."

"So when he asks you to see him, set up a meeting in a neutral place."

"A park?"

"No, an enclosed space. How about the public library? Or even someone's house. We can have several officers on hand."

Emily went back to work and set it up for Saturday.

"You were right," she told me, aghast. "He told me he'll bring me a present. He even told me what to wear."

I talked to Ron Legere, and he said he would handle it with Emily and two of his other detectives.

On Thursday, night Beth and Jeff came over, and we invited Bud and Janice Parker over for coffee. I had told Bud earlier to be mindful of his Nutting prints, and he asked me if we'd caught the art thieves yet.

"Not yet. Don't go broadcasting to anyone what you've got there." Bud loved woodworking, and I showed him my meager assortment of tools.

"I could help you with a project," he said eagerly.

"Yeah? Like what?"

"Maybe an end table, or a bookcase?"

"That sounds interesting. I think Abby could use a bookcase in her room."

"I'd love one," Abby said.

Eddie had become almost a permanent fixture at our house, and he sat next to Abby that night when we all settled in the living room to chat. While he was attentive to her, I didn't think he had the same look Jeff had when he looked at Beth.

"Jenny and I are going to Skowhegan the twenty-seventh and twenty-eighth," I told Jeff. "I've got two days of training at the Academy, and we're staying at your folks'."

"Bring the boys back," he said. "I'll be off that weekend." His younger brothers, Travis and Randy, had begged for weeks to come and visit in Portland.

"Eddie, you're staying *chez* Wainthrop, too," said Jennifer.

Eddie grinned. "Oh, boy. Apple pie."

"And I get to stay here alone and work," Abby pouted.

"Sorry," said Jennifer. "Maybe Leeanne can come back with us, too, for a consolation prize."

Nate turned in his essay on Friday, and I couldn't think of anything I'd want done differently. I faxed it to the commissioner of education in Augusta. The computer training wrapped up that day. I showed my class how to set up accounts and communicate electronically with state law enforcement agencies they might not have used before. The last thing I did was to demonstrate some sophisticated programs that allowed me to network with the FBI, Interpol, and other agencies. They wouldn't have access to it all without special training and authorization, but it whetted their appetites and showed them the capabilities we had.

"Good job, everyone," I said. "You don't get a diploma, but I'll send a commendation to each of your supervisors and ask them to bring you in on any cyber cases that come their way. You can always come to me for pointers."

"I'll miss the class," Cheryl said.

Emily nodded. "Me, too. Thanks so much for doing it, Captain Larson."

"One more thing." I opened a box on my desk. Jennifer had managed a rush order for six mugs that read "Certified Techie" on the side. I handed them out, and everyone seemed to like them.

Overall, I felt positive about a venture I'd thought began as punishment.

I took my lunch hour late and met Jennifer at Margaret's office. Everything looked great. Jennifer still hadn't gained any weight, but she was holding steady. The morning sickness seemed to be gone. Margaret measured Jenny's stomach and seemed happy with her progress, so I was happy, too.

Saturday dawned raw and rainy, and we stayed home. Eddie had vacillated so long he hadn't lined up a date anyway.

I sat in front of the fireplace that afternoon, reading and feeling lazy. Jennifer worked at her cross stitching, and Abby wrote letters. After a while, Jennifer put her stitching aside with a sigh and picked up the *Baby Names* book.

"What's the matter, gorgeous?" I asked.

"You were right. My cross-stitch horse looks like a moose with a saddle."

"So tell people it's supposed to look that way."

"I'll know it's not." She leafed through the book. "What do you think of Christopher?" Of course that made me think of Chris Towne, my old partner. I wasn't sure how I felt about naming a child after him.

The doorbell rang, and I went to the entry. Peter Hobart, from our church, stood on the doorstep in the breezeway. He owned a car dealership on the edge of town.

"Peter, what brings you out in this weather?" The rain was pounding down, and the wind had risen.

"I was wondering if I could ask you a legal question."

"I'm a cop, not a lawyer, but come on in."

We had a pot of coffee staying warm, and I offered him a cup. Sitting at the kitchen table, he said, "Um, this bike helmet law. Do both my boys need those all the time?"

"Yup. Any time they go out of the yard, anyway."

"Oh. Well, thanks." He poured milk into his coffee and sipped it.

"That's it?" I asked.

He looked as if he'd say something else, then nodded. "That's it."

"Well, have a cookie at least." I got them off the top of the refrigerator. I hadn't had a chance to get to know Peter, but he was in Jennifer's and my Sunday school class, and I had a feeling he wasn't really at my house to ask about bike helmets.

"Homemade cookies." He sounded like me when I was single, and it suddenly hit me that Peter was a widower. His boys were six and nine. Not many homemade cookies around his house.

"Hello, Mr. Hobart," Jennifer said, from the sunroom doorway.

He started to rise.

"Don't get up." She sat down, too.

"How are you feeling, Mrs. Larson?"

"It's Jennifer. I'm much better, thank you."

"Glad to hear it. You've had someone helping you while you were ill?"

"Yes, my sister came to stay with us."

"Oh," said Peter. "Has she gone back now?"

"No, she's still with us. She's got a job at the hospital."

"Ah."

The light was breaking. The helmets were an excuse. It was Abby he was there for. I got up and walked through the sunroom to the living room door.

"Abby, you want some coffee?"

She laid aside her stationery box and followed me to the kitchen. This time, Peter did stand up.

"Hello, Miss Wainthrop."

So, he knew her name and pronounced it correctly.

"Well, hello, Mr. Hobart. Nice weather we're having," Abby said.

He chuckled. "Nice for ducks." I'm not sure what it was exactly, but his whole face looked more animated when she entered the room, less uncertain, and more hopeful.

Abby got a coffee mug and fixed herself a cup. "What brings you out today?"

I said, "Peter was asking me about the bike helmet law. For his boys." I wondered if she knew Mrs. Hobart was dead. "How's business?" I asked him.

"Fair to middling. I sold a couple of cars this week."

"Good. Do you have any of those ones with the built-in car seats?"

"Yes, they're very convenient for parents. When will you need the car seat?"

"In April," I said. Jennifer was looking into her coffee cup. She was still self-conscious sometimes when people talked about the baby. She'd told me she felt like everyone at church was looking at her stomach to see if the baby showed yet.

"Are you thinking of buying a new car?" Peter asked.

"Well, Jennifer's Escort is pretty old. I was thinking I might get her something newer."

She looked at me in surprise.

"Well, come around when you're ready to look," he said.

"We'll do that. So how are the boys doing?"

"Good. Good. They're at their grandmother's today." He shot a glance at Abby. "I'll go get them tomorrow afternoon."

"I'll bet they miss their mother," I said.

"Well, yes, we all do."

"Let me give you some cookies to take home," said Abby. I wondered if she was trying to get rid of him, or if he thought she was. Maybe she pitied the cookieless boys. Every kid should get fresh, homemade cookies once in a while.

Jennifer said, "Harvey, is the patio door shut tight? I don't want the rain leaking in."

I went to look at it, and she followed me.

"What is going on?" she hissed.

"I think he's wife hunting."

"How long has he been widowed?"

"Three or four years, I guess. She had cancer."

"I know. I just feel like we're being overrun by suitors here."

"It's weird, isn't it?" I checked the patio door, and it was fine. "Should we invite Peter and the boys over sometime?"

"I don't know. I don't want to embarrass Abby."

We went back to the kitchen. Abby was bagging oatmeal cookies, and Peter was leaning on the counter, watching.

"We're going with the Nelsons," Peter was saying. "Do you know them?"

"I've met them," said Abby. "Didn't Mr. Nelson sing at Jennifer and Harvey's wedding?"

"Yeah, that's right." Peter's smile wasn't half bad, I supposed. Abby seemed to like it. "They home school. They've got kids about the ages of my boys. Rob asked me if we wanted to go with them, and I thought it would be good. If you're interested . . ."

I pulled Jennifer back into the sunroom. "Let her sort it out. She said no to Charlie. She can say no to Peter if she doesn't want to do whatever it is they're doing."

"Poor Peter." She put her arms around my waist, and I hugged her.

A minute later, Peter appeared in the doorway.

"There you are. I'm heading out. Thanks, Harvey."

I stepped forward and walked with him to the entry. He was carrying the bag of cookies. He wasn't bad looking, thirtyish and tall. He had a careworn air around the eyes, I thought, and he seemed a little tired now that he was out of Abby's sight.

"We're going to the circus at the Civic Center next week," he said. "Abigail and me and the boys. With the Nelsons."

"Terrific," I said. "On Saturday?"

"Yes. The six o'clock show. She has to work that night, I guess."

"Yeah, she's trying to get a different shift."

His brown eyes flickered with a little anxiety. "I didn't think she'd go."

I smiled. "You never know with Abby."

"Does she—have a lot of fellows hanging around?"

"Some."

"Your partner, Eddie—"

"He's one."

Peter nodded.

"Nerve-racking, isn't it?" I asked with a smile. "When I met Jennifer, I was a nervous wreck every time I asked her out. First you have to get up the courage to ask, then you have to sweat it out until she answers."

"Seemed like a million years," he agreed.

"Why don't you and the boys eat supper here that night, before you go?"

"Oh, we shouldn't. Your wife has been sick." Everyone at church knew, because Jennifer's name had been on the prayer list for a couple of weeks. I made a mental note to ask the pastor to take it off.

"She's fine now," I said.

"I haven't gone out much since . . ."

"You should. It will be fine."

Peter nodded. "Thanks." He went out into the drizzle.

I went back in, and Jennifer handed me the telephone receiver in the kitchen. It was Emily Rood.

"We caught him, Captain! You know, the computer guy." Her voice was charged with elation.

"Fantastic. Is he in the system?" I asked.

"Yes, he's been arrested before."

"What charge?"

"Molesting his girlfriend's daughter."

"You just did a really good thing, Emily."

"Thanks, Captain. I asked Sergeant Legere if I can spend some time at this detail, and he thinks it's a worthy project."

"That's great. I'm proud of you for making the collar."

"Thank you," she said. "It feels good."

"I'll bet it does. I wish we had a dozen people going after these guys, because there are a lot of them out there."

When I hung up, Jennifer was standing by the sink watching Abby peel potatoes. She asked Abby, "What made you say yes to Peter?"

244

"Oh, I don't know. The circus, Jennifer. Don't you love to go to the circus?"

"We never had many chances," she said.

"You want to go to the circus?" I asked. "I'll take you." I might never get another chance. Circuses had been hit hard by animal rights protests, and the one coming to the city was smaller than the old Ringling Brothers, but it should still be exciting.

"Super." Jenny gave me a distracted smile. "But why Peter and not Charlie? I'm just curious."

Abby sighed and put the vegetable peeler down. "Maybe it was the droopy eyes, or the motherless boys, I don't know."

There it was, the Wendy Darling Syndrome. I said, "Maybe it was just the tigers."

Abby smiled and looked at Jennifer. "Why did you say yes to Harvey the first time?"

This I wanted to hear.

Jennifer looked out the window at the back yard, where the rain was soaking the rose bushes. "I think it was his eyes," she said soberly. "That, and he seemed sort of nervous, as though he thought I was really something and he was holding his breath."

I put my arms around her from behind, and she put her hands over mine at her waist and leaned back against my chest.

I said, "I was scared you'd say no every time I asked you, right up until you said you'd marry me."

"The super hero with a tender heart," Abby said dispassionately. She took a saucepan to the sink and filled it with water.

"That's my guy," said Jenny, and her right hand came up to my cheek.

Greg walked into the church and headed our way as Sunday school ended. When Eddie and Abby came from their class, Eddie shook hands with him, and Abby sat down between them. Peter, pulling his boys into his pew across the aisle, looked fretfully toward Abby.

"Is this a comedy or a tragedy?" Jennifer whispered.

I shrugged. "As far as I know, Peter's the only one with a date confirmed for next weekend."

"So far."

Jeff was on duty, and Beth came to sit with Jennifer. She seemed very happy, and I wondered how many times she'd seen Jeff that week.

Lunch at our house was interesting. Jennifer had invited all the Bradleys, which included Beth, Rick and Ruthann, and their two kids. Eddie came along on principle. Jennifer had told him that he had a standing invitation at our house, and it seemed no church families with single daughters had invited him that day.

We also invited Greg, plus Pastor and Mary Rowland. The rain had abated overnight, and I cooked hamburgers on the back patio. Jennifer was a great, if casual, hostess. Lots of food, lots of laughter, lots of friends. It was too damp and chilly outside to use the picnic table, so I sat in the sunroom with the Rowlands, Rick, Ruthann and their kids. Jennifer stayed in the kitchen with Beth, Eddie, Abby, and Greg.

"How's Abby doing?" I asked when Jennifer brought in a pitcher of iced tea.

"It's a juggling act."

At dessert time, everybody came in the sunroom and ate cheesecake together.

"Jennifer, I can't believe you're eating so well now," said Ruthann.

"She's just a little pig," Abby said. "Has to make up for everything she didn't eat before." Abby looked tired, and I wondered if she was going to go to work that night without any sleep.

I caught her gaze. "I think both the Wainthrop sisters need naps."

"I know the Bradley children do," said Ruthann. She and Rick started looking for two-year-old Clarissa's shoes.

By two o'clock, everyone had cleared out except Eddie and Greg. Abby was yawning. I sent Jennifer off to bed.

"I guess I should go," Greg said regretfully, looking at Abby. I didn't think he'd managed a second alone with her.

"You don't have to," I said.

"I really should sleep, or I'll never make it

through work tonight," Abby said apologetically.

"Come back tonight," I told Greg.

"Sure," said Abby. "Come back after church. I'll have a couple of hours then when we can visit." She finally drifted off upstairs.

"Coffee?" I asked the men.

Greg said, "Am I outstaying my welcome?"

"Not at all, we just have certain sleep-deprived people here."

Eddie stayed, too. I wasn't quite sure why. He didn't seem to resent Greg. The two of them talked cheerfully about the airline and our computer work.

Greg pulled out around four. He said he wanted to see the waterfront and would eat out somewhere.

"I like him," Eddie said.

"That's good." I nodded slowly. "I do, too. We might see a lot more of Greg."

"I figured. Guess I don't need to come back after church tonight."

"Eddie, Abby hasn't made up her mind. She's going out with Peter Hobart Saturday."

Eddie's dark eyes widened. "He's married."

"Widowed. His wife had cancer."

"I didn't know that." He pulled out his truck keys. "Well, I guess Abby will always have all the dates she wants. She's just that kind of woman."

"What kind of woman?"

"You know, pretty, nice, smart. Like Jennifer."

I laughed. "She's nothing like Jennifer. Well, I shouldn't say *nothing* like her. But Jennifer never had many dates."

"Why not?"

"Well, for one thing, I think she was too reserved." We walked out to the driveway.

"Abby's not reserved," Eddie said.

"Nope. She's not overbearing, either, but she's certainly not reserved. In some ways, she's like you—mostly good ways."

He smiled wryly. "I'm glad you got Jennifer, Harv. She was what you needed."

He climbed into his truck, and I wondered what Eddie needed.

Chapter 15

Monday, October 18

Mike advertised the deputy chief's position again and had candidates coming in from as far away as Connecticut. He decided that when Terry left in two weeks, he would put Brad Lyons, the night patrol sergeant, on the front desk during the day, and he was training Cheryl Yeaton to take over as night sergeant.

"I thought she was hoping to make detective," I said.

"Not many detective spots opening up," Mike told me. "Just Arnie's and I figured you've picked somebody else."

"Not yet."

"You want Cheryl? Because we can sit down with her and thrash it out if you do. I talked to her about this sergeant thing, and she's willing, but she might change her mind if she's got a chance to join your unit. The thing is, I don't want to pass over her for sergeant and then have you decide you want someone else."

"Okay." My mind was racing. I didn't want to be unfair to Cheryl or anyone else. "I'm really not sure. Better put her in Brad's position."

"All right. We'll be getting a new batch of

recruits in January. I want her to be confident at what she's doing by then."

I needed to think harder about the vacancy. I had only about six weeks left with Arnie on board. As usual when faced with a major change, my stomach acted up and I found myself skipping meals when Jennifer wasn't looking. Why couldn't things ever stay the same for more than five minutes?

At nine o'clock Thursday evening, Jennifer and I were preparing to go to the art exhibit.

"Pretty late, isn't it?" asked Abby.

"No, it goes until midnight," I said. "That's the way people who don't have to work live, I guess."

I put on my good suit. It was Abby's night off, and she was looking forward to sleeping when it was dark. Jennifer called to her, and she came to the bedroom to arrange Jenny's hair for her.

"I don't know if we're any closer to cracking this art case," I said, working on the cufflinks I rarely wore—silver ones my sister Gina gave me when I graduated from Harvard. That was a million years ago.

"I hate to say it, but you may need another crime to give you some more evidence," Abby said.

Jennifer turned around on the dressing table

stool and looked at me. "Are you any closer to finding a deputy chief?"

"They interviewed a guy from Rhode Island today. I liked him, but the city council didn't. Too much of a maverick, I guess."

"Style similar to yours?" Abby asked with a teasing smile.

"Maybe. But Mike needs someone steady who can be chief in a couple of years."

"Mike's still planning to retire?" Jennifer shook her head.

"He and Sharon both say yes. It will be an official day of mourning at the PD."

Abby put Jennifer's luxuriant hair in little braids, up on her head, the way she'd had it for the formal wedding pictures. She wore the green silk dress I loved. It took me back to our courtship days, when she'd bought it for a big night out with me. Me! It had a little mandarin collar, and the buttons were strips of the silk twisted into fancy knots.

I smiled at her. "Everyone will stare at you at the gallery."

"You ought to wear more makeup," Abby said fretfully. "It would make you look more glamorous."

"She doesn't need it," I said. Jennifer wore a little lip gloss, but her lashes were a mile long without mascara, and her complexion never needed help. Her cheekbones were pronounced, and excitement over the task ahead had brought color to her cheeks.

I glanced at the clock. "We'd better get going. It's nine-forty-five, and we don't want to walk into the gallery at the last minute." We'd both boned up on Redwall's style and were primed to talk to art lovers. Jennifer picked up a white sweater, and we excused ourselves and went out to her car in the garage.

As I opened her door for her, I said, "You look so incredible in that dress."

"Well, take a good look, because I probably won't be able to wear it again for a while."

So I took a good look. Her tummy was still flat, but I could see that when the baby started getting bigger, that fitted dress wouldn't do at all. I kissed her, letting my hands glide over the green silk.

"I should take you to fancy parties more often," I whispered in her ear.

"No, it's fun once in a while, but being at home with you is better."

She always said the right thing.

At the door to the Alexi Gallery, I extended the invitation I'd managed to get from the gallery owner. When he'd gathered I had money, he took me for a potential patron and hadn't bothered to ask how I made my living.

The gallery was full of people. Most of the men wore suits or sport jackets. The women displayed a wide range of fashions, from flowing pants to provocative evening gowns. Most of their faces dripped eye shadow and lipstick. I wished I had stock in Maybelline. The hairstyles were even worse, from a near crewcut on one woman to myriad cornrows on another. Jennifer stood out as naturally beautiful, and several heads turned as we walked past.

Everyone held a wine glass.

"I wonder if they have anything else to drink," Jenny whispered.

A waiter stopped in front of us with a tray of filled glasses.

"Do you have anything nonalcoholic?" I asked. "My wife's expecting."

Sure enough, his eyes dropped to Jennifer's stomach, and she blushed.

"How about club soda?"

"Make it two," I said. He scurried away, and I smiled at Jennifer. "That wasn't so hard, was it?"

We looked at the Redwalls. "We saw a picture of that one." Jennifer gazed at a large canvas portraying a beach with lifelike sea grass in the foreground and sand awash with purple water beyond it. The waiter brought us two wine glasses full of club soda.

"Didn't I see you at the Visual Arts Society?" We turned to meet a middle-aged woman, escorted by a younger man. At the art club, she'd worn pants and a nondescript blouse. Tonight she had on a flame-red dress with a plunging neckline, definitely designed for a younger figure.

"Yes," Jennifer said brightly. "You paint water-colors."

"How flattering that you remember! I'm Lucille, and this is my friend, Eric."

Eric nodded, and looked Jennifer up and down.

I extended my hand to him. "I'm Harvey. This is my *wife,* Jennifer."

He didn't take the hint and kept staring.

"Where did you get the white wine?" Lucille asked.

Jennifer smiled a little and said apologetically, "It's club soda."

"Oh, on the wagon?"

"Uh, yes."

Lucille said, "I probably drink too much. But it seems to help my painting."

"Do you think these paintings are a good investment?" I asked.

"Oh, my, yes. Redwall is very much in demand now. Prices are going up as we speak."

Eric nodded. "He's a good investment. He's prolific, and affordable now, but definitely on the way up."

"I've been looking at a painting by Cecile Caron," I said tentatively.

"Oh, I know Cecile." Lucille drained her wine glass and looked around for the waiter.

"I like her style," I said.

"Traditional," Lucille shrugged. "Redwall's more exciting."

"Do you have any original Carons?" asked Eric.

Jennifer's hand snatched at mine.

"No, not yet. I've sort of got my eye on one. We're thinking about some art for our new home."

"Where do you folks live?"

Jennifer's fingernails dug into my palm.

"Here in Portland," I said.

Lucille spotted the waiter and went after another glass of wine.

"Do you paint?" Jennifer said to Eric.

"No, I work for a gallery in Manchester, New Hampshire. I just came up for the showing. Lucille invited me. We're old friends."

I judged him to be about Jennifer's age, and so I thought their friendship couldn't be too old. A waiter came around with crackers and cheese, and we took some. Jennifer moved me toward another painting.

"That guy gives me the creeps," she whispered.

"I wasn't especially taken by him," I agreed.

"He's nosy. It was like he wanted to get our address."

"Yes. I'll try to get his last name so I can check up on him."

"Maybe I can get Lucille alone and ask her."

Jennifer's gaze tracked the older woman in the red dress.

We made the rounds of the exhibit and chatted with a few more people. The gallery owner, Roger Blaisdell, was effusive and tried hard to sell me a Redwall.

"Maybe," I said, watching Jennifer chase Lucille, as Lucille chased another waiter. "I don't have the right decorations for my office, and I'd really like something special for the bedroom at home, too."

"Something by a local artist for the office?" he suggested. "It's good p.r."

"Do you ever have Landers watercolors?" I asked. Landers was one of the Maine artists we'd studied up on. One of his paintings was on our stolen list.

"I had one last spring. Occasionally one comes my way. Would you like to leave your card?"

My card had "Portland Police Department Priority Unit" on it. In the old days, I'd have given him a dummy business card that said I was an optometrist or an engineer. I said, "Perhaps my wife and I can come in one day when it's not so crowded."

He drifted off to find someone more eager to buy Redwalls. Jennifer came back, eyes glittering. "Eric Stanley. He interned at the Portland Museum of Art. That's how she met him."

"Good work."

"Isn't it Captain Larson?" I turned to face the inquirer. It was Thelma Blake, the widow of a famous author. Eddie and I had solved her husband's murder earlier that year.

"Mrs. Blake!" I shook her hand warmly. She wore a platinum wig, a sweeping lavender top over black chiffon trousers, and sequined high heels.

Jennifer clasped her hand, smiling. "So good to see you."

"How have you been since the wedding?" Thelma asked.

"Wonderful," said Jenny.

I looked around and then leaned toward Thelma. "Mrs. Blake, we're here incognito tonight."

"Oh, dear, I hope I didn't"—She leaned forward and whispered loudly—"blow your cover."

I said, "No, we're using our real names, but I'd just prefer no one knew my profession, if you get me."

"Oh, right, right." She smiled and looked quickly from side to side. "You can trust me."

I wasn't sure we could. Time to change the subject. "We're expecting a baby," I said with a big smile.

"How delightful!" She scrutinized Jennifer's figure. "Not for a while, I'd say."

Jennifer blushed. "Next April."

"My Ellen was born in April."

"How is she?" I asked, wondering how we could get away.

"Oh, fine. You know, Martin's book has been published. It will be in the stores next week." Her husband's last novel was being published posthumously. "They're coming out with an entire new paperback line of his earlier works, too. It's very exciting. I was on television in Boston a week ago."

We got home, exhausted, about midnight. I was supposed to get up and run at six the next morning, and I knew I'd be tired.

My phone rang at five. I rolled over and fumbled for it.

"Sorry, Harvey," Mike said, "but you'd better get downtown. An orthopedist's office was broken into. Guess what's missing."

"Not drugs?"

"Nope. Art off his office walls. A patrolman responded to the alarm, and the doctor's down there, but so far they can't tell that anything's missing except two original watercolors and four prints."

I rolled out of bed. Jennifer opened one eye.

"What's up?"

"Art theft, from a doctor's office this time."

"Not Carl and Margaret's?"

"No. Go back to sleep."

I called Eddie. "Ed, it's me. No running today.

We've got an art theft. Meet me as soon as you can." I gave him the address.

The lock had been picked, too easily. I could see that as soon as we got there and looked at the door.

"You need better security here," I told the doctor.

"The building owner is supposed to take care of those things." He sat unhappily on the corner of the receptionist's desk while we looked around. "We had the alarm, and the drug cupboard has a double lock. Still, I suppose I should have insisted on better door locks."

I scanned the patrolman's notes. "Art worth over ten thousand dollars."

"I never thought anyone would break in here. Can you get the pictures back?"

"Doubtful. They're probably over the state line by now."

He groaned and shook his head.

"Call your insurance agent."

"Harv," said Eddie, "looks like they broke something."

"The prints in the waiting room had glass," said the doctor. There were several shards on the floor below the bare spot where one print had hung.

"Must have dropped the frame." Eddie used tweezers to carefully pick up each piece of glass and drop it into a plastic bag. "Hey!"

"What?" I was right there, looking over his shoulder.

"Blood, maybe?" He held up a sliver of glass with the tweezers.

I whipped out another evidence bag and opened it. "This may be our break." I couldn't help remembering what Abby had said the night before—that we needed another crime to give us some evidence in the case.

Eddie and Nate spent most of the morning at the doctor's office while I went to the police station. There were no fingerprints, but they found two tiny drops of blood on the rug, and a smear on a piece of glass in the hallway.

I ate lunch with them at the café, and we went over the limited clues.

"Why did they pick an office this time, not a house?" asked Eddie.

"Must have heard the doctor had nice pictures," I said. "Maybe one of the thieves is a patient of his."

Nate stirred his coffee thoughtfully. "They've nearly been caught twice in homes. Maybe they picked an office because it was empty at night."

"Or maybe this is a different bunch of burglars," I said.

I flagged Eric Stanley's name on my computer and did a thorough background check that after-noon. He was young in the art field, and there wasn't much, but he did have a bad check record and had hopped from employer to employer.

A shadow fell across my screen, and I looked up.

"Human blood on the glass, Harv," Eddie reported.

I'd expected that. "Great. Send it to Augusta." The state was building a DNA database and required blood tests from felons. "If we arrest anyone on this thing, they have to give us a sample."

Saturday was circus day. I took Jennifer to the matinee, and Eddie brought Rachel Trueworthy. I didn't know her well, had only seen her around at church. She had curly brown hair and a nice smile, and she conversed well without chattering.

Jennifer loved the circus. All right, I loved the circus, too. We all did. It was one of those things that made me feel young. Jennifer in pigtails and striped shirt over jeans, face lit up as she watched the tigers pace and the costumed horses leap. She looked like the little girl on the fence in Cecile Caron's painting. Cotton candy and clowns and Jenny squeezing my hand. For once I was able to completely forget the age difference. It was part of the magic she pulled on me.

We went home laughing, and Eddie and Rachel stayed to supper. Peter arrived with the boys at four-thirty, and we sat down at five. The two boys, Andy and Gary, were quiet at first, but grew more and more excited as we told them about the show that afternoon. They couldn't wait to see it themselves.

When the Hobarts whisked Abby away, leaving us with the dishes, Eddie manfully grabbed a dish cloth. I couldn't weasel out of it then, so I helped, too, scrubbing out a few pans. Rachel cleared the table, and Jennifer loaded the dishwasher.

It was cooling off, so I lit the fireplace, and we drank hot cocoa and played Rook. I was warming up to Rachel, but still at the back of my mind was the image of dark-haired Leeanne, watching Eddie silently, wistfully. She was so young, but I found I had picked my favorite for Eddie. Maybe, in time, two of my favorite people would find each other. I smiled, remembering how she'd watched us with binoculars while Eddie heroically took a dive in the ocean at Fort Point last summer.

He and Rachel headed out soon after nine, and Eddie said to me low, in the breezeway, "Thanks, Harv. Nice first date. I've had worse."

"Anytime, Ed."

Jennifer and I sat companionably in front of the fire until Abby came in. Peter had left her at the door, with two sleepy boys in his car. She meandered into the living room, wailing, "Now what do I do? I love those little kids!"

"Think long and hard," I said. "That's a big job, being an instant mom."

"That Andy is so cute! Trying to be tough, but the tigers scared him. And Peter was such a good daddy!"

"He might have been on his best behavior tonight," I said cynically.

"And maybe not, too," said Jennifer. "He's a nice guy, and he has nice kids, and he's been through a lot."

"True," I said. "And don't get me wrong. I like Peter. How does he stack up against your other suitors?"

"Suitors, plural?" Abby flopped down into an armchair.

"Well, there's Greg and Eddie and Charlie . . ."

"I don't think Charlie qualifies as a suitor," said Jennifer. "He asked her for a date, and she said no."

"And Eddie doesn't really like me." Abby shook her head. "I mean, he does, but not that way."

"You sure?" I asked.

"He flirts with other girls right under my nose. He brought another girl here tonight. What does that tell you?"

I said, "Well, you don't seem too broken up about it."

Abby pursed her lips. "I think Eddie and I will always be good friends." I was glad to hear that.

"So that leaves the fly boy," said Jennifer.

"Yeah." Abby looked very somber.

"Make two lists," Jennifer suggested. "Car dealer versus navigator. Sporadic income versus huge salary. Instant family versus babies of your own."

Abby cried, "You mean, two adorable boys *plus* babies of my own versus just babies of my own. You're slanting things. And I think Peter has a pretty good income. He'd be home every night, too, which is more than I can say for Greg."

Jennifer threw up her hands. "It's your decision. Maybe neither of them's right for you."

"Take your time, Abby," I said. "Give them both a fair chance, and don't rule out anything yet."

Chapter 16

Sunday, October 24

Jennifer was impatient for our trip to Skowhegan. Six men from our department were going for the Integrated Ballistics Identification System training, and all would stay in the dorm at the Criminal Justice Academy in Vassalboro, except Eddie and me. On Sunday, Jennifer began packing. We would leave Tuesday when I got home from work.

Beth and Jeff came for lunch after church, and it seemed quiet. Abby, who had sat with Peter and the boys during the service that morning, went right to bed after lunch. Beth and Jeff sat on the wicker settee in the sunroom, and Jeff kept his arm around her shoulders. Yes, things were looking cozy in that direction.

While Jennifer showed Beth the new boots she'd bought, I had a chance to speak to Jeff in private.

"Did you talk to the pastor last week?" I asked him.

"Yeah. Thanks for helping me, Harvey. You were right—Pastor Rowland was a big comfort to me."

"What did he say about telling people?"

"He pretty much agreed with you. He said if it would help catch a criminal or ease grief, then do it, but the guy's incarcerated and . . . Well, you said it. Knowing what I told you would probably cause more hurt."

I nodded. "What about Beth?"

Jeff got the dog-who-fetched-the-stick look. "Yeah. Beth."

"You two are getting close," I said.

"Uh-huh. I told her, I've settled things with God. If she wants to know about the worst night of my life, I'll tell her someday. But right now, I don't think we need that between us. I'm okay."

"I'm glad." I, too, had a worst night ever to look back on—my partner Chris's death, and Carrie walking out on me. It wasn't something I wanted to talk about and depress my loved ones. The people who had to know knew.

Jeff smiled again, the sweet but slightly sorrowful look Jennifer got sometimes. "Everything's forgiven. I didn't think it could be this way."

A huge weight rolled off me. "It can. We'll keep praying for you, Jeff. This will make Jennifer very happy, you know. Well, it does me, too, but she's been very concerned about you."

"I'll talk to her," he said. "I know she's been wondering if I believed or not. I'll tell her she can stop wondering."

When I got home on Tuesday, Jennifer and Abby had supper ready, and we ate quickly, so we could hit the road.

"Be careful while we're gone, Abby," Jennifer said. She warned her about taking safety precautions when leaving the house at night and coming home early in the morning. Abby had been granted her request to change shifts, but had to work through Sunday on her old schedule. After that, she would leave for work in the afternoon and come home at eleven. She would sleep when we slept and be there for Jennifer during the day.

"We'll call you when we get to your parents' house," I said, "and you call us when you get home tomorrow morning, all right?"

Jennifer frowned at her. "We should have asked Beth to come stay with you."

"I'd hardly see her. She'd be here alone at night sleeping, and I'd be here alone during the day sleeping."

She was right, and there wasn't much we could do about it. We both hugged Abby and got into my vehicle. I picked Eddie up at his apartment, and we drove north, arriving at the Wainthrop's house in Skowhegan about eight o'clock. Jennifer was tired. She called Abby, and I encouraged her to go to bed early. When I'd tucked her in, I sought out my mother-in-law.

"Marilyn, I have to run an errand. Would you come with me?"

"This late?"

"Yes, I have an appointment, and it's not far."

"You're so mysterious!"

Eddie was playing a game with Leeanne, Travis, and Randy in the living room. Jennifer's father, George, had the TV on. Marilyn went in and told them we were going on an errand, then joined me in my Explorer.

"Where are we going?" she asked, pulling on knit gloves.

"To see Cecile Caron, the artist." I told her about the painting Jennifer and I had seen in the gallery in Portland.

"How exciting," Marilyn said.

"I was going to take Jennifer with me, but I decided to let it be a surprise." I was already planning how I would present the painting to her.

We found the house, and Mrs. Caron let us in. I apologized for being so late.

"That's all right. You told me it might be late evening."

I introduced Marilyn. Mrs. Caron sat us down in her pleasant living room. Nothing matched in her décor, but the mix of bright fabrics, shelves of books, and serene paintings was soothing. She brought a five-by seven photograph to me and said, "I think this is what you want to see."

I looked at it. The little girl was definitely the

one from the painting. She had the pixie face, the pigtails, and Jennifer's gray-blue eyes. I held it out to Marilyn, and she caught her breath.

"That's Jennifer, all right!"

"Your daughter?" asked Mrs. Caron.

"Yes." Marilyn turned it over and read, "Little girl at Wainthrop farm," and a date.

"Could it be Abby?" I asked.

"No, no, it's too early, and anyway, Abby and Leeanne had short hair when they were little. We kept Jennifer's long, but it was so much trouble I made the other girls wait until they were older to grow theirs out."

"I painted the old barn, from the back, that year," said Mrs. Caron.

Marilyn nodded eagerly. "I remember you setting up down there. Jeff and Jennifer wanted to go down and watch you. I tried to keep them from bothering you."

"They didn't bother me. I used to take a lot of pictures, when I saw something I might want to paint later. Your little girl looked so wistful, I took her picture. I don't know if she knew I took it at the time."

"She didn't seem to remember anything about it," I said. "She told me it couldn't be her in the painting."

"She was pretty young," said Marilyn.

I looked at Mrs. Caron. "I want that painting. I'll give you the money right now."

"Well, Mr. Larson, I've placed it with the gallery. I can call the owner, if you like."

"Sure. He has to get his commission, I guess."

She left the room, and I looked at the photograph again. My Jennifer, before anything had hurt her.

"Your kids had a good childhood," I said to Marilyn.

She smiled and squeezed my hand. I was glad Jeff had decided not to bring up his past trauma.

Mrs. Caron came back a minute later with a troubled expression. "I'm so sorry, Mr. Larson. Nicholas Dore tells me the painting is sold."

I slumped in my chair. I had waited too long. "I should have bought it that day."

Marilyn touched my arm. "I'm sorry, Harvey."

I stood up. "Thank you, Mrs. Caron." I walked for the door.

"Good-bye, Mr. Larson."

"Captain Larson," Marilyn said gently.

She followed me out of the house, and I opened the door of the SUV for her. She had the photograph in her hand. "She told me to give you this."

Eddie and I went for our training the next day. I was depressed. I told Eddie the whole story about the picture on the way to the Academy. He was sympathetic, but advised me to forget it.

"It's one of those things. You just have to move on."

"I loved that painting."

"Maybe she'd do another one."

I sighed.

The ballistics training was interesting. It combined my love of computers and guns with detective skills. I'd had minimal training on it ten years earlier, but the system had changed a lot since then.

Eddie did well, too, and we felt like we were learning something that would be useful. The system would match a spent bullet to the gun that had fired it, the way fingerprints were identified. The database of guns nationwide had grown huge, and the system was more useful every year. Already, several old murder cases in our area had been solved because of it.

Tony Winfield was one of the others taking the training, and he was having a ball.

"I'm so glad I took your computer training," he told me at lunch. "Some people are really lost on this, but I haven't had any problems as far as running the program."

"Beats traffic detail, huh?" said Eddie.

Tony grinned. The uniformed officers avoided traffic duty whenever possible.

That evening, we handed out the T-shirts I'd gotten from Jeff and helped Leeanne feed her goats. Eddie had grown up in the city, and he seemed fascinated by the goats. And Leeanne. I was beginning to see why so many women loved him. He gave his full attention to whoever he was with. That evening, I'd have sworn Leeanne was his favorite woman in the world—but Saturday I'd have said the same thing about Rachel.

Leeanne was commuting to classes in the daytime, and she sat up with Eddie and Jennifer and me that night. Marilyn shooed Randy and Travis off to bed at nine-thirty, and she and George followed at ten. We all had to be up fairly early, except Jennifer, but I thought Eddie and Leeanne wanted some get-acquainted time. Eddie's big brown eyes were saying something to me. I wasn't positive, so finally I got up and went to the kitchen for a glass of water, and he followed me.

"Is Leeanne coming back to Portland with you?" he asked.

"I think so. She's trying to fix it so she can take Friday off from school."

"Harv, I really like her. Do you think—is it okay if I—"

"If you what?"

"I want to ask her out. Or maybe I can just come visit her at your house."

I took a deep drink of water, considering. I honestly didn't think he realized the effect he had on young women.

"Whatever you want, Eddie. Just treat her . . ."

273

"How? How should I treat her?"

"Like something very precious. Like I treated Jennifer."

He nodded, then squeezed my shoulder. He got the picture.

I took Jennifer up to her old room, where Abby slept now whenever she was home. We crawled under a quilt their great-grandmother had pieced. The moon shone in through the window, and it was very quiet, even quieter than Van Cleeve Lane. No traffic sounds, just an occasional creak of old timbers or a goat's muted bleat. I heard Eddie climb the stairs soon after. Jennifer went to sleep with her head on my shoulder.

"Harvey, isn't your birthday coming right up?" Marilyn asked me at breakfast.

"Well, not for a while," I said. It was November twelfth. Jennifer must have told her.

"What do you need?" she asked.

"Me? Nothing."

"Oh, come on, you're family. We always give the kids birthday presents."

How many years since I'd been 'one of the kids'? I smiled at her. "T-shirts, I guess. Jennifer's always stealing mine."

Jennifer made a face at me, then told her mother, "He really does need a new Harvard shirt. I'm afraid I've about done in his old one."

274

"She wears it all the time," I agreed. I liked it when she wore it.

"Where do I get one?" Marilyn asked.

"I don't know." Jennifer turned to me. "Where did you get the old one?"

Jennifer didn't usually ask idiot questions. "At the college bookstore."

Leeanne grinned. "Where else?"

Marilyn brought a platter of pancakes to the table. "Oh, so I can't just run down to Wal-Mart?"

Jennifer shrugged. "I'm sure they have a website."

"They do," I said. Everybody seemed to think this was an odd thing for me to know, but I was sure they'd all been to the University of Maine bookstore in Orono.

"I'll get you one online, Mom," Leeanne said.

Eddie and I left for training, and I had a better day. I had put the painting out of my mind and concentrated on bullets and gun barrels and images on the computer screen. Tony seemed to be dividing his attention between that and a female officer from Lewiston, but Eddie stayed on target.

We all received certificates for completion of the training at the end of the day. Eddie and I went back to the Wainthrop's for supper, and Jennifer and the kids had things packed up. George and I made plans for hunting on November 13. Jeff would be off that weekend, and he would bring Beth up with him.

Travis and Randy were wound up, anxious for their stay-over visit with Jeff. Leeanne was going to drive her car down, so she could drive herself and the boys home Sunday afternoon. That seemed like a good plan to me. Somehow Eddie ended up driving her car, though, and Travis and Randy landed in the middle seat of the Explorer.

"I think I'd really like to go into law enforcement," Randy said as I drove toward the interstate highway. We talked a lot on the way down about the training he'd need. I thought he would be really good at it and told him so. Travis was more athletic, and had coaching aspirations. He was a senior at Skowhegan Area High School and had applied to UMO for the next fall.

"Do they have a criminal justice program?" Randy asked.

"I think so. They've got just about everything," Travis said. "Well, not medicine."

"You could go someplace else." Jennifer swiveled around to look at them. "Don't you guys ever think about going away?"

"Maybe I could get into Harvard," said Randy.

"Yeah, right," said Travis.

I looked in the rearview mirror and caught Randy's eye. "I'll bet you could."

He smiled. "It's really expensive, isn't it?"

"Very. But they have endowments."

"What's that?"

We kept talking about colleges for a while, then Travis asked about Jeff's schedule.

"He'll get home late tonight, and he has Friday and Saturday off," Jennifer said. "You guys can spend both days with him, or come over to our house whenever you want."

"Can we see the police station this time?" asked Randy.

I said, "Sure, and Jeff will probably take you to the fire station. What else do you want to do?"

"Play basketball," said Travis.

"Jeff and Eddie can get up a game in the neighborhood anytime," I said.

"Anytime?"

"Day or night. Maybe I'll come over and join you. There's always a bunch of Eddie's cousins around, too."

"Eddie's cool," said Travis.

Randy made a face. "Yeah, but he likes Leeanne."

Abby ran out into the garage when we drove in at the house. "My siblings!" She hugged the two boys fiercely. "I'll bet Mom and Dad don't know what to do with themselves tonight."

I said, "They'll probably catch up on sleep."

Chapter 17

We all sat up until eleven or so, then I took Eddie home and drove Travis and Randy to Jeff's apartment. Jeff wasn't back yet, but I still had a key, since it was my old place and Jeff had told me to hang on to one. We went in and pulled out the sofa bed. The boys arranged their sleeping bags and duffel bags, and I'd just told them to get ready for bed when Jeff came in. They started talking excitedly to him, telling him all sorts of things that had happened in Skowhegan lately. I could see they were going to be up for a while, so I said goodnight to Jeff. He gave me an amused wave, and I went home.

It was a hectic weekend, but lots of fun. When I got home from work Friday, Jeff and the boys were there, and Beth had come straight from school. Jennifer lined up the six Wainthrop siblings, and Beth and I took pictures. Eddie showed up while we were eating supper, and we played Risk, then went out for ice cream.

Saturday was a blur. We had a basketball tournament in the park near Eddie and Jeff's, with half a dozen Thibodeau cousins and neighbor kids. The girls went shopping. Everybody converged on our house for lunch, then Jeff took Eddie, Randy, and Travis to the fire station.

When they came back and everyone had eaten cookies, Eddie and I took Randy and Travis and Jeff to the police station, and at the last second, Leeanne came running out and hopped into the Explorer.

"Hey, it's a little crowded," Eddie said. "We can take my truck." He and Leeanne jumped out and got in his pickup and followed me.

"Did I miss something?" Jeff asked, looking in the side view mirror at Eddie's truck.

"Don't blink," I said.

Jeff looked sideways at me. "So, whatever happened to Sarah?"

"Who's Sarah?" Randy asked.

"History," I said. "Eddie hasn't taken her out in months."

Jeff scratched his head. "I thought for a while he liked Abby a little."

"So did he."

Jeff groaned. "I can't keep up."

"I know you don't get to church every week because of work," I told him, "but there's been a succession of girls stalking Eddie there."

"So, this thing with Leeanne is not serious?"

"Too soon to tell. Ask me again in a month, and I'll update you."

We got out at the police station, and Randy and Travis ran to Eddie's truck. Jeff and I followed at a more leisurely pace, and Eddie took the boys and Leeanne into the foyer.

"How's it going with you and Beth?" I asked Jeff as we ambled up the steps to the station.

"Really good."

"Glad to hear it."

Jeff paused on the top step. "In fact, I think I'm almost ready to ask her to make it permanent."

"No joke? That's great. I mean, if you both know what you want . . ."

"I do, and I think Beth does, too. Just don't tell my brothers yet or I won't get any peace this weekend."

We went inside, and Eddie was getting the sergeant on duty to show his guests the roll call room, the booking area, and the com room.

"Come on upstairs," I said to Jeff. I punched the code on the keypad beside the stairway door.

"So this is where you and Eddie spend half your waking lives."

"Well, a good part of it, anyway." We climbed the stairs and entered the unit office.

"Let me guess . . . that's your desk." Jeff pointed to mine in the window corner, with pictures of Jennifer on every flat surface.

"That didn't take ESP to figure out, did it?" I showed him Eddie's desk, and the interview room. Everybody likes to see that, and the observation room beside it. "Ours isn't as big or as intimidating as the interrogation room downstairs," I told him.

We went down the hall to the break room, and

I got two Pepsis out of the machine and we sat down.

"Beth's going to teach the rest of the year," Jeff said. "I'm hoping she'll be willing to stop after that. But if she wants to keep teaching for a while, I guess that wouldn't be so bad." He shrugged.

"If she keeps working, you might not get much time together, with your schedule," I said.

"Yeah, I hope she won't want to work forever." Jeff smiled. "First I have to get her to say yes."

Something told me that wouldn't be too hard. I rubbed the back of my head. "I'm not saying she shouldn't work, but it's really nice for your wife to be there when you walk in the door in the evening. Now, don't tell Beth I said that. She'll think I'm a chauvinist."

He smiled. "Some women like to work. Beth likes teaching. And Jennifer's still doing some computer work, isn't she?"

"Yeah, she's putting out a new software program. An old coworker of hers is marketing it. And she might want to keep on with that sort of thing. I don't mind. In fact, I think it helps her confidence. I just don't want to see her working someplace else and dragging home exhausted every night."

Eddie and Leeanne and the boys came into the break room.

"Hey, soda!" Randy went right to the vending machine like a magnet was pulling him. I stood up and pulled a handful of change out of my pocket.

"You're spoiling them," Jeff said. "They'll go home and run Mom and Dad ragged."

"No, they know this weekend is a treat, right fellas?" I looked pointedly at Randy, the younger boy.

"Sure, Harvey," he said.

I kept them in the break room with the soda, giving Eddie a couple of minutes to show Leeanne his desk. She'd been to the police station once before, but things were different now.

Five minutes was about as long as I could keep the lid on, and we walked back through the office, collecting Eddie and Leeanne. Travis wanted to test my statement that the stairs were faster than the elevator, so Randy and Eddie and Leeanne got in the elevator. Jeff and I took the stairs, with Travis running down them ahead of us. Travis did the two flights in about ten seconds flat, but even Jeff and I were waiting with him outside the elevator when it opened.

We drove back to the house. Beth had arrived with a fruit salad, and she, Abby, and Jennifer were getting supper ready. After we ate, the evening degenerated into a cutthroat game of Trivial Pursuit.

At nine o'clock, Jeff stretched his long arms.

"I guess I'd better get these hooligans home and into bed." Randy and Travis protested.

"Why don't you take Beth to her car first?" I asked. "I'll hog tie them here for a few minutes." It was the least I could do for Beth, who had paved the way to romance for me many times, back when she was Jennifer's roommate. She said goodnight and went out through the kitchen with Jeff. I kept the boys occupied with putting away the game and straightening up the living room. Eddie and Leeanne sat talking on the couch.

The lights from Beth's car swept the walls, and Jeff came back in for Travis and Randy.

"I go in to the station early, so you'll pick these guys up for Sunday school, right?" he asked me.

"Sure thing." I looked at the boys. "You guys have your luggage ready in the morning."

Jennifer and I walked out to the breezeway and watched them pile into Jeff's pickup. We waved, then went back inside. Abby was on the phone in the kitchen.

"Where are you?" she was asking. "Really? Pittsburgh? Is it a nice airport?"

"Greg," Jennifer and I said at the same time.

I put my arm around her, and we walked through the sunroom. I stopped to check the patio door and pull the drapes. Jennifer started into the living room, then turned back with alarm on her face.

"What?" I asked.

"Hand holding. Leeanne and Eddie." She pointed over her shoulder toward the living room.

"Here we go again," I said. "Maybe we should open a matchmaking service."

"What is it about this house?" she asked. "We don't do anything. They just come here, and it happens."

I kissed her. "Love must be in the air."

"I was fretting over Jeff and Beth, but now I've got Abby juggling two men, and Leeanne holding hands with Eddie."

"Don't worry," I told her. "Eddie's been confused, but he's also been thinking. You saw him hang back on commitment with Sarah, and he sorted out his feelings for Abby. He won't do anything until he's sure it's right this time."

"So, that means he's sure it's right to hold hands with my baby sister?"

"I guess so. And she's growing up fast. She's almost twenty-one. Did Leeanne take French in high school?"

"I think so."

"That should be interesting."

Jennifer looked up at me. "Jeff told me some good news tonight."

I smiled. "Yeah, he told me. Beth seems happy. They both do."

"She's got no reason to hold him off now." Jennifer looked up at me with glittery eyes. "It's really serious with them."

"Yeah. We'll get more good news soon, I guess. No regrets?"

"None here," she said.

Leeanne and Eddie came out into the sunroom, and Eddie said, "Getting late. Guess I'd better go. I'll see you guys in the morning."

"Sure, Ed," I said.

He started walking toward the kitchen, and Leeanne stood there. Jennifer made little hand motions, telling her to go with him. Leeanne looked at us, embarrassed, then tagged after Eddie.

"What have I done?" Jennifer threw herself at me.

I laughed. "Don't worry."

A couple of minutes later, Abby and Leeanne came back into the sunroom together.

"I've got to get ready for work," Abby said. "Greg's got next Friday and Saturday off, and he's coming up here."

"Driving from Brooklyn?" asked Jennifer.

"No, he can probably get a seat on a plane for nothing."

"Okay. And you're working three to eleven on Friday," Jennifer said, with a "complete this sentence" tone.

"We're going out Friday morning," said Abby. "And Saturday."

Jennifer looked at me, but I didn't know what she wanted me to say.

"Goodnight." Abby went upstairs.

"Poor Peter," said Jennifer.

"Who's Peter?" asked Leeanne.

"Abby's other guy," I told her.

"Oh, right, the widower. Do I get to meet him tomorrow?"

"Probably him and several other young men," said Jennifer. "Just go to the singles class with Eddie, and you'll have your dance card filled in five minutes."

Leeanne frowned at her and then laughed.

Jennifer, Abby, and I went to Jeff's for the boys in the morning, then drove to the church. Leeanne had informed us that Eddie was coming to get her, and they arrived at the parking lot just behind us. The boys were sent to the teen class, and Eddie, Abby, and Leeanne went to the singles class. Jennifer and I enjoyed sitting with Rick and Ruthann Bradley and feeling very settled and married.

Mike and Sharon came in and sat beside me when Sunday school was over. I was surprised, since they hadn't been back for the last three Sundays, but thankful. Mike chatted away about the latest batch of deputy chief candidates. When the singles class let out, Eddie and Leeanne sat down in front of us, and Abby sat with Beth on the other side of her brother, Rick.

Jennifer poked me as the pianist began to play. I looked at her with raised eyebrows.

"They're holding hands in church," she whispered.

"Who?"

She nodded forward, and I peeked over the seat. Eddie had a firm grip on Leeanne's hand.

I sat back and smiled.

Jennifer poked me again.

I whispered, "What? We're holding hands. We held hands the first time we came here."

"But we were serious."

"Think about it, Jenny. A girl Eddie can hold hands with in church. This is a good thing."

"I was thinking of my sister."

"I was thinking of my brother." Eddie was the closest thing I'd ever had to a brother, at least until I married into the Wainthrop family.

Mike leaned over and whispered, "Eddie's dating your sister-in-law?"

I shrugged a little. "Apparently."

Mike shook his head. "I never could keep up with that kid."

"The worst thing is, he doesn't even have a little black book. He keeps it all in his head."

Mike chuckled. "Smart phones. You should know that, Harvey."

Pastor Rowland spoke on marriage that morning. The husband's responsibilities. The wife as a perfect complement to her husband.

I'd heard it before, but it was good to hear it again. Halfway through the sermon, I noticed that Mike was holding Sharon's hand, too.

"It's catching," I whispered to Jenny. She looked at me, and I jerked my head just a little toward Mike. She looked a little startled, then smiled at me and settled back against the pew, squeezing my hand.

Leeanne, Travis and Randy left mid-afternoon, to be sure they'd arrive in Skowhegan before dark. Eddie put Leeanne into the car and talked to her for a minute through the window, then stood back and watched silently as she drove out. The boys waved vigorously.

I went over and stood beside Eddie, and he said, "I'm going up to Wainthrop's Saturday, Harv."

"Got a date, huh?"

"Yup. Going to spend the day there and take her out for supper."

"That's nice. Don't stay so late you'll be tired driving home."

"Right. Now I'd better go see my folks. My mother's been complaining that she never sees me anymore."

Visiting home was a good thing for Eddie, in my book. He'd had trouble connecting with his family since he'd quit going to Mass and confession at their church. Jennifer and I waved him off. I sent up a silent prayer for him.

Sometimes the people you love most are the hardest to feel comfortable with.

"It's my last night on the late shift," Abby said before she left for work that evening. She would have Monday off, then report for her new post in obstetrics on Tuesday.

"Congratulations, sweetie," Jennifer said, giving her a hug.

Peter had asked Abby to sit with him in the evening service, and she had gone, sitting between him and six-year-old Andy. He'd asked her for a date for Friday, and she'd told him she was busy, but perhaps another time. He asked for Thursday, which she had off, and she agreed to go out for ice cream with him and his boys. Jennifer and I kept our mouths shut.

I liked to be in bed by ten o'clock Sunday night, because Eddie and I would be running early, so we said goodnight to Abby about nine-thirty and went into our room.

"I refuse to worry about Leeanne and Abby," Jennifer said. "I spent way too much energy fretting about Jeff, and it's turning out great. But I wish Abby wouldn't keep Peter and Greg both on the string."

"If she marries Greg, she'll probably move to New York," I said.

"I don't want to think about that."

"Stop worrying about it, then. Just pray that God will bring the right husbands to them."

"Yeah."

I winked at her. "And get rid of all the rejects painlessly."

Just on the edge of consciousness, I heard Abby drive out at ten-thirty. Jennifer was lying beside me in one of my T-shirts, breathing softly, and I lay on my side with my right arm across her tummy, over the baby. I'd gotten used to sleeping that way. It was part of my fantasy ideal life, and I had pleasant dreams.

The next thing I knew, I jerked awake and lay there, not breathing, listening, trying to determine what had made my heart race. It was too dark for Abby to be home. I pushed the light button on my watch. Three-twenty a.m. I heard a stealthy sound in another room, not one I recognized. I stiffened. Another sound, like something being moved on the carpeted floor, then soft footsteps. I looked toward the door, but I'd closed it the night before. A tiny gleam of light flickered at the crack beneath the door.

Reaching out with my right hand in the moonlight, I carefully picked up my cell phone from the nightstand. Star-two.

The dispatcher was loud in my ear.

"This is Captain Larson," I said quietly. "I've got a burglary in progress at my house. Send a unit here immediately, please."

"Yes, Captain." A pause. "137 Van Cleeve Lane?"

"Yes." I put the phone down and sat up on the edge of the bed. Jennifer slept on. No time for clothes. I had on a pair of boxer shorts. I heard another sound, and I thought it was in the study, where our computers were. I stood up slowly, willing the bed not to creak. It didn't. I went quietly across the rug to the dresser. I could just make out my gear, where I laid it out every night. Badge, handcuffs, keys, gun. I drew my Beretta from the holster, then tiptoed to the door.

Chapter 18

I listened. Muffled sounds. Slowly, I turned the knob. I thought the tiny noise I caused could be heard throughout the house, but nothing changed. I drew the door in toward me. When it was open a crack, I looked out into the sunroom. It was dark. I had drawn the drapes over the patio door. I waited while my eyes adjusted, absorbing every smidgen of available light.

Another sound, this time from the living room. I waited. I thought I heard a low voice, but I wasn't sure. Someone walked away from the living room, through the study, into the kitchen. By looking out through the sunroom, I could see a beam of light, and a shape moving toward the entry. But someone still moved stealthily in the living room. I waited. The unit should arrive soon.

The person came back through the kitchen, and instead of turning into the study, shined his light into the sunroom. I ducked back beyond the door frame. The beam of light swept around the room outside. Across from me, I could see the doorway between the sunroom and the living room. A dark bulk suddenly obscured it.

"Anything in here?" The whisper was so loud I jumped. They were both in the sunroom. Could they possibly not know there was a bedroom so near? They thought the family was asleep upstairs. The add-on master bedroom wasn't in their plan.

I braced myself, heart pounding. They shined a flashlight on Jennifer's Van Gogh.

"Want that?" asked one.

"Nah, it's a fake."

The thief nearest me swung his flashlight around and focused it on the bedroom door and me.

"Hey!" He raised a pistol. The barrel gleamed.

I pulled the door open and dropped to one knee. "Police! Freeze!"

I got one round off and dodged behind the door frame. Three bullets went past me, into the door and the room beyond.

Jennifer jerked upright on the bed.

"Get down!" I cried.

She dove over the side of the bed, onto the rug.

I held my gun ready and peeked out the doorway. One man held a weapon pointed in my direction. He took a step toward me. The other backed toward the kitchen.

I squeezed the trigger at almost the same moment a slug whizzed past my ear, then I heard his shot. I flattened myself on the floor and prayed.

My ears rang, and I couldn't tell if there was movement in the next room or not. I took a deep breath, stood up, reached around the door jamb, and flipped the light switch, flooding the sunroom with brilliant light. I ducked back behind the wall. Nothing. Slowly, I peeked out.

One man was lying on his back on the floor, his hand to his chest, bleeding profusely. His gun lay beside him on the rug. A second man was just disappearing out the door to the breezeway.

I ran out past the fallen man, kicking his .45 across the room as I passed him. I tore through the kitchen and the entry, out the open door. A dark figure bolted down the driveway. He dodged left along the sidewalk. A light came on across the street in Bud Parker's house.

I took off diagonally across the front yard and the driveway. The cold air hit me, and my feet touched the frost-covered grass in the yard next door. I dodged the neighbor's bird bath and judged my stride carefully. I jumped over the fence, landing on the sidewalk just behind the fleeing man. A parked car loomed dark against the curb a few yards beyond, but I'd tackled him before he reached it. A pistol went flying off the edge of the sidewalk. He struggled, and I kneeled on his back.

"Police, you imbecile! Freeze!" Handcuffs. I needed my handcuffs. I put my Berretta's muzzle against the back of his head and said, "Hold still or you'll wish you had." He lay still.

I said, "I'm going to get off you. Don't move,

or I'll kill you." My adrenaline surging, I eased off him. Jennifer came running down the sidewalk, panting. She'd grabbed her white robe, and it flew out behind her with her long hair.

"Harvey, are you okay?"

"Give me the belt to your bathrobe. Quick." The man had tensed when she spoke, and I prodded him with my gun. She pulled the tie belt from the belt loops and put it in my outstretched hand.

"Go get my handcuffs," I said. "On the dresser."

She turned around and ran back along the sidewalk in her bare feet. I quickly secured the man's hands behind him and stood up.

Bud Parker was coming hesitantly across the street, squinting at me.

"That you, Harvey?"

"It's me, Bud."

"What's going on? Should I call the police?"

"They're on the way, but call an ambulance."

He turned back and ran toward his house.

Jennifer came gasping, holding up the handcuffs.

"Good girl!"

I could hear a faint siren, finally. I snapped the handcuffs onto the burglar's wrists, untied the belt, and started tying his feet.

"Harvey, that man grabbed me." Jennifer's voice caught on a sob.

"What man?"

"In the sunroom. When I came out with the handcuffs, he grabbed my ankle." She shuddered. I hadn't factored him in when I'd sent her back into the house. Stupid of me.

"You okay?"

I stood up and held her for a second.

"I think so."

I looked along the curb, located the burglar's .357 magnum and kept an eye on it.

Bud was coming back.

"Janice is calling the ambulance," he said. "What happened?"

"Burglary. Don't let anyone touch that gun over there. I'm going back in the house. There's a wounded man in there. Don't let this guy get up. The cops are coming. Just keep him here until they get here."

"Harvey—"

"Jenny, stay here with Bud." She was holding her white robe around her. The siren was louder. My heart racing, I ran down the sidewalk, up the driveway, and in at the breezeway, flipping on more lights. He was halfway across the kitchen, crawling with the .45 SIG in his hand. A wide trail of blood stained the floor behind him.

"Drop it." I pointed my Beretta at him.

He started to raise the pistol.

"Drop it," I repeated. "If you don't, you'll go straight to hell." For just a moment I wouldn't have cared. He looked at me, then lowered his head. His hand relaxed, and the gun fell onto the linoleum. His head hit the floor with a dull thud.

"Don't move." I went a step closer, then another. Keeping my gun trained on him, I stuck my foot out cautiously and dragged the weapon out of his reach. Then I stood still and waited, expecting him to look up at me. I was panting, not so much from exertion as from terror. I could have gotten Jennifer killed. I didn't want to consider the trauma she had just gone through.

The squad car had stopped outside, and there was a general commotion in the neighborhood. I heard more sirens approaching.

It occurred to me that the man on the floor hadn't moved. He could be bleeding to death while I stood there. My training said to cover him until someone else arrived. I took a cautious step toward him and kicked at his outstretched hand with my bare foot. He didn't react.

Someone stepped through the doorway behind me.

"Okay, up against the wall."

"I'm the homeowner," I said.

"Just drop the gun and step up against the wall," the officer said.

I knew I'd do the same thing in his position, although common sense might tell me the guy in boxers wasn't the burglar. I laid my Beretta down carefully and stepped to the wall beside the refrigerator, my hands shoulder height.

"I'm Captain Larson," I said. "My badge is on the dresser in the bedroom. So's my ID."

"Just hold on," he said. Another man came through the front door.

"Captain Larson?"

I turned my head. Finally, someone I recognized. "Aaron. Good to see you."

Aaron O'Heir said to the other officer, "Tommy, this is Captain Larson, you know."

The officer bending over the burglar stood up. "Sorry, sir. We had to be sure."

"I know." I lowered my hands and stepped toward him.

"This guy's dead," said O'Heir.

I took a deep breath. "I'm sorry about that. It was him or me."

"We understand, sir."

"Did you get the guy outside?" I asked.

"Yes, sir, he's in custody."

"Can I go get my pants now?"

The first officer went with me, apologizing.

"It's okay." I went into the bedroom.

Tommy stopped at the door and looked at the bullet holes in the woodwork.

"Three rounds there, another one into the bedroom," I said, pulling on a pair of jeans. The first three bullets had gone through the pine door or the jamb, and on through the wall on the opposite side of the room.

Tommy stepped in and looked at the wall

opposite the door, over the bed. Just above where I slept, another bullet hole pierced the gray wallpaper, between a pink blossom and a trellis.

"Is that your wife outside?" Tommy asked.

"Yeah. She was in here with me when it happened."

"Jiminy."

I found my Portland Fire Department T-shirt and pulled it on, then stepped into my sneakers and went out with him, sidestepping the blood on the carpet in the sunroom. Two EMTs were in the kitchen, bending over the dead man.

"You call the M.E.?" I asked in Aaron's direction.

One of the EMTs stood. "Harvey, you okay?" It was Jeff.

"Yes, just a little shook up. Where's Jennifer?"

"I saw her out in the driveway."

I went outside and down the driveway. She came running to meet me, clutching the white robe around her.

"Are you okay?" I choked out, squeezing her hard against my chest.

"Yes. Are you?"

"Yes."

"Jeff's here," she said.

"I saw him."

"That man in there . . ."

"He's dead."

She collapsed against me, crying then. I

couldn't take her inside. There were at least six patrol cars in the driveway and the street now. I walked slowly with her to the nearest one. It was empty. I tightened my arm around her and took her to the next one. An officer was standing beside it, and I could see the prisoner in the back seat.

"I'm Captain Larson. You make sure I get my handcuffs back, okay?"

"Yes, sir."

We walked on to the end of the driveway, and Bud and Janice stood there with a dozen other people from the neighborhood.

"Janice," I said, "could Jennifer go over to your house and sit down for a little while?"

"Of course. Come on, honey." Janice put her arm around Jennifer.

Bud looked at me. "You'd better come, too."

"Just for a second," I conceded.

"My feet are cold," said Jenny. I scooped her up and carried her across the street and up their driveway.

When we stepped into their living room, I set her down. Janice took Jennifer to a chair. As she turned, I saw blood on the hem of her bathrobe, soaking the terry cloth for an inch-wide band on the left side. Jennifer was oblivious to it, but Bud nudged me, his eyes on the stain.

I turned toward him. "Has Janice got something she can put on?"

He headed down the hallway toward their bedroom and came back a moment later with a plaid robe. I took it from him.

"Jenny." I stepped to her chair and bent down to her eye level. "I want you to put this on."

She looked at the robe, then at me. "I'm fine."

"No, you're not, gorgeous. Take your bathrobe off and put this on."

She stood up slowly. Bud turned his back. She looked down at her robe and saw the stain at the bottom.

Janice screamed a little and stepped back. "I'm sorry," she said. "I was startled."

Jennifer wriggled her arms out of the sleeves and dropped the white robe to the floor, then stepped away from it. I held the plaid robe open, and she put it on over the big T-shirt and tied it securely. I led her to the sofa, and she sat down.

"Anything else I should know?" she asked quietly.

"Just let me take a look." I knelt beside her and twitched the hem of the plaid robe aside, studying her ankles. Bud went out of the room and came back with a damp cloth.

"He grabbed my foot," Jennifer whispered, as I scrubbed away at the drying blood on her left ankle. His hand and the bloodied robe had left smears half way up her shin.

"Your robe must have dragged across him,"

I said. "It's all right, baby." I knew she was remembering another time when a man had grabbed her.

Janice held her hand while I worked. When I finished, I gave the bloody cloth to Bud and sat down on the couch beside Jennifer with my arms tight around her.

"I'll wash the bathrobe," said Janice.

"Burn it," I said. I knew Jennifer would never wear it again.

She looked into my eyes. "I was running past him, and he caught my ankle. I almost fell over. I jerked away and kept going."

"You're safe now." I kissed her hair and her temple and her cheek.

"Can we go back over?" she asked.

"Not yet. Stay here with Janice. I'll go see how they're doing. It's pretty messy inside."

The car with the prisoner was pulling out when I crossed the street. O'Heir met me at the door.

"Captain, they're taking the dead man to Augusta for an autopsy." It was standard. "We've got the survivor, and we'll question him. I've got men taking evidence. Is there someplace else you folks could sleep?"

As if we could sleep. I looked at my watch. It was barely four o'clock.

"We'll figure it out. Listen, Aaron, there are things you need to ask him. My unit has been investigating a burglary ring, and this could be part of it. If they were looking for artworks, it's imperative we know who hired them."

"You have artworks in your house?" he asked. "Looked to me like they were after electronics."

"I've inquired about art undercover. I didn't think anyone knew where I lived, but they might have been able to find out. My wife and I were posing as collectors."

"Okay, we'll ask him."

Another officer came up the driveway to the breezeway. "Captain?"

"Yes."

"Officer Barnes asked me to give you these." He held out my handcuffs and the tie belt to Jennifer's bathrobe.

"Thanks."

"You want to sit down and tell me what happened?" O'Heir asked.

"Sure." I took him inside. Men were still working in the kitchen, and we stepped into the study.

I sat down at my desk. My computer was disconnected and sitting on the floor. Jennifer's was gone. O'Heir looked at the poster of me in the Kevlar vest, then sat down in Jennifer's chair and pulled his notebook out. I started my narrative with waking up out of a sound sleep and told him everything from there.

When I'd finished, he had me go through the

rooms and tell him what was missing. Jennifer's computer and printer, the TV, DVD player and CD player from the living room, the small framed Murillo print Mr. Bailey had left in the house as our wedding present, the flow blue plate I had bought Jennifer before we were married, an antique side table, a jar of state quarters we'd saved on the mantle. That was about it.

"There's a car out by the curb, where I tackled that guy," I said. "If that's their car, you'll probably find our stuff in it."

I stayed there with them until the body was removed and the dark car had been checked. Jennifer's computer and the other things were in the back seat and the trunk. Officers carried them into the house for me, and I put things back together. The ambulance was long gone.

I went over to the Parkers'. Janice had put Jennifer to bed in their guest room. When I looked in, she stared back at me with huge eyes. I sat on the edge of the bed and smoothed her hair back from her forehead.

"Can you sleep a little, gorgeous?"

"No. I'm trying not to worry about you."

"Nothing to worry about now. I'll go through an investigation. That always happens when you shoot somebody. They'll find it was justified, send me for counseling, and that will be that."

"They shot at you, didn't they?"

"Yes. We need a new door on the bedroom.

There are holes in the bedroom wall, too, and the rug in the sunroom is a mess."

"Can somebody clean it?"

"I think I'll have it ripped out. You know, the baby crawling on it and everything. It's pretty bad. I don't think you can ever get the residue out from something like this."

She closed her eyes.

"I'm sorry." I should have spared her the details. "I wish you could forget what you saw." She sat up, and I held her. "I should never have sent you back inside. I'm sorry."

"We should call Abby," she said. "She can't come home and walk into that mess."

"All right, I'll try to get her." I kissed her gently and laid her down on the pillow. "Try to sleep."

Chapter 19

I called the hospital and, after a lengthy hold, spoke to Abby. She was upset and wanted to come right home, but I told her not to, and that she might not be able to get inside when she did.

"If you don't see me when you get there, go over to Bud and Janice's. That's where Jennifer will be."

The eastern horizon was lightening when I went back over to our house. Only two officers were left, and they had dug one bullet out of a stud in the bedroom wall. The rest had gone through, but they'd checked with the neighbors on the next street and couldn't find any damage over there.

"Sorry things are such a mess, Captain," one of the men said. "There are people that clean up after suicides. Maybe you could get them to come in."

It was too early to call anyone, so I started mopping up. The kitchen first. That wasn't too hard, just time consuming. The rug in the sunroom was hopeless. I scrubbed at it with a rag, but there was no way it would look like anything other than a battlefield. I found splatters on the walls and the furniture and cushions, and most of those I could deal with.

At six I put a load of laundry in the washer and started calling contractors. The fourth one didn't hang up. He agreed to come right away and give an estimate.

Eddie came to the door while I was talking. He walked in slowly and got the story. He looked at the blood and the bullet holes while I made coffee. I drank two cups and he drank one and ate two English muffins.

"I don't think I can run today," I said.

"No problem."

I left him there in case Abby came home early and walked across the street. Bud met me at the door.

"I think Jennifer's asleep," he said. "Janice went to lie down, too."

I checked on Jennifer, and sure enough, she'd drifted off. I tiptoed out.

"You want some coffee?" Bud asked.

"No thanks. I just had some. I've got someone coming to look at the damage."

I went back home and told Eddie, "I guess I'd better show my face at the station later and let Mike tell me I'm suspended."

"No hurry." Eddie left to change and said he'd see me at the office as early as possible.

I'd just changed my clothes when the contractor arrived and gave me an estimate for the door and the rug and the holes in the wall. At 7:30, I was in the station, talking to O'Heir.

"Well, sir, we've questioned him, but he's a stubborn one," Aaron said.

"I need to know who they were working for."

"I understand, sir."

"Has he got a lawyer?" I asked.

"The court will get him one."

"What have you got so far?"

He handed me a report, and I read the names. The prisoner was James Hubble. The dead man was Ian Foster. Both lived in the area and had records. Robbery, breaking and entering.

"Let me see their effects."

"Well, I'm afraid Foster's went to Augusta with him."

I felt like swearing. I'd been right there when the M.E. took the body, and I hadn't thought a thing about it. I looked up at the ceiling and took a deep breath.

"Show me Hubble's effects, and request Foster's from the M.E. immediately."

"Yes, sir."

I waited while he got an envelope from Evidence. He moved slowly, and I realized O'Heir had been on duty all night, and it was past time for his shift to end. I tried to speak courteously.

"Thanks, Aaron." I dumped the things out on his desk. A pocketknife, a key ring, some change, a set of lock picks, a small flashlight, and a wallet with three driver's licenses, each with Hubble's picture and a different name. I shook my head. "Call me upstairs, please, if you get anything out of him, and I want to see Foster's things when you get them."

"Yes, sir. I'm leaving soon, but I'll make sure the patrol sergeant knows."

"All right, Aaron. Thanks for getting there as fast as you did." He watched me go out into the foyer. I climbed the stairs wearily.

Eddie was just removing his jacket.

"Harvey, did you talk to the prisoner?"

"No. They did. Nothing good."

"Think we could question him?"

"I dunno. Maybe later." I flagged Foster and Hubble in my computer program and searched for information on them. Most of it I already knew, from O'Heir's report. Foster had a prior conviction for transporting stolen antiques, along with his other accomplishments. At ten minutes past eight, I called Mike, and he told me to come right up. He met me at the door to the outer office.

"You all right, Harvey?"

"Yeah."

Judith said, "Good morning, Captain," without moving a muscle.

"Morning."

Mike and I went into his office and sat down.

"I'm okay, and I think Jenny's okay, but it was not a restful night," I said.

"Why did they pick your house?"

"I'm not sure." I rubbed my chin. I hadn't shaved. "It's possible someone thought we had art. A guy at the art exhibit last week was asking us where we lived and what we owned. And the dealer we showed the Turner to might have had the impression we invested. Or someone could have picked us off the mailing list for the art club. I don't know."

"Mm. But you were careful. I know you."

"I didn't use an assumed name. I'm in the phone book."

"Hmm. This truth-telling can be hazardous."

"Can I question the prisoner?" I asked.

"Well, technically, you're on suspension. You know that."

"I know, but, Mike—"

"I've also known you to get riled when it gets personal. Not often, but now and then."

"I'll stay cool."

He raised one eyebrow, as if he'd take that with a grain of salt.

"You know what's funny?" I said. "It turns out we did have art. The guy we bought the house from left a little picture as a gift to us, and they stole it. I'd almost forgotten about it. I'll try to find out what it's worth. Maybe they were after that, but I think it was coincidence."

"Where's Jennifer?" Mike asked.

"Across the street at the neighbors'." I swiped

my hand across my eyes. "I should call her."

"I'll see that the investigation into the shooting goes through quickly. There's no question you were in the right on this thing."

"Thanks. Any chance I can skip the shrink?"

"That's negative. I'll set it up."

It was what I'd expected. "Okay."

"Go home, Harvey."

"Is that an order?"

Mike gritted his teeth. "I should probably say yes."

"There's a lot I can do here, Mike."

"Keep a low profile?"

"Absolutely."

He swiveled his chair back and forth a couple of times. "I'll put this through as fast as I can."

"Thanks."

I went back to my desk and called the Parkers'. Jennifer was up, and she talked to me shakily. I told her about the contractor and asked if she wanted me to have him do the repairs. She did, ASAP. Abby was there, too, and I talked to her. I told her they could go in, and to put Jennifer to bed upstairs in the guest room next to hers. They could get to the stairs by going from the kitchen to the study, to the living room. Not through the sunroom. If Jennifer needed anything from the bedroom, Abby could go get it.

Next I called the contractor to confirm I wanted

to hire him. He said he couldn't come right away, so I offered to pay him extra, and he said he'd come after lunch. I called the Parkers' house again. Jennifer and Abby had gone across the street. I called our house and told Abby to expect the contractor, but to check his ID first. The fatigue was catching up, but I shook it off.

Eddie and Nate went with me downstairs, and I asked to see the prisoner. Terry was on duty, and he told me I could go in with one of his officers. Eddie and Nate had to wait. Jimmy Cook was the man he brought me.

"Jimmy! How's the leg?" I shook his hand.

"Pretty well, Captain. Plagues me when it rains."

"Good to see you." I felt better, just knowing Jimmy was back on duty and mostly recovered.

They took Hubble into the interrogation room down there, and Eddie and Nate went into Observation. Jimmy and I went into the room with the prisoner.

"Well, genius, remember me?" I asked.

Hubble sat handcuffed at the table, staring at the chain that held him down.

"Answer the captain," said Jimmy.

"Yeah," Hubble said.

"You do? Well, good. I thought maybe the necktie threw you off, since I was a little less formally dressed when we last met."

He didn't bat an eyelash.

"You and your pal Foster broke into my house. That wasn't very smart."

No response.

"What were you after?"

No answer.

Jimmy leaned over the table. "Talk."

"Just whatever we could get."

"And who were you getting it for?" I asked.

"Nobody."

"Then who were you taking it to?"

"Nobody."

"Oh, you and Foster wanted a couple of computers for yourselves, huh?"

No answer.

I was losing patience, but I'd promised Mike I would stay calm. I said slowly, "Listen, moron, your partner is dead. I could have shot you, too, and nobody would have thought a thing about it. But I didn't. Now, tell me who you were lifting stuff for."

"What's in it for me?"

"Oh, I don't know. Maybe I don't tear you apart?" I paced a little. Jimmy looked sympathetic, but I knew I was close to losing it. I took a deep breath. "You didn't like the Van Gogh. It was a cheap print. You took the print from the other room, though. One of you knew enough to tell which one was worth something. You were after artworks for somebody with some money."

"Can I get a lawyer?"

"What, you haven't had a lawyer come see you yet?" I said. "You poor thing. Of course you can."

Hubble scowled. "Look, Ian made the arrangements. He told me what to look for. Anything not on the list we could have."

My fist came down on the table a foot from his nose. "What was on the list?"

"Paintings, mostly. He'd tell me to look for a certain picture. A portrait or something."

"And what paintings were you after last night?" Patience, calm and patience.

"One of a ship and . . . I can't remember."

"For whom?"

"I told you, I don't know."

"I think you do. You and Foster worked together a long time. You've done at least a dozen jobs in this area, looking for art."

"I think I want to talk to a lawyer. Now."

I hesitated, then gave up. We had to give him the lawyer. I should have stopped the first time the word came out of his mouth.

"Thanks, Jimmy." I went out. Eddie and Nate came after me from Observation. I stopped at Terry Lemieux's desk and said, "Hubble wants his lawyer."

"Okay. I've already spoken to the D.A.'s office about it."

"And we want a DNA test. We've got some blood from the scene of the last burglary that we want to test him for."

"I'll start the paperwork," Terry said.

I looked hard at him. "Don't let him bail out, no matter what. This guy was in on all the art burglaries, and one of them has an attempted murder, not counting the gun battle at my house this morning."

"I'll call you if anything happens."

I nodded. "Your men got a bullet out of my wall. I want to run it on IBIS."

Terry made a note on a memo pad. "I'll have Winfield do it. You really shouldn't be the one, Harvey."

"Fine." I rubbed the back of my neck and sighed. "I hear you're leaving soon."

"Yup. Going to Fairfield."

"Congratulations. I hope it works out for you."

"Thanks." Terry was one of the good ones, and I knew he'd be missed.

We went up the stairs. Eddie could barely contain his anger. "Boy, that bozo Hubble makes me mad."

"Maybe the lawyer will convince him to deal," Nate said.

I loosened my necktie. "Let's call the M.E. and ask if he'll send some of Foster's blood to the lab right away, so they can try to match it to the blood sample from the doctor's office burglary."

"I'm on it," Eddie said.

I called Jennifer's cell phone. It rang six times, then Abby answered.

"Sorry, Harvey. We forgot to get her phone out of the bedroom."

"I figured. How is she?"

"I think she's all right. I've got her in the guest room, but she wants to get up."

"Did you check her pulse and all that?"

"She was distressed this morning, but she's all right now."

"What about the baby? Should I call Margaret? If I call Margaret, she'll come."

"I don't think you need to."

"Well, keep an eye on her," I said.

"Will do."

Ryan Toothaker, of the *Press Herald*, had learned of the burglary at my house during his routine check of the police log that morning. He asked for an interview, and I talked to him and reporters from two TV stations. So much for my undercover work on the art case.

When the press conference was over, Mike was waiting for me.

"You questioned the suspect?"

"Not much," I said.

"I knew I should have sent you home. You can't do that, Harvey."

"You said I could stay."

"*You* said you'd keep a low profile, but here you are talking to reporters."

I looked at my watch. "I need to check on Jennifer, so I'm taking my lunch hour now."

"Don't come back."

"Aw, Mike, come on."

"No. This is one investigation you don't want to compromise."

I couldn't argue with that. "Okay. I'm sorry."

He nodded and clapped me on the shoulder. "We got this, Harvey. Stay home, at least for today."

I took a moment to apologize to God for going off the track again and then gave my detectives some suggestions for their afternoon activities.

"Arnie, you're in charge this afternoon."

"We got your back, boss," Arnie said.

I drove home, eager to see for myself how Jennifer was doing. She was sitting at her computer, and she jumped up when I walked in.

I put my arms around her. "You should rest."

"I'm okay," she said. "I had to do something, so I've been working on my flagging program."

I understood that feeling. When something really bothered me, I threw myself into my work. That was one reason I felt so helpless, not being able to head up this investigation myself.

Abby came to the study doorway. "Lunch is served."

"You ought to be in bed," Jennifer told her.

Abby shrugged. "The contractor's here. He just drove in."

I looked out the window and saw a gray pickup with a utility cap on the back.

"I'll take care of it." I went out, and he showed me the door he'd brought, a match to the six-panel pine door on our bedroom. He would mount that and patch the bedroom walls first, then tear out the carpet in the sunroom. I'd found some leftover wallpaper in the utility room cupboard, and I gave him that.

Abby, Jennifer, and I ate lunch together. I told them I had interviewed the prisoner, and he had committed other art thefts but hadn't given us his contacts' names yet.

"I hope you can find out who's buying stuff from them and stop them," Jennifer said. She stretched and yawned. "I really want a shower."

"Take it upstairs," I said. "Abby can help you take your things up there."

Abby started clearing the table. "Just tell me what you want, and I'll get it for you."

"I can do it," Jennifer replied. "I'm not sick. Abby, you should go to bed."

"Honey, are you really okay?" I moved my chair closer to Jennifer's and put my arm around her.

"Yes, I'm fine."

"Is the baby okay?"

"Everything's fine."

"Do you want to see Margaret, or Carl?"

"No." She leaned over and kissed me. "Please stop worrying. I admit, it was a shock. When I woke up, I didn't know what was going on."

"I'm sorry. I was afraid if I woke you up, they'd hear me, and I couldn't get the drop on them."

"Well, you sure did."

"Yeah. At least you jumped off the bed when I told you to."

She laughed. "I almost crawled under the bed."

"That's what you should have done if I went down."

"Don't say that. Seeing that guy's blood was bad enough." She looked toward the sunroom, where blood soaked the carpet under the Van Gogh print, and the smears extended toward us as far as the kitchen doorway, where I'd scrubbed the linoleum.

"Maybe you should have just yelled at them and scared them off," Abby said.

I looked at Jennifer. "I suppose that might have been better in some ways." I hated that I'd put her in more danger.

"No," she said firmly. "You needed to catch them. We'd have both been furious if they got away."

The truth was, Foster was in the shooting mode before I yelled, but I figured replaying it wouldn't help Jennifer. I squeezed her. "Let's go in the study." I didn't want her to be able to see the bloody rug. She went with me and sat down in her desk chair. I wheeled mine over close and sat down, reaching for her hand. "You know, I was so mad at him. When you told me he grabbed

319

your ankle, I just wanted to go in there and shoot him again."

"Oh, baby. But you didn't."

"No. I didn't. I made him drop the gun."

"He had the gun when you went in?" Jennifer searched the depths of my eyes.

"Yes. He'd gotten to it and picked it up. I told him if he didn't drop it—" I broke off. She didn't need to hear that either. My next words came out before I'd really thought them through. "And then I stood there while he bled to death." The stark words lay between us for a moment.

"Come here." She pulled my head down against her shoulder and stroked my hair.

My lungs constricted. "I didn't know he would die before the ambulance got there."

"Things happened really fast," she said gently.

I sat up, and she looked up at the poster of me in the body armor. "God is good," she said.

I pulled in a ragged breath. "Maybe I ought to take a day or two off."

"Mike would let you."

"He'd love it. But we've got Hubble. I can't ease up on this case now. I'll stay home this afternoon, but unless Mike locks me out, I'll go back in the morning."

She put her hand up to rub my scratchy cheek and smiled. "I'd love to have you take some time off, but if you don't want to, I'll understand. I'm going take a shower now."

"I guess I'll be in here on the computer." I kissed her, and she went upstairs.

I got up and looked into the bedroom. The new door was on its hinges, and the contractor was smoothing joint compound where the hole had been in the wall over the bed.

"Hey, I lifted the corner of that rug out there," he said when he saw me. "You've got hardwood underneath. Were you going to get a new carpet, or do you want the oak?"

"I don't know. Let me look at it." I went to the patio door, where he'd loosened the edge of the carpet and pulled it back. Beneath the rug and the padding was a fine oak floor similar to the one in the dining-room-turned-study. I went upstairs and told Jennifer.

Her reaction was, "I wonder if there's a good floor under the living room carpet, too."

I went down and told the man to pull the carpet out and, if it was all good, leave the wood floor bare. "Tell me if it needs refinishing."

I went to my computer, mulling over my conversation with Hubble. A picture of a ship. Had he meant the Turner print Jenny and I had shown Dore at his gallery?

I was able to check the crime updates remotely via my home computer. Hubble and Foster showed up in O'Heir's report. I glanced through it again, and stopped at the list of items stolen from our house. The Murillo print. I went to the art auction sites I'd bookmarked and looked for it. After a half hour of browsing, I took out my phone.

"Eddie?"

"Yeah?"

"You know that picture in our living room? *The Divine Shepherd*?"

"Huh?"

"You know, over beyond the fireplace."

"Oh, Baby Jesus with the sheep?"

"Yeah."

"What about it?"

"Hubble and Foster took it."

"You got it back, didn't you?"

"Yes, but, Eddie, it's valuable."

"I didn't know that. I thought it was just a copy."

"It is, but the print itself is old."

"Like Mike's that you took to the gallery?"

"Yes. His is worth eight hundred bucks or so. The Murillo is worth five times that."

"Wow. Where did you get it?"

"Mr. and Mrs. Bailey had it. When he moved out, Mr. Bailey left it for us, and he told me it was a wedding gift. He left a lot of stuff, but that was special, I guess. I knew it was nice, but I never tried to find its actual value."

"Pretty decent wedding gift."

"Yes. I'm wondering now if that was on Foster and Hubble's list."

"Hold on, Harvey." A moment later, he said, "Terry called up here. Foster's effects just arrived from Augusta. You still want to see them?"

"You handle it," I said. "Mike told me to stay home."

"I'll call you," Eddie said.

I went to the kitchen and heated up leftover coffee. Twenty minutes later, Eddie called me back.

"Okay, Nate and I made a list," he said. "You ready?"

"Yeah. What did he have?"

"His wallet, a pocketknife, cigarettes, a lighter, keys, penlight, contact lenses, wedding ring, and a chain with a metal arrowhead hanging from it."

"What's in the wallet?" I asked. I could hear him and Nate talking to each other, then Eddie came back loud and clear.

"I put you on speaker. There's a little cash, some store cards, and his driver's license. Oh, what have we here? Three business cards, all from art dealers."

"Where are they located?"

"Uh, South Portland, Boston, and Dover, New Hampshire. And there's a piece of white paper off a small tablet."

"You guys see what you can find out about those three art dealers this afternoon, without scaring them," I said. "What's on the paper?"

Eddie said slowly, "Landers still life, N. C. W.

nautical sketch, Braden abstract." He paused just a second. "Harvey, this is weird."

"What's weird?"

"It has your address."

"You're kidding."

"No, I'm not. One-three-seven Van Cleeve Lane. That's you."

I felt like my heart stopped for a moment. "Take a picture of it and send it to me. Have Nate do it right now."

"Okay."

Less than half a minute later, the photo came in on my screen. I squinted at it.

"Look closer, Eddie. That's not a three."

Chapter 20

"You're right," Eddie said. "It's an eight. The pen skipped a little or something."

Nate said, "Captain, Landers is one of the artists we studied from another burglary."

"A-plus," I said. "Braden is a living artist, too."

"Who's N.C.W.?" asked Eddie.

I looked at the photo again.

"Oh, no." I looked across the room, remembering Jennifer saying, 'Mrs. Harder has several nice paintings.' "

"What?" Eddie asked.

"They broke into the wrong house."

"Who lives at 187 Van Cleeve Lane?" Nate asked.

"Our neighbor, Mrs. Harder. Jennifer told me she's got a Wyeth illustration."

"Andrew or—" Nate stopped short in recognition. "N.C. Wyeth."

"Right. Andrew's father. That must be the ship picture Hubble said they were after. I thought he meant the Turner from Mike's office, but they had a list of Mrs. Harder's artworks. I'd better talk to her."

"Want us to come out there?" Eddie asked.

"No, I'm close. I can go see her as a neighbor."

"Okay, Nate and I will check on these art dealers."

"Call me if anything turns up." I stopped by the bedroom and said to the contractor, "I'm going down the street for a few minutes, but I'll be right back. If my wife needs anything, please tell her to call me."

"Got it," he said.

Mrs. Harder's forty-something niece came to the door. "Miss Hutchins, isn't it?" I asked. "I'm your neighbor up the street, Harvey Larson." The toy poodle sniffed at my pantleg.

"Oh, yes, Mr. Larson. You had some excitement at your house this morning. One-thirty-seven, isn't it?"

"Yes, ma'am. Is Mrs. Harder in? I really need to see her right away."

She looked puzzled, but was well-bred to a fault.

"Won't you come in? I'll tell my aunt."

I stepped into the entry and glanced around as she left me. It was right there, at eye level. A detailed pencil sketch of Hornblower's ship, *The Indefatigable*. It was framed and matted under glass. My chest tightened, just looking at it and knowing what might have happened last night.

"A study for a book jacket illustration."

I turned around to face Mrs. Harder. Her white hair was swept back, and her blue eyes twinkled at me. Her face had some wrinkles, but she was still attractive at seventy-five.

"Yes, ma'am, my wife Jennifer mentioned it to me once, and I recognized it just now. A fine piece of art. I love the Hornblower books, and I've always admired Wyeth's illustrations."

"Yes, I think some of his finest work was done for boys' books," she said.

I smiled. "I have an old copy of *Treasure Island* with his paintings in it."

"Did you come to see the Wyeth?" she asked. "My father purchased it a long time ago."

"Actually, ma'am, I need to speak to you about something else. It's indirectly related to the sketch. Maybe your niece should be here, too."

"Please sit down." She passed into the living room and sat on the sofa. I followed and sat in a chair facing her.

"Min, would you join us?" she said to her niece, who stood in the doorway to the kitchen. Miss Hutchins came in and sat down in a recliner.

"Mrs. Harder, I'm not sure if you're aware of it, but I'm a police officer."

"Oh, yes, I've seen you on the news. I felt so safe when I heard you were moving into the neighborhood."

"Thank you," I said. "And you heard that our house was broken into this morning."

"Yes. Terrible. Just terrible. Min and I heard the sirens. Were you at home?"

"Yes, ma'am. My wife and I were sleeping, and two men came into the house."

"How awful," Mrs. Harder said.

"Is she all right?" asked Miss Hutchins.

"Yes, she's fine. And that's taken care of now, but I have reason to believe they were working for someone else. Someone who trades stolen artworks."

Mrs. Harder's eyes widened.

"Ma'am, the burglars broke into the wrong house. The address they had on a piece of paper was yours. They misread the number and broke into our house instead."

She put one hand to her lips and stared at me. "Oh, dear."

"Yes. Do you have an alarm system?"

"Yes, but I hear they aren't always a deterrent to professional thieves."

"Well, they're a big help, but these two have bypassed alarms in at least two cases I know of. And they had a list of items they were looking for."

"Sort of a shopping list?" her niece asked.

"Yes. The Wyeth sketch was on it, and a Landers still life, and a Braden abstract."

Mrs. Harder gasped.

"You own a Landers and a Braden, ma'am?"

"Yes. That's the Landers, right behind you." I turned around and looked at it, then stood up and went closer. It was about three feet long and two high, a potted African violet, a ship in a bottle, and a pocket watch, together on a windowsill. Through the window, a rocky shore was visible. "I like it."

"Thank you. So do I," she said. "The Braden is in the dining room. I also have several other pieces I enjoy."

"Only the three were on the list," I told her. "We're not sure how they knew you had them."

"Could someone who's been in the house have seen them and hired someone to steal them?" she asked.

"It's possible. Or someone may have told them what you had. It may have been purely innocent. For instance, you told my wife you had a Wyeth, and you don't know us very well."

"Oh, dear. You're saying I talk too much. But your wife is so sweet and good, and you're a policeman. I wouldn't tell just anyone."

"But you never know, ma'am. Jennifer might casually say to someone else, 'Yes, my neighbor has a valuable painting that is just wonderful,' and never think about what they might do with that information."

She was thoughtful. "That oil is worth quite a bit as well." She nodded toward a landscape over her stone mantle. "If someone came in here and saw the Landers, they'd have seen it, too. I've kept it there for years. But it wasn't on the list, so it must have been word of mouth, as you say. What can I do?"

"Just be very careful what you tell people, and don't let strangers into the house. Maybe install a few more deadbolts, and think about upgrading your security system. Does your dog bark when people come around?"

"Sometimes. Oh, what a nuisance. I don't know if it's worth having the pictures, if my niece and I are in danger just having them to look at."

"Well, ma'am, as I said, these particular burglars are out of commission, but that doesn't mean no one will ever try it again."

"Are you sure you and Mrs. Larson are all right? They didn't harm you, did they?"

"We're fine. Our house is a mess."

"Oh?"

"Bullet holes and . . . well, I'm glad they didn't come to your house, Mrs. Harder."

"They shot at you?" Miss Hutchins asked.

"Yes. But we're fine. Really."

"Oh, dear," Mrs. Harder said.

"You two talk it over," I said. "Be alert. And maybe you should get a bigger dog."

As I reached home, Terry called me. "Captain, Hubble's lawyer is with him if you want to talk to him again."

"I'm at home now, Terry."

"Suspended?"

"Yeah, you know the drill. Could Eddie come down and talk to him with his lawyer there?"

"I suppose so. Oh, and Captain, I just got Winfield's report on that bullet from your house."

I gave Tony mental brownie points for acting so quickly. "What's the upshot?"

"Winfield says it was fired from the same gun the Westbrook guy was shot with. The one who surprised the burglars, and they took the gun off him and shot him, you know?"

"I get you. Thanks, Terry." I went in the house, told the contractor I was back, and settled down at my computer again. Eddie had e-mailed me an update on the work he and Nate had done. Nate had called the art club president and told her he was thinking about buying a painting from the South Portland gallery. She was cagey and told him to check around before he dropped any money there. While she didn't say anything specific, Nate got the impression the place had a bad reputation.

Eddie had checked out the Dover, New Hampshire gallery. The owner had fired a man a couple of months earlier for taking a stolen painting on consignment. He hadn't found much on the Boston gallery yet, except that it had changed hands within the last three months. I shot back a detailed message on what he should focus on when he questioned Hubble.

I figured it would be at least half an hour before

he reported back to me on the interview with the prisoner, so I made myself pull up my budget figures and do some work on that. I hated it, but it was the kind of task I had to concentrate on, so it was a good distraction for that moment.

When Eddie called again, I realized with satisfaction that I'd accomplished a lot and the budget was close to completion.

"Yeah, Ed?"

"I did what you told me and zeroed in on that list. Harv, you should have seen his face when I told him they were in the wrong house."

That was worth a grim smile on my end. "Wish I'd been there. What did he say?"

"He blamed it on Foster. Said the person who hired them wrote down the address and a list of the items he wanted stolen. Foster read it wrong. The lawyer wanted to know if we could prove that, and I told him to look at the paper in Foster's effects. It says 187, but they were inside 137."

"Excellent," I said.

"Yeah. Hubble said that Foster told him they wanted a ship picture. They were looking for it at your house and couldn't find it. But the client had said the homeowner at that address had all the items on the list, including the ship picture. They were starting to think it was a little strange when they couldn't find anything on the list in your house. They were going to look upstairs when you surprised them."

"Perfect. You got this all on videotape, right?"

"Yeah. The lawyer told him he didn't have to say anything, but Hubble was so mad at Foster for messing up like that, he just spilled it."

"They didn't know we slept downstairs."

"That's right," Eddie said. "You scared the socks off both of 'em."

"They scared me, too. If Abby hadn't been at work, they might have walked into her bedroom while she was sleeping." I let out a slow breath.

"I'd say God was watching over you," Eddie said.

"Yeah."

"Oh, and the Baby Jesus picture?"

"You mean the Murillo?"

"Yeah. Hubble said he thought that was a bonus, because it wasn't on the list. But Foster didn't think it was very good."

"Ha!"

"Hold on," Eddie said. "Okay, I'm putting you on speaker. Nate's got something to tell you."

"What have you got, Nate?" I asked.

"I've found something in common for those three art dealers from the business cards."

"Yes?"

"A guy named Eric Stanley worked for them all at one time or another."

"Excellent. Jennifer and I met him at the Redwall opening." I pulled out my pocket notebook and flipped back through it.

"How does he fit into this?" Eddie asked.

"I'm not sure, but he could be the go-between. Foster and Hubble would get their instructions and steal a painting or two and take them to Eric Stanley. Then Eric would sell them to art dealers he knew and take his cut."

"That makes sense to me," Eddie said.

"Get hold of the Manchester P.D. and have them pick up Eric Stanley immediately."

"Will do, boss." Eddie clicked off.

An hour later, Arnie called me with news that Hubble was ready to plead guilty to breaking and entering. "I'll go to the D.A.'s office with Eddie," he said.

"Good. Thanks, Arnie. But he can't just plead out on this. They shot a Westbrook man in July. Hubble's not going to just be forgiven that one."

"He said that wasn't him."

"He's blaming his conveniently dead partner again?"

"Yeah," Arnie said. "He claims he wasn't there and that Foster was working with someone else then. A guy named Carey."

"What happened to that guy?"

"He said Carey got busted in Portsmouth, so Foster took Hubble on. We've got the samples for the DNA testing."

"Good, because when that DNA match comes back, it's another B&E charge at the doctor's office. Then there's the job in Rosemont, where they stole a Redwall painting the end of September."

"We told him we'll charge him with every one of the thefts, even though he wasn't the one who nearly killed you and Jennifer."

"You got that right. Is Nate there?"

Arnie put him on the phone.

"Nate, I want you to check on this Carey guy that Hubble says used to work with Ian Foster. Start with Portsmouth P.D., and if they don't have anything, try New Hampshire State Police."

"Yes, sir." I knew Nate would go into action.

When Jennifer woke up after several hours of sleep, I told her about the burglars' mistake. It seemed to comfort her and take away some of the anxiety to know they hadn't meant to terrorize us. But then she got to thinking of what they might have done at Mrs. Harder's house.

The contractor's truck was still in the driveway, with the sunroom carpet rolled up in the back. When Jennifer saw the hardwood floor, she got excited.

"Wow, I love this. Can we get an area rug?"

"Sure," I said, glad the stain was pretty much gone.

The contractor was packing up his tools, and I made a quick inspection tour with him.

"I'll be back tomorrow to sand that joint

compound and patch the wallpaper," he said. "Your insurance should cover all of this."

I'd found a chicken pie in the freezer and thawed it in the microwave. We sat down to eat with Abby at six. Jennifer did pretty well with the meal, and I was pleased, but there were still dark shadows beneath her eyes.

"Can we sleep downstairs tonight?" she asked.

"Are you sure you want to?"

"I'd rather," she said quickly.

"Okay. But I think we'd better have a security system installed right away," I told her.

"A burglar alarm? You said they got the wrong house. No one will bother us now, will they?"

"Jenny, we have things people want to steal. The Murillo print, for instance. I think it's worth about four thousand dollars."

"Really?" She and Abby both stared at me.

"Some of the furniture Mr. Bailey left us is valuable, too. They were going to take one of those little tables in the living room, maybe more, and your plate, and all of the electronics. They hadn't even gotten to my guns." Besides my Beretta, I had a shotgun and a hunting rifle upstairs in a closet.

"I don't think I'd like having alarms," she said. "I'd hate to live like that."

"So, what do you want to do? Get rid of all the valuables? Buy a guard dog?"

"Please don't get a dog," said Abby. She was a cat person.

Jennifer sighed. "We should have just lived in your apartment and not had all this stuff."

"Jenny, Jenny, you need beautiful things. Besides, even in my apartment I had the computer and the guns. Unfortunately, the way the world is today, we have to take security measures. I never worried too much about it before, but now I'm responsible for you and Abby and the baby."

"All right," she said. "Whatever you think would be best."

I squeezed her hand. "How would you girls like to go out for ice cream?"

"Too cold," said Abby.

Jennifer smiled. "How about hot cocoa and doughnuts?"

"You got it, gorgeous." I was getting to be good pals with the personnel at the doughnut shop.

I went to work Tuesday morning. I figured if Mike didn't ask, I didn't have to tell him I was there. New Hampshire State Police Detective Ainsley called me the first thing. "We've got Eric Stanley, and I have some information for you."

"He's talking?" I asked.

"Oh, yes. He's very eager to cut a deal. He's confessed to accepting stolen property, fraud, check kiting, and embezzlement."

"Embezzlement?"

"From a former employer. I'll fax you a complete report later today. Most of it's New Hampshire stuff, but he was behind several thefts in your area."

"He hired Foster and Hubble to steal art."

"Yes, and others. He had crews working for him in several areas."

"The man we have in custody, James Hubble, says Foster had another guy, name of Carey, working with him, and Carey shot a home-owner in Westbrook, Maine, during a burglary in July. Then Carey was arrested on some other charge in Portsmouth. I've got one of my men checking on it, but you may want to look into it."

"I will. Stanley says he met people at the gallery where he worked, and other places. Art shows, openings, auctions. He'd strike up acquaintances with all sorts of artists, dealers, collectors, and find out who had bought expensive pictures. Then he'd send his crews out to steal them."

"Where did the artworks go?"

"Always out of state. Sometimes as far away as Florida or Ohio. Lately he'd been sending a lot to a fellow in Massachusetts."

"And you've got the name?"

"Yes," Ainsley said. "We've contacted the Lexington P.D. They're going to the art museum to question the man."

I raised my chin when I heard that. "Lexington, huh?"

"Yes. That's where Daniels is."

The adrenaline shot through me.

Chapter 21

"Did you say Daniels?"

"Right. Neil Daniels," Ainsley said. "Works at the art museum there. Some kind of assistant curator or something."

"And this guy was buying stolen paintings?"

"That's what Eric Stanley claims."

"Hoo, boy."

"What?"

"I know that guy."

"You know him?"

"Well, not personally, but my wife knows him. Went to college with Neil Daniels."

"Small world," Ainsley said.

"Getting smaller every day."

I just sat there at my desk for about twenty minutes, staring at the cartridge display on the wall over Clyde's desk. It was hard to breathe at first, but I made myself calm down. I thought of several things I might do, but rejected them all.

Nate came to me with a computer printout.

"That Carey guy is in the New Hampshire State Prison on an armed robbery charge. Twelve-year sentence. I talked to their warden about the art theft where Hubble says Carey shot the guy. He wasn't in jail then, and they'll question him about it."

"Good." I was still staring at the cartridges.

He laid the paper on the corner of my desk and went back to his computer.

"Harv, you okay?" Eddie was looking at me from where he sat. He'd turned around in his chair, so his back was to his computer.

"Eddie, I need to be very careful right now to do things right. Something's come up."

"Can I help?"

"Come with me." I got up and went to the interview room, and Eddie followed me. The other men, working at their desks, barely looked up. I sat down at the table where we interviewed suspects. Eddie took a seat opposite. It crossed my mind that I had maneuvered him into the investigating officer's chair.

I hauled in a painful breath. My chest hurt, and it wasn't the old injury. "That guy I had Nate do the background check on a few weeks ago—Jennifer's old boyfriend?"

"I remember," Eddie said.

I bit my lip. There was no way to ease into it.

"I was just talking to Detective Ainsley of the New Hampshire S.P., and he brought up Daniels's name. Eric Stanley claims Neil Daniels is buying stolen paintings from him. He could be behind the art burglary ring."

Eddie's eyes widened. "You've got to tell Jennifer."

"Do I? I don't want to upset her. The break-in at our house was quite a shock."

"But you can't hide it from her. It will be on the local news because of all the stuff stolen around here. You'll probably have to tell the press yourself, and she'll see you on TV."

That was true.

"But this guy . . . he's the one who . . . and then the burglar, Foster, grabbed her . . ." I put my head in my hands.

Eddie said softly, "It's tough, but you've got to tell her."

We did a lot of communicating with New Hampshire and Massachusetts State Police that morning. At eleven-thirty, I called Jennifer and told her I couldn't make it home for lunch, and I kept at it. I wasn't avoiding telling her about it; I just wanted to have as much information in hand as possible before I sat down with her.

Eddie went out to the diner with Nate and Arnie, and they brought me back a sandwich. We began to get a trickle of faxes, telling us where stolen items had been sold. Later, because of the information we'd uncovered, authorities started locating more stolen artworks, and a couple of recoveries were reported. The police were able to contact two more owners and tell them some of their belongings had been found. I tried to be patient as it unfolded.

Clyde and Arnie worked on the electronics end of it. They learned through informants where Hubble and Foster had fenced high-end electronics. The cheaper stuff we despaired of ever tracing. The antiques were going to another middle man, the owner of an antique shop in Kittery. Late in the day, Arnie called Kittery P.D. and filled them in. The contact there said he knew the shady antique dealer and would pay him a visit. I faxed him a list of antiques taken in the burglaries we knew Foster had been involved in.

The motorbike surfaced in a shed at Hubble's brother's house. It was the address Hubble gave as his own. I had Arnie delegate that to the patrol sergeant, and Aaron O'Heir took a unit to search the place and Foster's. They didn't find any stashed loot at Hubble's, but at Foster's apartment, they found three TVs, a DVD player, and seven guns.

The handgun Hubble had carried Monday morning was one reported stolen in another burglary. The list of charges against Hubble was getting longer. I talked to his lawyer, and he called me back an hour later and told me Hubble was ready to talk to O'Heir again. He was adamant that he didn't want to see me, but he would spill everything he knew in exchange for whatever breaks we could give him.

Ainsley sent me the lengthy report on Eric Stanley's arrest, including lists of items he'd commissioned the thieves to steal and dealers to whom he had shipped them. I kept my eyes peeled for something on Daniels, but so far there was nothing. Apparently he worked with a variety of clients. Whenever one of them had a market for an artwork, Eric would set up the theft.

Ryan came to the office for a follow-up on that morning's page-one story, and I told him Eddie was in charge of the art case while I was on suspension. Mike would hit the ceiling if Ryan quoted me in the next morning's paper. Eddie gave him a rundown on stolen property recovered and a widening circle of arrests, but didn't mention Daniels.

At three o'clock I called the Lexington, Massachusetts P.D. Neil Daniels was on a business trip. The museum expected him back on Thursday. The police would question him then.

"Where did he go?" I asked.

"Uh, let me see . . . He was going to appraise four paintings the museum is considering purchasing from a private collection. The owner died, and the heirs offered the paintings for sale. The museum gets first refusal, because the deceased loved it so much. Spent a lot of time there."

"Did the collector live in Massachusetts?"

"I think so, but the paintings were someplace else."

"Where?"

"Just a second, I'm looking for it."

I tapped my desk with a pencil.

"Here it is. Cottage in Scarborough, Maine. Someplace called Prout's Neck. His summer home."

I sat up straight in my chair. "Let me get this straight. Daniels works for the Lexington Museum of Art. The museum sent him up here to Maine today to look at some paintings in Scarborough. He's going back Thursday."

"Yes. Well, he may come back to Massachusetts tomorrow. They expect him at work Thursday morning. We plan to question him then."

"And what if he happens to pick up a newspaper while he's up here and reads about the arrests we've made, and the art theft ring we're busting?"

"Didn't realize he was going into your territory. Sorry. Nothing we can do about it when he's not in the state."

"Have you got the name of the deceased collector?"

"Uh . . ."

I tried to stay calm while I waited, tapping deliberately with the pencil.

"John W. Carpenter."

"Thank you."

I tapped the desk again, then broke the pencil in half.

"Eddie!"

He was at my side immediately.

"We're going for a ride."

I gave Nate, Arnie, and Clyde instructions for the rest of the day. Eddie and I headed south in his truck. The Scarborough town manager allowed us to look at the tax map of Prout's Neck, and we located Carpenter's property.

"Better get a Scarborough cop or a state trooper to go with us," Eddie said. I hated the delay, but he was right. We went around to their police station. It took me half an hour to convince their deputy chief to send a man with me. It was nearly five when we arrived at the cottage. A white-haired man was locking the front door. A black Lexus with a Maine plate sat in the driveway.

I showed him my badge. "Sir, I'm Captain Larson with the Portland Police Department. I understand this was the summer home of John W. Carpenter."

"Yes, sir, I'm his executor, Marvin Wallace."

"Mr. Wallace, did a man named Neil Daniels come here to appraise some artworks for the Lexington, Massachusetts, Museum of Art?"

"Yes, Mr. Daniels left here about five minutes ago."

"Five minutes? Where was he headed?"

"Back to Massachusetts, I suppose."

"Did he appraise the paintings?"

"He examined them and bought them on the spot for the museum. Took them with him."

"How did he pay for them?"

"He wrote a check to the estate on the museum's

account. You're not telling me this Daniels was a phony, are you?"

"No, sir, I don't think so. He *is* employed by the museum, and they did send him up here to see the paintings. I didn't realize he was going to purchase them today."

"Is there a problem?"

"No, I don't think so. It's just that we're trying to locate Mr. Daniels quickly. You don't know for sure where he was going?"

"No, but he had four paintings in his car, and they were worth $23,000 together. I don't think he'd stop overnight at a cheap motel. I assumed he was going straight back to Lexington."

We left the Scarborough patrolman at his station, and I called Jennifer and told her I would be late.

Everyone had left the office when we got back, and I sent Eddie home. I went to the file cabinet and pulled out Nate's file on Daniels. It was quite thorough, including a description of his car and the Massachusetts tag number. I called the Maine State Police, asking them to watch for the car on I-95 south. We had some license plate readers along the busiest parts of the interstate, and they would notify me if Daniels's plate number showed up. I tried to call the Lexington Museum of Art. It was closed, and I got a recording with the hours of operation.

On my computer, I pulled up the museum's

website. Daniels was listed among the staff, and his credentials seemed to be in order, beginning with his art history degree from UMO the year Jennifer graduated, then an internship and a master's, then employment at the museum as a cataloger, then promotion to assistant curator of modern paintings.

I jotted down the names of three administrators and then looked for home phone numbers. I finally got hold of the museum's special programs facilitator, but she couldn't tell me a thing.

I sighed and leaned back in my chair. I had to go home and talk to Jennifer.

Nate's folder lay before me, and I opened it again. Daniels grew up in Caratunk, a tiny town on the upper Kennebec. His parents still lived there. Would he drive that far to see his family briefly?

He'd done pretty well for himself for a small-town boy. Instead of driving a pulp truck, he held a responsible position in an urban art museum. Why should he jeopardize that?

He had a brother, Justin, employed by a white-water rafting outfit in The Forks. Sister Lynn, married and living in Missouri. Sister Jodi, employed as a buyer for a large department store at the Maine Mall, living in Stroudwater, Portland.

I took a deep breath. It was right under our noses. Wouldn't a nice guy like Neil want to see his sister when he was going to be within a few miles of her house anyway?

The stairway door opened, and Eddie came in. He was wearing his winter jacket over a flannel shirt and black jeans.

"Cold out?" I asked.

"Yeah, it's going to go down in the teens tonight. Maybe snow a little."

"What are you here for?"

"I wanted to see if you'd gone home."

"Not yet."

"Harvey, don't let this thing get out of control again."

"Thanks. I don't think it will, but I just found out Daniels has a sister living about three miles from here."

"Within the city limits?"

"Yes."

"Let's go."

Eddie parked his truck at the curb in front of a modest brick house. In the driveway sat a gray Toyota Corolla with a Massachusetts plate.

"You're good, Harv," said Eddie.

"Nate had it in his background check. I never read it 'til tonight."

"Looks quiet."

A couple of lights were on in the house. We got out and walked up the driveway to the door, and I rang the bell.

A young blonde woman opened the door. She was attractive, but her face was too thin, and her lips were thin, too. Like Neil's. She couldn't be more than twenty-two. She looked at us expectantly, then a little apprehension crossed her face. Single women shouldn't open the door wide like that.

"May I help you?"

"Miss Jodi Daniels?"

"Yes." Definite apprehension.

I pulled my badge out, and Eddie unzipped his jacket so his showed. I said, "We're from the Portland P.D. We're trying to locate your brother, Neil. Is it possible he's here tonight?"

"Well, yes, I—let me—just a minute." She turned away into a sparsely furnished living room, leaving the door open, and called into the next room, "Neil!" Her voice rose as she said it.

He came in from the kitchen, tall and loose jointed. He was wearing dress pants and a tailored white shirt, but the jacket and tie of museum formality had been left somewhere, and his collar was open. He surveyed me and Eddie through steel-rimmed glasses. His hair was shorter than it had been in the yearbook picture, but he had the same serious, calculating look.

Eddie nudged me just a little, and I realized I was staring and thinking about Jennifer liking this guy, believing herself in love with him. I turned a little toward Eddie and said quietly, "Take over."

He stepped forward, and I closed the door behind us to keep from heating the outdoors at Jodi's expense.

Eddie said, "Mr. Daniels, I'm Detective Thibodeau, of the Portland P.D., and this is Captain Larson. We need to talk to you, sir."

"What about?"

"There's been a string of art thefts in the area, and we thought you might be able to help us."

"In what way? Do you need appraisals?"

"No, sir, we wondered if you knew some of the people involved."

"I'm sure I don't—unless you mean people whose artworks have been stolen?"

"No, sir." Eddie glanced at Jodi, who stood with her hands on the back of a chair, watching her brother. "Maybe you could come over to the station with us, and we can talk there."

"Is that necessary? Can't we talk here?"

Eddie looked at me, and I nodded curtly. I surveyed the room. The girl didn't have much in the house, but what she had was nice. The chair she was leaning on was a Shaker ladder back, with acorn finials at the top. She had a Sheraton card table, and the painting over the bookcase looked like a Landers. It had the same quality I'd seen in the one Mrs. Harder owned. Bright, clear colors. A weathervane jutting above a roof of old cedar shingles, with a maple branch in the red blossom stage reaching toward it.

"Sir," Eddie said, "an Eric Stanley has been arrested, and he told us that—"

"Just a minute," Daniels cut him off. He stood looking Eddie in the eye for a few seconds. He licked his lips and glanced at Jodi. "Perhaps I *should* go with you. Just let me get my jacket." He turned away, and Eddie followed him out of the room.

I looked at the signature on the Landers. "Nice painting."

"My brother gave it to me for my birthday," Jodi said.

"He's an art curator," I said mildly.

"Yes, he told me this is an investment for me."

Should I tell her? She looked uncertain, but not frightened.

Eddie came back with Daniels, who was scowling, but ready to travel.

"Neil, I don't understand," said Jodi. "What about dinner?"

"I'm sorry. I'll call you if I'm going to be late." He faced Eddie. "Should I drive my car?"

"Ride with us," said Eddie. "Someone can bring you back."

"Are the Lexington Art Museum's new paintings in your car?" I asked.

He turned and stared at me, then said, "In the trunk."

"They should be safe," I said.

We drove in silence with Daniels in the back seat, and at the station we went in through the garage to the foyer. Cheryl Yeaton waved at me through the security window. I punched the elevator code, and we went up.

"Let's sit in here, sir," Eddie said pleasantly, opening the door to the interview room. Neil sat at the table, and Eddie sat opposite him. I hit the video cam switch and stood near the door.

"Mr. Daniels," Eddie began after giving the date and our names, "you've been named by Eric Stanley as having received stolen artworks from him during the last few months. This is a very serious charge."

"Are you arresting me?" Neil asked.

"At this point, we just want to hear what you have to say. Are you acquainted with Eric Stanley?"

"I've met him. He makes himself known to people in the art world."

My cell phone rang. I excused myself and stepped out into the office.

"Harvey? It's Beth. Are you all right?"

"Yes, I'm fine."

"Where are you? It's after eight o'clock. Jennifer's very worried about you."

"I'm sorry, Beth. I told her I'd be late. We had a break on a case, and I had to stay. Is she with you?"

"Yes, I'm at your house," Beth said. "She called me an hour ago. She was scared to be alone."

"Oh, boy. Where's Abby?"

"She had to go to work at three o'clock. She's starting a new shift."

"That's right. I'm so sorry. Eddie and I have a man we're questioning right now. Let me talk to her for a second."

Jennifer came on the line, tearful and shaky.

"I'm sorry, Harvey. I didn't think I ought to call, but Beth was mad."

"No, it's my fault. I should have called you again. I forgot Abby was going in early tonight. Honey, everything's okay. We've got a break on the art case, and Eddie and I are here together working on it."

"Have you arrested someone?"

"Not here. That Eric Stanley guy we met at the exhibit was picked up in New Hampshire, and now we've got someone else in here for questioning. He may have bought stolen goods from Eric. We're making progress, but I may be a while longer, gorgeous."

"That's okay, as long as I know you're safe."

"I am. Beth said you were a little nervous tonight."

"I shouldn't have been, but I couldn't help

354

thinking about that man grabbing my foot, and it got dark and you weren't here, and we don't have an alarm yet." She was crying bigtime, which really wasn't like Jennifer. I put it down to hormones and the recent trauma. "Did you wear your Kevlar vest?" she choked out.

"No, baby. We didn't have anything like that tonight. It's been very routine. We just went to pick a guy up and brought him in for questioning."

"He didn't shoot at you?"

"No, he was very polite. He works for a museum. On the surface, he's very respectable. He wasn't running away, we just had a little trouble locating him."

"Oh. I'm sorry."

"Don't be. Just ask Beth if she can stay with you a while longer. I may be another hour. If it's going to be any more than that, I promise I'll call."

I put the phone in my pocket with a sigh. On my desk was the framed photo of Jenny on the breakwater in Rockland. I picked it up. Her hair swirled around her in the ocean breeze. Her eyes shone with eager happiness. The day I proposed.

Foster's touch had unnerved her for sure, but would it have disarmed her so if Neil Daniels hadn't shattered her security three years earlier? Jennifer shouldn't have to live with fear. I had wanted badly to shield her, to provide an atmosphere of invulnerability for her and our baby. I should be home, holding her securely.

I put the picture down and went back into Interview.

"You seem to know a lot about me," Neil was saying.

Eddie had Nate's folder open in front of him on the table. "Yes, sir, we've compiled quite a lot of information on you."

I sat down quietly.

"So, am I free to go now?"

Eddie said, "What are your plans?"

"I was going to spend the night at my sister's and go back to Lexington tomorrow. I was going to return to work Thursday, but since I was able to purchase the paintings, I'll deliver them to the museum tomorrow."

Eddie looked at me, and I could read his eyes. Daniels had denied everything, and would go back across the state line. The Massachusetts State Police might look into it, or they might not.

"Sir, what about the Landers painting?" I asked.

"What painting is that?" Neil's eyes widened, but his lips narrowed.

"The one hanging in your sister's living room."

He was quiet a moment, then said, "I purchased it for her as a birthday gift last month. She hasn't been in her present position long and doesn't have much money. I gave it to her as a start toward decorating her own home for the first time."

"That's nice. And where did you buy it?" I asked.

"From a dealer."

"What dealer?"

He hesitated too long. I followed up with, "And do you have a receipt?"

"I—of course. Someplace. At home. In Lexington."

"You're not married," I said.

"No, what does—"

"You live alone?"

"Yes."

"So, there's no one at your house who could locate the receipt and fax us a copy?"

He looked bewildered.

"Name the dealer you bought it from," I said evenly.

"Nicholas Dore."

"I know him," I said.

He shrugged a little.

"Eddie, go pull up Arnie's notes on the case, please, and pinpoint the last Landers theft."

While he was gone, I said, "Mr. Daniels, I can't figure out why you would do this. Was it the money?"

"I didn't do anything." A sheen of sweat shone on his forehead.

Eddie came back in. "Stolen September

twelfth, here in the city. Rooftop with clipper ship weathervane."

Neil sat very still.

I took out my pocket notebook, flipped through it, and handed it to Eddie, "Please call Nicholas Dore. His gallery and home numbers are right there. Ask him if he's sold a Landers lately. If he has, I want the date, the seller, the buyer, and a detailed description."

Eddie went out of the room again, and I said, "Mr. Daniels, you'd better pray he comes back here describing that weathervane."

Neil said nothing, but stared at the cheap landscape print on the opposite wall. The interview room was the only place we pretended to have art in Priority, and it was a K-mart special.

When Eddie returned, he said, "Mr. Dore hasn't had a Landers in six months, and the last one was a boy in a rowboat. He says he knows Mr. Daniels by sight, but doesn't recall doing business with him."

I didn't say anything for five seconds, waiting to be sure my voice would be under control. Then I said, "Detective Thibodeau is placing you under arrest."

Neil stirred. "May I call my sister?"

"You might do better to call an attorney."

"I wouldn't know who to call. I've never needed one."

Eddie stepped forward and started reading

the Miranda. I went out and left the door open. A quick phone call put in motion the process of getting a search warrant. I walked over to the corner beside my desk and looked out over Franklin Street, at the lights and the traffic.

"Can I call my sister now?" Neil asked when Eddie brought him out in handcuffs.

I picked up the receiver of my desk phone. "What's the number?" He gave it, and I pushed the buttons and handed the receiver to Neil. I turned back to the window.

"Jodi, it's me. I'm not going to be able to come back tonight. No, no, it's just—this is going to take longer than I thought."

I heard Eddie say, "You should tell her. She can help you make bail or call you a lawyer."

"Jodi, listen. They—they've arrested me. Oh, it's all a mistake, but you need to help me out. Can you come to the police station? And please call Dad. No, don't call them. No, no, Jodi, just—please, call Dad. Then come down here. Okay."

I heard Eddie hang up the receiver.

"What the—"

I turned around. Neil was staring at the breakwater photo of Jennifer.

Chapter 22

My stomach lurched. I didn't even want him looking at her picture. I should have turned it around. His eyes leaped around my work station, and I realized it wouldn't have done any good. At least four other photos of her were highly visible, on the shelf of reference books, next to my in-box, and tucked between the monitor and the router. The formal wedding portrait, with the crown of braids; Jennifer and me at Stonehenge; the five-by-seven Cecile Caron had given me of the pigtailed girl looking out over the rail fence; and the snapshot he focused on next, taken at Fort Preble. She had the Rapunzel look, one long braid hanging over her shoulder, and her face was sweet and trusting. Her navy-blue T-shirt said UMO in huge letters.

"I can't believe it." He took a step toward it and bent toward the pewter-framed picture.

"Sir, you'll have to come with me now," Eddie said quietly.

"I'm going home, Ed," I said, and he nodded.

As he guided Neil toward the elevator, I called the sergeant's desk. Cheryl answered.

"This is Captain Larson. Eddie's bringing a

prisoner down for booking. Please have an officer meet them at the elevator."

I picked up my briefcase and took the stairs, beating them down there. Neil turned and looked at me as they stepped off the elevator. Cheryl Yeaton punched the security code to the booking area for Eddie. The incredulous look was still on Neil's face.

Beth left as soon as I got home. She had to be up early for school. I made myself a mental note to send flowers to her classroom the next day.

The furnace was on, and it was cozy in the house, but I lit the fire anyway. I brought the log cabin quilt from our bedroom and wrapped it around Jennifer and sat in a big armchair by the fireplace with her on my lap.

"What happened tonight?" she asked, every muscle in her body tense.

"Like I told you, we took in a suspect for questioning. After we'd talked to him, Eddie took him into custody." I looked into her solemn gray eyes. "Jenny, it was Neil Daniels."

She didn't blink, but sat there staring back at me for about ten seconds. "You arrested Neil?" she finally asked in a small voice.

"I had Eddie do it."

"You didn't hit him or anything?"

"No. I didn't so much as spit on him."

"Thank you. What did he do?"

"We're pretty sure he bought a stolen painting, but it's bigger than that. He works at the Lexington Museum of Art, and it's looking like he commissioned art thefts through Eric Stanley and sold the paintings Eric's crew stole to private collectors."

She put her hand up to my stubbly cheek.

"That was hard for you."

"Extremely."

She nodded. "He had a good job at the museum?"

"Yes. Assistant curator."

"What he always wanted to do. Why would he risk losing that?"

"Got greedy, I guess. His salary wasn't very big."

She looked toward the snapping blaze in the fireplace. "Will the charges stick?"

"I think so. Eric Stanley has given us quite a list of paintings he sold to Neil. He sold stuff to other people, too, but lately they've done a lot of business. I'm surprised we hadn't made the connection earlier, except that he lives out of state."

"He had a position of trust," she said.

I sighed. "His big mistake was giving one painting to his sister. He must have thought it was safe, and if someone saw it and made the connection, he could claim he bought it in good faith and didn't know it was hot. Must not have realized it was stolen from a house just a couple of miles from his sister's." I shook my head. "I felt sorry for Jodi."

"I met her a couple of times," she said. This merging of unwanted episodes from our lives was too unsettling, and we sat in silence. Her boyfriend's little sister. They probably got along. If she'd married Neil, Jodi would have been a bridesmaid. I felt mildly nauseated.

My phone rang, and I answered. It was Eddie. Jennifer took the quilt and headed for the bedroom.

"Jodi's been here," Eddie said. "She tried to bail her brother out, but the bail hearing won't be until morning, so she left alone."

"Good. Let him sweat tonight. She didn't drive his car, did she?"

"No," Eddie said, "and we got the keys from him. I sent a marked unit to Jodi's house to recover the Landers and the four paintings belonging to the museum, and to search the house and Neil's luggage and car."

"The warrant came through that fast?"

"Yeah. I called Mike to ask for help expediting it. And when Browning speaks, minions listen."

I laughed. "And judges, apparently."

"Oh, and I got hold of the chairman of the museum's board of trustees, and they will send someone up here tomorrow to take possession

363

of their paintings at the police station."

"You've been busy. Good work, Ed. Go home and get some sleep. We'll want to check on Jodi's antiques tomorrow, I think."

"You think they're all stolen?"

"It wouldn't surprise me."

"Oh, I called the Lexington P.D., too," he said. "They're getting a warrant to search his house down there tonight."

"Great."

"Is Jennifer okay?" Eddie asked.

"Yes. I told her, and she's coping."

She was spreading the quilt out over the comforter on our bed when I got to the doorway. She had changed into her Portland Fire Department T-shirt, and it hung halfway to her knees. She folded back the blankets on her side.

"You okay?" I asked.

"Yeah, I think so."

I caught the faint sound of an engine. "Abby's driving in."

I went out to meet her, and she came in through the kitchen to the sunroom.

"How'd it go?" I asked.

"Great! I love it. Much slower pace than the ER. I hope I'm still in Obstetrics when you guys have your baby."

"Me, too," said Jenny, coming to the bedroom doorway.

"Get enough of those T-shirts and you won't need maternity clothes," said Abby.

"I couldn't wear my favorite jeans today. I'm getting fat." Jennifer rubbed her stomach, but it didn't look any different to me.

Abby laughed and headed for the stairs with a cheerful, "Goodnight. I'm beat."

"I'll tell her about Neil in the morning," Jennifer said. "After I've slept on it and you've made up for being so late tonight."

"I'm really sorry about that." I reached for her and pulled her close. "I didn't intend to leave you alone. Are you upset that I didn't tell you earlier it was Neil?"

"No. You had to go where the evidence led you, and I'm glad you didn't just drop it on me over the phone."

I started unbraiding her hair. "I wanted to be here with you. It was so hard, meeting him like that." She tucked her hand into my holster strap, and I sighed deeply and kissed the top of her head. "Get into bed, gorgeous."

I went around turning off lights and checking the dying fire and the locks, then shaved quickly and climbed into bed beside her. She burrowed in on my shoulder, and I put my hand over on her tummy. Finally, I could feel a tight firmness that hadn't been there before.

She covered my hand with hers. "That's him," she whispered.

I went to Eddie's in the morning and ran with him and Jeff, and I told Jeff about the arrest of Neil Daniels.

"I never liked that guy. He was arrogant." He eyed me speculatively. "Is Jenn okay?"

"I think so."

When I went home to shower and change, Jennifer was up and making breakfast. She looked okay. No, she looked great. She had on black pants and a coral-colored blouse.

"Going somewhere?" I asked.

"Just into the study to work." She looked down at her clothes. "I wanted to feel a little professional. I think I can wind up the program for John today, and I figured I shouldn't be in my p.j.s when I call him."

While we ate, Abby staggered into the kitchen in her bathrobe.

"What are you up to today, Harvey?" she asked. "You're dressed to kill." I was wearing my best suit and Jennifer's favorite tie.

"I'll probably be at the courthouse this morning, and this afternoon Eddie and I want to get over to the shooting range and see if we can qualify with the new .45s we're getting."

"New weapons. Wowzer!"

"Yup."

"Anything happening in the art case?"

"Yes, actually, we've pretty much cracked that

case. Cops in several states are scurrying around as we speak, tracking down middle men and stolen property."

"So we're not going to any more art club meetings? I was hoping you or Eddie would take me to one of those fancy exhibits."

"I think we're done with that for a while, but that doesn't mean you can't go and hobnob with the art people."

"No, thanks," Abby said. "It was only fun because it was mysterious."

Jennifer walked to the garage with me in her sock feet. I tossed my briefcase into the Explorer and turned around to kiss her. She stood on the bottom step, which brought her nearly to my height.

"I hate to go off and leave you again," I whispered.

"I'll be all right."

I said, "Call me after Abby leaves. I promise I won't be late tonight."

She clung to me for a few seconds, then said, "Go make Portland safe."

I considered sending Eddie alone to the court-house but changed my mind. I needed to see it through. Jodi Daniels and her father came into the courtroom together. I sat near the back, as inconspicuous as possible, and Eddie did the talking for the department. The judge had dealt with Hubble the day before, and he set Neil's bail high. The prisoner would stay at the county jail to await arraignment the next day.

Throughout the hearing, Neil sat with his eyes averted. His father seemed the stoic type, but Jodi constantly batted at tears with a tissue.

Later, an assistant D.A. came to our office to gather information. Word had come in from Lexington that the police there found a small amount of cocaine in Neil's house. They'd also confiscated his computer and an address book, which had Eric Stanley's name and number in it, among others.

They were calling the rest of the people listed in the book and had found a collector in Philadelphia who admitted buying a Redwall from Neil recently. Mr. Daniels had helped arrange the purchase privately, said the new owner, very hush-hush. He was offended when the police suggested his acquisition might be stolen. I faxed descriptions of the stolen Redwalls to the Philly P.D. They would pay him a visit and see if the painting was a match.

I called a florist and ordered yellow roses for Beth, to be delivered to her kindergarten classroom, with a note reading, "Thanks for being there when I couldn't be. I'm glad you're Jennifer's friend."

When I hung up, I looked up to find Mike striding toward my desk.

"Figured you'd be here. I pulled some strings and pushed my weight around. Your I.A. hearing's at one."

"Today?" I asked.

"You want your suspension lifted, don't you? Because if you don't, I suggest you go home. It's already going to be hard for me to explain what you were doing in Scarborough last night."

"Right." I pulled in a careful breath. "I'll be there. Your office?"

"No. The conference room on the first floor. Don't you screw this up, Harvey."

I nodded. Mike whirled and stalked to the stairway door.

I sat down and tried to catch a deep breath. Eddie walked over to my desk frowning.

"Everything okay?"

"I'm not sure." It was a long time since I'd made Mike really mad. "I need to pray about this. They're holding my hearing at one o'clock."

Eddie blinked. "We were going to the shooting range then. Want to go now?"

I really, really felt like shooting something, so we went. Our purpose in the outing was to try out the new side arms the department had ordered. Ron Legere had delivered five to our unit that morning.

"I could like this," I said, hefting the Heckler & Koch .45.

Eddie pulled his out of his holster and dropped it back in a few times. "Not too bad. It will take some getting used to."

It took a lot of prayer to not imagine the target was Neil Daniels. Eddie and I qualified with no problems.

"Too bad we're so good," he said. "Now we have to go back to the office."

As soon as we got back, Eddie went to get some lunch, and I went to the locker room and took a shower. I put on a clean shirt, but even so, I was sweating through it by the time I got to the conference room. I knew Eddie was praying for me, and I gave Jennifer a quick call from the stairway.

"Send up some prayers, sweetheart. I'm about to go into my hearing about the shooting."

"Okay." She sounded scared.

"Everything will be all right," I said, though I wasn't a hundred percent sure. "What are you up to?"

"Janice Parker is here. We're having tea and cookies. Well, she is. I'm drinking milk."

I smiled, thankful for the normalcy of it, and that Jennifer wasn't alone.

At 12:59, I walked into the conference room. I knew everyone at the table—Mike and every division head, plus two officers representing the internal affairs department.

They grilled me pretty hard about the incident

at my house, but I'd expected that and handled it all right.

"I understand you were back on the job yesterday," Lieutenant Kirby said.

That stopped me cold. I glanced at Mike, but he just sat there like a stump.

"Actually, I mostly sat at my desk all day, catching up on paperwork and things like that. I had sat out most of Monday, and I guess I was getting a little antsy."

"You went to the courthouse this morning."

"Yeah, but only as an observer. One of my detectives was appearing."

Ron Legere looked down at a printout in his hand. "What about this jaunt to Scarborough with Detective Thibodeau?"

I swallowed hard. "We got a tip about a suspect we'd made contact with previously, and we learned the person buying stolen art from him was in Scarborough. It was urgent, because he could have left the state with stolen goods, so we rode down there. He'd left already, but we were able to trace him to a family member's home here in the city."

"Who made the collar?" Mike asked. He already knew, and I figured he just wanted that asked and answered on the record.

I met his gaze. "Detective Thibodeau. I was just along for the ride."

They asked me a few more questions, and it

was finally sinking in that it would have been smarter for me to stay away from the station for the last three days.

Finally Mike said, "I think we all know Captain Larson has an excellent record. I happen to know that he pretty much stuck to non-essential stuff this week and spent a lot of time at home. Officers are allowed to observe in the courtroom on their own time, and to use the shooting range when they're off duty."

I shot him a glance. I hadn't realized he knew about that. Even if he was mad at me, Mike still had my back.

"The captain's stayed away from his desk most of the time since the incident," he went on. "But we can't afford to keep him off the job much longer."

A woman in I.A. cleared her throat. "It looks to me as if the shooting was justified."

They took a quick consensus, and Mike stood. "Okay. Suspension lifted. Harvey, you'll see the psychologist next Friday at eleven."

"Sure. And thank you. All."

I hurried out into the hallway on Mike's heels.

Once we were in the stairway, he turned around and cocked an eyebrow at me. "Don't do this to me again. You shoot somebody, you back off and don't come near this building until I tell you to."

"Right."

He sighed. "I'm glad it doesn't happen often. Now, get back to work."

Chapter 23

I got home fairly early, and Jennifer wanted to hear all the details. I was honest with her, even though it set her to worrying again. We sat down and prayed about it, then and there. I felt a little better, but not completely.

She started getting supper ready, and I sat at the kitchen table, too fatigued to even go change my clothes.

"It's shocking, this impulsive side of yours." She threw me a fretful glance. "I had no idea work would get to you like this. You were always so calm and efficient before."

"Sometimes the façade slips. I'm sorry."

"No, don't be." She turned down a burner, came over to stand behind me, and started massaging my neck, which felt great. "Tell me when things are tying you in knots, baby."

I nodded. "I never had anyone to share it with before. I'll try to do better."

The doorbell rang.

"I'll get it." She walked into the entry and opened the door. "Mike! Come on in."

"Thanks, Jennifer."

My stomach fell about three stories, and I wondered if he was going to chew me out worse than he had that afternoon. I shoved my chair back and stood.

"Mike. What's up?"

"Just thought I'd stop by on my way home and look at that floor you had refinished."

"Oh. Okay." I took him into the sunroom. Our house wasn't on his way home.

"Looks pretty good," he said, eyeing the oak floorboards. "You did a good job getting rid of the blood. Where was the body?"

Jennifer stayed out of the room while I retold the story of the burglary, showing him where Foster had stood and where the lead had hit the door and the bedroom wall.

"I read Eddie's report tonight." Mike turned to face me soberly and lowered his voice. "He also gave me a few details that weren't in the report. I wasn't aware that Jennifer had a connection with Daniels. But he's not going anywhere for a while. We'll make sure of that. I wanted you and Jennifer to know."

"Thank you."

He nodded. "I'd have probably done the same thing, or worse. But tell me next time, Harvey."

"Yeah. You know what?" I met Mike's gaze. "I can honestly tell you I don't hate him any-more."

"I'm guessing that's a big leap for you." Mike smiled then. "I've got to get going, but you guys did excellent work."

• • •

Abby came into the kitchen as I was about to leave for work Friday morning. She had to be at the hospital that evening, but would have Saturday off.

"I'm going out to the airport and meet Greg," she said brightly, pouring herself a cup of coffee.

"Drive safely," I said.

Jennifer's brow wrinkled. "Does Peter know Greg is coming?"

"I don't think so," Abby replied. "He didn't ask."

"Abby, you can't keep going out with both of them. Not unless you're up front with them both." Jennifer's intensity surprised me and told me how concerned she was about Abby.

"But I'm not sure which one is right for me." Abby plopped down in the chair opposite her. "They're so different."

"Do you really like Peter?" I asked.

"Yes, lots. He's shy, but he's really nice. And I love his boys!"

"Have you two talked much?" Jennifer asked.

"Some. It's hard to get very personal with the kids around."

"Maybe it's time you two went out without the boys," I said. "The Larson baby-sitting service might be able to help you."

"Oh, that's sweet." Abby ate a banana and went off to the airport to meet Greg.

"What are we going to do with her?" asked Jennifer. "Peter will be so hurt!"

"What about Greg?"

"I think he'd take it easier."

"I don't know." I tried to wrap my head around Abby's predicament. "Greg's only been really in love once, and it fell apart on him. Peter's wife didn't reject him, she just died."

"You have an odd way of looking at things," Jennifer said.

The office routine soothed me. We had a new case to work on, and plenty of paperwork and loose ends to tie up from the old ones. To my surprise, Mike walked in a half hour before noon.

"Morning, chief," Nate and Clyde said, almost together.

"Hey." I raised my eyebrows at Mike.

I'd been helping Nate with a report, but Mike drew me off to the corner where my desk was situated.

"I wanted to give you the news myself," he said. Of course, I immediately thought something bad was going down. "That Bangor captain. You missed the interview during your—" He coughed lightly—"suspension, but we're going to hire him as deputy chief. He'll start in a few weeks."

"Finally!" The relief was huge. "You couldn't have made me happier."

"I wish you could have met him, but I think he'll be okay."

"Mike, if you can work with him, I'm happy."

"Well, he likes fishing, so I figure he can't be too bad."

Greg was at the house with Jennifer when I got home at half past five. Jennifer had dug out a jigsaw puzzle of a Charles Wysocki painting, and they had it a third put together on the card table in the sunroom. Outside the patio doors, snowflakes hovered in the twilight and fell, then melted on the dead grass. We were only five days into November, and I knew we had a long snow season ahead.

"Greg, good to see you." I shook his hand warmly and couldn't help thinking he was ten times as colorful as Peter. It was the first time I'd seen him out of uniform. He was wearing a gray sweater instead, over a checked cotton shirt, and dark pants.

"Hope you don't mind my being here," he said.

"No, I don't like Jennifer being alone much right now. Did she tell you about what happened Monday morning?"

"Yes. I'm sorry you guys went through that."

"I wouldn't want to again, I'll tell you."

"So, what happened to the man you arrested?" Greg asked.

"He's been indicted on several burglary counts. He didn't fire his gun that night, so we didn't charge him on attempted murder, but we've got him on several thefts. He'll do some time."

Jennifer had stew in the Crockpot, and Greg ate supper with us.

"You're staying here tonight?" I asked.

"Well, no, but thank you. Jennifer said I could, but I already checked in at the hotel. I'll stay there this time."

"If you come up this way again, plan to stay here," I said. "We've got extra room, and you're welcome."

"Thanks, I'd like that. If there is a next time."

"Why do you say that?" I asked.

Jennifer was cutting pie, but she stopped in the middle of a slice to watch Greg.

"Well, Abby told me this morning I have some competition."

"I'm glad she told you," Jennifer said. "I didn't think it was fair of her not to."

"Did it upset you?" I asked.

"Well, I'm not thrilled about it. Do you think she feels strongly about him? She mostly talked about his kids."

"I'm not sure," said Jennifer, and I shrugged.

"They really haven't gone out much," I said carefully.

"Well, neither have we." Greg shook his head. "I'd like to think I have a chance here."

"Take her someplace fancy tomorrow," I advised.

"She'd like that?"

I told him how much she'd enjoyed the under-cover assignment at the art club, and how wistful she'd been when I took Jennifer to the exhibit.

"Hmm," said Greg, "where can I take her?"

Jennifer brought the newspaper over, and I pulled out the weekly entertainment section that came on Fridays.

"Theater?" I asked. "Concert? The university's having a faculty recital."

"Take her to this," said Jennifer, pointing to the theater section. "Gilbert and Sullivan. She'll love it."

Greg phoned the box office and spoke for two tickets.

"Now I need to call the airline, if you don't mind. I was going to fly out at eight tomorrow night." He was able to get a seat on an 11 p.m. flight and was obviously relieved.

Eddie called me shortly after Greg left. "Harv, I'm a little nervous. I'm not sure where to take Leeanne tomorrow night. I wish it was down here. I know where things are in Portland."

"She'll know a place. Tell her you want the best restaurant in Skowhegan. Or take her down to Waterville. There are some nice places down there." I was starting to feel like Jennifer and I ran an event planning agency, along with the matchmaking business.

"That's a good idea," Eddie said. "You know, I'm starting to feel like I could be done looking."

"Take your time, Ed."

"I know. You're right. Maybe I'm just panicking because I'm getting old."

That made me smile. "You don't want to do that. Go slow, and talk a lot. Find out how she feels about things."

"Right. Then what?"

"Talk some more. And listen."

Greg came for Abby at nine in the morning, and they were gone all day. She came back flushed and dreamy after a visit to the Longfellow house and the waterfront. They'd eaten lunch at the floating restaurant, then gone to an antique show at the Civic Center. During the hour she was at the house, she showered and dressed meticulously in Jennifer's green silk.

"I don't know if I can stand it," I said to Jennifer. "That's your Grace Kelly dress."

"Sisters always share their clothes," she said. "Don't take it too hard." She arranged Abby's hair for her, and Abby put on a little makeup and a necklace of amber beads.

"Pretty classy," I had to admit.

"Thanks, Harvey," Abby said. She kissed me on the cheek. I felt really old, as if I were sending a daughter out on a date in her mom's high heels.

Greg came back in a really nice suit. Charcoal gray, with a shirt so crisp it had to have been ironed by some minion at the hotel. The tie had little airplanes all over it. Jennifer took a picture before they left. Abby's warm parka went over the silk dress, spoiling her sophisticated look just a little. Jennifer mother-henned her, making sure she had gloves and a hat along.

Jennifer and I spent the quiet evening perusing the baby names book and talking and laughing together. It was so precious to hear her laugh. I kissed her so often she sent me off to shave, then welcomed me back for more.

"I'm trying not to think about Abby and Leeanne tonight," she confessed about nine o'clock, as we settled into bed.

"They're both out with good men."

"Yes, and I want them both to have good husbands. But Abby especially seems so uncertain. I want my sisters to love their husbands madly, and I want them to be loved as much as . . . as you love me."

She could always thrill me and make me want to give a little more to make our marriage better. I didn't want to kill her joy for one second. My lapses in that since our wedding were my biggest regrets.

She looked up at me intently. "I really wonder about Eddie and Leeanne."

"Don't. Eddie will behave himself."

"That's not what I mean. I think she's very loving, and maybe ready to love. For life. Eddie's been so unsettled. I'd hate to see her get hurt."

"Well, Casanova is showing signs of being ready to put down roots," I said.

Abby came in quietly at eleven-thirty, after she'd left Greg at the airport, and went lightly up the stairs. She'd have to work every evening until the next Friday, when we were all heading north for the weekend. Abby, Jeff, and I had managed to get one weekend off together, and the hunting trip was scheduled. I wondered if Eddie wouldn't end up going with us.

Eddie was back from Skowhegan in time for church the next morning but missed the singles Sunday school class. Dropping onto the pew next to me before the worship service, he smiled. The song leader stood to open the service. Jennifer leaned across me and touched Eddie's hand, looking anxiously at him. He smiled again and squeezed her hand before taking a hymnbook.

As we sang the first hymn, Mike and Sharon slipped into a pew across the aisle, beside Peter Hobart. Abby wasn't with him. I turned quickly to Jennifer. "Where's Abby?"

"Behind us."

I sneaked a quick look. Charlie Emery and Joshua Wright sat on either side of her. She met my eyes for a fraction of a second and gave a tiny shrug, as if pleading helplessness.

I glanced over at Mike again, a little surprised he had shown up. I'd let him down twice, quite badly, but he seemed ready to forgive my flaws. He nodded at me with what might have passed for a smile. God had given me friends I didn't deserve.

We rounded up an impromptu luncheon party when the service ended. Jennifer loved bringing friends into our house, and now that she felt better, she was in the entertaining mood. Today it was the Driscolls with their two younger children, sans Amanda, who hadn't made it home from school that week, plus Mike and Sharon, Eddie, and the Rowlands. I grabbed Abby's arm and said in her ear, "You can bring one of those guys to lunch, but not both."

"Thanks, but I don't think so."

All of the women huddled in the kitchen, and Jennifer had recruited Eddie and Bill Driscoll to help arrange tables. We had converted the dining room into our study, but dinner seating was problematic for such a crowd. Jennifer set up the card table in the sunroom with the oak library table, so some could eat in there and the rest in the kitchen.

The sunroom was pleasant and bright with the patio door and wicker furniture. Jennifer had picked out new area rugs for the wood floor, and no signs of bloodshed remained. Baskets and books and lots of cushions made it one of Jennifer's favorite places, and she didn't seem to let the room's bloody past prejudice her against it.

Mike and I stepped into the study for a few minutes.

"I was proud of the way you handled yourself at the hearing Friday," Mike said.

"Thanks. I was glad you were there. Even though I knew it was a good shooting, I was kind of wound up with the Daniels thing. I felt like I was in the hot seat."

"Been through it few times myself." He looked at Jenny's poster of me in the vest and smiled a little.

"I gotta get rid of that thing," I said.

"No, it's cute. You look ready to take on the world."

"I keep forgetting it's there. It's embarrassing when people see it for the first time." I didn't take many people in there. The room held our computer stations with all the peripherals, Jennifer's file cabinet, and five bookcases. A utilitarian room for serious work. But it seemed lately that dozens of people had been in there, gaping at the poster.

"This Daniels," said Mike.

"What about him?"

"The chief in Lexington called me last night. He was trying to reach Eddie, but he was out of town. The dispatcher gave him my home number. Should have given him yours, but that's the breaks."

"So?"

"The museum is frantically checking its inventory. They think they may be missing a piece or two that was in storage. They don't display everything at once, but rotate the exhibits. Well, they're checking, I'll just put it that way."

"Thanks for telling me."

"It made me feel bad for barking at you Friday. You oversaw it because you needed to be sure he was secure. And you were right about him."

"That doesn't mean I should have halfway ignored the suspension."

"I could go either way on that, so we'll just leave it there."

We started to go into the kitchen, but it was so hectic I took Mike around through the living room. Eddie, Pastor Rowland, and Bill Driscoll and his son, Perry, were sitting there, talking about hunting. Bill was an enthusiast, and he'd taken a deer the day before.

"So how was Skowhegan?" I asked Eddie when the hunting tale was finished.

"Great." A contented smile stayed on his lips.

"Find a nice place for dinner?"

"Yeah. And we went to this theater last night that was really cool. It's old and fancy. Leeanne was real excited. They had pictures in the lobby of all these famous old actors who'd starred there."

"What did you see?"

"*Arsenic and Old Lace.* Pretty funny play."

"I saw the Cary Grant movie. Never saw it on stage."

"Leeanne liked it a lot. Her sense of humor is kind of like mine, I guess."

"Cold last night," I observed.

"Yeah." He glanced around. The other guys were listening to Mike. "I kissed her, Harvey."

"Yeah? You don't have to tell me. You don't have to tell George, either."

He grinned and said, "I didn't. But you're my friend."

"Then, as a friend, congratulations. If you hurt Leeanne, I'll break every bone in your body."

"I'll be extra careful," he said.

I nodded. "Big step in the relationship."

"I'll say. I don't think she ever kissed a guy before."

"Oh, come on, she's twenty."

"Well, yeah," he said. "Okay, school kids, maybe, but I don't think she's ever kissed a grown man, and I know she hasn't ever kissed a cop before."

I felt like I was missing the point. "A little awkward?"

He looked surprised. "No way."

I nodded with satisfaction. "Take your time, Ed. Don't rush things. Remember, her neural cortex isn't fully formed yet."

"Huh?"

Mike said to me across the room, "So, Harvey, what do you think?"

"About what?"

"Did the trees in the Garden of Eden have rings?"

I laughed. "The pastor's sitting right here. Ask him."

We spent most of the week mopping up from the art case. The circle kept widening as one contact led to another. Reports drifted back to us from other states. I let Eddie handle anything directly related to Neil Daniels, and he told me on Wednesday that the Lexington Museum of Art had confirmed three paintings missing from its storage.

"Feeding his coke habit," I hazarded.

"Maybe," said Eddie. "Stupid, no matter how you look at it."

"Neil is a smart man. He couldn't have thought he'd get away with it when he was sober."

"There's a new wrinkle." Eddie's eyes were troubled.

"What is it?"

He looked around. Clyde and Arnie were working at their desks on the other side of the room. Nate was at the copier near Paula's desk.

"When they told the museum employees that Neil had been arrested, it was a shock, of course.

But after it soaked in, something else came out. They had a couple of interns this fall, college kids. One girl told her supervisor today that Neil had—" he stopped short and turned to the window.

"Had what?"

"He assaulted her, Harv."

"Oh, man."

"She says he took her out a couple of times. That's against the museum's rules with underage kids. She was 19, and the museum staff was in a mentoring program with the students. They weren't supposed to date anyone under 21, and even then, they had to have permission if it was a student."

"Her word against his?"

"Yeah, she didn't make a report at the time."

"How long ago?"

"Mid-October."

"So, just three or four weeks ago," I noted. "Are they pressing charges?"

"The detective down there says yes, if she'll go through with it."

I considered. "Let's not tell Jennifer. I want *him* punished, not her. She's had enough trauma lately."

"What if they need other people to testify—you know, establish a pattern."

I thought about that. "Not unless it's absolutely necessary to convict him."

"All right. I'm sure glad she didn't wind up with him."

"Me, too." I sent up a silent prayer of thanks.

"George asked me to come back to Skowhegan this weekend," Eddie said.

"George? Not Leeanne?"

"Well, she did, too, but he asked if I wanted to join you all for hunting."

"Great. Ride up with us."

Chapter 24

Friday, November 12

The alarm woke me at six for running. Jennifer catapulted onto my chest.

"Happy birthday!" She kissed me and stroked the back of my head, where my hair was getting long again. I wished she'd forgotten about my birthday.

"You want to be married to an old guy?"

"I want to be married to you, no matter how old you are." She ran her hand through my hair, scrutinizing it. "Nope, no gray yet." Next to her, the running routine looked very unattractive.

She told me to bring Eddie back for breakfast, and she had pancakes and bacon ready when we got there. Abby came down, and we fixed the last details of the trip. Eddie and I would come straight home at five. Jeff couldn't get off until six, and he and Beth would leave then. I'd gotten my gear ready the night before, and Jennifer had packed our clothes.

"When do we eat birthday cake?" Abby asked.

"Mom's fixing it. When we all get up there, we'll party," Jennifer said.

I pouted a little. "I have to wait all day for my presents?" Jennifer slugged me.

Mike called while we were still at breakfast. "New homicide, Harv. Your unit needs to take this one. Illegal alien with a bullet in his head at the Custom House Wharf."

"I'll put some men right on it."

I told Jennifer I had a new case, but didn't give her the details. Much better to keep her thinking pleasant thoughts.

"This isn't going to put the kibosh on our trip, is it?"

"Not if I can help it."

"Hey, you know the Invincible Duo," Eddie said with a grin. "We'll probably wrap this one by noon."

Jennifer looked skeptical. I finished my coffee, trying to give her the illusion that I wasn't in a hurry.

She was just beginning to need maternity clothes, and I wanted to be sure she and the baby were warm and comfortable on the trip. As Eddie and I left for the station, I told her sternly, "You go to the store today and buy yourself some clothes. Abby, make her go."

"We're going," Abby confirmed.

"All right." I kissed Jennifer. "Love you."

Eddie rode to work with me, like old times, and I told him what I knew about the homicide, which wasn't much.

The sky was gray, and it was spitting snow. "I hope they get enough snow for tracking the deer in Somerset County," Eddie said.

As soon as we reached the police station, I sent Arnie and Clyde to the wharf. Arnie called in a little later and asked if Nate and Eddie could go down and help. I sent them, hoping Eddie wouldn't be needed for very long.

I was alone with paperwork until eleven o'clock, when the psychologist came. We'd met before, and we got along. We stayed at my desk with a fresh pot of coffee, and I told Paula she could go home before the snow got any worse. I gave Dr. Slidell the basics on the shooting at my house. He asked me a few questions, and then we swapped hunting stories.

"Guess you're all right, Larson," he said as he headed for the elevator at noon. "I'll give the chief my report this afternoon."

I drove home and ate a quick lunch with Jennifer and Abby. Jenny was modeling maternity jeans and a fuzzy blue, long-sleeved top that made her extra cuddly.

"I like it, but you should have bought more," I said.

"The snow was getting heavy, and we figured we'd better get home."

That made sense. I hoped it would taper off by the time we left for Skowhegan.

"This trip is going to be great," I told her. "No seminars, no homicides. Just fun."

· · ·

Mike and Arnie were going hunting on Saturday, too, and they were drinking coffee in our break room when I got back from lunch, arguing good-naturedly over where to be at the crack of dawn.

"How's it going?" I asked Arnie.

"Not bad. We've got a couple of witnesses. I think we'll have a suspect in custody this afternoon." He looked at his watch and stood up. "Time for me to get back down there. I left Clyde in charge."

"What about over the weekend?" I asked. "You and Eddie and I are all planning to be gone. Do we need to cancel our trip?"

"I don't think so," Arnie said. "Clyde was getting a line on the suspect. I can stay tonight if I need to, but I think things will be under control."

He left, and Mike said, "Sorry, Harv, I shouldn't have shot the breeze with Arnie."

I shrugged. "He's entitled to lunch."

"You got his replacement picked out?"

I sat down across from Mike. "I'm down to two. Jimmy Cook or Tony Winfield."

He tipped his chair back against the side of the snack machine. "I'll look them over. I'd lean toward Jimmy, all else being equal. Tony's too young. Keeping Eddie's history in mind, of course."

I nodded. "That's all I ask. Jimmy must have

enough experience to qualify for the detectives' exam in the normal way. But I'd be happy with either of them."

"Think Clyde will be?"

I hesitated. "If he's not, I'll switch things around and put him with Nate."

Mike nodded. "Clyde working out all right?"

"His work is fine. I haven't gotten close to him."

"You won't."

"Too bad."

"Wishing you hadn't picked him?" Mike asked.

"Maybe. I like a tight unit. I miss Pete like crazy. Every time I want a legal opinion I have to call somebody outside."

"You had quite a bit of legal training yourself."

"Mostly pre-law. I didn't get that far into the good stuff."

Mike shrugged. "We could see if one of the officers wanted to take legal training."

"What, pay to educate a man and have him leave us for the private sector?"

"We'd have to get a commitment out of him."

I shook my head. "The city council wouldn't approve it. Your budget would go down in flames."

"Speaking of budgets—"

"Let's not." I didn't have a lot left to do on it, but I'd ignored it for the last couple of weeks.

He laughed. "Okay. So, Jimmy or Tony."

• • •

At five o'clock I left, feeling a little apprehensive. The suspect wasn't in custody, but Arnie had called in and assured me they would have him soon. He released Eddie, but kept Nate and Clyde, and he asked for a contingent of uniformed officers from the evening shift for backup.

Jennifer ran out to the driveway when Eddie and I pulled in. I'd had Eddie put his truck in the garage that morning, to leave it inside while we were gone.

"Everything's ready," Jennifer cried, embracing me.

"Great. We've just got to change. You want me to shave?"

"Take your razor and shave at Mom and Dad's."

Abby packed sandwiches and drinks for us to eat on the road. Eddie and I loaded the luggage and hunting gear into the Explorer, and I wondered which bag my present was in. The snow was falling steadily now, and as we went north it accumulated. Plows were out, keeping the interstate clear, but when we got off in Fairfield, the side roads weren't so well groomed. Several inches had piled up on the flat by that time.

Leeanne greeted us all with hugs except Eddie. She was still a little shy around him. They smiled at each other, and he took off his Winchester cap and put it on her, then pulled his duffel bag and Marlin 336 rifle out of the back of the Explorer.

Everybody helped unpack, and we were pretty well settled by the time Jeff and Beth pulled in.

Beth hadn't had her mittens off ten seconds when Jennifer let out a scream hugged her, laughing and doing her happy dance.

Abby went over and joined them with a whoop.

"What's going on?" George looked at his oldest son.

Jeff gave him a guilty smile.

By this time, Marilyn and Leeanne were also swarming Beth.

"Let me see," Leeanne cried, and Beth held out her left hand. A diamond sparkled on her ring finger.

Everyone talked at once. The girls all wanted to know when Jeff had proposed, and where. Randy and Travis gawked at the ring, but seemed at a loss for words. Finally things settled down, and I went out to Jeff's truck with him to bring in their luggage.

"Congratulations, brother," I said.

"Thanks." He grinned from ear to ear. "Beth wants to set an early date. She said it worked for you and Jennifer, it can work for us."

"Things got a little crazy at our wedding," I reminded him.

Jeff laughed. "No offense, but Beth doesn't hang around with all the crazy people you do. We're talking about Christmas Eve."

Marilyn had done some creative organizing

to fit everyone into the farmhouse. Jennifer and I had her old room again. Winter coats filled all the hooks near the back door and piled onto the bench beneath. The row of boots made walking near the back door hazardous.

The girls were all giggling and carrying on in the pajama party mode, and Travis had Eddie, Jeff, and Randy playing ping-pong in the barn. It was chilly out there, and I didn't think the game would last long.

George was settled in his armchair with the paper, and I sat down on the couch and picked up a *Field & Stream* off the coffee table.

"How's my daughter doing?" George asked, folding the local section.

"Jenny's good."

"Done being sick?"

"I think so."

He opened the sports section. "Didn't like that burglary business."

"I didn't like it, either."

"Jennifer sounded a little upset when we talked to her the next day."

I laid down my magazine. "Well, it was pretty traumatic. I wish it hadn't happened, but it did. I'm having an alarm system put in."

He lowered the newspaper and locked eyes with me. "You think you can take care of Abby, too?"

"Well, I'm doing my best, George. We like

having her there. She's a big comfort to Jennifer."

He nodded. "And what about Leeanne?"

I swallowed. "What about her?"

"You trust this man?"

"With my life, every day."

"But with my daughter?" He was anxious, and I knew all his girls were dear to him.

"Yes. Eddie's rock solid." I was glad I could say it and mean it. A year ago, I couldn't have done that.

Before he had time to grill me about Beth, Jennifer and Abby came pounding down the stairs and went into the kitchen. "Mom! We're ready for the cake!"

Abby pulled on a jacket and went to the barn for the guys. They came in blowing on their hands and laughing, telling about Travis's super serving technique that popped three balls into the goats' pen. They got two back, but one of Leeanne's pets beat them to the last one.

When all the preparations were ready, they called us into the dining room, and Marilyn carried the cake in with forty-two candles blazing.

"Quick, Jeff, where's the hose?" Abby said.

I couldn't blow them all out at once. "You won't get your wish," mourned Leeanne.

"I already got it." I smiled at Jennifer.

There was a pile of wrapped boxes on one end of the table, and they made me sit there while they sang to me. I hadn't had such a blowout for my birthday since . . . well, ever. Marilyn dished up ice cream for the girls to distribute with the cake, and I picked up the first box. A new pocketknife from Eddie. I opened the blades, inspected them, and nodded, content.

Beth had cross stitched a montage of detective motifs—magnifying glass, smoking pistol, badge 373, and a dagger. Mysterious little footprints sneaked around the edge, and in the middle, "Captain Harvey A. Larson, Priority Unit."

I said, "Guess I've gotta hug you on this one, Beth."

Marilyn was snapping pictures. "So nice to have all the children home," she said. "Can we do this again at Thanksgiving?"

"I think we need to visit Harvey's sisters, Mom," Jennifer said.

"And I've got to work on Turkey Day," Jeff added.

Abby scrunched up her face. "Me, too."

"That's what comes of having half your family in public service and medical jobs," Beth said with an apologetic smile.

"Christmas, then," George suggested.

Leeanne said, "Jeff and Beth will be on their honeymoon."

"That's a little sudden, isn't it?" Marilyn looked wide-eyed at Jeff.

Jeff just grinned. He sat with his arm on

the back of Beth's chair, and she was firmly established as part of the family.

"We'll be together in Portland for the wedding," Abby said.

George frowned at her. "I thought the wedding would be in Freeport."

Beth winced. "We decided my family's church isn't big enough, so we thought we'd have it at Victory Baptist. It's our home church now, anyway."

"You could have it in L.L. Bean's, by the fish pond," said Randy.

"Right, and the reception in the camping display," Jeff said sarcastically. Beth's father worked for Bean's, but there was a limit to employee perks.

Jennifer handed me another package. Marilyn and George's box for me held two Harvard T-shirts, cranberry and forest green. They'd updated the logo a little.

"Great," I said. "His and hers?"

"No, those are both for you," said Marilyn. I gave Jennifer a wink.

Next I opened a book on the lighthouses of Maine from Leeanne and a deer call from Jeff. Abby had made good her promise and bought me an up-to-date version of Trivial Pursuit.

"Okay, are you ready?" asked Jennifer.

"What, more?"

Jeff went out and came back in carrying a large

package. A very large, flat package. It reminded me of the one we'd found in the tobacco smugglers' SUV, and my pulse quickened. Jeff brought it over and set it down on edge in front of me. I looked at Jennifer, then at the package, then back at Jennifer.

"Open it," she said.

I took a deep breath and started peeling off the paper.

The Caron, of course. My girl before I'd known her, the full color, hand-painted, two-thousand-dollar, jumbo version of the little framed snapshot on my desk. I stood up and hugged her fiercely. "I'm going to cry," I whispered in her ear.

"It's okay."

I dug out my handkerchief. "So how many people knew about this?"

"Just Beth. She's been hiding it at her house for a month. She and Jeff brought it up in Jeff's truck tonight."

"A month?" I said. "When did you buy this?"

"The day after we first saw it."

I eyed her with new respect. "You told me it would be foolish to spend so much on it."

"I know, but when I thought it over, I could see how much it meant to you, even if it wasn't really me, so I decided to use some of my software money."

"Jennifer, it *is* you," said her mother.

"Sure," said George, setting the frame on the

buffet, leaning it against the wall. "That's the fence in the lower pasture. You used to wear that little green shirt all the time."

Jennifer stared at the painting. At last she shook her head. "I don't remember anything about it."

Jeff said, "That artist lady camped down there for days, painting pictures of the barn. We sneaked down to watch her."

Jennifer just shook her head.

"Selective memory," said Jeff.

I reached for Jenny's hand. "She took your picture and painted this later. She gave me the photograph when we were up here a couple of weeks ago."

"You didn't tell me."

"No, I didn't want to disappoint you. The painting had been sold, and I thought we'd lost it forever." I laughed and hugged her again. "The snapshot's on my desk at work. I'll show it to you when we get home."

"Wow." She gazed at the painting. "Where are we going to hang it?"

"In the sunroom. Where the Van Gogh is."

"Where does Van go?" Abby asked, and everyone laughed.

I said, "I think he goes in the study, where the picture of me is, and that comes down."

"Absolutely not," said Jennifer.

Everyone started giving suggestions for rearranging our art, and the phone rang. Marilyn answered it in the kitchen and came back to get me.

"It's your man, Arnie Fowler."

I frowned and realized I'd left my cell phone upstairs. I strode to the kitchen and picked up the receiver. "What's up, Arnie?" Marilyn swung the kitchen door to, and the noise from the dining room died away.

"It's Clyde."

"What happened?"

"I'm at the hospital with him."

"He took a bullet?"

"No, I think it's a heart attack. We had to chase the guy. We got him, and one of the patrolmen was cuffing him, and Clyde just went down."

"Is he going to make it?"

"I don't know. I rode in the ambulance with him. His wife's coming in." Arnie sounded drained.

"Okay, I'll come down," I said.

"You don't need to. Mike's coming in."

"No, I should be there." Clyde was one of my men. I couldn't not go. "I'll be there before midnight."

Chapter 25

Jennifer begged to go with me.

"Stay here, gorgeous. I want you to rest."

"No, I want to be with you."

I was hastily shaving in the upstairs bathroom, and she sat on the edge of the tub, pleading her cause.

"You need to sleep and drink milk and take vitamins and make that baby grow."

"Please."

The bathroom door was open, and Eddie came hesitantly down the hall and stood in the doorway. "I'll go with you, Harv."

"No sense in us both losing sleep and missing out on the hunt."

I finally persuaded him to stay, but Jennifer was still not mollified. I drew her into our room and put my arms around her. "I'm going to kiss you, and then I'm going to leave. My wife is staying here with her family. I'm not asking, Jenny."

She lay quiet in my arms, then took a deep, ragged breath. I rubbed her back a little and kissed her hair. "I really think this is best, gorgeous. Please don't fight me."

"I won't. I just—wanted to give my opinion. If you still feel that way, I'll stay."

"I do. I love having you with me, but I don't

want to have to worry about you and the baby on this trip. This is about Clyde. It's snowing, and if anything should happen—which it won't—then I'd have to take care of you."

"All right." Her arms went up around my neck. "Come back to me."

"That's a definite yes."

When I went downstairs, George had the late news on.

"It's wild out there, Harvey. The wind's blowing hard, and the snow's drifting. They're saying there are white-out conditions on I-95."

I didn't like it, but I stuck by my decision and put on my coat, hat, and gloves.

I put the Explorer in reverse to back out of the driveway with the lights off so I could concentrate on the backup light. Snow had drifted, six or eight inches deep, across the gravel drive. Visibility was close to zero. Just as I was going to turn out into the road, Jeff ran out of the house, waving his arms. I braked, then drove up beside him and put my window down.

"Mike's on the phone."

I parked and we went in, stamping the snow off our boots.

"Harvey, where's your cell phone?" Mike asked.

"I left in the bedroom. Sorry. You just caught me."

"I'm glad I did. Don't try to come down."

"I need to be there, Mike."

"Not tonight. Come back tomorrow if you want, but take it easy. This storm is nasty. We've got four multi-car accidents within the city limits, and it's probably worse where you are than it is down here."

"You're at the hospital?" I asked.

"Yes, with Arnie."

"How's Clyde?"

"Pretty bad, but hanging on. Deborah's here."

"I'm his captain, Mike."

"I know, but she understands. It was dangerous even for us to get here. Clyde and Deborah's daughter had a fender bender driving in. You stay put tonight, Harv. I'll call you in the morning."

"But—"

"That's an order."

I sighed. "All right. But do call me. I'll have my cell phone with me."

"Go hunting. I'll call you after we talk to his doctor."

"Mike, you'll let me know if—I mean, anytime, okay?"

"Sure."

Jeff and Beth sat up for a while with Jennifer and me. I think they were too keyed up to sleep yet, and my mind kept turning over every interaction I'd had with Clyde over the last few months.

The wind howled around the house and rattled the old window frames. Jeff went to the living room window and looked out. The snow was still swirling.

"If this keeps up, the deer won't come out in the morning," he said. "They'll all hole up in the woods."

I hated to admit, but I thought he was right. The snow was getting too deep for our expedition.

Jeff went back to the couch and sat down beside Beth.

"So, what advice do you have for us?" Beth asked, smiling at me and Jennifer.

"Just love each other," Jennifer said.

I looked at Jeff. "And don't take anything too seriously when it comes to the wedding preparations."

He chuckled. "You nearly went nuts during your engagement, didn't you?"

"Yes, and I shouldn't have. Just do whatever you can to help Beth, and forget about the rest."

"Are you wearing tuxedoes for the wedding?" Jennifer asked.

"Not if I can help it," said Jeff.

Beth smiled and patted him on the chest. "You don't have to."

"Thanks." Jeff turned hopeful blue eyes on me. "Harvey, will you be my best man?"

"Well, Jeff, that's quite an honor. Are you sure?"

"Yes. Randy and Travis are too young, and I don't know the guys at work very well yet. I might ask one of my old friends in Skowhegan to usher, but I feel closer to you and Eddie than anyone else. Maybe Eddie will usher for me, too."

I winked at Jennifer. "Just don't invite his whole family."

"We're keeping it small," said Beth.

"Good luck." Our wedding had turned into a mob scene.

"You have to invite the church," Jennifer said.

Beth frowned. "Well, yes."

"And the fire department," said Jeff.

"Good luck," I repeated. It sounded too much like our guest list.

"So, anyway, will you do it?" Jeff asked.

I looked at Jennifer. "Sure, I guess so. Any objections?"

"No," she said.

Beth smiled at me. "Good, because I want Jennifer for my matron of honor."

"I'm pregnant," Jenny said.

"Duh." Beth laughed. "I have a catalog I'll show you tomorrow. There's a sweet velvet dress with a pleat in front. It will still fit you at Christmas time. You'll hardly be showing by then, anyway."

"Everyone will stare at me."

"No," said Jeff, "they'll be staring at Beth that day."

Beth smiled and nestled against his shoulder,

and Jennifer gave in gracefully. I was glad, because I wouldn't have to walk down the aisle with some other girl, and I could eat with Jennifer at the reception. I'd have done it for Jeff anyway, but going through it with Jennifer was a whole lot better.

I had set my phone alarm to wake me at 4 a.m., but I had doubts about the hunting conditions. I got up and dressed by flashlight. I kissed Jennifer in the drowsy darkness and told her to sleep for a few more hours. Beth wasn't going hunting, either, so Jennifer had agreed to sleep in.

Marilyn was up, and Leeanne and Abby were in the kitchen with her, fixing an early breakfast for all of us.

"Dad and Jeff went out to look around," Abby said. "I have a feeling we're not going anywhere."

Leeanne and Abby had planned to go with us. They were dressed warmly, with L.L. Bean boots, wool socks, and wool pants. Abby had a thick flannel shirt over a turtleneck, and I recognized Eddie's black sweatshirt on Leeanne, *Province de Québec* on the back, and *je me souviens*—I remember—on the front.

Travis and Randy came down the stairs yawning.

"So, we gonna do this?" Travis asked.

"Don't know yet," Leeanne said.

Eddie came into the kitchen just as George and Jeff opened the back door.

"Well?" Marilyn asked. "What's the verdict?"

"I don't think we could even get out the driveway without plowing first," George said, "and then I doubt if we'd find any deer this morning."

"They won't come out in this weather," Jeff said.

"How deep is the snow?" Leeanne asked.

"More than a foot, and deeper where it's drifted," Jeff replied.

Marilyn shook her head. "Well, that's too bad."

"How about breakfast?" Travis asked.

"It's ready on schedule," his mother replied. "Sit down. You might as well eat it while it's hot."

It was strange to be sitting in the farmhouse kitchen eating eggs and toast before dawn. The boys were disappointed. Travis especially was eager to shoot his first whitetail. Randy had planned to pack his camera, along with a Remington .30-06. I thought George took it hard, too. He was counting on showing us all his favorite hunting spots.

Abby and Leeanne rebounded first. Before I poured my second cup of coffee, they were thinking up alternate plans for the day.

"Well, I guess we postpone the hunt for another time," George said. "Can you get off next weekend, Jeff?"

"No, but maybe the week after."

"How about you boys?" George looked at me and Eddie.

"We'll have to see how things go," I said. "It sounds like I'll be short one man for a while. I'll have to let you know."

"That's the breaks," Jeff said. "Everybody put your weapons away."

I was surprised how confidently Leeanne and Abby handled their rifles. Jennifer had told me their father taught them all to shoot when they were teenagers, and apparently it was part of the growing up ritual in their family.

Marilyn brought the coffeepot around again. "I think it's a wise decision for you all to stay home this morning."

We all helped clean up after breakfast and put the hunting gear away. Jennifer woke up when I peeked into our room.

"Back already?" she asked.

"We're not going. The storm outplayed us."

"Oh, I'm sorry."

I lay down beside her, but I couldn't go back to sleep.

"Do you want to go back today?" she asked.

I turned my head and looked at her. Apparently she couldn't sleep either, now that I'd woken her thoroughly.

"I'd like to. I'll wait a couple hours and call Mike for an update."

The snow had tapered off when we went back downstairs at seven. Eddie and Leeanne were sitting on the sofa, and Leeanne looked comfortable, leaning on Eddie's left shoulder. He stirred when Jennifer and I entered the room, but didn't take his arm from around Leeanne.

"What's the plan?" he asked softly.

"We packed our stuff," I said. "Jenny's going to eat, and then I'll call Mike."

I drank more coffee while Jennifer ate breakfast, and Eddie ate again. The sun came up, and George assessed things in the driveway.

"Guess I can get to plowing," he said.

Jeff and I got shovels and went out to clear the walk and the steps. Meanwhile, Eddie got the less strenuous job of helping Leeanne feed her goats.

Jennifer, Abby, and I headed back to Portland that afternoon, a day earlier than we'd planned, but I was concerned about Clyde and felt I needed to be there. Eddie opted to stay a bit longer and go tobogganing with Leeanne and her brothers.

I dropped Jennifer and Abby at the house, unloaded the luggage, and made sure they had heat and electricity. Then I went to the hospital. I was directed to the cardiac care unit. Arnie met me in the waiting room.

"Harvey, glad you got here okay."

"How's Clyde?" I asked.

"He's stable, but still serious."

I stayed three hours, talking to all the cops who

came in, and I went in once to see Clyde, but he wasn't conscious. His wife, Deborah, accepted my sympathy. She looked worn out.

Sunday morning, we went to church. Eddie came in time for Sunday school. After the service, Mike ate lunch with us. He and Arnie had missed their hunting trip, too, and were hoping to go together the next weekend.

"I'm going to give you your recruits tomorrow," Mike said as we sat in the kitchen beneath the flow blue plate, eating Abby's apple crisp. It was a small luncheon party that day, just us and Abby, Eddie, Mike, and Sharon.

"My recruits?" I asked.

"Cook and Winfield."

"Both of them?" It was almost too good to be true.

"I'm thinking Clyde's going to be out a while."

"Yeah, that's the impression I got, too. But I've got Arnie for six more weeks."

"It's his idea," Mike said. "Get them in there now to train and get used to the unit. Less confusion when he leaves."

"I like it. Arnie will be a great asset in training them. But are you saying Clyde's not coming back?"

Mike poked at his dessert with his spoon. "It was pretty serious. The doctor told me he needs to take it easy for a while. Maybe several months."

"All right. Are Tony and Jimmy officially part of Priority now? Or are they just on loan?"

"Permanent. I'll push the paperwork through tomorrow so Lyons can start filling their slots downstairs."

"Do they know?" I asked.

"Not yet. I spoke to Jimmy Friday afternoon and told him he was Arnie's replacement, but he's expecting to start in January."

"Can I call them and tell them to come to our office in plain clothes tomorrow?"

"Sure."

Eddie looked pleased.

"Can you work with Winfield?" I asked him.

"You putting Nate and Jimmy back together?"

"I think they'd like that."

"It's okay. Arnie's going to train them, though, right?"

I grinned. "What, you don't think you've got the patience to train a young hotshot?"

Eddie shrugged. "I'm pretty sure I couldn't do as good a job as Arnie. Or as you did."

Chapter 26

Monday, November 15

Flowers arrived for Abby as I left for work Monday morning. She wasn't up yet, but Jennifer accepted the box. The security man drove in as the florist's truck drove out. I spoke to him for a few minutes and agreed on the alarm system that would be best for us. I left with him counting windows. I had the feeling Jennifer was going to be exhausted before lunch.

Jimmy and Tony were waiting upstairs, standing together near the windows. They both wore neckties and jackets, ready for detective work. I shook hands with them and welcomed them to the unit.

Tony's grin burst out. "Thank you, Captain. It's a real pleasure to be here."

Jimmy's smile had less wattage, but was as genuine. "Harvey, thanks. I really wanted this."

"I don't suppose you want your old partner back?" I asked.

"I'd love to work with Nate again."

"All right, you got your wish." His smile rivaled Tony's then. "Winfield—no, wait." I took a deep breath. I always told myself his relationship to the governor didn't matter, but somehow, in my struggle to treat him equally with all the other men, I'd gone too far in not treating him special. I looked at him sharply. I called all my other men by their first names, and I made myself say it evenly. "Tony, you'll be with Arnie. He's going to train you in our procedure. Starting New Year's Day, you'll be with Eddie."

"Wherever you want me, Captain."

I went on, "We get a lot of homicides, but we handle other things, too. This unit got a homicide case Friday, and it extended into the weekend. We try not to work weekends, but when we need to, we do."

Tony and Jimmy nodded. I told them about Clyde's heart attack, and Tony said, "So, if Wood comes back later, will I still be here?"

"The chief says your assignment is permanent." I thought his cheeks would split if he smiled any wider. I needed to talk to Mike again, to clarify Clyde's role when he was ready to return to work.

Eddie and Arnie breezed in, and Nate wasn't far behind. I put Tony at Clyde's desk, asking Arnie to put Clyde's personal things in a box, so that I could stow them in his locker.

"Jimmy, I have no desk for you yet. We need to move some furniture, I guess. I'm going to talk to the chief as soon as I can, and you can use my desk when I'm not at it. Meanwhile, pull up an extra chair near Nate, there, and he can brief you on what we've been doing. He was in on this homicide thing, and the art theft case before that. We've got some loose ends to tie up on both cases, and one of our older collars is coming to trial this week. You can go over the files on those. Eddie and Nate will be in court tomorrow. Jimmy, you have court experience, but, Tony, I'll probably send you along to observe."

I caught sight of a five-by-seven of Leeanne, newly perched on Eddie's shelf of phone books and criminology references. It had been taken at our wedding, with her wearing the royal blue gown, and her dark hair in the braided up-do. She looked sweetly at the camera from under lashes as long as Jenny's.

"Nice picture," I said appreciatively.

"*Merci, mon ami.*" Eddie normally spouted French only around his grandmother, when he wanted to be funny, or when duty demanded it. Yes, Eddie was in love.

Ten minutes later, I let myself into the outer office of the chief's suite, reflecting on how comfortable I felt going up there now. I visited Mike upstairs several times a week, and it seemed ludicrous that I'd quaked on the rare occasions I'd gone up to see former Chief Leavitt.

"Morning, Harv!"

I smiled and shook Mike's hand. "I need a desk for Jimmy Cook. Is there an extra one kicking around?"

"Fill out one of these"—he opened a desk

drawer and took out a triplicate requisition form— "and send it to Supply—"

"You're kidding. I can't just go snooping around the basement and see if there's an old desk gathering dust down there?"

"Afraid not."

"How about if I just go buy one at the used furniture store and make it a present to him?"

"Nope. Can't give personal gifts to an officer."

"Ha! What do you call that Hudson Bay blanket you and Sharon gave us?"

"A wedding present. That's different."

I sighed and took the form. I bent over his desk, fished a pencil out of my jacket pocket, and prepared to write.

"Uh-uh," said Mike. "Use ink."

I grabbed his pen out of his breast pocket and wrote in big block letters, where it said "Items requisitioned," ONE DESK. I signed H.A. Larson at the bottom and held it out to him.

"No, that has to go to Supply, then they send me the pink copy. You, my friend, keep the yellow copy."

"Mike, I'll give you the pink copy. Supply doesn't have to send it up to you."

"No, no, see, you have to send them both, then they tear off their white copy and send me the pink."

I tried to stay calm and rational. "Does it really matter who tears off the pink copy?"

He looked at me, then started laughing. "You don't deal well with bureaucracy, do you, Harv? I'll have to jot that down on your next evaluation."

He tore off the yellow copy and gave it to me, then ripped off the pink copy and dropped it in his wastebasket. He took the white sheet into the next room and said, "Judith, would you please get this right down to Supply? And tell them I have my copy. Thank you."

When he came back, he spread his hands. "You see? You just do it. The masses understand that. That's why we have procedure. Do it their way and you'll eventually get a desk, and no one complains."

"Eventually. What does poor Jimmy do in the meantime?"

"Just improvise, Captain. Let him work at the table in the interview room."

I shrugged. "Okay. Now, let me update you on the art case. The blood from the doctor's office break-in was Hubble's."

"Good. He'll stay behind bars for a long time."

"Right. Him and Eric Stanley."

"What about Daniels?"

"They're indicting him here for theft and accepting stolen merchandise. Then he goes back to Massachusetts for more of the same and an assault charge. Maybe a drug charge, too."

"Good. I hope it's a comfort to Jennifer."

"Well, she doesn't know about the assault thing. I figured she's been through enough. Lexington P.D. will handle it down there."

"Well, speaking of your wife," Mike said in a more portentous tone, "we're buying six copies of Jennifer's program from that fellow who bought the rights. What's the new company?" He picked up a piece of paper from his in box.

"Macomber Software. I'll tell Jenny. She'll be pleased. Who gets it?"

"Me, Eddie, Nate Miller, Joey Bolduc, Cheryl Yeaton, and Emily Rood."

"What about Tony? You're giving it to everyone else who took the advanced computer training. Why not Tony?"

"Does Winfield have a desk?"

"Yes, Clyde's. I put him there so he'd be close to Arnie."

"All right, seven copies. I wouldn't want to waste the city's money by ordering software for a cop who had no desk and no computer."

"That's right, Jimmy needs a computer, too."

Mike opened his desk drawer and pulled out another requisition form.

I said, "Maybe he can just buddy up with Nate for six weeks, until Arnie's computer is free. But he definitely needs a desk."

Mike put the form away and closed the drawer.

"Now I have a really important question," I said.

"What's that?" Mike went to the table where he kept coffee going all the time and poured two cups.

"What happens when Clyde comes back?"

He turned to face me and held out a white mug with the Marine Corps emblem on it. "Sit, Harv."

I sat. "So?"

"Drink."

I drank, and then I raised my eyebrows at him. I wasn't going to let him dodge the question.

"Clyde's not coming back," he said.

"Never?" I set the mug down.

"I spoke to his physician this morning, and with Deborah." Mike sat down behind his desk. "Clyde had another coronary last night. Massive. He's very bad, Harvey. If he makes it, he'll be granted early retirement."

I shook my head. "I'm sorry to hear that. I wouldn't wish it on anybody."

Mike nodded soberly.

I skipped lunch and met Jennifer at Margaret Turner's office. A nurse weighed Jennifer and took her blood pressure. Margaret came in, reading the chart on a clipboard.

"Great. You gained a pound this month. Fantastic. Let's try for two the next time. Blood pressure's good. How do you feel? Morning sickness all gone?"

Jennifer grinned. "I haven't even thought about it for the past week or two."

"That's good news. So keep eating. How's Harvey doing?" She looked at me.

I spread my hands. "I'm fine."

"Why don't you just run down the hall to see Carl?" Margaret said. "He was concerned about you after we heard your house was broken into."

I opened my mouth and then closed it. Margaret was not a person to argue with lightly. I went, and Carl switched off the machine he was dictating to and jumped up when he saw me.

"Harvey, how you doing?"

"Great." I shook his hand. "Margaret seems to think you need to eyeball me."

"You didn't get hurt in that shoot-out?"

"No, but you should see the other guy. Ooh, boy, that was sick. Forget I said it."

"Sit down and let me take your b.p." He reached for a blood pressure cuff. "So tell me, what on earth happened? Were you asleep?"

"Yeah, we both were. They just jimmied the front door and walked in."

"One-seventeen over ninety. Not too bad. You shot one guy?"

"He started it."

"I'm sure. How did Jennifer take it?"

We walked slowly down the hall toward where I'd left Jennifer, and I told him about the burglary. "You know those jerks had been in a doctor's office the week before and stolen the art off his walls?" I asked.

"No joke? Margaret's got some expensive framed posters in her exam rooms. They're nice. Limited editions."

"Are they insured?"

"I think so. Guess I'd better check on it."

Margaret was setting Jennifer up for an ultrasound. "Just because," she said to me, when I walked in. Jennifer was covered with rose-colored drapes top and bottom, with just her middle exposed. Carl stood in the doorway, his arms folded.

"Hey, Goldilocks," he said to Jennifer.

"Don't you have someone to cure?" she asked. She didn't want some other man looking at her stomach.

"Let's try that again," said Carl. "Hello, Jennifer."

"Hello, Carl. It's nice to see you, but I'd rather see you when I'm fully clothed."

"No problem. See you, Harv." He drifted off down the hallway toward his office.

"That's the way you have to handle him," said Margaret. "Just give it to him straight." She put slippery junk on Jennifer's stomach and started moving the hand piece around. I still didn't think Jennifer was any fatter, maybe just slightly less thin.

"Been feeling any movement yet?" Margaret asked.

Jennifer said hesitantly, "I thought I felt something this morning, but it was just little flutters."

"He'll be kicking the stuffing out of you soon enough," she said. "There he is."

I looked at the monitor. The baby was bigger, nearly twice as big as before, and his little arm flailed as I watched. I put my hand on Jennifer's head and smoothed her hair. She grabbed my hand and watched the monitor, an eager light in her eyes.

"Now, Margaret, when you say 'he,' do you mean that in the generic sense?" I asked. "As in '*man*kind' or 'each person must bring *his* own pencil?' "

"Yes, Harvey. It could be a she."

"So, when can you tell?"

"Sometimes you can tell at this stage. It depends on the position of the baby, mostly. Sometimes you can't tell until the delivery. Do you want to know, if we can tell?"

Jennifer said, "Yes, yes, of course he wants to know."

I said, "Well, I don't know about that." I'd be ecstatic if I knew it was a boy, but how would I feel if I knew it was a girl? A little girl like Jennifer. Protective feelings welled up in me. Yes, I could be content knowing I was the father

424

of a tiny baby girl. "Do *you* want to know?" I asked her.

Jennifer said, "I think it would help us be ready for the little person we're getting in April." She squeezed my hand, and I laced my fingers through hers.

"Okay," I said. "I want to know, too. If it's a girl it will be . . . really nice."

Jenny smiled. "But if it's a boy . . ."

I shrugged and nodded a little, smiling. Her look was so tender. I bent down to kiss her.

Margaret said, "Oops. Uh, are you sure you want to know?"

"Yes," we both said together.

"Okay, Mommy, Daddy, take a good look. It's a boy."

Discussion questions for *Found Art* for Book Clubs and other groups

1. Harvey agonizes over his choices for new detectives in his unit. Who would you have picked first? Why?

2. "Wonder Boy," the governor's nephew, is slowly working his way into Harvey's enclave. What factors work against Tony? What does he have in his favor?

3. Lying becomes a bigger stumbling block for Harvey in this book. He has intended to talk to his men about not lying in a professional capacity, but then has to admit he lied to some of them for personal reasons. Harvey is demoralized and convinced he's a failure in a lot of ways. Does lying have a place in undercover or other law enforcement operations? Do you have any words for Harvey?

4. Jennifer's sister Abby starts a new relationship with an airline navigator. Is Greg just too good to be true? How does one tell, at

the start of a new acquaintance? What would you tell Abby to look for?

5. What do you think of the way Harvey handles his first meeting with Neil Daniels? Is he wimping out or taking the high road?

6. Nate is so eager to succeed in his new position, he'll do anything to please Harvey. How does one temper one's enthusiasm without losing the forward momentum?

7. How do you protect your more valuable possessions? Have you ever wondered if it's worth having "nice things"?

8. Eddie has avoided spending time with his family for weeks because they are vocally opposed to his spiritual conversion. Is this just one more area in which he needs to grow up, or could he use some counsel on this topic?

9. Jeff agonizes over an incident that happened when he was a child. Do you think Harvey is wrong when he advises him not to tell his family or Beth about it?

10. While Harvey finds orderliness and routine soothing, he doesn't deal well with the rules

of bureaucracy, whether it's a mandatory suspension or a triplicate requisition form. However, he has a history of learning to cope. Where do you see Harvey five years from now? Can he accept all the new changes and survive?

About the Author

Susan Page Davis is the author of more than seventy published novels. She's a two-time winner of the Inspirational Readers' Choice Award and the Will Rogers Medallion, and also a winner of the Carol Award and a finalist in the WILLA Literary Awards. A Maine native, she now lives in Kentucky. Visit her website at: www.susanpagedavis.com, where you can see all her books, sign up for her occasional newsletter, and read a short story on her romance page. If you liked this book, please consider writing a review and posting it on Amazon, Goodreads, or the venue of your choice.

Find Susan at:
Website: www.susanpagedavis.com
Twitter: @SusanPageDavis
Facebook: https://www.facebook.com/
susanpagedavisauthor
Sign up for Susan's occasional newsletter at
https://madmimi.com/signups/118177/join

| Books are produced in the United States using U.S.-based materials | Books are printed using a revolutionary new process called THINKtech™ that lowers energy usage by 70% and increases overall quality | Books are durable and flexible because of smythe-sewing | Paper is sourced using environmentally responsible foresting methods and the paper is acid-free |

Center Point Large Print
600 Brooks Road / PO Box 1
Thorndike, ME 04986-0001 USA

(207) 568-3717

US & Canada:
1 800 929-9108
www.centerpointlargeprint.com